"Heartwarming, tender, memorable...
Sweet Jasmine is
well worth reading."
—Kathe Robin, *Romantic Times*

Unforgettable

"Maybe you should go back inside," he said, his voice gruff as he pulled his hands from the waves of her hair. In an instant, Wade was off the seat, around the wagon, and whisking her into his arms to take her the last few yards back to the house.

His steps slowed as he neared the porch, the fresh scent of jasmine once again filling his mind. He let her down, her body slowly sliding against his hard form, and when her feet touched the wooden planks, he held her tight, reluctant to let her go.

"For some reason that I don't understand, I am drawn to you." His voice was a faint whisper in the night. "Why is that, Madeline?" he demanded, his eyes searching, his voice hoarse with emotion. His arm held her close like a band of iron, capturing her to him. "You are not part of my plan."

He lowered his head to hers as though he had no will to resist, and captured her lips with his own . . .

SWEET JASMINE

ALYSSA LEE

DIAMOND BOOKS, NEW YORK

This book is a Diamond original edition, and has never been previously published.

SWEET JASMINE

A Diamond Book/published by arrangement with
the author

PRINTING HISTORY
Diamond edition/November 1992

ISBN: 1-55773-810-6

Diamond Books are published by The Berkley Publishing Group,
200 Madison Avenue, New York, New York 10016.
The name "DIAMOND" and its logo are trademarks
belonging to Charter Communications, Inc.

PRINTED IN THE UNITED STATES OF AMERICA

10 9 8 7 6 5 4 3 2 1

For Michael

SWEET JASMINE

One

Central Texas, 1879

WADE ALEXANDER WAS furious. He sat perfectly still, his eyes cold and dark, the quiet intensity of his ire evident in every inch of his hard, chiseled form. "You mean to tell me you didn't get the land?"

Harold Mackenzie cleared his throat. "Well, you see, Wade . . ."

"All I see is that you told me the purchase was as good as done, that an old spinster desperate for money owned it."

Wade leaned forward, his light-colored shirt pulling tight against broad shoulders, and slowly began to rise from the high-backed leather chair. He looked away, and for the moment he ignored the other man so completely it was as if he was unaware of Mackenzie's presence. A thick, uncomfortable silence filled the room.

Harold seemed unable to move, his pale green eyes magnified by wire-rimmed spectacles, his thin hands clasped tightly to the papers he held. "I'm sorry!" he finally blurted, shattering the quiet.

"You're sorry! Sorry doesn't cut it, Harold. I need that land." Wade's voice was low and threatening. The result was numbing.

Harold sat down heavily in the chair behind him, an audible sigh escaping his lips.

Struggling for control, Wade raked a large hand through his black-brown hair, then placed both hands flat on the desk. "Tell me what happened."

"Well . . . um . . ." Harold sputtered, his eyes casting about the room, searching desperately for a place to rest other than on the towering height of his employer. "It seems the owner of the property isn't willing to sell, after all."

"Why not?"

Harold shrugged his shoulders and braved a glance at Wade. "I'm not sure."

"I told you to up the bid if necessary."

"I did!" he exclaimed with a sudden burst of energy. "But the answer came back as 'No amount of money is going to buy that land.' Period. End of discussion."

"I can't believe a woman outwitted you on a simple land deal." Wade's hard stare never wavered from the other man. "A *woman*! All you needed to do was pay her a few compliments, ask her about things she likes to do. Escort her to one of those senseless soirees they're so fond of having over there in Austin. Women love that sort of thing. You would've had her eating out of your hand."

"But, Wade," Harold protested as if wrongly accused, "I never had the opportunity to speak with her."

If Harold thought this statement would justify his dismal results, he was sadly mistaken. Instead, Wade's ire grew tenfold. "You mean to tell me you said everything was wrapped up when you hadn't even spoken with the landowner yourself?" His strong hands, tanned golden brown from the hot Texas sun, balled into fists on the smooth mahogany surface. A muscle tightened in his jaw.

"All my dealings were through her solicitor. A pleasant fellow, actually." Harold grinned, seeming to forget his precarious position. "Took me to a real nice restaurant for lunch."

"I don't give a *damn* where the solicitor took you or what kind of fellow he is!" Wade closed his eyes for a moment and took a deep, agitated breath. His anger permeated every crack and crevice of the room. "Just tell me exactly what he said."

"Well," Harold mumbled warily while shrinking back as if to lose himself in the folds of the soft leather chair. "At first he told me there'd be no problem. It was later, after he spoke to her, that he came back and said he couldn't help us. I asked to meet with the lady personally, of course, but the man outright refused."

Wade sighed and walked to a large window that overlooked the bustling town of Fielding, Texas. "What in the Sam Hill would an old maid need with a tract of land a good ten miles from her home in Austin? Holding on to it for sentimental value? Sounds like something a fool woman would do. Harold, I find it hard to believe there isn't *some* amount of money that won't change her mind. In fact, I'll bet the solicitor is trying to squeeze every penny out of the land to set her up for life. He knows a good thing when he sees it." Wade shot Harold an impatient scowl before turning back to the window.

Horse-drawn carriages rolled through the crowded streets of the small central Texas town his grandfather, William Fielding, had founded in 1839. Founded, Wade supposed, was not exactly the word for a town that had sprung up more by accident than by design. Wade's grandfather had traveled south from St. Louis with his wife and daughter to lay claim to a piece of land so he could ranch full time. From his new home, William, or Bill as he'd been known, had found that travelers who were making their way west from Houston often stopped by in search of provisions and a decent place to stay. Realizing he could make a great deal more money catering to passers-through than by tending cattle, Bill Fielding opened up shop selling dry goods and necessities while Mrs. Fielding rented out rooms and cooked meals. Word spread quickly, bringing a flurry of saloonkeepers and bawdy houses to the outpost to tap the lucrative flow of wayfarers.

Bill Fielding took to the idea of founding a town so much so that he put his full energy into making his prodigy grow and prosper. He mapped out streets, wrote up some rules, and walked about the fledgling community with a six-shooter in one hand and a shot gun in the other to let everyone know who was in charge. And sure enough they found out. Bill Fielding hadn't been a man afraid to use his gun.

But now, forty years later, Bill was gone, along with a good many of the bawdy houses, leaving his only daughter's son, Wade, to run the show.

A reluctant swell of pride nudged its way between the anger and frustration as Wade gazed out through the glass panes. Newly built boardwalks lined most streets. He had recently convinced the township of the need to pave Center Avenue. The bricks should arrive any week. He was pushing and pulling Fielding, Texas, into the next decade and he was proud to do it, proud to follow in his grandfather's footsteps. But his true love was the ranch, the ranch his father had started, the ranch Wade was bound and determined to turn into the vision his father had always dreamed of.

He owed his father that.

All of which brought him to the fact that he needed the spinster's land—regardless that Harold said it was impossible to acquire.

Wade drew a deep breath. Slowly, steadily, a look of pure determination replaced all remnants of anger and frustration. He knew what he had to do.

Harold eased to the edge of his chair, desire to worm his way out of trouble possibly making him brave, and interrupted his employer's reverie. "I still don't understand why you can't simply use the land across the river that you already own."

At first there was no response. The room was silent save for the distant clang of the blacksmith's hammer as Wade turned back from the window. "Buying the new land," he eventually replied, "would be a great deal less expensive, not to mention more convenient, than building a five-hundred-yard bridge across the Colorado River. Given that, the only feasible locations are the West Tract and the Patterson acreage. Since I've dropped the Patterson deal because you told me we had the other tied up, I'll have to go over to Austin and talk to the West Tract owner myself."

"But, Wade, as I explained—"

"Who's her solicitor?" he asked sharply.

Harold sighed. "Edward Leister."

Wade's eyes flickered with surprise, but only for a moment. "Ed Leister? It couldn't have been more than three and a half, four months since I last spoke with him. He didn't mention representing a new landowner to me. And anyone who uses Ed can't need the money all that bad," he said more to himself than Harold. "What's the woman's name?"

"He wouldn't tell me. Just said it's not proper for a woman to be involved in such things."

"Sounds like something Ed would say. Hmmm." Wade returned to his desk. "We've wasted too much time as it is. I'll ride over to Austin tomorrow and pay Ed a visit." He looked directly at Harold. "I want the file on the West Tract and a complete report detailing everything you have done so far—*excluding* your 'real nice lunch.' Have it to me by the end of the day."

Wade picked up a letter and began to read, effectively dismissing the other man. "On your way out tell Nathan I want to see him."

No sooner had the door shut than it opened again. Wade's assistant of the last two years, Nathan Caldwell, entered briskly, full of cheer. "I received a vague nod of the head in this direction from Harold. I guess that was a lesser man's version of announcing a summons."

Wade merely scowled at his assistant before saying, "I have to go to Austin tomorrow."

"What brought this on?" Nathan asked, placing a short stack of letters in front of Wade to be signed.

"I need to talk to Ed Leister."

"Ed Leister? What for?"

"As it turns out, we don't have the West Tract. Ed is representing the landowner," he said, glancing over the letters and starting to sign, "and it looks as though I'll have to be the one to convince him to get us that property."

"Little Harold couldn't pull off the deal?" Nathan cocked his head and glanced at his boss. "I still can't figure out why you keep that dimwit around."

"Because he is family." The words were said deliberately, each syllable stressed.

"Third or fourth cousin at best," Nathan offered, either disregarding or failing to notice Wade's menacing tone. "Not to mention an inept cousin at that. Have you given any thought to the fact that you have an awful lot of relatives floating around out there for someone who is an only child and whose parents died years ago?"

Wade's hand stilled. The words cut to the core. He would have winced had another man not been standing there to see such weakness. Instead, he merely looked out, beyond Nathan, to a place in years past.

In his mind's eye he saw the charred remains of the house he once called home. Darkness threatened to consume him as it had so many years before, when it had sent him on a wild journey to escape the pain, bringing him back only two years before to try to make things right.

Guilt, to this day, followed him around like an unwanted companion. If only he had been there, he wished for the thousandth time. But he hadn't been there, he reminded himself harshly, turning his mind back to the present and his assistant who had been rambling on the whole time.

"Speaking of family," Nathan continued, "it seems a long-lost cousin of yours has died."

A shadow passed across Wade's eyes. "Who now?"

"James Daniels."

Wade leaned back. "Jim Daniels. Lord, I haven't seen him in what . . . nineteen years, I think. He wasn't that much older than me, couldn't have been more than thirty-seven years old."

"He died of the fever. Went in his sleep."

"When's the burial?"

"Last month. Sorry. Nothing you can do. There's an inheritance involved, however." Nathan set a document on the desk in front of Wade. "If this is correct, the bequest should arrive any day."

"What is it?"

"Doesn't say. Just says that you are the sole beneficiary of the late James Dawson Daniels, formerly of the Nebraska Territory."

"The Nebraska Territory?" Wade brought steepled fingers to his chin. "I wonder what he was doing up there?"

"I wonder what the inheritance is?"

A low chuckle rumbled in Wade's chest. His face brightened slightly with subtle hints of mirth. "It's probably something crazy. A stuffed hog's head wouldn't surprise me." Wade shook his head. "Well, anyway, send whatever it is over to the house."

The door clicked shut, leaving Wade alone in the office

his grandfather had used solely for dealing with town concerns. Wade's concerns, however, had grown to encompass not only the management of the nearly sixty-five percent ownership of everything in Fielding, Texas, but the running of the ranch his father had started, as well.

The office was filled with proof of Wade's wealth and success—the wealth he had inherited, but the success he had worked tirelessly, day and night, to achieve. It was as if he felt the need to prove to his dead parents, or perhaps solely to himself, that he deserved it all.

He ran one strong finger along the edge of the handcarved mahogany desk, his dark countenance unfathomable. Dark wood paneling hugged the walls; Persian rugs covered the hardwood floor; an ornate grandfather clock announced the quarter hour.

The news of Jim's death left Wade feeling unusually dispirited. He had always hoped that one day Jim would walk through the door, a fat cigar clamped in his mouth, to brag about his escapades. Now, with the arrival of a single document, all hope of seeing his cousin again was snuffed out as thoroughly as was the man's life.

The sun lowered in the western sky. Long rays of golden light filtered through the glass-paned window. The brass handle of the top desk drawer reflected the diminishing sun. He pulled the drawer open and found a small black box among the neatly placed items, reminding him of his impending engagement.

Lorraine Wilcox was everything a wife should be. Blond hair, blue eyes, shapely. And, more important, she knew a woman's place.

A year ago he had set out to catch her, and catch her he did. He had pursued her with the calm determination that characterized all his dealings. She was the prettiest girl in town and from one of Fielding's finest families. And in a few short months she would be his.

Strangely, though, the thought of spending the rest of his life with her didn't fill him with the excitement he thought he should feel.

But that's absurd, he scoffed at himself. It was just the news of Jim's death making him think such ridiculous thoughts.

Pushing himself up from his desk, he put the box in his pocket. His parents would have been proud, he told himself. His carefully planned life was falling into place.

And he was determined that nothing or no one would get in his way.

Two

WADE LEFT FOR Austin the following day. It was just past noon, and after settling comfortably in the saddle, he had a chance to mull over what he knew about the West Tract deal. He had been surprised to learn that Ed Leister was handling the purchase, and as he approached his destination, this fact, more than any other, seemed most important.

The Leister family, with the oldest brother, Richard, at the helm, was an integral part of the Austin community. If Ed was dealing with the West Tract, could that mean a Leister owned it? But then, who would the mysterious lady be?

For the life of him he couldn't think of a single old, un-married woman who belonged to the family. He knew Ed and Richard's mother was still alive, but she certainly wasn't a spinster. Could Harold have been mistaken and the woman wasn't an old maid at all, but perhaps just *old*?

He realized then that if indeed the woman was a Leister, it was Richard more than the younger brother, Ed, Wade would have to deal with if he wanted the property.

Once in Austin, Wade left his horse at the livery before walking the short distance to Edward's office.

"Mr. Alexander." The receptionist, who was not only young but a woman as well, blushed crimson when she turned to find Wade standing at her desk. "It's so good to see you. . . . I mean, good that you're here . . . to see Mr. Leister, of course." Her hand fluttered to her light brown hair, then down to smooth some nonexistent wrinkle in her gingham skirt.

"It's a pleasure to see you, Miss Judith. Is Edward in?"

"Yes . . . yes, he is. I'll tell him you're here."

She left momentarily, then returned, her smile and red-tinged cheeks still glowing.

"Go right up. His assistant will be waiting."

The offices of Edward Leister were nicely done in a very traditional, manly kind of way. Dark woods, lots of supple leather, and books lining every wall. Wade went up the stairs expecting to find Ed's assistant, but found his carousing buddy from younger days waiting instead.

"I see you've redone the place. Not bad for a younger son," Wade joked and extended his hand to the short, wiry man.

"Good to see you, old buddy." Ed slapped Wade on the back and led him to a door with EDWARD LEISTER boldly etched on a shiny brass plate. "So you like it. Rosalind deserves the credit. Redecorated the entire place. Had furniture and material shipped in from all over the country. Took her forever to get it done."

"Sweet Rosalind. How is she? Beautiful as ever?"

Edward smiled. Being a man of small stature, nondescript brown hair, and plain looks, he always beamed at the mention of his striking wife. "Just fine, just fine."

They spoke at length of shared escapades and mutual acquaintances before Edward asked, "So tell me, what brings you to town? Or should I guess? The land Harold Mackenzie was out here trying to buy?"

Wade gave a slight nod of acknowledgment.

Edward sighed. "I figured it wouldn't be long before you showed up and tried to convince me to see things your way. But I'll tell you up front, just like I told Harold, there's nothing I can do. My . . . um . . . the owner won't budge."

The *my* confirmed Wade's suspicions but instinct told him to proceed cautiously. "Can't you at least set up an appointment for me to meet with the woman?"

Ed shook his head. "I'd like to help you, Wade. You know I would. But I'm just not in a position to do anything else."

Wade leaned back in his chair and looked closely at his friend. "Is Richard?"

The nicely appointed office suddenly crackled with tension. Edward scowled. "Yes, he is, but if I were you, I wouldn't press it with him. It's a sore subject."

"Sore subject? Who owns the property?" Wade asked, one dark brow arching in question.

"That's a sore subject, too." Ed grimaced. He sat quietly for a moment as if trying to make some sort of decision, the tension slowly beginning to settle. Finally he spoke. "Look, I'm really not in a position to do anything for you, but"—he paused, shuffling a few folders on the desk—"Rosalind and I are having a little party this evening around seven. Come by. Rosalind would love to see you." Edward Leister hesitated before adding, "And Richard will be there. But tread lightly, my friend."

"Is it some scandal?"

The words seemed to amuse Ed, and for the first time since the land discussion began, the tension eased entirely and he laughed out loud. "Scandal, no—at least not yet. It's simply a case of someone usurping brother Richard's precious control. So, will we see you tonight?" he asked, still smiling.

Deciding the party was his best bet for seeing Richard Leister, Wade agreed. "Sure, around seven. And Ed, I appreciate it."

Wade had a few hours before he had to be at the Leister's. After making overnight arrangements for his horse, Wade registered at the Cedar Creek Hotel. He'd have to stay the night because of the party, but things could be worse. He could be on his way back to Fielding no more effectual than Harold Mackenzie. Wade hoped the overnight stay would be worthwhile.

With accommodations taken care of, Wade called on several businesses to place orders for ranch supplies he couldn't get in Fielding. It was six o'clock when he made it back to his room; just enough time to grab a bite to eat, change into the only set of decent clothes he had brought along, and make his way to the party.

Edward Leister and his wife lived about a mile from town. Not having the time to go to the livery and saddle his horse, Wade had an attendant from the hotel drop him off at the Leister home. The driver asked when he should return, but Wade told him he preferred to walk back.

As Wade approached the cream-colored stone house, the imposing front door opened immediately. A butler in formal attire and spotless white gloves stood at attention. "Good evening, sir," he said, running a disdainful eye over Wade's attire. "May I take your . . . um . . . hat?"

"Wade!" Edward called out, greeting his friend with a huge smile and a warm handshake. "Good of you to come."

"Some 'little party,' " Wade said while handing his black Stetson to the butler. "Had I known, I would've brought my top hat and tails."

"But you didn't know." Ed pulled at the stiff shirt collar and bow tie. "And I'm sure you'll get over it."

"Where's Rosalind?"

A delicate woman of no more than five feet came forward with arms outstretched, blue eyes shining, blond curls perfectly coiffed. "Wade Alexander. Where have you been hiding yourself?"

Pulling her hands to his lips, Wade smiled warmly. "Rosalind, you are lovelier than ever."

Rosalind laughed, a welcoming smile spreading daintily on her lips. "Still the charmer, I see."

"Tell your brother-in-law that. I'm hoping to charm him out of some land."

"I should have known you'd have some reason for coming. But reason or not, I'm glad you're here. Come on, let's go in so you can see everyone." Rosalind took hold of both men's arms.

"You know you take a great risk of ruining your party every time you invite me," Wade remarked as they entered a high-ceilinged room brimming with well-heeled guests.

"Oh, pooh. It just keeps those girls in line to have their mamas keeping track of where they are for a change. Besides, you know that every one of them will be thrilled to death to find out you're in town."

As if in proof, a nearby trio of young ladies smiled becomingly at Wade, fluttering fans and waving prettily, in obvious anticipation that he, perhaps, would pay them a bit of attention. But in the same picture, Wade couldn't help but notice the mothers who moved closer to their daughters' sides. It was a strange sensation to know he was thought of as a ruiner of women, all because of one careless affair—an affair, thank God, that had not produced a child.

He had been with the girl only once, and while he took complete responsibility for the mess, it wasn't he who had instigated the liaison. Of course, that part of the story never got around, only the part about the girl having to move to St. Louis to live with an aunt. He still felt bad about the situation. But he knew for a fact he was neither the first man she had given herself to, nor the last, merely the one she had tried to snag with her lies and stories.

Ed noticed the coquettish smiles. "Just wait a while. As

usual, once they sneak a few sips of punch, they'll be brave enough to slip away from their mamas and find you."

Rosalind shook her head. "There's not a mama here who doesn't want you for a son-in-law, Wade. It's just finding a way to get their daughters to the altar with their virginity intact that poses the dilemma." With that Rosalind sauntered away, leaving the men wide-eyed and speechless.

"She's never been one to mince words," Wade finally said with one raised eyebrow, his lips quirked up in an incredulous smile.

The men joined Rosalind and a young girl of medium height, golden hair, and ample chest. "Why, Wade Alexander," Emma Jean James said in a practiced voice, holding out her hand. "How good it is to see you."

"Miss James," Wade replied, dutifully accepting her hand.

"So formal?" She turned to Ed and Rosalind. "What did you do to get him here?" But before anyone could answer, an older, less comely version of Emma Jean stepped forward. "Hello, Mr. Alexander."

Wade could have sworn she was out of breath.

"What brings you to our city?" Emma Jean's mother asked.

"The fine hospitality of my good friends and the opportunity to visit with such lovely ladies as yourself." Where he hadn't kissed Emma Jean's hand, he did so to her mother's. Henrietta James actually blushed.

"Good God," Rosalind mumbled.

"Pardon?" Henrietta asked, her blush fading with the narrowing of her eyes.

"How odd." Rosalind smiled. "Over there. Edward's brother. Richard, dear," she called. "Come see who's here." She turned to the James women. "If you'll excuse us."

Wade laughed once both mother and daughter were out of earshot.

" 'Such lovely ladies as yourself,' " Rosalind mimicked. "That was a bit thick, even for you. Unless, of course, you're getting desperate in your old age?"

"No, Rosalind, not me. In fact, you'll be pleased to hear that I'm going to ask Lorraine Wilcox to be my wife."

"The girl who was with you the last time you were in town? The judge's daughter?"

"Yes."

"Oh."

" 'Oh'? I tell you I'm engaged, and all you can say is 'oh'?" Wade looked to Edward. "Is this the same woman who has tried to marry me off to just about every female in Austin who's under fifty?"

"Rosalind just doesn't know what to say she's so happy for you. Isn't that right, dear?"

"Well, if you really want to know . . ."

"Come on you two, Richard is waiting for us." Ed took his wife's arm and led her toward his brother, forestalling Wade's attempt to question Rosalind further.

Richard Leister was a big man, almost as tall as Wade, though several inches wider. He had Ed's brown hair and ordinary features, but when combined with his height and girth, those same characteristics turned out as anything but plain.

"Richard, honey," Rosalind said to the brother-in-law who was a good twelve years older than she. "Look who blew in with the wind."

"Wade." Richard extended his hand. "How's Fielding?"

"Good. We're growing all the time."

"I hear Judge Wilcox is up for another award."

"Yes. As a matter of fact, I'll be joining the judge and his family this year at the award ceremony."

"Wade seems to be quiet serious with Wilcox's daughter," Ed supplied.

Rosalind made a sound that sounded suspiciously like a snort. Wade looked at Rosalind but was prevented from questioning her yet again when Richard threw a meaty arm over Wade's shoulders.

"The judge's daughter. You don't say. I hear she's a pretty little thing."

"Yes, she is."

"So what brings you to town?" Richard asked, turning his gaze to the scores of guests who ambled through the room.

Ed visibly cringed.

"I came over to see about the West Tract."

Richard's arm dropped as his glance darted from the crowd to Wade before finally glaring at Ed. "I thought you told that idiot Mackenzie the land was not for sale."

"I did," Ed protested.

"And Ed also told me there was nothing else that could be done," Wade added. "I simply find it hard to believe that someone with your business acumen wouldn't take the profit from that land and invest it in something more lucrative."

Richard grumbled. "I know, I know. Damn! I've said that very same thing a thousand times. That land's useless just sitting out there so far from Austin." With narrowed eyes he looked at Wade. "Why're you so hot-fired about it? What do you want with it?"

"To expand my ranch. Plain and simple. And I'm willing to pay a fair price. Why don't we at least sit down and talk it over?"

Richard's head wagged back and forth, his lips pursed tightly. "Hell, it couldn't hurt."

"How about in the morning?"

"Tomorrow's not good. Every Friday I ride to New

Braunfels. If you want to stay the weekend, or come back, I could meet you first thing Monday morning."

The idea of the two-hour ride to Fielding, then another to return didn't do much for Wade, but neither did the prospect of going back to square one with Herb Patterson to try to secure his acreage. "Eight o'clock, Monday, then."

After shaking Wade's hand, Richard turned to Edward and said, "Your office at eight." Without another word to his younger brother, and merely a nod to Rosalind, Richard strode from the small group.

Ed muttered. His eyes shot daggers.

"There, there, dear. You know how he is," Rosalind said, placing a hand gently on his sleeve. "Now that Wade has his business taken care of, let's go enjoy ourselves. It's a party, after all."

Knowing he couldn't leave for Fielding until first light, Wade decided to try to relax. He had always enjoyed Ed and Rosalind's company and so rarely got to see them. But he was left to his own devices a few moments later when his hosts were waylaid by an assortment of guests.

The orchestra started up in the next room, and several couples glided across the hardwood floor. The ladies were lavishly dressed, bedecked with jewels that sparkled under the substantial crystal chandelier. The men stood by uncomfortably in attire so unlike the loose chambray shirts, trousers, and boots they usually wore.

Wade walked through the crowded house to the tall French doors swathed in golden silk draperies tied back with braided ropes and tassels. The doors were open to a veranda overlooking a spacious lawn and garden. The night air was cool, and he looked forward to the walk back to his room. He'd stay at the gathering only a short while longer, then content himself with the clear night sky and possibly a brandy back at the hotel. His days of hearty drinking and lusty women were over.

He lit a hand-rolled cheroot and pulled slowly at the heavy smoke. Leaning against the wooden doorframe, he glanced about the room. He knew just about everyone and recognized the rest, but no one he particularly wanted to talk to.

And then he saw her, no more than a few steps from where he stood. He was sure he'd never seen her before—he would have remembered. She stood alone at a side table, surveying the assortment of extravagant delicacies with a discerning eye. He stared openly, the cigar held forgotten in his hand.

She tasted a strawberry dipped in sugar, and Wade could see traces of white powder left upon her full lips. She dabbed the sugar with a napkin. He longed to have wiped it away.

She turned then as if sensing his gaze. Their eyes met and held. She looked at him, directly, no lowered lashes or simpering smiles, and he wondered who she was. Her eyes were green, a rich, deep, blue-green encircled by long, thick lashes. And her hair—soft flames of fire, pulled loosely up and back from her face. Her lips were red—red without paint. And her skin—porcelain white with a faint smattering of freckles across the delicate bridge of her slightly upturned nose.

At length she broke his gaze and spoke to a woman who had approached.

His eyes wandered. Though tall for a woman, she was no less shapely because of her height. Her breasts swelled, her narrow waist fell gracefully into rounded hips. His heart beat faster.

Then she smiled, a wide perfect smile that brightened her already perfect face and dazzled her eyes. He caught a strand of her laughter floating across the crowded room, and for one untamed second, Wade had the urge to take the few steps that separated them and pull her into his arms, to feel the softness of her skin.

His tumultuous thoughts were interrupted, however, when a short, balding man approached her, laying his hand upon hers. The man's eyes traveled the length of her, a lewd smile settling on his lips. Wade felt an inexplicable surge of anger and started toward the pair.

An image of Lorraine loomed in his mind, checking his steps. She was the woman he was to marry, the woman with whom he would spend the rest of his life. The girl with waves of fiery hair and penetrating eyes was none of his business. But despite his commendable intentions, Lorraine was banished, replaced by visions of the other.

Drawn by a pull he didn't understand, Wade stepped quickly outside to get rid of the cigar, crushing it under his booted heel, intent on approaching the unknown woman. But when he returned, she was gone, disappeared into the crowd of wandering guests.

Disappointment reverberated through the air.

He searched the room, his face a dark, unreadable mask, looking for any sign of the fiery tresses. He went from corner to corner, winding his way through the crush of guests. But she was nowhere to be found.

He took a drink from a passing waiter and swallowed the whole thing down. With the glass returned to the tray, he took one last look to prove to himself that she was really gone. And she was.

The cool air beckoned. He walked out into the garden and looked up into the endless heavens. Pinpricks of light dotted the black sky, thousands upon thousands of distant stars shining brightly. Eventually his heart slowed.

Turning to lean against the balustrade, Wade looked back at the house. From this distance the windows turned to glimmering rectangles filled with animated guests, framed by the darkness of the solid house walls.

He took a deep breath. His world straightened, no longer seemed askew. What had happened in there? What had he been thinking, he asked himself with a shrug of his broad shoulders, ignoring the memory of that intense disappointment he had felt when he found her gone. It must have been the heat, he told himself as he pushed away from the railing to return to the party.

Redheaded temptresses weren't a part of his plan.

Three

MADELINE MONTGOMERY DESCENDED the long curving staircase from the upper regions of Ed and Rosalind Leister's house, bringing her reluctantly back into the throng of guests. Near the bottom step she overheard an irate older woman reprimanding a younger woman who Madeline assumed must be her daughter.

"Emma Jean, you stay away from that man," Henrietta James demanded, holding securely to her daughter's arm and pulling the girl down onto the Queen Anne bench that sat against the wall.

Madeline took the remaining steps and didn't listen to the rest. She had been hearing a good deal of the same talk ever since she arrived at Aunt Rosalind's party. Every mother in the room, it seemed, was keeping a watchful eye on her daughter. And all apparently because of one man—the man who had stood so casually in the doorway, causing her heart to flutter in her chest when their eyes had met. His look had held such dark depths that she had wondered what he was thinking. She imagined he heard all the whispers about him, and she just knew his feelings were hurt. Poor man. People could be so cruel. Was that what caused the brooding she had sensed when she had watched him without his knowing? Probably so, she told herself. Who wouldn't brood in the same situation? You had to respect a man who did not turn and run from such vicious tongues.

Or so she told herself, as it was easier to attribute her fluttering heart to sympathy rather than attraction. His striking good looks and his bold stance had nothing to do with it. She wasn't the type to get carried away by such things. Their eyes had met and her heart had skipped a beat, she thought disdainfully. Really! If there was one thing she was not, it was a romantic fool.

Madeline slipped through the room, trying to avoid standing in one place for any length of time. Every time she did, some man would strut toward her, practically foaming at the mouth. Good God, it was disgusting!

She didn't understand why they all clamored for her attention. Certainly it wasn't her looks. With red hair and pale white skin, she knew she wasn't anyone's idea of a prize. Therefore, she decided, it must be her money. It appeared that word had gotten around that Dale and Katherine Montgomery's only child, Richard Leister's niece, had come to America from England to take control of her deceased mother's estate. She could just imagine the uproar her decision had caused, if her uncle's reaction was any indication. An unmarried maiden returning to take control. Madeline could only hope that more people were of her sweet grandmother's ilk rather than her uncle's.

It was her grandmother, in fact, who had convinced her to make the voyage across the Atlantic to take up the reins of an inheritance she hadn't known existed. She also hadn't known Uncle Richard had been overseeing the estate since her mother had run away with her father twenty-seven years ago, the year before Madeline was born.

Well, Uncle Richard's control had come to a halt, much to his annoyance. It would seem, Madeline mused, that she had done nothing but irritate her mother's older brother since the day she set foot within Austin's town boundaries.

Pausing at a table laden with food, she picked up a finger

sandwich at random and popped it in her mouth. The salty taste of raw fish and cream cheese pulled her features into a mask of pained surprise. She chewed bravely and swallowed as quickly as possible, washing the whole mess down with a cup of punch.

Just as she pressed a linen napkin to her lips, she noticed Frank Pearson, a fellow who worked for her uncle, pushing his way toward her. Instantly she spun around on soft kid slippers, the folds of her simple dress billowing in her haste. But her attempt to flee was thwarted when her quick turn brought her face to face with Mark Webster, another young man of whom her uncle approved.

"Miss Madeline, you look marvelous," Mark gushed.

"Hello, Mr. Webster," she said reluctantly.

He was no taller than Madeline, and it was from her new maid, Jane, that she had heard him referred to as "the short, fat fellow in need of a rich wife." When Madeline had probed, Jane regaled her with stories of the man's exploits in Guy Town. She was sure he wasn't there doing good works. And to think, her uncle approved. Whether the gossip was true or not, Madeline had learned that she had best watch out for herself. Uncle Richard certainly wasn't.

"Miss Montgomery!" Frank Pearson had managed to arrive at her side, elbowing his way between her and Mark Webster. "Has anyone said you look marvelous this evening?"

"Yes, just a moment ago. In fact, you and Mr. Webster have so much in common I think I'll leave you two to chat."

She quickly stepped away, saying her hellos to nearby guests as if she didn't know the young men heatedly watched her retreating steps.

Wandering through the house, she stopped at a fountain that bubbled with champagne. She started to fill a glass but decided against it. The bubbly stuff, as her father had always called it, went straight to her head, leaving her with what could only be compared to bells and hammers clanging and banging away at her the next morning.

She opted for more punch, and with a cup in hand, she roamed about, watching the clock, waiting for a reasonable amount of time to pass so she could leave without hurting her dear aunt's feelings.

Uncle Richard had demanded she attend. Arriving at Madeline's home first thing that morning, he had barged in while she sat at the breakfast table sipping coffee and reading the local newspaper.

"Good morning, Uncle."

"Morning," he said as he pulled off his hat, his skin blotchy and damp. "No one answered the door. I just walked right in here." Richard looked around. "Where's your grandmother?"

"In the rose garden, enjoying the morning sun." Madeline turned the page. "Would you care for some coffee? Jane just made it."

"Who's Jane? Some new runaway you've taken in?"

"No, Uncle. She's my maid. Your office sent her over, remember?"

"Oh, yeah, well anyway. I came to talk."

"To me?" she inquired, feigning surprise, her eyelashes batting coquettishly. "Whatever can I do for you?"

He glanced at her with a scowl before he pulled out a Chippendale chair and lowered his girth into it. "For one, you can get rid of that damn fancy talkin' of yours."

"You'd rather I curse and blather like you?" Before he could respond, she set the paper down and held her hands up in the air as if framing a picture. "I can see it now. Miss Madeline Montgomery sitting next to Harriet Winslow at the Women's League Social. 'Damn, Harriet, that hat of yours beats all.' " She did a fair job of imitating his southern drawl, only adding heat to her uncle's already steamy face.

"Don't get smug with me, young lady."

"Of course not, Uncle," she said with lowered lashes and a mischievous smile. "What was I thinking? I must have lost my head."

Richard brought his fist down on the cherrywood table with more force than he intended, causing delicately flowered china and high polished silver to dance about on the white linen cloth. "I don't know why I put up with this."

"Neither do I. And you really shouldn't have to. You needn't bother yourself about me. So why don't you just go home and send my love to Aunt Alice." She pushed back her chair. "Let me see you to the door."

"Sit down, young lady. This discussion isn't over yet."

Madeline sat down with a sigh, a few more wisps of red hair falling from her once secure chignon. "I was afraid of that."

"You have a smart mouth on you, and I'm getting sick and tired of it. I can't imagine what my sister was thinking when she brought a child up in such a way." He shifted in his seat, rearranging his bulk to a more comfortable position. "Must have been that husband of hers. Told her not to marry the man."

"And is that why you forbade her name to be mentioned ever again?" The words were spoken slowly, filled with scorn. The smiles and sarcasm were gone, replaced with a voice of icy steel any man would take notice of. Her green eyes darkened as they fixed on his blotchy countenance. "Uncle Richard, my father was a kind and decent man. You will not speak of him in such a manner."

"I'll do what I please, little lady. You understand me?" He said the words with force, though he shifted in his seat and looked away.

"What I understand, Uncle, is that you are not welcome in this house if you continue to be so hateful. And we both know who owns this home." Her eyes turned to chips of jade, daring him to contradict her.

Richard shifted again and studied his niece in indecision. "Hell, I didn't come here to talk about your father, anyway, or this damn house for that matter. I came to make sure you attend your aunt Rosalind's party tonight. A girl with your kind of money needs a husband to take care of it properly."

Married to someone he could manage easily, or possibly someone who would be advantageous to him, she thought, but replied instead, "I am not getting married, Uncle. Not now, not ever. Period, end of discussion. Do you hear me?"

His blotchy face became a solid color—red, bright red, with a telltale vein bulging out on his forehead. "Why, you impertinent little . . . Yes, I hear you, but I won't take no for an answer."

"You'll have to. I'm an adult and there's nothing you can do."

When Madeline set her coffee cup aside and made ready to leave the room, Richard attempted to calm himself. "Madeline"—he sighed—"your mother and I had some unfortunate times between us. But that's water under the bridge at this point. The important thing to consider is you. You are a headstrong girl who needs a stabilizing force. Someone to make decisions for you, to take care of you, make sure you are never in need. I think we both would agree you don't exercise the best judgment at times."

"What's that supposed to mean?"

"Do I have to remind you of the little incident last week where I found that harlot's daughter in this house, under the very same roof as your grandmother—my mother!"

"Little Lucy is an orphan. She needed help. Grandmother

didn't mind. I had the child here until I found her a home. I promised her mother that."

"And that's another thing. What were you doing that put you in a position to meet up with a woman of such nature?"

"You know perfectly well what I was doing. Helping Reverend Marshall down in Guy Town."

"Well, I don't like it. If you feel the need to do good works, then raise money or join the Women's League like the rest of the ladies do. A Leister shouldn't be mucking around with poor and sick people."

"I'm not a Leister. I'm a Montgomery."

"In name. But you've got the Leister blood running through your veins. Not to mention Leister money and a Leister house." He clenched a silver fork in his meaty hand. "And as long as you live in this town, young lady, you're not going to run around embarrassing the rest of your family."

"You mean embarrass you. Grandmother doesn't mind."

"Your grandmother is another story altogether these days." Richard scowled and looked out a window that led to the rose garden. "After thirty-one years of my patient guidance, my widowed mother suddenly decides she should be making decisions for herself." He shook his head and glanced back at Madeline. "But that's neither here nor there. You're going to start acting like a lady. Now, go to Rosalind's party so you can meet some nice young men. Frank Pearson is partial to you. I'd approve of him."

Madeline clutched the edge of the table, afraid if she let go she'd pick up her plate and throw it at him.

"I've got to get on now. Think about what I said. I don't want to have to force the issue," he stated.

Closing her eyes, she sat very still and waited until she heard the front door click shut. "He can't make me do anything," she reassured herself. "I'm an adult and my mother's estate was left to me unencumbered. I own everything out-right. Uncle Richard can't do a thing."

"Is something wrong, miss?"

Madeline opened her eyes and found her maid hovering in the doorway. "No," she said as she heaved a long, frustrated sigh. "I was just talking to myself."

The servant turned to go.

"Jane," Madeline called. "If Mr. Leister calls again, tell him I'm not in."

The sounds of the party brought her back to the present. She had ended up coming but only because her aunt Rosalind had sent a message.

Darling Madeline,

Do please come by this evening, if only for a little while.

Yours, Rosalind

Rosalind the peacemaker. Madeline didn't know for a fact that Rosalind was trying to avoid a scene, though she had a pretty good idea. And even though she was a bit put out with the lot of them just now, she truly liked her younger uncle Edward and his wife and wouldn't do anything to dampen their elaborately planned party. So she went, but she had managed to avoid her uncles and aunt all evening.

She had been in Texas only two months, and from the be-ginning Richard had treated her like a child, attempting to make decisions for her as if she couldn't make them on her own. She was twenty-six years old, for heaven's sake, and had traveled from London to Texas without any help from her uncle. And she didn't need his help now.

The thought brought her blood to a boil. Then she heard another vapid remark about the poor man whom no one seemed to like. And Richard said she didn't have good judgment. Hah! He had poorer judgment than she if he would allow an obvious outcast to attend the party and then make no attempt to make him feel welcome.

It didn't matter that it was Ed and Rosalind's party, that Richard was only a guest. Outrage surged through her. Outrage that her uncle was so obtuse, outrage that she was at this stupid party, and outrage that these people would treat another human being so shabbily.

Just because he didn't wear the black formal attire the rest of the men wore was no reason to snub the man. He probably couldn't afford top hat and tails. Or for that matter, maybe he didn't know any better. She felt another surge of sympathy for him. Not everyone could afford all the luxuries her family and their friends apparently could.

In all her dismay, Madeline failed to notice the men who tried to strike up conversations with the man, or the girls who slipped away from their mothers to seek him out. She also didn't realize that the mothers, who in one breath scolded their daughters on the dangers of him, in the next extolled their offspring's many accomplishments to the very same fellow.

As a result, Madeline decided impulsively she for one was not going to put up with these mean-hearted and ill-bred people any longer. She was going to make the man feel welcome.

With purposeful strides and spine held straight, she walked right up to the outcast, ignoring the whispers and murmurs she heard all around. "Hello, I'm Madeline Montgomery," she stated, tapping his shoulder to get his attention.

The man turned, his eyes widening a fraction at the sight of her. He started to smile, but something stopped him. Instead, he looked at her closely, his eyes hard in a questioning stare.

Regardless of his intense scrutiny, Madeline noticed that

up close he was even more handsome than she had realized. Black-brown hair, fathomless eyes, chiseled jaw, massive shoulders . . . Oh, stop this nonsense, she chided herself. You're not a shallow little twit. This is a humanitarian effort. Nothing more. She pulled her shoulders back as if to bolster her confidence, and then the stranger smiled.

"Is something funny?" she asked, her hand coming self-consciously to her hair.

"No," he responded simply, one dark brow rising.

His deep voice rumbled through her, and Madeline fleet-ingly looked away. "Well, aren't you going to introduce yourself?" she asked, returning to his bold stare.

His smile widened, though not with friendliness, and Madeline suddenly suspected she had plunged into waters too deep. But that couldn't be, she assured herself. She had seen with her own eyes the wretched loneliness that had filled him as he stood alone, the profound hurt at being shunned. So she chalked his ill behavior up to skepticism that anyone would treat him kindly.

"I'm Wade Alexander," he finally said. He studied her for a moment. "I'm sure I don't know you."

"You're right, but you looked lonely and I thought I'd ask you to dance."

"I looked lonely?"

"Well, yes," she said casually, though inwardly she cringed, wishing she could bite back her words. How could she be so cruel to comment on his obvious status as outcast? The last thing she wanted to do was embarrass the poor man.

"What made you think I looked lonely?"

Madeline smiled at Wade kindly, trying to think of the best possible way to muddle through this one. "It was just that I haven't seen you dance all evening."

Wade leaned back against the windowsill and crossed his arms, making it perfectly clear he wasn't on the verge of doing the gentlemanly thing and escorting her to the dance floor.

"You've been watching me?" he asked in a low voice that didn't sound as though it should be used to address a woman, or at least not a lady.

Her smile vanished, red surged through her cheeks. "Not watching you . . . exactly." And then suddenly a thought occurred to her. She glanced about the room before leaning forward and whispering, "Don't tell me you don't know how to dance?"

His eyes followed her gaze. "After you braved the wilds, you'd be terribly embarrassed to be sent on your way, especially in front of all these people who're watching this little tête-à-tête with great interest, is that it?"

Her mouth gaped open in astonishment. She was stunned with disbelief. He obviously warranted all the horrid things she had heard. The man was a cad!

Angry at herself for having so wrongly judged his character, she managed a "Go dance with yourself" before she turned on her heel, endeavoring to get just as far away as she possibly could. But her attempt was foiled when he reached out with one strong arm and pulled her into a German waltz.

The instant their bodies came together, Madeline felt a jolt of something she didn't understand. She glanced up into his dark eyes, and she thought he must have felt it, too.

They glided across the floor, underneath crystal teardrops sparkling from the chandelier, and for the first time Madeline could ever remember, she wasn't counting, one, two, three, one, two, three, with her feet trying desperately to follow along. She forgot about everything—the death of her parents, London, her uncle, the mean remarks—and lost herself to the pleasures of being held in the arms of this contrary man.

His arm held her close, her hand held securely in his grip.

He smelled faintly of expensive brandy and the fine cigar she had seen him smoke, but his look was of an untamed predator. Their eyes held, though neither one spoke, as if unwilling to break the fragile spell.

Around the room, floating on a tidal wave of sensation, they danced as if they had danced together all their lives. She followed his lead with an ease she didn't think possible. Their bodies fit together like two pieces of a whole as they moved around the dance floor, unaware of any other.

Perhaps it would never end.

But then the music ceased, the magic vanishing into the flickering light of the candlelit room, and the spell was broken.

It was a moment before her mind broke from its floating, dreamlike state to the harsh edge of reality, and Madeline caught sight of several pointed stares. Her anger revived. She forgot that only minutes ago she had deemed the others correct, that the man was indeed a cad, and she wondered anew how people could be so cruel. Her lips pursed and her green eyes darkened. "I've had enough, I'm leaving, and if I were you, I'd leave, too."

He looked down at her with eyes half closed, his lips settling into a hard line. "Perhaps I'll do that."

Nodding her head, she turned away, leaving him to follow or not as she walked from the dance floor.

Upstairs, she found her things. Catching sight of herself in the mirror, she frowned at her reflection. No wonder the man had found her so amusing. Just then she wished she had not worn such a plain dress, had worn instead something that would have made something of her unattractive features.

Her heart sank. Her hair, once so painstakingly pulled back, as usual, stood out about her head like wisps of fire. Perspiration glistened on her forehead from the dancing, and already the rust-colored tendrils were trying to curl. With a sigh, knowing she could do nothing about the errant strands, her cocoon of heady sensation fully dispelled, Madeline left the room.

Slipping out the back door, she shushed the dogs that started to bark. She hadn't said goodbye to anyone for fear her uncle would insist she stay and find herself a husband. The vision of Wade Alexander's dark handsomeness loomed unexpectedly in her mind. The way he had held her, his strong arms pressing her close, too close for propriety's sake. Corded muscles and softly waving hair that she longed to run her fingers through. His hand on the small of her back sending tingling sensations coursing through her body. And his eyes, deep and dark, almost black, searching hers . . . though for what she had no idea.

A horse and an old wagon that had seen better days stood amongst many others. Old Betty, Madeline's recently purchased steed, was tethered to the railing, though Madeline didn't notice the harness dangling undone. If she had gone out the front door, the valet, obviously practiced in such precarious maneuvers, would have brought her transportation conveniently to the front stoop. But to leave by way of the front door would have entailed an explanation; therefore, it was left to her to extract Old Betty and the wagon from the tight-knit row of carriages and buggies.

Grasping the high wooden seat, Madeline pulled herself up into the wagon, then gathered her skirts and shoved them beside her. When she looked up, she saw a tall figure crossing the road. Wade Alexander. The way her heart had palpitated earlier and his rugged handsomeness were forgotten as the sight of him walking reminded her of the man's sorry plight. Poor man, not only did he not have a carriage of some sort, he didn't even have a horse to carry him home. Before she thought about what she was doing, Madeline stood on the floorboard and called, "Mr. Alexander!"

Wade turned at the sound as if expecting her call. "Miss Montgomery," he drawled.

"You should have told me you didn't have a ride home. I'll be more than happy to take you."

"You're too kind, but—"

"Nonsense. I'm not kind at all. Now get in."

He approached the wagon with a reluctant smile. He hesitated when he drew up alongside and looked into Madeline's guileless eyes as if yet again he searched for the answer to some plaguing question. Then, with a shrug, he started to get in. "Is this thing safe?" he asked, warily eyeing the rickety contraption.

"Of course it is," she reassured him. "I've been riding around in it for days now with only the most minor of problems."

Suddenly she looked down at the horse.

"Something wrong?"

"No, no," she said, catching her lip between her teeth. "You sit tight, I'll just be a second."

Before he could respond, she was out of the wagon and walking around to stand in front of the horse, having finally noticed the unattached harness. After a bit her red head peeked back out, and with smiling green eyes, she said, "Just a minute more."

Wade sat on the hard wooden seat, a beam of moonlight catching a look of great incredulity stretched across his face. "Miss Montgomery," he called in disbelief, "what are you doing?"

Madeline straightened and smiled wryly. "I hadn't noticed they took the harness off Old Betty. Don't worry, though," she added through gritted teeth as she reached up to hold the harness to Old Betty's head. "I just about have it done."

The wagon rocked as Wade jumped down and followed

her to the front. His obsidian eyes snapped with irritation. "Get away from there."

Madeline straightened, pushing wayward strands of hair from her eyes. "Don't get huffy with me. I'm perfectly capable of harnessing my own horse. I've done it before, I'll do it again."

"Not with me around, you won't. Now get back in that wagon."

"One of these days you men are going to realize women are every bit as capable as you are."

Wade didn't bother to respond, merely gave her a look that sent her scurrying back to the wagon. With a huff she climbed back in.

Old Betty whinnied and stomped her hoof, then whinnied a few more times. Wade stepped to the side of the wagon and looked at Madeline. "Are you sure this horse will take the bit?"

"Of course she will. I got here, didn't I?"

"For all I know you pulled the wagon yourself," he remarked sarcastically.

Madeline stifled a snort of laughter and merely rolled her eyes. "If you hum a few bars of 'Dixie' it seems to take her mind off the bit, and you can slip it right in."

"You expect me to sing to this old bag of bones?"

"No, just hum. Like this . . ."

Wade was saved the chore when, sure enough, as no more than a few notes of the melody floated through the air, the bit slipped past the horse's huge teeth.

When Madeline heard the sound of metal passing over teeth, she said, "Assuming you didn't take the bit yourself, it seems to have worked."

Mr. Wade Alexander didn't bother to stifle his snort of disbelief, bringing a hot blush to Madeline's cheeks. Sometimes she couldn't believe the things that came out of her mouth.

"We'd probably get a lot farther and a lot faster if I pull this thing myself," he grumbled when the wagon squeaked dangerously as he pulled himself up onto the seat.

"You really have a disagreeable temperament. If you had been a student of mine, you would have spent a great deal of time in the corner."

"You're a teacher? Of children?" he asked, clearly surprised or perhaps outraged.

"Was. I haven't been able to secure a position since I arrived in Texas. I hope I'll find something soon." Madeline sighed. "The kind of work I've been doing recently, while necessary, is harder to deal with on a day-to-day basis." Consciously pushing thoughts of the sick and helpless she dealt with every day from her mind, Madeline carefully guided the horse from the clutter of other carriages. "Where to?"

"Where to?" he repeated. "Oh, yeah. Pine Avenue. Better yet, why don't you give me the reins?"

"Nonsense. I may have succumbed to your domineering wishes about harassing Old Betty but I insist I drive. Now, hold on." Madeline snapped the reins and the horse and wagon lurched forward, jerking its occupants about, causing the old boards of the wagon to squeak in protest at the sudden movement.

"I thought you said this thing was safe."

"It is. It's just the starts and stops that are hard on Old Betty."

"Old Betty," Wade murmured. "Why would anyone strap a horse with a name like that?"

"You'd have to ask the previous owner. She came with the name. Though it suits her, don't you think?"

Wade could only shake his head.

They rolled out onto the road, running over ruts and

bumps indiscriminately. Wade sat back, pulled out a cheroot, and glanced in her direction. "Your family approves of this?"

Madeline smiled. "Good heavens, no! They hardly approve of me. They only put up with me, I suppose, because they have to."

"Montgomery? I haven't heard that name around here before."

"It's not surprising. My parents moved away in 1853. My father was a diplomat attached to the American Consulate in Paris and then in London."

Savoring his cigar, Wade surveyed the passing scenery. "I wonder what it would be like to live over there."

Assuming he had never been himself, and longed to go, she was silent for a moment while the rhythmic clatter of horse's hooves filled the air. "You'll make it one day," she finally said with determined cheeriness. "And you'll love it."

Madeline nodded then as if she had convinced herself.

"Tell me about yourself," she asked a short time later. "It must be tiring for you to go to such parties. People can be so awful."

Wade remembered Henrietta James and her daughter Emma Jean. "Yes, I suppose so."

"If you'd like, I could introduce you around a bit. That might help." The idea made her chuckle. "Or then again, it might make things worse."

Wade's eyes narrowed, but before he could question her, they took a corner and the front wheel hit a rut.

They bounced around on the seat, and Madeline lost hold of one rein. Old Betty veered to the right as Madeline leaned over to retrieve the missing rein, taking them over a small rocky mound. Wade grabbed the side of his seat with one hand and held Madeline with the other to keep them both from flying out onto the dusty road.

"This wagon may be safe, but you're not," Wade growled. "If you don't watch what you're doing you're going to get us both killed." He glanced over at her and would have told her to stop right then and let him off, but something stopped him. Probably the same thing that had sent him in search of her when first he saw her. Intrigue, which grew with every second he was in her company. He wasn't sure just what to make of her. Something inside told him she was different from the rest, that she was sincere in her interest. But then another voice, one he was better acquainted with, told him she was like all the other women who chased him around, she just happened to be more ingenious. As a result, he didn't tell her to pull over and let him off, rather held tight and decided to see where the night might take them.

"Do you think it was wise to have asked me to dance?" he asked while studying her profile.

"How do you mean?"

"Your reputation and all."

She laughed. "You mean, won't I ruin my reputation?" She gave him a wry smile. "A twenty-six-year-old female who hasn't managed to get herself married and rides around without a chaperon or companion has no reputation left to lose. My family has made that particular point perfectly clear."

He had been right after all. A lonely female searching for a husband, though how she thought this display of hers would secure one, he couldn't imagine. But a voice inside of him came up with the answer. By the very method he half hoped she was leading him to. A liaison.

While his interest lay in the feel of her body against his, her interest most assuredly was in the feel of a ring around her finger. Yes, a ruined woman. A shotgun wedding. Was she desperate? Maybe so. Though she had looks, she must not have money, if the state of her transportation was any indication, not to mention her lack of escort to the party. What father in his right mind would permit his daughter to gallivant around as she apparently was free to do?

He glanced at her practical dress, and a thought occurred to him. Could it be that she was part of the help? Could working as a servant be the work she spoke of that was not quite as rewarding as teaching? Would a servant be bold enough to ask a guest to dance?

The room *had* been rampant with outrage when she had so brazenly approached him. He had thought at the time it was because of him. Maybe not.

Questions swirled through his head, but despite his skeptical musings, he was still filled with uncanny attraction and desire that surged in his loins every time he looked at her delicate features. He remembered the jolt of sensation he experienced when he took her in his arms for the waltz. Not in years had he felt such intensity. He thought of her suggestion that he leave the party. Having set up an appointment with the Leisters for Monday morning and knowing he wouldn't have a chance to discuss the land any further that night, he'd decided to take her advice. And when he had walked out into the night, he had half hoped his instincts were correct and he'd find her waiting for him. And sure enough he had.

"Penny for your thoughts?" Her voice was sweet in the springtime air.

Wade looked at her, across the wooden seat, the silver moonlight washing over her. He tried to see her face in the dimness, to see those blue-green eyes and full red lips that had made his heart pound with desire as he stood at the edge of the room. She turned to look at him, and they gazed into each other's eyes, she forgetting she was on a humanitarian mission, he forgetting his skepticism of her motives, both unaware of their surroundings until with a crash they came to an abrupt halt, tossing them into a tangled heap.

They each lay dazed, until eventually, Madeline extricated herself with a sigh, pulling herself up to inspect the damage. Chickens squawked and feathers flew, disrupting the peaceful nighttime sky.

"Apparently, someone has put a bale of hay and some old wood where it doesn't belong," Madeline said with a careful shrug, then looked to Old Betty to make sure she was unharmed.

Wade shook some straw from his hair and began to laugh. "You're right. A barn should never be built so close to a road."

"At least not a road I might travel on."

The entire night and the frustrations each had brought to it bubbled up in the form of laughter, and they laughed until tears gathered in their eyes. Wade experienced a moment of simple unencumbered pleasure, and it felt good to laugh so hard.

After a bit, while feathers and straw settled around them, they sat quietly in the night, aware only of each other. Wade reached out and gently touched her face. She closed her eyes as his fingertips traced a path down her cheek to her lips. He thought to kiss her, despite the fact he knew he shouldn't. He had no business with this woman, whoever she might be. But just then, none of that mattered. He only wanted to feel the fullness of her lips, to hold her body against his. Wade leaned forward, his eyes on her sweet lips. But the moment came to a screeching halt when yet another crash reverberated through the air.

"Damn kids. What the hell. Gallivantin' 'round town, kissin' and carryin' on, destroyin' a person's property. No respect, I tell ya, no respect!" The man started to grab hold of Wade's shirt but stopped at the look he received. "Well, what you gonna do about this wreck, mister?" he asked, taking a step back.

"Oh, sir, it's all my fault," Madeline confessed. "I'm to blame. You see, one minute we were riding along without a problem, then in the next"—Madeline scrunched her shoulders and wrinkled her nose—"we clipped the side of your barn."

"Clipped, my backside. You ran the damn thing down. It's a wonder someone didn't get kilt."

The farmer took another step back when Wade started to rise, his features pulled into a dangerous mask. Madeline put a restraining hand on Wade's arm and shook her head.

"You kids have got ta learn," the farmer continued once he was convinced Wade wasn't getting any closer. "So I'm gonna go up to the house and send for the sheriff. Don't even think about runnin' off. If ya do, I'll track ya down, and then the goin's gonna be worse."

Madeline sat quietly as the farmer marched up the hill. As soon as the old man was far enough away, Madeline slapped the reins, and after a few ominous creaks and groans, the wagon pulled off into the dark, the culprits heedless of the shouting farmer.

"Whew, what a night," Madeline said once they were out of sight of the man and his barn. "I've heard Mr. Tucker is not terribly kind when riled. I'll go back tomorrow and make amends. Supposedly his wife is the more understanding of the two. I guess I better make certain I go back when she's at home."

"Hmmm," was all Wade said.

One long finger of the Colorado River crept toward the town. The flowing water lapped at the bank. Crickets beckoned to their mates. The night was simply beautiful, and without thinking about what she was doing, Madeline stopped the wagon and climbed down, leaving Wade alone on the wooden seat.

"It's beautiful, isn't it," she called back as she approached the water, a light skip carrying her across a sandy path.

Wade sat in the wagon and watched. An unfamiliar tightness surged through him. After anticipating this very opportunity all evening, he was surprised by the disappointment he felt. Disappointment that she would so obviously, and so easily, throw herself at him. Asking him to dance, offering him a ride, and now stopping at a secluded spot. He was torn between disappointment over her character and hunger for her body.

His emotions stirred. Why did she have to be like all the rest? he asked himself. For some reason, he had hoped she was different, unlike the many women who threw themselves at him whenever they were given a chance. But apparently she wasn't any different. He shrugged his shoulders. And what did it matter, anyway? After tonight he would never see the girl again.

Lorraine loomed in his mind. The idea of dallying didn't sit well. Loyalty, he had been taught by his father and grandfather, was ever important. But then he looked at Madeline, at the soft sway of her hips as she skipped along to the river. His chest tightened, though this time with something else, with the same sensations that had overcome him when first he caught sight of her fiery red hair and bright smiling eyes. And in that moment he knew he had to have her.

Lorraine was pushed from his mind. His primal needs prevailed, and Wade followed the fair Madeline to the river's edge.

She stood on the bank, the silver moonlight dancing on her hair. Looking up into the sky, she appeared to be lost in thought and lovelier than any woman Wade had ever seen. His desire grew. His pulse raced. Yes, he wanted her, regardless of the repercussions.

She lowered her eyes and looked up the length of the Colorado. Wade quietly came up behind her and followed her gaze. Gentle swells of water flowed toward them, mesmerizing, peaceful.

His loins grew taut with longing. His breath became shallow. And there, on the sandy edge of the gently rippling river, he reached out and lightly touched her shoulder. Anticipating the feel of her soft curves pressed against him, he was unprepared for Madeline to twirl around with a gasp, and for her arm to catch him unexpectedly hard in the midsection. He exhaled a startled "umph" as his feet teetered precariously on the sandy ledge. And in only a few interminable seconds, he realized he was going in.

"Oh! Mr. Alexander!" Madeline cried, her hands clasped to her cheeks. Without another thought she inched down the bank to help the man out of the murky waters.

"I'm so sorry!" she exclaimed as Wade groped around for something to pull himself out with, refusing her outstretched hands. "You startled me."

Wade stared at her with a mixture of amazement and disbelief, not daring a word for fear of what might come out.

"Quick, let's get you home," she said once he had managed to pull himself from the river.

They retraced their steps, Madeline running ahead in search of something to use to dry him off, Wade sloshing a muddy path back to Old Betty.

"Fortunately," she said, as if trying to reassure the soaking wet man once they were back in the wagon and on their way, "it's warm enough out here that the wet drive home won't be a problem. In fact, it might do a body good to cool it down. There's a tinge of humidity in the air, and I find it always makes the temperatures seem warmer somehow. Thank goodness this didn't happen in the dead of winter, though I hear the winters in this area are nothing compared to winters in England." She turned to Wade. "I've heard there are people around here who've never seen snow. Surely this can't be true? Is it?"

Wade didn't answer, merely gave her a look that said as clearly as words that she should be locked up for the safety of others. He couldn't believe the inane chatter that drifted across the seat.

When the river-soaked man didn't respond, Madeline ignored his look and drove on without another word until they approached Pine Avenue. "I don't know where on Pine to take you," she finally said.

"Right here is fine."

Madeline glanced about and saw nothing that resembled a family dwelling. Stopping the wagon at the side of the road, she was awash with feeling. She didn't want to see him go. She longed for more of those unfamiliar moments when time seemed to stand still as he gazed into her eyes. But then she told herself she just felt badly for the man. Pity. That's what she was feeling. He had had a humiliating time at the party, and now he was obviously embarrassed of his home and didn't want her to see it. "You don't have to get out here. I'll be more than happy to take you home, wherever you live."

"I'm not going far." Wade jumped to the ground, water squashing out of his boots when he landed.

Deciding it was best to leave what remained of the man's obviously tattered pride intact, she didn't insist. But wanting to let the man know she would never intentionally embarrass him, she said, "Mr. Alexander, I'm sorry for the way you were treated at the party. Just remember, you are as good as anyone there. One day you'll have achieved whatever it is you want to achieve. Just so long as you never give up. And then every one of those people that were there tonight will be clamoring after you . . . if that's what you want."

Wade stared at her in confusion until comprehension finally dawned. All this time, she had thought him an outcast, a man unwelcome. He began to explain but was given no chance as she snapped the reins once again and pulled off into the night, leaving him to stand alone on the boardwalk, the stars twinkling their amusement from the dark sky. He watched until she was out of sight, then shook his head. What would he have said, anyway? *No, you misunderstand, they really do like me. In fact, those very people continually seek me out.*

No, he wouldn't have said that, even though it was true.

Wade turned toward the hotel, and then he smiled. Madeline Montgomery *was* different from all the rest. Her only interest in him was to help a person who she thought was less fortunate than herself. Wade shook his head in wonder.

To think, a poor little servant girl was trying to help the notorious Wade Alexander.

Four

MADELINE SNAPPED THE reins and turned toward home. Old Betty trotted down the road with more enthusiasm than she'd had all night, anxious for the comforts of her straw-filled stall.

Home for Madeline stood just a bit north and west of downtown, practically a straight shot up the way, and it would take Madeline but a few minutes to arrive. On a road made for riding, Madeline didn't have to worry about things getting in her way. This was especially nice as Madeline had the dangerous habit of daydreaming while she held the reins and had clipped more than one ill-placed cart or fence. The barn incident was only unusual in the size of the object she had hit.

In fact, Madeline had gained something of a reputation in the short time she had called Austin home, the same reputation she had managed to procure while living in London. Eccentric, reckless. And she would have been ostracized completely for going about unescorted or unchaperoned if it weren't for the fact that everywhere she went, she spent endless hours doing the good works no one else wanted to do. If only she'd learn to control a horse and wagon, more than one person was heard to remark, they'd love her even more.

Tonight, however, there were no children on the road or obstacles in Madeline's path, leaving her thoughts free to run rampant in any direction they so chose. And they chose

Wade Alexander. Not intentionally, of course, but for some reason, she couldn't quite keep him out of her mind, despite the fact that she told herself the evening had been nothing more than a good deed done.

After a minute or two she pulled through a tall wrought-iron gateway. Hooves and wheels crunched on thick gravel. Small stone walls lined the long drive, guiding her to the front doors of the structure she had come to find she owned.

Reining in, Madeline looked up at the house that had been left to her mother when her mother's father had died. Her mother, Katherine Leister Montgomery, had never even known she owned the house because of the long-standing feud she'd had going with her brother, Richard. But now Katherine was dead, and Richard and Katherine's mother had been determined that her granddaughter know of the inheritance that had waited for so many years in Austin, Texas.

No matter how often Madeline viewed her new home, it always surprised her. Made from a chalky white stone that was abundant in the area, the house both sprawled with long wings and rose with high towers. From what she could tell, the house had grown as the family had, adding a bedroom here or porch there whenever the need arose. It reminded her of an odd combination of Tudor and Victorian, though hewn from native Texas stone. Despite its English influence, the dwelling resembled none of the town houses or hotels Madeline had resided in while living in London.

Unlike Edward's and Richard's houses, Stony Way, as Madeline found her new home was fondly called, was but minutes from the heart of town. Madeline's grandmother had moved in just months before Madeline's arrival, moving out from underneath her eldest son, Richard's, domineering thumb after nineteen years. And oh, how he hated that act of willful independence.

Gathering her skirts, Madeline leapt to the ground. Her

mood was light and gay, so different from the gloomy one she had set out with earlier that evening.

With a dreamy sigh she thought again of the man in the doorway, Wade Alexander. She danced a few steps, her beaded handbag swinging on her wrist. His hard good looks appeared to have been chiseled out of granite. Dark brown eyes, almost black, looking down at her with a hint of a smile. Cheekbones and jaw, shoulders and waist, and thighs encased in snugly fitting pants. And his hair, dark waves caressing his neck, just waiting for her fingers to run through it. What a sight, she murmured.

And the near kiss. Her heart fluttered at the memory. His strong finger reaching out to caress her cheek. The weakness she had felt in her knees. Sitting in the moonlight aware only of each other. His head moving closer. What would have happened had the farmer not interrupted?

With a shake of her, by now, wild tresses, Madeline navigated her thoughts onto safer grounds, away from the man's heart-stopping image. She remembered his inappropriate attire, the people who appeared not to like him, and the lack of a ride home, which was hard to fathom in a part of the world where a man's horse and gun were his most prized possessions. Wade Alexander was a charity case, she told herself firmly, nothing more.

But that didn't seem to make a difference to her errant mind. If anything, it seemed to add to his appeal. Wade Alexander was different, so unlike the practiced, though unperfected, gallants she had previously encountered not only here but in London as well. Standing alone at the party, Mr. Alexander had not cared one whit what people thought of him, of that she was sure. And he obviously wasn't ensconced in money and obligation, as his lack of material goods announced. He probably was fighting tooth and nail to make a success of himself, to pull himself up by the bootstraps, to realize the promise this country, America, proclaimed. Here in America, she remembered, every man was equal.

For a moment she was taken back by the thought that if the man was in need of money, perhaps he was like all the rest and was merely after hers. But then she shook her head in denial. He'd said he had never even heard of her before.

An inexplicable wave of relief washed over her, bringing a smile to her lips. Having spent her entire life around the wealthy and the arrogant, someone like Wade Alexander was a refreshing change.

She wondered if she would ever see the man again, and the thought sent her heart into an odd cadence. In the months she had been in town, this was the first time she had laid eyes on him. But Austin wasn't that big, she reminded herself. If she ran into him once, surely it would happen another time. Yes, she'd make sure of that.

Just as she placed her hand on the doorknob, the front door burst open and Selma—her grandmother's longtime companion and a woman who had taken instantly to Madeline—stepped back in the entrance, her arms akimbo, feet spread wide. She had gray hair and ample girth, and the warmest brown eyes that just that second blazed with annoyance.

"What do you think you're doing? You told me you were going to run over to your aunt's and be right back. Here it is a' ut three hours later, and you come waltzing in like no-s business."

"I did waltz tonight, Selma. With the most striking man I have ever seen. Tall, dark, handsome . . ." She giggled as she danced a few more steps. "Isn't that what every girl is supposed to dream of?"

"She's supposed to dream of a husband, child," the other woman admonished, "and I don't see you wanting one of those, so I can't see how any of this is pertinent. What is pertinent, however, is your not letting your grandmother know what happened to you. You're grandmother and I have been worried sick."

Madeline hooked arms with Selma, taking comfort in the smell of lavender, and led her inside. "Where is grandmother?"

"Upstairs, finally nodded off to sleep, no thanks to you. But she told me to have you go in and wake her when you got home from the party. And there's another thing," the companion continued, "if I've told you once, I've told you a thousand times, it's not proper for you to be gallivanting around town without an escort. In the daytime it's bad enough, but at night it's unacceptable. Riding around in that godforsaken old wagon with that nag pulling it, and at all hours of the night to boot."

Madeline glanced at the clock.

Selma's heated gaze followed. "So it's only a little after ten. It might as well be two in the morning for all the difference it makes to your reputation. Not to mention all the worrying I've done."

"You're right, absolutely right. I apologize, sweet Selma. What would I do without you?"

Setting her handbag aside, Madeline stepped away from Selma and began to waltz with an imaginary beau. "Daa, daa, daa, da da da da, daa, daa, daa," she sang as she glided about the white and black Italian marble floor, gas globes of frosted glass casting shadows of gold about the foyer. Her licks of fiery tresses had finally managed to escape all semblance of respectability, flowing wildly down her back, curling about her face. She closed her eyes and swayed to her notes of music.

Selma stepped closer, her nose sniffing the air, a scowl etched on her face. "You've been drinking!"

"Yes!" Madeline said dramatically. "Oh, yes. Drinking the nectar of life."

"Good God," Selma said, briefly closing her eyes. "It sounds as though you've been drinking the nectar of corn mash. Or else you've lost your wits."

Madeline laughed, a full-bodied sound that filled every crook and corner of the spacious room. "Perhaps I have. Who knows? But I do know that I have had the most wonderful evening." With a final twirl about the room, Madeline added, "Why don't you go on to bed, Selma. I'll close up the house."

"I can't leave you alone down here. No telling what kind of mischief you'll get yourself into."

"I'll get into no trouble, I promise. The groom is putting Old Betty to bed, and I will follow shortly. Just a sip of milk, then I'm on my way upstairs myself."

Selma grumbled. "Dancing, carrying on, talking about a horse like it's a person." She moved toward the stairs. "You'll come up right after?"

"Yes, I promise."

With a sniff to reaffirm her indignation, Selma pulled her ample girth up the red carpeted steps. Halfway up Selma stopped and turned. "Do you think you might marry this man?" she asked with obvious hope, her irritation suddenly gone.

Abruptly Madeline stopped, the joy extinguished from her eyes as quickly as if she had put wet fingers to a candle flame. She looked at Selma for a long moment, then, forgetting the milk she had spoken of, she carefully began to turn down the lights.

Selma sighed. "I'm sorry. I shouldn't have said anything. It's just that I thought perhaps . . . maybe . . . Well, I care about you, child," Selma said with a desperate sound in her voice. "I know you've been telling your dear grandmother that you're not going to marry, but don't you want a family of your own?"

Madeline's step faltered. Her throat constricted. Marriage. Isn't that where dancing and flirting were supposed to lead? What had she been thinking? How could she forget? "Well, get it out of your head." She started up the stairs. "I will never marry."

A bit of Selma's anger revived. "Hogwash! You're being—"

"Stop! This discussion is over. Good night." She continued on to her bedroom, not looking at Selma as she passed her on the steps for fear the dear woman would see the tears that filled her eyes.

Madeline took a deep breath as she walked down the hall. What was wrong with her these days? she wondered. One minute she was on top of the world; the next she was fighting back tears. But she knew exactly what was wrong.

She closed her eyes against the unwanted images that lay menacingly just at the edges of her consciousness. Her thoughts grew dark with tormented memories. "No!" she cried out into the dimly lit hall, her hand flying to her mouth to stifle the scream.

She hurried to her room, unable to face her grandmother and her loving concern, which would surely make Madeline break down and run into her arms and cry like a little baby. And that wouldn't do.

With quiet steps Madeline passed her grandmother's room and went instead to her own. Tomorrow she would say she had hated to wake her—tomorrow after she had banished the dark memories and Wade Alexander completely from her mind.

After shedding her clothes, she washed her face, then crawled into bed. Despite the warm night, Madeline pulled the covers up to her chin. She had come to accept her parents' deaths and had learned with the help of her grandmother to carry on. But sometimes, such as this night, Madeline felt alone and helpless. She could never marry, she who had spent the night filled with fancy dreams of Wade Alexander. She chided herself for a fool. Though all night she had told herself the man was nothing more than a charity case, she realized that in her heart she had felt a great deal more.

Tears welled up in her eyes again. Her life stretched before her, empty of love, without a family of her own. Of course there were her aunts and uncles, even her grandmother. But they had their own children and responsibilities; it just wasn't the same.

Eventually, knowing sleep would elude her, she threw back the covers, went to the window, and pulled back the curtains. Overhead, the moon hung in the heavens, huge and silver, a greater work of art never to be achieved. The night was peaceful. And somehow, the silvery moon in its dark heaven always managed to calm her, to reassure her that everything was going to be all right.

A soft knock sounded on the door. "Madeline, dear. Are you awake?"

Her grandmother's voice floated through the door.

Turning away from the window, Madeline closed her eyes and took a deep breath, filling her lungs. Slowly she exhaled and opened her eyes. Buck up, girl, she chastened herself, quit feeling sorry for yourself.

When she felt certain she had a hold of her emotions, she called to her grandmother. "Yes, Gran. I'm awake."

A woman in a white cotton nightgown and matching wrap entered. She had silver-white hair and the same blue-green eyes as Madeline, only slightly faded with age. "When did you get home?"

"Not too long ago. I would have come in, but I hated to wake you."

"Such a sweet girl, you are. But tell me, how was the party? Better than you anticipated, I hope."

Madeline smiled a reluctant smile. "I suppose."

Gran studied her granddaughter closely with wise old eyes. She looked away, then walked over to the window and looked out at the same scenery Madeline had earlier viewed. "Is something the matter, dear?" she asked without turning away from the land.

"No, I'm just tired." Madeline hated to lie but hated burdening her dear Gran with her silly problems even more.

"Thinking about your parents again?"

Madeline sighed. After only two short months in the same house, Madeline knew Gran wasn't going to give up. "I was just thinking about life, and what a mess it can be."

"Ah, I see. Well, don't spend too much time thinking about the messes. It's a waste of precious time. Life is curly, I've learned. Just like a pig's tail. And no matter how hard you try to straighten it out, it always curls right back up again. Enjoy the good and muddle through the bad, I always say. You can't let the messes slow you down. Live your life as best you can, making decisions every day. Some will be good, some bad—the trick is to make the best of the good and learn to turn the bad to some advantage." Gran shifted her weight and pursed her lips. "Don't make my mistake and let others make decisions for you because you're afraid to make them yourself."

"Oh, Gran—" Madeline began, only to have her grandmother wave her sympathy away.

"I'm not bemoaning my state. I simply don't want you to make the same mistakes. You're a smart young lady, Madeline. You need to go out there and follow your dreams—now, while you're young. Things are changing for women. Unlike in my day, you can do most anything you like." Gran turned to face Madeline. "You must always follow your heart."

Madeline's brow furrowed and her throat grew tight. "If only I could."

Gran's shoulders slumped. "You could if only you'd let yourself. I hope in time you will learn that. But enough of an old woman's ramblings. Tell me all about the party. How many beaux tried to attach themselves to your side? And how about Rosalind? Tell me about her dress."

They chatted until midnight. Madeline tried to be enthusiastic and fill her grandmother in on all that had transpired at the party—all, that is, except for her encounter with Wade Alexander. That, she had no wish to share, at least not yet.

Later, when Madeline was left alone, her thoughts tumbled around in her head. There really was a great deal she could do with her life, she told herself as she remembered Grandmother's words. Marriage would always be out of the question, but . . . She was reasonably smart, fairly practical, educated, and most of all she was good with children.

Her grandmother was right. She *could* follow her heart. She could go out and make something of herself. Maybe she couldn't have a family of her own, but she could go out and make a difference for a few of the families of this world.

She would start a school!

If there was one thing she knew central Texas needed, it was a quality school for the less fortunate. But how to start one, she wondered. And then it came to her. The land her uncle wanted her to sell. If she sold it after all, she could use the money to start a school. That was it! She'd go to Uncle Edward first thing Monday morning and tell him to go ahead and sell the land.

Feeling better as a result of her renewed resolve, Madeline returned to her bed and pulled the covers up to her chin.

Ideas and plans filled her head, and gradually, slowly, excitement began to build. Perhaps she wouldn't have a life of dancing and romance, but she would have a purpose. And always she'd have the memory of once being held in a man's arms and dancing like a queen.

Five

FRIDAY MORNING WADE woke to a sparsely furnished, sun-filled hotel room. How had he slept so long? he wondered groggily as he ran a tired hand through his dark hair. When he stretched his rippling muscles, he caught sight of his clothes hanging from doors and chairs, and in a rush he remembered. Madeline Montgomery and their amazing ride through the night. His lips twitched with amusement. The girl was unbelievable.

He shook his head as he stood up from the bed and went about the room gathering his now stiff but dry clothes. After a quick bath down the hall and a hot meal, Wade packed his saddlebags and was ready to make the ride to Fielding. But something held him back. Despite everything—Lorraine and his well-ordered life—he had the preposterous fancy to go and search out Madeline Montgomery, to laugh just a little bit longer. But he knew himself better than that. He really wanted more. And that was unacceptable.

Self-recrimination filled him. He had worked tirelessly for the last two years to get his life in order. His parents truly would have been proud. Everything was just as it should be. He didn't need a dalliance to mix up his life. He owed his parents that.

Wade made it back to Fielding in good time and went straight to the office. It was nearly six o'clock that evening when Nathan stuck his head in the door. "Aren't you supposed to pick up Lorraine at six-thirty?"

Wade cursed. He'd forgotten all about the plans he'd made with Lorraine. He looked at the clock. "Did you call over to the Hilltop Hotel?"

"Everything's set. Naomi has Lorraine's favorite table set with flowers and candles, even champagne. You're going to an awful lot of trouble to propose to a woman you know is going to say yes."

Wade pulled up in front of the Wilcox home in his brand-new brougham to a swarm of children who gathered round the buggy. There were plenty of wagons in Fielding, but a sleek brougham was a novelty in a town whose citizens' primary mode of transportation was by foot.

"Let me drive 'er, Mr. Alexander," an older boy pleaded as he ran a loving hand over the prized thoroughbred.

"Not tonight, Tommy. I'm stepping out with Miss Wilcox." Then he winked at the girls who broke into a burst of giggles before he strode up the petunia-lined flagstone path of the large whitewashed two-story affair on Elmview Street.

"Wade, dear, do come in." Mrs. Wilcox stood graciously next to her husband and welcomed their guest with a knowing smile. "I hear you two have a very special evening planned."

"Margaret, hush," Judge Wilcox reprimanded his wife.

"That's all right, Judge. We do have a special evening planned. Is Miss Lorraine ready?"

The judge snorted. "Women are never ready when they're supposed to be. Irresponsible lot if I've ever seen one. And to think they want the vote. Good God, what's this country coming to?"

"Cornelius, mind your manners. I will not have you using our Lord's name in vain."

"What did I say?"

"You know what you said. . . ."

Wade cleared his throat. "If you'll excuse me, I'll just wait for Miss Lorraine in the parlor." Wade left the Wilcoxes standing at the door.

Judge Cornelius Wilcox was a man a person didn't want to get crossways with, a peculiar sort who had lived in Texas all his life. "Born and raised," he was fond of saying. In fact, if stories were to be believed, the only time he had set foot outside a hundred-mile radius had been to travel to Boston and bring himself back a wife. Well, of course, Wade knew at some point the man had left to pursue his education, but that fact didn't make nearly as good a story.

Regardless, Wade knew that Mr. Wilcox didn't travel much. His wife, however, always seemed to be going somewhere. The man didn't even bother to accompany Mrs. Wilcox on her many jaunts far and wide to see the world. Though Wade felt the judge needed to take a firmer stance with his strong-headed wife, the Wilcoxes still were just the kind of family Wade wanted to marry into—a respectable, homegrown family with a little city breeding and culture thrown in for good measure.

Minutes ticked by as Wade paced impatiently until, finally, Lorraine appeared at the top of the stairs. Her golden blond tresses were pulled up in an elaborate design of twists and curls, and a seductive smile graced her perfectly painted lips. She came down the stairs to pirouette at the bottom, her skirts billowing out around her ankles. She wore a dress that even in Paris would have been considered fashionable— Lanvin blue crepe de chine trimmed in a delicate white guipure. The gown was cut low and daring, made decent only by a fichu of creamy lace.

"What do you think? Mother bought it for me while she was in France."

Wade crossed the room and slowly pulled her to him. "Lovely." His deep voice was like a caress, and for a moment both Wade and Lorraine forgot that at any minute her parents could walk through the door.

She pressed against him for a fleeting second, just long enough for him to feel the curves of her body. When he would have pulled her closer, she stopped him with one dainty hand and a coy smile. "Now, now, Wade. I'm a respectable woman," she said in a sultry voice as smooth and thick as honey. "I'm saving myself for the man I marry."

Without releasing her, Wade nipped at her ear. "You're also the biggest tease I've ever met."

Lorraine laughed. "And you love it." Then she pushed away. "Wade, please, my parents."

In one quick movement he pulled her back, then dipped his head to her breast to kiss the swell of one ample mound through the exquisite lace. "Your parents will be arguing the rest of the night. Maybe I should carry you upstairs right now and have my way with you. Cornelius and Margaret would never know."

"Really!" she gasped playfully and slapped at his hand. "Those are the very people who brought me into this world. I'd be careful what I said if I were you."

"You're right. I'm indebted to them for life." He brought his hand up to cup the fullness of her breast. "I will have to compliment them on their admirable accomplishment."

Her head tilted back and her eyes closed. "Oh," she moaned. "Wade."

"It only gets better. Now come on," he said, suddenly standing her up straight and pulling her into the foyer to say good night to her parents, her eyes still clouded with passion.

"Have her home early," the judge called after them.

* * *

The neighborhood children still surrounded the shiny buggy.

"Take us for a ride, please, please, please!" several cried as if they all could fit in the sleek two-seater.

"Later, kids." He helped Lorraine up onto the cushioned seat, then paused. "Anyone who sneaks a ride on the back this time will get a strapping he won't forget."

Tommy Teeple instantly appeared from behind the brougham, a guilty smile stretching his lips wide across his young face. "Everything's in order in the rear, sir."

"In order, my foot!" Wade chuckled. "Get out of the way before one of you gets run over."

The Hilltop Hotel was a mere stone's throw away, easily walked if Lorraine hadn't made it clear from the onset that she preferred to ride.

They were met at the door by the proprietress of the small hotel. "Wade, darlin'. We've missed you around here." The widow, Naomi Edwards, turned her painted face toward Wade and smiled a smile filled with unspoken promise before she reluctantly turned her attention to Lorraine. "Miss Wilcox. Good to see ya. We have your favorite table all shined up and ready."

After a lingering glance at Wade and a flounce of her full skirts, Naomi led her guests to a quiet nook overlooking a small stream. Lanterns flickered through the windows, casting faint shadows about the room.

"Thank you, Naomi," Wade said as he held Lorraine's chair.

Naomi looked up into Wade's dark, fathomless eyes. "You're welcome."

Pulling off her gloves with a scowl, Lorraine waited for Naomi to leave. "It's shameful the way that woman flaunts herself. She's been throwing herself at you since the day she moved to town," she hissed.

Wade glanced from Lorraine to the swaying hips of Naomi Edwards. "I hadn't noticed," he said with a grin, ignoring Lorraine's unattractively contorted features.

Lorraine studied him for a moment, the scowl slowly softening, until she actually returned his smile. With a delicate hand she smoothed her perfectly arranged hair. "That's probably true."

The few words, with the vanity they implied, sliced at his good humor. His jaw muscles tightened, his full lips narrowing unnaturally. But he had worked for this night for a very long time, and determined that the evening be a success, he put her words from his mind.

After champagne was poured, Lorraine inhaled deeply. "Wade," she purred, "how simply divine."

"Where'd you pick up that phrase?" He leaned back, crossing an ankle over his knee, his arm resting casually on the wooden table.

"You terrible, terrible man," she said with an exaggerated drawl. Picking up her glass, Lorraine sipped at the wine and giggled much the same as the young neighborhood girls had earlier. "Don't you like simpering females, love? It's all the rage these days."

Reaching across the table, she took his hand, unmindful of the glances they received from nearby patrons. Her voice grew deep and throaty, her blue eyes sparkling with promise, much like the painted Widow Edwards's. "Do you want me to tell you what else is all the rage?" Her fingernails gently raked the palm of his hand, a knowing smile spread across her lips.

The determined good humor he had fought to maintain slowly began to evaporate. His hand closed around Lorraine's, almost too tightly, and he stared at her for one interminable moment. What was amusing in a widowed acquaintance was decidedly unamusing in his future wife. The disquiet he had felt upon receiving the news of Jim's death returned, only stronger than when it had first accosted him.

He thought of their embrace at the foot of the stairs, when Lorraine had pressed against him with the intimate, none too obvious pressure of her body. A subtle promise of what was to come. At the time his heart had pounded at the thought. But now, as he remembered, he wondered if this was what he wanted—from a wife.

Extracting his hand and reaching for his wine, he looked closely at Lorraine. He looked at her expecting to see someone different. But everything about her was familiar. She was the same woman he had set out to marry all those months before. If he were truthful with himself, he knew she hadn't changed. She had taken his hand before and had even made suggestive remarks. Then why did it seem different tonight?

The fiery image of Madeline Montgomery loomed unexpectedly in his mind. But that was absurd. There was no place in his life for someone like Miss Montgomery, and that was that, he told himself, mentally washing his hands of the unpredictable woman.

He then remembered the ring in his pocket. He had planned this for months. It was the loss of his cousin that disturbed his thoughts. Surely.

"Hello." Lorraine waved a well-manicured hand in front of his fathomless eyes. "Where are you?"

He focused on her, then he shrugged his broad shoulders. "Wool-gathering I suppose."

"Anything wrong?"

"No, nothing's wrong."

The handwritten menus with the restaurant's nightly

choices lay on the table. He picked one up. "What are you going to have?" he asked without looking at her.

Lorraine seemed to ponder this question, her eyes shrewd as she watched Wade study the menu, before she sweetly asked him to decide for her.

Wade relaxed, the creases of tension visibly melting from his face. Yes, he thought, things were going to be all right. The life he had worked so hard for, the wife and children he wanted, the expanded ranch, were all going to be realized.

They had roast beef with a potato soufflé and creamed spinach on the side. Champagne flowed freely, and by the time dessert was served, Wade thought coffee was in order. Women, he felt strongly, shouldn't be allowed more than one or two glasses of wine.

"Coffee." Lorraine pouted. "I'd rather have a brandy."

"But you'll have coffee instead," he said as he motioned to Naomi.

"Mother and I had a brandy the last time we were in New York." Lorraine scowled as Naomi poured two cups of coffee.

"What they do in New York City is not my concern," Wade replied in a voice filled with censure while he thought not of the northeastern city but of Lorraine's mother and her headstrong ways.

Lorraine opened her mouth as if to protest, but snapped it shut and snatched up her cup. The coffee was hot, and in her temper, she scalded her mouth.

"Careful."

"Oh, careful yourself, Mr. Alexander," she hissed while setting down the steaming brew. "You're not my father, nor my keeper."

He noticed her pouting lower lip, so full, so ready to be kissed, the tilt of her haughty chin. Forgetting his earlier reservations, he reached across the table and touched her hand.

"No, I'm not your father nor your keeper, but I would like to be your husband."

Her pale blue eyes widened as Wade took the small box from his pocket and placed it on the table. Lorraine could only stare, her breath held in anticipation.

"Go ahead, open it," he urged, leaning back in his chair to watch with a satisfied smile.

She held the black satin box between her hands and closed her eyes as if making a wish. Then, carefully, she pulled it open and gasped at what she saw. "Oh, darling! It's the most beautiful ring I have ever seen." With great ceremony she slipped it on her finger and held it out to catch the light. "I was so afraid you were going to give me that old ring of your mother's. Not that it's bad, it's just not to my taste. But this, darling," she cooed, failing to notice the tension that suddenly charged the air, "is splendid. Not even Sally Peters has a diamond. I'll be the envy of every girl in town."

A sharp jab cut into Wade's gut and his satisfied grin evaporated. His jaw clenched. But still Lorraine failed to notice her newly betrothed's altered countenance.

"Jason and Sally just came in. Let's go over and show them," she gushed.

But when Lorraine started to rise, Wade's hand snaked out and took her arm in a steely grip, forcing her back into her chair. She looked up at him with questioning eyes. "What is it?"

With great restraint and tight control over each word, he said, "There is time enough to tell everyone."

"Oh, you're right!" She leaned forward, unperturbed by Wade's actions, and clasped her hands together. "I'm just so excited. We'll have a huge wedding with a reception for everyone in town. I have it all planned. It will be marvelous. I'll walk down the staircase, my hand resting delicately on the banister, my chapel-length train trailing behind. Everyone gazing up at me, every man in the house crushed because I am not his." She stopped abruptly and through demurely lowered lashes, studied her fiancé. "Oh, how silly of me to go on about such paltry little things. It's you I should be thinking of, and believe it or not, I am." She moved even closer, the swells of her lily-white bosom pressing against the table. "You have made me the happiest woman alive. I'll be so proud to be the wife of Wade Fielding Alexander."

Lorraine waited as if she thought her words would settle over him like a soothing balm. Then she ran her tongue slowly over her lip and whispered, "Why don't we go for a ride, then back to your house for a bit. Mother and Daddy will never know. They're always asleep when I get in."

Wade wasn't sure which caused him to act, the promise of her creamy breasts or the need to erase the growing doubt that had surged up within him; regardless of the provocation, he called for the check, paid the amount, and pulled Lorraine up from the table, then drove her toward his home.

The night air was warm and heavy. A gentle breeze rustled in the trees. Brittle leaves left over from winter tumbled along the dusty road. The black thoroughbred trotted smoothly toward Wade's home on the outskirts of town. Wade took in the sights and sounds of the darkened sky while the rhythmic sway of the buggy gradually rocked his concerns away.

After a while they talked more easily, and Wade began to feel a great deal better than he had all day. They spoke of dates and bridal parties, and of all the people they would invite to the wedding. It wasn't until they neared the house that he remembered his cousin and the inheritance that should arrive any time. "A cousin of mine has died and left me an inheritance," he told her.

"How much?" she asked excitedly, turning to him on the seat.

"Not *how* much, Lorraine, but rather, what. Jim Daniels didn't know the first thing about making money, just an awful lot about having fun."

"Humph." Lorraine grimaced. "It's probably an old watch or something."

Wade laughed.

Lorraine crossed her arms. "Or a box full of debts. That family of yours comes to you for everything. Now they're even coming to you after they die."

Wade pulled the buggy to an abrupt halt. "My family is important to me, Lorraine. You've known that all along. And it's not going to change."

Her newly received diamond ring caught a beam of moonlight, causing the stone to shimmer in the night. With outstretched fingers, she moved the ring to catch more light before folding her hands in her lap. "I'm sorry, darling. I was just a bit pesky. It's because I feel so badly for you. All that responsibility," she said, her voice velvety while she looked at her folded hands.

Wade reached across the seat and pulled her close. "I appreciate your concern, but it's nothing to worry your pretty little head over. I'll take care of my family." With one finger under her chin, he lifted her face so he could look into her eyes. "And I'll take care of you, too."

Reaching up, she kissed him. It was all he needed before he plundered her mouth, his hands caressing her back.

"Wade," she murmured as his lips trailed a fiery path down her neck to the coveted white swells.

It wasn't until her hand tugged on his shirtfront that he realized they were stopped in the middle of the road no more than a half mile from his house. "Wait." He took her hand and kissed it. "We're almost there."

She laid her head on his shoulder as they rode the rest of the way down the dirt road. The moon shone brightly, casting long shadows of twisted oak and cedar across their path. Her hand circled on his thigh, and just as she raised her head to kiss his neck, his sudden curse stopped her.

"What the hell?" Wade jerked up in his seat when he caught sight of his towering home, so recently completed, ablaze with light. His first thoughts were of fire. Memories of a past fire intertwined with the sight before him, making him momentarily paralyzed with fear. In seconds he cleared his mind and urged the horse on at a wild pace. He pulled through the wrought-iron gates, then reined in so suddenly that a spray of dust and gravel flew into the night sky. The promise of the evening was forgotten as he told Lorraine to wait in the buggy, and he raced up the front steps.

He burst through the door, his heart pounding in his chest, those memories of another time, another fire, testing his sanity, pushing him on. This time he would save anyone who was left inside; he would not let anyone die. But the sight that met him stopped him dead in his tracks, for it was not the fire he expected. Rather the house seemed full of children, running here and there like a pack of wild Apaches.

Long, interminable seconds passed while his mind tried to assimilate the spectacle before him. His first thought as the fear began to recede and his arms and legs were left weak from the passing emotion was that Tommy Teeple had followed him home wanting a ride. But on closer inspection, he realized he recognized not one of the wild youths.

And wild they were. Two kids crawled up the stairs backward as if racing; another slid down the banister, whooping Indian war cries the whole way down. One boy held a porcelain china doll over his head, laughing as a much smaller girl jumped and screeched trying to obtain the prize. Wade was too stunned to tell the two youths that the doll had been one of the few things of his mother's that had been saved, that if broken it was irreplaceable. Instead, he turned away, and it was a moment before he found his longtime family servant in the melee. "Phillips!" Wade bellowed.

Phillips, looking frayed, his neatly tailored black suit smudged and askew, stumbled his way toward the front door with a tiny redheaded bundle attached to his arm. "Good evening, sir."

Wade pried the youngster from his servant and set the boy down. "What the devil is going on here?! Who are these ruffians?"

Phillips cleared his throat and with a tired sigh replied, "Your inheritance, sir."

"My inheritance?!" Wade looked about the room as if the world had gone mad.

Phillips produced a letter that had arrived with the children. "I believe this is supposed to explain."

Seizing the dispatch from the man, Wade almost tore the page in his haste to read it. Once he reached the bottom of the handwritten note, he started again from the top. "This can't be," he stated as he reread the missive. When he finished a second time, Lorraine, who had slipped in unnoticed, took the letter and read for herself.

"This says you're now the guardian of these children. Seven children!" Lorraine's arm fell to her side, the letter fluttering to the ground.

Phillips retrieved the piece of paper just ahead of the small redheaded child.

"This cousin of yours died and left you his kids." Lorraine's voice raised an octave.

"It would appear so," Phillips answered for his employer who still hadn't moved.

A young girl of about five or six approached the entryway. She looked from Phillips to Wade, then gazed up at Lorraine with worshipful yearning in her large blue eyes. "You're pretty," she pronounced before hurtling herself into Lorraine's arms. "Are you my new mama?"

Lorraine nearly fell back from the force but was saved when Wade reached out distractedly and steadied her.

"Well, are you?" the girl asked again, gazing up from the elegant folds of Lorraine's Parisian skirts.

"Mama?!" Lorraine cried before peeling the child off and turning to her fiancé. "What is this all about? You told me this Jim person was sending you some stupid little memento." She twirled around with her arm outstretched, encompassing every child. "These, let me tell you, are not mementos."

Wade flashed her an angry scowl before demanding the group's attention. But despite his command, children still slid down the banister and hopped up the steps.

Phillips cleared his throat. "It would seem, sir, your new charges did not hear."

Wade glared at the servant and clenched his fist, then bellowed into the room, "Quiet!"

Motion stopped. Every child froze on the spot and looked curiously toward Wade. Silence reigned. The quiet seemed deafening. The only sound came from the tick of the clock and the heavy breathing of an overexerted child. No one spoke as they all stood perfectly still, each group warily eyeing the other.

Finally a boy stepped forward. He had carrot-red hair, thick and wavy, and pale white skin with a hefty dose of freckles. He was long and lean, appearing too tall for his slight frame, and Wade had the fleeting thought that the boy looked just like Jim. Yes, Jim. Wade knew without a doubt these were his cousin's children. Every one of them had some shade of their father's bright red hair.

Wade smiled, forgetting the problematic, not to mention unbelievable, situation he found himself in, thinking only of a lost cousin and his children. "How old are you?" he asked with an encouraging smile.

"How old is he?" Lorraine demanded before the boy could answer. "Age is not the issue here, rather, who is he really? How do we know they are your cousin's children? How do we know that letter isn't a fraud?"

Lorraine had a thunderous glare turned her way but was saved a setdown when the boy pulled his wiry shoulders back and replied, "I am James Dawson Daniels, Jr. And these here are my brothers and sisters. Who're you?" He finished by pointing his finger practically in Lorraine's face.

"Why you impertinent little—"

"Lorraine! That's enough." Wade looked at the children. "This is Miss Wilcox, and I am Wade Alexander, your—"

"Cousin!" The cheer was deafening as the remaining four children came bobbing toward him at full speed to attach themselves to any available body space.

For a moment Wade was caught up in all the excitement, but when he glanced around the room and observed Lorraine's mutinous rage, Phillips's rumpled coat, and James Dawson Daniels, Jr.'s unhappy scowl, the reality of his predicament about knocked him off his feet where the children hadn't been able to.

"Enough!"

Wade practically had to shake the youths from his body, and even then they tried to jump back on. It wasn't until the oldest boy instructed his siblings to get back and be quiet that amazingly enough they did. Wade eyed James Dawson Daniels, Jr., and would have complimented him on his control had the boy not stepped in front of the gaggle of siblings defensively, his thin chest puffed up as if ready to do battle.

"Pa said you'd take care of us if anything were ever to happen to him. I told him I could do it. I'm fourteen. Plenty old to take care of us. And I will." He picked up the smallest child, the redheaded boy who had earlier attached himself to Phillips's arm. "Come on, you guys, we're going."

"Where, Jimmy?" they cried in unison.

"Quit your bellyachin' and come on."

Jimmy started to open the front door but was stopped when Wade's huge hand slammed it shut.

"You're not going anywhere," Wade said with an exasperated scowl.

Lorraine gasped, but when Wade turned to her she didn't speak, simply glared at the man and his brood of children.

Pulling Jimmy and his young brother back from the door, Wade said, "We'll get all this straightened out in the morning. For now, it's late and everyone needs a good night's rest." He turned to the servant. "Phillips, take them upstairs and put them to bed."

"Me, sir?" Phillips's eyes grew wide with possible mutiny.

"Yes, you. Now, all of you, go on, get upstairs."

They piled up the stairs in a herd, Phillips grumbling behind them like an irritated sheepdog, leaving the newly betrothed couple to stand alone in the entry.

The sounds of the children grew faint as they were swallowed up by the huge corridor leading to the bedrooms. Wade leaned against a table.

"What are you going to do with them?" Lorraine asked ruthlessly.

"I haven't the foggiest idea," he replied as he looked toward the second floor. "No idea at all."

"Well, you'd better think of something, or you're going to be stuck with seven squalling brats, most of whom belong inside the nursery. Good God, what could your cousin have been thinking? I thought you said you hadn't seen him in a great many years. How would he even know you're still here? Or that you'd take them? You're a bachelor, for mercy's sake."

He had no answer for his outraged fiancée, no answer at all. After running a tired hand over his face, he stood and opened the door. "I'll take you home."

Thoughts of what they had come to the house for ran through each of their minds but nothing was said. They simply got back in the brougham and rode silently to the whitewashed home on Elmview Street.

Six

THE ROOM WAS dark, the only light provided by fading silver moonbeams filtering through the mullioned window. Heavy green velvet curtains hung open as they always did, regardless of the hour.

With a sheet draped casually over his legs and lower torso, Wade lay sleeping in the massive bed. His granite-hard shoulders and well-muscled chest covered with curling black hair remained exposed, caressed by the silver light. He had spent the night in a series of fitful dreams filled with the wilds of the Nebraska Territory and seven redheaded Indians. The quiet, restful sleep he had sought when he lay down the night before eluded him.

Somewhere between the last dream and waking, something fluttered across his face. He swiped lazily at the annoyance before rolling onto his side, one large, hard thigh peeking out from underneath the white muslin sheet. A moment later the nuisance returned, this time from the other side, tickling a feathery path across his forehead. In his sluggish state he swatted at the irritant only to have it return anew to attack the tip of his nose.

Wade mumbled a rebellious growl and turned away, the sheet slipping even farther, leaving only one thigh and the essentials of his manliness concealed from the early morning air. An unfamiliar, high-pitched gasp suddenly resounded through the room.

Wade jolted upright, his heart pounding, only to find himself staring into the largest cornflower-blue eyes he had ever seen. A small child, who looked remarkably like one of the Indians from his dreams, was staring him in the face.

"What the devil!" he snapped, struggling to cover himself in the tangle of sheets.

"Why, Cousin! You're indecent!" The young girl who had wanted Lorraine to be her mama stood at the side of his bed, a goose feather in her hand.

"Indecent!" he sputtered when finally he had the sheet back around him. "What are you doing in here? You have no business in my room."

The child merely smiled, revealing a telltale hole from a freshly missing tooth. With great ceremony she held out her tiny hand to display the extracted incisor. "I want to put this under my pillow, but I don't think the Tooth Fairy knows I moved to my cousin's house. You need to tell her."

In the aftermath of his disconcerting dreams, Wade's mind filled with conflicting images of Indians and torture, blue eyes and teeth. Wade looked from the tooth to the girl, then back to the tooth as if unable to comprehend her words.

"You can tell her today." With that seemingly settled in her mind, the curly headed child studied his bed. "I like your room better than mine." Then she scrambled up next to him as fast as her little legs would take her and began jumping up and down, arms flailing, screeching for joy.

Wade cursed the fates that had led him to cease his childhood habit of wearing pajamas. But he knew, just as the Tooth Fairy was not to be found, that pajamas were not miraculously going to appear. With no apparent alternative, he called to his servant. "Phillips!"

In seconds the door burst open, admitting not the ever faithful Phillips, but rather three additional children of varying sizes—two boys who looked identical with matching short-cropped hair and loads of freckles, and a plump little girl, older than the one with the extracted incisor.

"Look," the new girl squealed. "His bed is huge!"

Desperate, knowing what was to come, Wade vaulted from his berth, pulling the sheet with him just as the young girl and her missing tooth were on the upswing, and stormed to his dressing room, slamming the door in his wake.

With the plank of solid oak safely lodged between him and the children, Wade, cursing, jerked on a pair of pants. "Damn blast it," he growled as he hopped on one foot when the other got stuck in the trouser leg.

A discreet knock sounded, and with growing outrage he yanked the door open, ready to blast the little scoundrels. "You—"

"Good morning, sir," Phillips said at the same instant he stepped back with eyes opened wide.

Wade could only stare back at the man, wanting nothing more at that moment than to vent his spleen. But years of control forced him to curtail the flow of words and look beyond his servant to the bed he had so recently fled. His *empty* bed.

"Is there a problem, sir?"

If Wade hadn't caught sight of a lone feather lying on the rug, he might have thought he had dreamed the whole episode.

"Where'd they go?" he demanded.

"Who, sir?"

"You damn well know who." Wade studied the room before turning away with a mumbled "never mind," then pulled out his razor and strap.

"What are you doing?" Phillips asked with growing concern.

"What does it look like I'm doing? I'm getting ready to go into town."

"You're leaving?"

Wade heaved a weary sigh and looked at the other man. "What else would you have me do?"

"Why, I . . . well, I thought you might do something with the children, sir."

"And what do you propose I do with them?"

"I don't know, but surely they can't stay here." Phillips's shoulders slumped, and his stiff upper lip seemed to falter.

Wade grabbed a towel and went over to the giant copper bath. "I know. What was Jim thinking?" He shook his head. "I'm going to the office and see what I can arrange. Those children need a home. But not this home. As Lorraine pointed out, I'm a bachelor. And this is not an orphanage."

"That's the spirit, sir." Phillips's eyes brightened. "Perhaps you should contact Father Hayes. Men of God always know what to do about orphans. He'll help us."

Wade turned on the water faucet. The house momentarily shook and shuddered as the newly installed steam pump brought water to the upper region.

"I'll leave you to your preparations," Phillips said distractedly as he left the room muttering to himself.

After his shave, Wade slumped into the bath of steaming hot water and examined his mixed emotions. His ever-important sense of family conflicted with the reality of his inability to take care of seven children, not monetarily, but as a true parent. And if he was truthful with himself, the fact was, he didn't want the headache—this morning had convinced him of that. But even if he wished to keep them, children needed guidance, he reasoned. What kind of guidance could he possibly provide? However, in spite of all his justifications, the fact remained—they were family.

Wade's thoughts swung back and forth like a pendulum. Family or not those kids needed the stabilizing force of a father figure *and* a mother figure. Unexpectedly, Madeline

Montgomery came to mind, and he almost laughed at the thought that she'd fit in quite well with the band of heathens. But Madeline Montgomery was not an option, and as far as the kids were concerned, neither was Lorraine.

Wade shook his head. Lorraine had shown in a matter of five minutes what kind of a mother she would make his young cousins. The thought disturbed him more than he liked to admit. But he told himself it was an unfair judgment. He didn't want to take care of the brood any more than she did.

"Damn you, Jim Daniels," he cursed under his breath, grabbing a bar of soap and lathering his body.

By the time Wade had rinsed his long limbs, which never proved an easy task no matter that he had purchased the largest tub available, he felt he had come up with the solution. Surely there were other relatives on the mother's side. Jim probably hadn't put them in charge because they lacked the money. Who, in the wilds of the Nebraska Territory, assuming that was where the mother was from, had extra money to feed seven hungry mouths? Wade had the funds. He would provide the money and let another long-lost cousin provide the home.

Relief washed over him. He wasn't shirking his responsibilities, but he also wasn't going to have to keep seven children. All he had to do was find another relative. His mind raced with a course of action as he finished his bath, pulled on fresh clothes, then headed for the bedroom door.

On his way out the downy goose feather caught his eye. He chuckled at the memory of the children romping on his bed. They were definitely Jim's kids. He thought back to the days he had spent with his cousin.

With no father and a mother who drank most of the time, Jim had virtually lived in the Alexander home. Jim had always been a hero to all the other kids. A little older, and a little more daring, everyone had thought he could do no wrong. Including Wade. And then, with tales of great far-away places, Jim had set out to live a life of adventure. Even now, so many years later, Wade missed the lust for life his reckless cousin had brought with him wherever he went.

Wade smiled, and in a burst of goodwill he pocketed the feather before making his way downstairs to sate his appetite.

"Good morning," he said, entering the breakfast room, a bit surprised to find the table full and amazingly quiet. He didn't notice the mutinous stares or sullen looks, simply thought that after only mere hours in his well-run home they were already learning to behave. Nothing like a little discipline to bring them around, he mused. The fact that he had not once given them one ounce of discipline, had only blustered and bellowed, didn't cross his mind, nor the fact that it had only been a matter of minutes since they had ransacked his bed.

Ham, eggs mixed with cheese, biscuits and gravy, and coffee waited on the sideboard. Wade filled his plate before going to his seat. The children still hadn't said a word.

"You know," Wade began, dipping a biscuit in his gravy, "other than Jimmy here, I don't know any of your names."

Still they were silent.

"Come on, tell me your names." Wade glanced from child to child with an encouraging smile.

The girl of feather fame sat up. "My name is Grace. I'm five and a half. Almost six," she added proudly, her dark red curls bouncing on her head. "And this is little brother William. We call him Billy, though. He's only two."

Two-year-old Billy was a chubby little boy with silky golden-red hair, filthy hands, and a mostly toothed smile.

"Hello, Grace, Billy." Wade nodded at each.

He looked to the others. Not one of them spoke, only

stared down at their plates of food with great interest. Eventually, Grace continued.

"That's Jimmy, you already know him, and she's Bridget. She's twelve."

"Not either. I'm thirteen," Bridget said with an unladylike harrumph of importance before sitting back gracefully in her chair.

She was tall like Jimmy, with the same thick red hair, though not a single freckle marked her creamy skin. With those big green eyes and porcelain features, Wade knew she'd be a beauty one day.

By this time tension had eased a bit, and Wade was feeling quite pleased with himself. Only Jimmy sat morosely in his chair, which Wade chose conveniently to ignore.

"That's Elizabeth." Grace pointed across the table to another redheaded child who Wade guessed was about ten. "She's seven and a big meany." Grace punctuated her sentence by sticking out her tongue.

"Am not!"

"Are so!"

"Am not!"

"Stop it!" Jimmy grumbled, his voice surprisingly low.

All eyes turned toward the oldest brother, and Wade was yet again impressed by the boy's ability to control his younger siblings.

"I'm Garrett—"

"And he's Garvin," Grace said interrupting the brother who had chosen to finally speak up, pointing to another child who sat staring at his plate. "They're twins. Papa said it was a fluke. No twins in our family ever before."

The boy, Garvin, grew red.

"Ah, shut up, Miss Know-it-all." This from Garrett. "You're just jealous cuz you're not a twin. And everyone knows no one would ever want to be a twin with you."

"Liar, liar, liar!" Grace cried, jumping up from her seat, knocking the table and sending a glass tumbling forward, spilling milk over the white linen cloth.

"Grace!" several of them cried as they leapt from their seats, trying to avoid the streams of flowing milk.

"You dumbhead!"

"Am not! You made me do it!" Grace said, her eyes shining with tears.

Wade looked about the table. Only he and Jimmy remained in their seats. How could things so quickly get out of control? he wondered. Shouldn't a person get some forewarning of impending disaster? Wade grimaced when suddenly he became aware of a small trickle of milk dripping steadily on the newspaper in his lap. He jerked back and tossed the paper aside, using his napkin to blot up the liquid.

Thank God this situation was only temporary—a few days, a week at the most, he promised himself, the children still raging out of control.

When he'd had enough of the screaming and bickering, and he realized Jimmy was not going to quiet his siblings this time, Wade decided there was no alternative but to take action. Discipline. Wasn't that what he had been so sure of?

"Children, control yourselves!" He said this in a tone that had cowered more than one full-grown man but failed to procure even the slightest glance from these squabbling parties. He noticed a small, quirking smile from Jimmy. "Think this is funny, do you?" In one swift motion he was up from his chair, his hands landing flat on the tabletop, and he bellowed, "Sit down!"

Six varying sizes of children's bottoms slapped against their seats. Wade turned his head to Jimmy, hands still planted on the table, and gave a slight nod of the head. But if he expected some acknowledgment of his prowess, he was to be greatly disappointed. All he received was a snort and a shake of the head.

Wade grunted before he sat back down, folded the wet tablecloth back, and dug into his meal as though nothing had happened. Silence at the breakfast table, he decided, was golden. He had certainly learned his lesson about encouraging conversation.

He took a sip of coffee that by then was lukewarm. Glancing about the room, he noticed for the first time that neither Phillips nor the serving girl were anywhere to be seen. "Oh, well," he mumbled and got up to freshen his cup. When he did, something stuck his leg. Reaching into his pants pocket, he found the feather. With a smile he pulled it out and held it out to Grace.

In a flash havoc reigned once again.

"There's my feather," Garrett said, snatching it out of Wade's hand. "How'd you get it?" he asked with something very close to accusation in his voice.

Wade froze nonplussed, his arm extended, his body half out of the seat. Grace fought for the feather while everyone else seemed to join in for no more than good measure. Closing his eyes, Wade pushed the chair back and without so much as a good day was out the front door, telling himself it was nothing more than a bad dream.

"Harold, get me the file on the West Tract. Nathan, get Jack Barnes over here, right away. And bring me a cup of coffee—hot."

Both Harold and Nathan jumped, not having heard their employer enter. Harold hurried out and Nathan smiled. "Mr. Barnes should arrive any minute."

Wade scowled at his assistant as he walked straight from the entrance of the building to his office door without missing a beat. "One of these days you're going to think I'll want something done and I won't."

Nathan chuckled and followed, grabbing the coffeepot and a cup on the way. "Rough night with your inheritance, eh? Let me see." Nathan cocked his head in thought. "You hung the stuffed hog's head that you swore it was going to be over your bed so you'd always remember your dear departed cousin. In the middle of the night, you woke up and it scared you half to death."

Wade grunted.

"No? Not a stuffed head? My goodness, what could it be? An old clock? Or no, wait. Seven little children perhaps?"

"You know damn well what it is, and the least you could have done was warn me."

"What? Send a messenger over to Hilltop Hotel and ruin your lovely betrothal meal? I'd never dream of it," he said with a grin that revealed huge white teeth.

Wade picked up some mail and looked at Nathan. "You may be the closest thing I have to a brother, but you'd better watch your step or you're going to be out on the boardwalk looking for a new job."

Nathan laughed as he started to pour Wade a cup of coffee.

"Just leave the whole thing," Wade said, gesturing to both the cup and the pot.

Nathan merely shrugged and set both the cup and the pot of steaming coffee on some files on the desk. "So tell me, really, how was it?"

Tossing the letters aside, Wade slumped into his chair. "Well, they've about scared my newly betrothed wife into breaking our engagement—"

"Not with the size of diamond you gave her."

"Phillips is one step away from walking out the front door never to return—"

"Phillips? Nah. I've seen ornery bulls who couldn't scare old Phillips."

"And apparently I need a locksmith to put a new lock on my bedroom door. Maybe a throwbar would keep them out."

"Knock, knock. Anyone home?"

Both men turned to the door.

"Jack," Wade said. "Come in."

Nathan gathered up some papers and started to leave. "Can I get you some coffee, Mr. Barnes?" he asked the lawyer on his way out.

"No, thanks, Nathan. Had plenty before I left the house," Jack replied, rubbing his stomach.

Jack Barnes had been Wade's solicitor for the last two years. A short man with a balding head, the lawyer was a good thirty years older than his client. More than once Wade had questioned something Jack had done, but the fact that he was a Fielding man and the only solicitor in town made it damn near impossible for Wade to justify to himself using anyone else.

Wade grimaced. How was it possible for a man such as himself, with reasonably intelligent mental faculties, to surround himself with such ineptitude. Perhaps he had gone a bit overboard with his loyalty to family and friends.

Just as Jack set his satchel aside and lowered himself into a chair, Harold timidly knocked at the open door. "Here's the file you wanted."

"Put it with the others," Wade said, motioning toward the credenza. He turned to Jack. "I'm glad you're here."

"Nathan tells me you got yourself a passel of kids." Jack chortled. "I'm not sure who I feel worse for. You or your inheritance."

"I'm glad someone is finding some amusement in this situation. I, myself, don't see it." Wade leaned forward and rubbed his temples. "I've got to do something. I have no business keeping seven children."

"What do you want me to do?"

Wade's hands stilled. "You tell me. You're the lawyer," he snapped.

Jack shrugged his shoulders. "As I see it, there are only three possibilities. You keep them yourself, find another relative, or send them to an orphanage."

Wade leaned forward in his chair and looked Jack straight in the eye. "Orphanage is out. Jim's kids are not going to grow up without family."

"Well, then," Jack said, taking off his spectacles and wiping them on his shirt, "that leaves you or a relative."

"That's what I thought. Well, then, find a relative. Make a country-wide search if you have to. Spare no expense. You'll probably need to start in the Nebraska Territory. But whatever you do, just find someone."

"Sure, Wade, I'll do what I can. I'll need the official document that came, and the letter that arrived with the children might be of some help."

"Harold will get you whatever you need."

"Right away," Harold announced enthusiastically. "If you'll come with me, Mr. Barnes, I'll get the documentation."

Jack pushed himself up from the seat. "I'll let you know how things go."

As soon as the door closed and Wade was left alone, he poured himself a cup of steaming coffee. With a smile of anticipation, he brought it to his lips. Hot coffee and solitude. Such precious commodities.

"Damn blast!" he shouted when the coffee seared first his lips, then his fingers when he jerked back and spilled a good portion of it all over his desk, turning a pile of unread mail a murky brown.

* * *

Wade lingered at work as long as he could and would have slept on the sofa in his office had it not been so uncomfortable. The idea of some good, sound sleep finally drove him home.

The house was dark except for one solitary light burning in the entryway. Normally, Phillips left a light burning at the top of the stairs, but normal no longer seemed to exist around here.

He took the stairs slowly, one at a time. Despite the lack of lighting, experience helped him maneuver the distance unscathed.

He entered his room, shut the door quietly behind him, then leaned up against the frame with closed and tired eyes. He'd made it without a single glimpse of anyone under the age of fifteen. But as luck would have it, no sooner did he open his eyes than he confronted three sleeping little heads on pillows, all in a row, peeking out from underneath the sheets and covers.

His first instinct was to yank them out of his bed and send them on their way, but the ruckus that was sure to result caused him to reconsider. Following great indecision, the allure of the soft comfort of his bed battling the certainty of an uproar, peace and quiet won out and Wade snuck back out the door to find another place to sleep. With seven new bodies to accommodate, every bedroom was taken. Thinking better of using one of the beds vacated by the kids in his room for fear one might return, Wade went in search of a sofa that could fit his large form. "I should've stayed at the office," he muttered before running his knee into a low table in the darkened hallway.

Morning arrived just as Wade found a semi-comfortable position on a divan that was better suited to seating ladies sipping tea and eating cakes than sleeping a man well over six feet. Flinging back the covers he had pilfered from the laundry, Wade stomped to the breakfast room in stocking feet. The children were already there.

"Good morn—" Elizabeth began but got no further when Wade turned an ominous glare in her direction.

"Anyone who says a word won't eat for the rest of the day—maybe the rest of the week!"

A gasp echoed through the room. Wade ignored their outrage, telling himself he wasn't an ogre, that he simply deserved a bit of peace and quiet.

After serving his food, Wade sat down and concentrated on his meal, his eyes never wavering from his plate, daring anyone to speak. Gradually he began to notice a soft weeping. With a sigh he looked up and found the seven-year-old, Elizabeth, whimpering in her seat. "What is it?" he asked reluctantly.

Elizabeth raised her head and looked at him. "You're so angry." The last word was long and drawn out, sounding a great deal like a moan.

Wade shifted in his chair at the twinge of conscience that pricked him. "If you hadn't been sleeping in my bed, maybe I wouldn't be so angry."

Her mouth snapped shut as if just remembering, and she grew silent once again. Wade felt justified in his response. They knew they were wrong, he told himself, and now they were contrite.

Returning to his plate, Wade buttered a hot roll and was just putting it in his mouth when Grace began to weep. With determination he bit the roll, ignoring the sound. Soon the weeping grew noticeably louder.

"What is it now?" he demanded of Grace, dropping the remainder of his roll to his plate.

"You didn't tell the Tooth Fairy we live here now."

"What are you talking about?"

"You told me you would tell the Tooth Fairy where to find us. She's supposed to put coins under my pillow when I lose a tooth. Papa said. And she didn't. Now no one will ever find us 'cause you won't tell anyone. We'll never see anyone again, not the Tooth Fairy, not even Saint Nick."

Her crying had turned into an all-out wail, and Wade hadn't the slightest idea what he was supposed to do. "I never told you I'd tell anyone anything."

This only intensified the sobs.

"What the devil do you want me to do?"

Before matters could deteriorate any further, Jimmy banged his fist on the table and said, "Grace, quit your cryin'. You didn't even sleep in your own bed last night. How do you know if the Tooth Fairy came or not."

The tousled red head slowly rose, and Grace looked at her brother with huge blue eyes swimming in tears.

"Go on. Go look," he insisted as he went back to his meal.

Hesitantly she pushed back her chair and walked from the room with all the grace of a princess. A few minutes passed before a squeal sounded from the upper regions of the house and Grace came barreling down the stairs. "She came, she came! She found me!" When she returned, she held out her tiny hand and showed everyone the two copper pennies she had found under her pillow. "I forgot to look there."

Wade glanced over at Jimmy. Their eyes met for a moment before Jimmy looked away. Wade went back to his meal, trying to ignore the uneasy feelings that welled up inside him.

Wade went straight into town as he had been doing for the last week. It didn't matter that it was Sunday morning; he had work to do. Between the land purchase and the children's arrival he had virtually no time to spend out at the ranch. Just the thought of his beloved ranch made him long for the smell of fresh hay and the feel of silky horseflesh. But first things first, he told himself as he tossed the reins of the big chestnut to the young boy who would see to his horse.

A message waited for Wade when he arrived at the office.

"Jack has initiated a search for a relative, but it could take some time," Nathan said as he followed his employer into his office.

"How long?"

"Didn't say. Just said to sit tight. He'd find one as fast as he could."

"Sit tight, my foot! He'd better find one soon before someone is terrorized to death."

"You really should be nice to those kids. If that letter that arrived with them is any indication, those kids have been through a lot. Mother dying, father dying, left alone in this big, bad world."

"I know what the letter said, Nathan," Wade remarked impatiently. "I read it, too. And when did you become such a kind-hearted soul? Besides, it's me who's in danger of not surviving. Those kids are tough as nails, and they look out for one another."

"So, the all-powerful Wade Alexander has been brought down a peg or two. What greater men couldn't accomplish, seven little children have."

Wade pointed to the door. "Out!"

"I have everything ready for your return trip to Austin," Nathan said quickly. "All the papers and documents you wanted drawn up for the West Tract," Nathan added as he turned to leave.

"Damn! The trip to Austin. I'd forgotten all about it. Who knows if I'll be able to get back by nightfall. Those kids will kill poor Phillips, and that's only if I can convince him to stay."

"Sounds like you need a keeper for those kids."

"Absolutely! A governess. I'll need her there first thing in the morning. Take care of it."

"Me?"

"Who else is going to do it?" Wade looked at his assistant with a mocking smile. "Yes, you with the kind heart."

Wade went to the Men's Club in hopes of getting away from the problems of his inheritance. Not more than a block from his office the old establishment catered to the men who ran the small town of Fielding. Unlike in his grandfather's day, Wade had set up a council of sorts to deal with the day-to-day problems of running the small town. It was in this building that brothels were closed, fines were determined, and plans were made. Anything that went on in Fielding was talked about in this locale.

"There's the new daddy." This pronouncement was accompanied by an assortment of hoots and hollers.

"Where're the cigars?"

"Who's the lucky mama?"

"What does Lorraine think about all this?"

Questions came all at once, quick-fired and full of glee.

"I take it Jack Barnes has been in here," Wade said tightly with a deep scowl.

"Yep. And Judge Wilcox, too."

With a shake of his head, ignoring the rest of the comments, wanting nothing more than a peaceful meal where he wouldn't have to speak to anyone, he wondered why he thought he could have gotten it there. Those kids had rattled his brain.

Never having gotten much farther than the door, Wade turned on his heel and left.

Later, at the end of the day, Wade went to visit Lorraine. Tommy Teeple met him when he pulled up to the house.

"I hear there's a boy come to live with you who's about my age."

"How old are you?"

"Twelve."

"If I've got my numbers straight, there are two about your age. Twins. Garrett and Garvin."

"Gosh! Can I go over and see 'em?"

"Sure," he said, then hesitated, thinking about how all he needed was one more troublemaker around the house. "But stay out of mischief."

"You kiddin' me?" Tommy tilted his head and smiled. "I never get in trouble."

Wade chuckled and ruffled the boy's hair. "No, you just never get caught. Now, get on out of here."

Lorraine waited on the front stoop, her golden locks pulled up from her face, her lush figure shown off in a pink muslin day dress. "You'll have every child in town over at your house before long. If I didn't know better, I'd swear you were actually enjoying this little fiasco you've gotten yourself into."

"You obviously don't know me very well."

"There was a day when I thought I did," she replied before she spun around and went into the house.

They sat in the parlor. An old Mexican woman served them lemonade.

"How are your parents?" Wade asked, wanting nothing more than simple conversation, something Lorraine was always good at providing.

"Fine. You know Mother and Daddy. How are things at your house? Daddy said he heard Jack Barnes is looking for another relative to take the kids."

Wade rubbed a weary hand over his forehead and made a mental note to let Jack know how he felt about his telling everyone his business. "Yes, he is. Someone should turn up soon. Everything's going to work out fine."

"Really, darling?" Lorraine moved closer on the divan.

"Really."

"I'm so happy," she said, then pulled him back and began to rub his temples. "You must have had a time. You look awful."

"Thank you." He tried to sit up. "Your mother or father could walk through that door any second."

"Oh, phooey. Mother is out to supper with Daddy. They'll never know."

"What about Maria?"

"She won't tell. She wouldn't dare."

The tips of her fingers pressed against his temples. "Just relax."

And finally he did, succumbing to her ministrations. His body began to relax, and for the first time since he walked through his front door to find the children, his mind began to wander. Lorraine kept up a constant line of chatter, but she needed no response; in fact, she rarely did.

Memories of a time long ago, a time filled with fun and family, filled his mind. He remembered Jim and how he had never been far from trouble. Wade chuckled.

"What's so funny?" Lorraine asked, her fingers having stilled.

"I was just remembering Jim and the time he—"

"Oh, that cousin of yours. Well, that's sweet. Have I told you yet that Mother is having lace shipped in from Paris for my gown? I tell you, it's going to be the loveliest wedding dress this side of the Mississippi. Every girl in town is going to be green with envy. And I want to invite several people to come in from Austin. I thought they could stay at your house."

Wade abruptly pulled away and stood. "I've got to go."

"But you just got here."

"I only wanted to let you know I'm leaving for Austin in the morning."

"Again!"

"It's business."

Lorraine's eyes narrowed. "You were just there last week."

Wade leaned over and kissed her on the forehead. "Something's come up and I have to take care of it. If I have to, I'll stay overnight." Walking to the door, he told her goodbye. "If it's not too late when I get back, I'll come by."

"Well, maybe I'll be here, maybe I won't," she said petulantly.

Wade smiled, pulling her to him and kissing her pouting lips. His hand traveled down her back until he reached her hips. The kiss became more intense, Lorraine's arms wrapping around his shoulders. She moaned. But when she brought her fingers around to sneak between the buttons of his shirt, he pulled away.

Disappointment stretched across her face. "I'm beginning to think you're the tease, Mr. Alexander."

Wade shouted his laughter, slapped her on the rear, and walked out into the night.

Seven

A GENTLE MORNING breeze rustled through the twisted oak and cedar, carrying the scent of hyacinth blossoms along in its path. Wade stood at the window as the first rays of light colored the darkened sky.

He needed to be in Austin by eight o'clock, making it necessary for him to leave as soon as the sun was high enough to light his way. Half an hour at most. Actually, he didn't mind returning to Austin. In fact, he chuckled to himself, a reprieve from his cousins would do him good. It might even be nice if he had to stay overnight again. But no, he reasoned, he needed to get back and finalize arrangements for the transfer of the cattle to the new land.

Yes, the new land.

Wade was confident that once he had the opportunity to sit down with Richard Leister himself, instead of relying on someone else, he could convince the man to sell. And then he could get on with his expansion plans.

Wade was determined to become the largest breeder of Angus and longhorn cattle in central Texas. The Anguses had already arrived, the longhorns were on the way, and with new outbuildings and a modern barn he could reach his goal. The thought pleased him. The only thing left now was to finalize the land deal with Leister. Wade smiled with expectation. But first, he reminded himself, he had to get out of the house.

With his saddlebags already packed and secured, Wade hoped to eat his meal, enjoy a cup of hot coffee, and be gone before any one of the seven children ventured from beneath crisp white sheets.

A twinge of something bothered him. Conscience, yes, but pride as well. He had not run from unpleasant situations since his return to Fielding two years before. He faced his problems head on, unflinching.

Nathan's words came to mind. Something about what stronger men couldn't do, a few kids had. Well, that was a pile of horse manure, he assured himself; he wasn't reluctant to deal with anything, least of all mere children. He could handle a few measly youths.

Nevertheless, he closed his door softly and made his way through the hall and down the stairs as quietly as possible, his hat in his hand and his gear slung over his shoulder.

The aroma of fresh-brewed coffee met him as he entered the foyer. With a sigh of anticipation combined with relief that he had made it downstairs without disturbing his pint-size guests, Wade set his things at the front door. But his furtive plans were thwarted when he entered the breakfast room and his eyes lighted upon young Jimmy.

Breakfast was definitely becoming a meal to be missed.

At first neither spoke. Both simply stood on opposite sides of the room sizing up the other one, Jimmy in dungarees, his hazel eyes determined; Wade in shirtsleeves, restless to be gone.

Wade cleared his throat. "Morning," he said, turning to the sideboard to fill his plate, hoping the boy would disappear. He made Wade feel damn uncomfortable.

Long moments passed. Jimmy didn't reply, but he didn't bother to leave, either.

"Breakfast looks good," Wade remarked, trying for a paternal tone. "You should have some. Protein, meat on the bones. You know, growing boys and all that."

"Forget it."

Not sure if these frugal words masked some hidden meaning, Wade decided to ignore them altogether and hold the retort that if Jimmy didn't plan to eat, then why not mill around somewhere else? Instead, he sat down, picked up the morning paper, and tried to pretend the boy wasn't there.

Multipaned windows stood open, brocade curtains draped gracefully from velvet sashes, chirping birds frolicked in the birdbath no more than a few yards from the house. The day was growing older, and Wade was on the verge of forgoing the now not so appealing meal and getting on the road when Jimmy approached the table.

He wore a disreputable pair of overalls which had seen better days. His hair was partially wet and partially dry as if he had run wet hands through the coarse mass to bring some semblance of order to it after a long night's sleep. He apparently hadn't wanted to miss his older cousin. His fist was clenched, his pale face grim with purpose, and for a second Wade wondered if the boy could throw a decent punch.

However, it wasn't a blow Jimmy doled out when he extended his freckled fist. Instead, he opened his hand and set two copper pennies down next to Wade's plate. Understanding came slowly to Wade, and when it did it was all he could do to hold back the burst of laughter that threatened to ensue. He had expected a punch and was dealt instead a dose of youthful pride.

"She's my sister and I'll take care of her." James Dawson Daniels, Jr., pulled his wiry shoulders back with all the dignity of an Indian chief who knows in his heart he is about to lose his land.

Wade's threatening burst of laughter died as quickly as was born. He wasn't so old that he couldn't remember the heartfelt pride of youth. "I was only trying to help," Wade said, crumpling the newspaper as his hands dropped to his lap. "After all, she asked *me* to approach this Tooth Fairy character. I'm the one who fell down on the job, not you."

Jimmy stopped, eyes blazing and narrow, throat tight, and said, "We don't need your help. I already told you that."

Then he was gone, out the door and up the stairs, before Wade was given a chance to convince him otherwise. And he *would* have tried to convince him otherwise, Wade realized in a startled afterthought, despite all his assertions that the kids didn't need him.

Carefully setting the paper aside, Wade felt confused. But his own concerns were overshadowed by something else— the sorrow, yes, but more important, the admiration Wade felt for Jimmy. The young boy was a fighter, willing to take on responsibilities whether or not it was realistic he could handle them. Wade thought of Jimmy standing there in old clothes, ready to do battle against a man more than twice his age and double his size, all to protect his younger siblings.

James Dawson Daniels, Jr., was too young to be forced into such a position of duty. Hunting and guns, dancing and girls, those had been Wade's greatest concerns at that age. And those should be Jimmy's concerns, as well, Wade thought, not the responsibility of six brothers and sisters.

Wade sat back in the chair, his dark hair catching golden rays of early morning sun as his eagerly-waited-for cup of coffee grew cold.

The pennies caught his eye. Last night he had come home and remembered his total disregard of the Tooth Fairy episode. Cornflower blue eyes, swimming in tears, had come to mind, followed by the memory of his glance meeting Jimmy's, fleetingly, before the younger male had looked away. Passing the room that Jimmy occupied, Wade had stopped and pulled a silver dollar from his pocket. He would have left that, but instinct had told him the boy would never accept the amount. Now, as he listened to Jimmy's retreating footsteps, he understood the boy's pride made it impossible to take even the two copper pennies Wade had left instead. If he hadn't been so discouraged by the whole situation, he would have smiled as he came to realize the boy was a great deal like him.

Rumblings from upstairs disrupted his thoughts. The children were coming. He hesitated for a second. Perhaps he'd stay just long enough to say hello. But then he shook his head with a start, feeling he had experienced, yet again, another moment of insanity.

Tossing the badly crumpled newspaper on the table, Wade started to make his escape. But he was not to get more than a few steps into the foyer when someone knocked at the door. Hell and damnation, they were coming at him from every direction!

Phillips was there in an instant to greet the caller.

"Good morning. I am here to see Mr. Alexander," Wade heard a woman say to Phillips.

The door opened farther to reveal a female of indistinct years and indeterminate looks, standing at the entrance, her spine ramrod straight, her steel-wool hair pulled back severely, and wireless glasses pinched on her nose.

Phillips hesitated.

"Is there a problem?" the woman asked. "I was instructed to arrive promptly at six o'clock."

Wade knew on sight that she must be the governess he had told Nathan to find. Surreptitiously he glanced at the clock, knowing as he did that it was in the process of announcing the hour. It flashed through his mind that she must have stood on the stoop watching the time, waiting for the exact moment. The idea made him grimace. Was this the woman who would take care of the children? Would she be the one to mold their minds? But then, hadn't he thought, just days before, that strict discipline was just what these youths needed?

Catching sight of Wade, the woman stepped through the doorway, her stiff black skirt swinging like a bell. She held out her hand. "You must be Mr. Alexander. I'm Esther Merriweather. Mr. Nathan Caldwell, your assistant, has procured my services in your stead. If we could sit down, I will go over the schedule I have planned for the children. If there are to be any changes, I want to know about them right away. We wouldn't want to disrupt a schedule. Rules and regulations. Organization is everything, Mr. Alexander. Children must be taught to follow a prescribed path, never to deviate. Children must have order." Esther Merriweather looked about the entry. "Where shall we sit?"

Wade scowled. Not only was the woman a shrew, she had the audacity to give him orders. He had the urge to issue a sharp retort and put the woman in her place. But then he remembered his young unruly cousins upstairs and the trip he had to make to Austin. For the time being she would have to do.

"Miss . . ." he started, then looked at her in question. "You are unmarried?"

"Well, of course."

Yes, of course, he repeated silently. "Miss Merriweather. I am hiring you on a temporary basis. We will see how the next few days go. For now, I've got to go to Austin. This is Phillips. You can talk to him about your schedule." Wade ignored his servant's widened eyes. "I'm sure you'll have no problems."

"But, Mr. Alexander." Miss Merriweather's forehead grew so furrowed that her hair threatened to pop out of its confines. "These children are *your* responsibility. Not," she said, turning a disdainful eye on Phillips, "the butler's."

Phillips's widened eyes bulged even more as shock turned to outrage.

"Rest assured, Miss Merriweather," Wade said tightly, "I don't take my responsibilities lightly. Nathan Caldwell would not have hired you if you were not capable of the job. Furthermore, I will not be here and Phillips will. He'll show you around, make you feel at home, and introduce you to the children."

With strong hands Wade leaned over to pick up his Stetson and saddlebags, then stepped through the open doorway.

Miss Merriweather sputtered for a moment. "When will you be back?" she managed.

He looked back over his shoulder. "Tonight, maybe later." With a slight tip of his hat, Wade pulled the door shut between him and his inheritance and their new keeper. "Good luck," he quietly added.

Wade arrived in Austin in record time. He made it to Edward's office by a quarter till eight and found Richard Leister already there. The man was obviously anxious to sell the land. Just as Wade had thought, he mused. Well, he wouldn't make the man suffer. He'd get right down to brass tacks and then, once the deal was sewn up, he'd take the man out for breakfast.

"Wade," Richard brayed heartily, taking Wade's hand in a firm grip and pumping it like he was trying to get water. "I take it you went on back to Fielding. Didn't want to miss a second with your little woman, I'll bet." Richard threw his meaty arm around Wade's shoulder and smiled a knowing smile. "I'd hurry home myself if I was hurrying home to such a pretty young thing." Richard turned to his brother. "Ed, get Wade here some coffee."

Wade walked over to the window while Ed stepped outside the office.

"Coffee will be here in a minute," Edward said stiffly to his brother upon his return.

"Good, good, good," Richard said, ignoring his younger brother's icy glare. He walked over to Ed's desk and retrieved a cigar from a mahogany humidor, then pulled out a fine gold watch from his vest pocket. "Where's that coffee?" he demanded after looking at the time, then crossed the room with heavy strides, looked at his watch again before replacing it in his vest, and turned back to Wade. "Best be gettin' on with this. Have to be at the Capitol Building soon.

"Now, about this land. It's a shame you came all this way. At least for now. Damn blast it, Wade. I just can't sell it yet. Maybe we can work something out later."

The only sign of Wade's mounting disbelief was the slight tightening of his jaw. His dark eyes never wavered as he patiently waited for Richard Leister to finish his obviously planned speech. "Why can't you sell the land, Richard?"

"Why? Well, uh, because it's just not the time, I tell you. Yes, that's it. You see I thought about it long and hard. It's just not time to sell."

"The market's up and you know it. It's the perfect opportunity for someone like you who's had the land for years to sell and make a sizable profit." Wade could see the stubbornness in his opponent's eyes, and with it his frustration grew by leaps and bounds, leading him down a careless path. "This sale could set your old spinster lady up for life."

"Old spinster lady?" Richard and Ed chimed simultaneously, but further response was curtailed when a knock sounded at the door.

"The coffee," Ed said in unnecessary explanation before he called for the person to enter.

"Hello, hello, I hope I'm not disturbing you." Madeline Montgomery stood in the doorway, one hand on the brass knob, the other holding a pot of steaming coffee. "Oh, excuse me," she said, looking straight at Richard. "Jim Curfew asked me to bring the coffee in. His hands were full. I didn't mean to interrupt. I'll just set this down and come back. . . ."

And then, as she began to turn away, her eyes found Wade. "Oh," she said with surprise, her graceful hand coming up to smooth her, as usual, errant waves of fiery hair. "Why, Mr. Alexander. I didn't see you, either."

Her full lips curved into a devilish smile, and her dazzling eyes sparkled with mischief. "I'm glad to see you survived." As if realizing the inappropriateness of her comment, her smooth white cheeks stained red from obvious embarrassment.

Wade stood awash in the sudden unexpected pleasure of seeing her again. He wondered anew how any one person could be so lovely. He remembered the night he met her, the night he had spent feeling so alive, and afterward, wanting so badly to see her again. And here she was, standing before him, his gallant young servant girl, or perhaps, being here with the coffee in her hands, a new office girl. But either way, she was still the one who had deigned to help a person whom she had thought was a less fortunate soul. The thought pleased him immensely.

Wade stepped forward to stand before her. "Not only did I survive, Miss Montgomery, but in hindsight, I find I even enjoyed myself."

Madeline's crimson cheeks turned a flaming red, but her pleasure at his words was written clearly in her eyes. She managed a deprecating chuckle. "I'm glad, Mr. Alexander. I'd hate to think you went away with terrible thoughts of me."

Wade suddenly thought of the children, all seven of them in their red raging glory. Maybe it was the color of Madeline's hair, or possibly the gay laughter that graced her lovely lips, but he smiled as he thought again that she would fit in quite well with his pack of youngsters, could easily have been an older sister—maybe even their mother.

The thought unsettled him. His brows furrowed. Why, he wondered uncomfortably, was he thinking such things? He was there to talk business.

Richard stepped forward, breaking the silence. "You two have met," he stated, though not without a touch of puzzlement.

"Yes, we have," Wade responded, still looking at Madeline.

"Well, this changes things considerably, I suppose." Richard extended his arms to Madeline in an unfamiliar welcoming gesture.

If Madeline hadn't been so preoccupied, she might have been suspicious. But her thoughts were all too caught up with the man who had set her mind to whirl like a schoolgirl's. Wade Alexander.

Her heart beat wildly at the sight of him. Unlike at the party, here in an office of business he fit right in. His light-colored shirt and vest and perfectly tailored pants fit him like a glove, and his hair was perfectly groomed. He was more striking than she remembered, though in a hard sort of way. No pretty boy here, she mused.

"You two must've met at Rosalind's party." Richard glanced at Wade. "I see you made good use of your time."

Richard turned back to Madeline, took the coffeepot from her hand, and gave her a meaningful smile. "I suspect you're here to let us know you've reconsidered about that piece of land."

Madeline didn't respond at first, merely stood with her hand still outstretched, her pleasure at seeing Wade again fading just a bit. "The land?" she finally asked, dread tingeing her voice.

Wade visibly stiffened.

Richard, however, failed to notice the change. "You two must have discussed the West Tract over a cup of punch, eh?" Richard looked at Wade. "Well, you're a better man than I if you could make her see sense where I couldn't. Damn. My niece is a stubborn one. Should've known it would take some pretty talkin' to turn her around." Richard handed the coffeepot to Edward, then walked over to Wade and clapped him on the shoulder. "Good man, Alexander. Now, let's get down to details. Edward, take notes."

"This is your niece?" Wade asked tightly. "This is the—" Wade stopped in midsentence as Richard began dictating information that Edward wasn't taking down.

Madeline's heart pounded even harder in her chest, but no longer from excitement. The excitement was rapidly replaced by outrage—and something else. She closed her eyes and fought back the lump that formed in her throat. Disappointment loomed before her, disappointment that this man apparently was like all the rest—he wanted her for her money. She had been a fool. To think she had cherished the memory of being held in his arms. How could she have been so naive, telling herself he was different, when all the while proof stared her in the face. He wanted to mingle with the rich, so how better to do it than snag one of them. And if she were truthful, she had no one to blame but herself.

He hadn't tried to hide his situation by borrowing proper clothes or hiring a coach. No, Wade Alexander had confronted her as he was, his dire straits laid out before her as plain as day. It was she who had chosen to tell herself he didn't want her for her money. It was she who had wanted to believe in fairy tales. Reality told a different tale, however. Wade Alexander was the man who wanted her land.

Gradually her uncle's persistent chattering broke into her thoughts.

"I'm amazed you didn't tell me you two had this land

thing licked. Wanted to surprise me, did ya? Fine, fine. I'm not opposed to a surprise now and again. Now, where was I? Oh, yes, a legal description of the land." Richard turned to his brother. "You gettin' all this?" Leaning over the younger man's shoulder, Richard peered at a tablet that lay on the table. "You haven't gotten a word I said!"

The harsh words went unnoticed, however, when Madeline turned to Wade. "You told me you were poor!" she accused irrationally with her hands on her hips and blue-green eyes burning.

Everyone stopped. Richard along with Ed looked from Wade to Madeline, both perplexed by the turn of events.

"I never told you any such thing." Wade stepped past the brothers, his eyes dark with anger.

"What about not having a ride and those pitiful clothes you had on?"

"Madeline!" Ed protested.

Wade waved Ed's comment away. He looked at Madeline for a long time, then took her hand in an almost painful grip. "It seems to me you're the one with some explaining to do. A poor servant girl? Trying to help a person in need? No, I suspect you just wanted a little time alone with me. Is that why you're here now? To have your uncles force me to marry you?"

"A little time alone!" Richard bellowed.

But Madeline paid him no notice as Wade's insulting words penetrated her mind. With a jerk she snatched her hand away. "Force you to marry me?! Who do you think you are? I'm not marrying anyone! And if I ever considered marriage, I wouldn't marry you even if you were the last male in the world under age ninety-eight—a hundred and ninety-eight, for that matter," she added with a toss of her head. "And don't think for one minute that I can't figure out why you wanted to dance with me. For my land!"

Wade scowled. "You seem to forget that you were the one who did the asking, not the other way around."

Red surged into her cheeks. "Only because I felt sorry for you."

Richard, it appeared, was getting the gist of the situation. "It would seem, my dear niece," he remarked dryly, "you have gotten the facts mixed up. Poor judgment, perhaps?"

Ignoring her uncle's jibe, she turned to Ed. "I told you I will not sell that land, not now, not ever, and I mean it." It didn't matter that the very reason she had come to her uncle's office was to sell the land, after all. She would not let the likes of Wade Alexander make a fool of her. Forced marriage, indeed!

Richard's face was suffused in red. "What could you possibly want with that piece of scrubland? If I were you, I'd get it off my hands."

Suddenly her plans and ideas shifted, then jelled. She could raise money, then build the school on the acreage. It was perfect. Her frown curled up into a smile, her chin rose in defiance. "Well, you aren't me, and I'm going to build a school on my land."

"A school?!" Richard shouted. "For your information, young lady, that piece of property is a good ten miles from town. What parent on God's good earth would send their child way the hell out there? It's certainly no place to build a school. Even if you were smart enough to do it."

"I'm not talking about a school for average children. I'm going to build a school where parentless children can go to live and learn."

"Live and learn! You need to live and learn—about the realities of life!"

"Enough!" Wade stood before Richard, his dark eyes growing darker, his chiseled jaw clenched. "I will not be a part of your badgering her this way. If she doesn't want to sell, then so be it. I won't waste any more of your time."

With a stiff nod to each of the three dumbstruck relatives, he strode to the door. He pulled the door open, then hesitated. Turning back, he looked at Madeline, directly into her eyes. It was the same look he had given her the night of the party. Questioning, searching, but for what, Madeline again had no idea. Her heart clenched with yearning, her anger momentarily forgotten. But then he turned away and was gone, the door shut securely in his wake.

"What was that all about?" Richard asked heatedly.

Madeline turned to Richard, saw his blotchy countenance, and knew she couldn't spend one second more in the same room with him. She had to get out.

She left her uncles without so much as a wave of goodbye. Upset and hurt, she walked through the streets unmindful of where she was heading. The loneliness that had plagued her before returned. Her newfound enthusiasm waned. And she knew it was for no good reason. But the mind and the heart sometimes see things differently, and it hurt to find he had used her as a means to an end. And then she remembered the look in his eyes. Why did he have to turn back and look at her, to fill her again with longing?

It wasn't until she was several blocks away that she heard someone calling her name. With a start she turned hopeful eyes toward the voice.

"Oh. Reverend Marshall. I didn't see you."

"No, you didn't. Moving along just as fast as a jackrabbit with a hunt dog on its tail. Where you off to in such a hurry? Where's that horse of yours? Tuckered out, is she?" Reverend Marshall chuckled. "I wouldn't be surprised if that old thing just plain up and quit on you one day."

Madeline managed a cheerless smile.

The reverend looked more closely. "What's this? Something wrong, child?"

"No, nothing's wrong. Just lost in my thoughts is all. How about you?" she asked, wanting desperately to change the subject. "Is everything all right at the church?"

"Just fine. You're kind to ask. But there is a sheep of another flock in need of help."

"Really, who?"

"Father Hayes, from out Fielding way, sent me a wire. Seems there are some orphans in need of help." The reverend looked somewhat sheepishly at Madeline. "You have done so much for us in the short time you've been here, and I hate to ask you to do more. But I don't know of anyone else who could take the time to ride out to Fielding and deal with these poor children."

"What exactly is the problem?" Madeline asked, worry creasing her face.

"I don't rightly know. The wire was a bit cryptic. You know how wires are. Pay by the word and all. But apparently there are some orphans who need some help, and I couldn't think of a better person than you to give it to them. If you can't, I'll understand. Again, you've done so much already."

Not being one to go into a situation unprepared, she didn't particularly want to take on this when there were so few details to be had. No telling what she would find in Fielding. Though she had never been there herself, she knew the town was about half the size of Austin, maybe even smaller. What kind of an orphanage could a town that size have? But on the other hand, this seemed to be the perfect opportunity to flee from her uncles as well as Wade Alexander. Just the thought of running into the man made her stomach tighten. No, for now, it was best to get away for a while. Take her mind off her own insignificant problems and help someone less fortunate.

"Reverend, I'd be happy to help. Is next week too late? I'll find someone else to take over the ladies' luncheon at the Pavilion, but I don't think I could get it all squared away before then."

"Good heavens, that's fine. I knew I could count on you. Bless you, child."

Madeline waved goodbye and turned toward home, determined to put as much distance as possible between her and Wade Alexander.

Eight

W ADE LEFT E D Leister's office at an angry pace, though it was an anger born more of frustration than anything else.

Why was his well-ordered life suddenly going awry? his mind raged. He had worked tirelessly to get his life in order, and things had been going so well. Then bang, in a matter of days his plans, his house, and his heart were as settled as a chicken coop with a fox running wild inside. Wade shook his head in dismay.

Kicking a rock that lay in his path, he cursed to the skies before dropping onto a bench. He lowered his head into his hands. You're a fool, Wade Alexander, he scolded himself, you lost your head over a pretty face.

But despite his chastisement, the thought of one Madeline Montgomery, in all her glory, brought a reluctant wave of desire to surge through him, just as it had again and again since he had met her. And for the life of him, he could come up with no reason to explain his infatuation.

She was beautiful, yes, in an unusual sort of way, but Lorraine had the kind of beauty he had always been attracted to. Madeline was tall and slender, so unlike Lorraine with the lush curves he so enjoyed. Red hair versus shimmering blond, bright blazing blue-green eyes versus gentle blue ones. Hadn't he always pictured the woman of his dreams as a blond-haired, blue-eyed, lush-built woman to capture any man's imagination, the very picture of Lorraine? And furthermore, Lorraine was everything else he expected in a woman—fashionable, socially inclined, so very different from this woman here in Austin. Dressed as though she bought her clothes from Henry's Clothes by the Pound, Madeline Montgomery was about as socially adept as a toadstool. Not to mention the fact that he was suspect of her morals, and she appeared to be the chattiest female he had ever met.

But still his mind raced in imagination.

Wade looked out over the busy street. The townspeople were well about their day, while he merely sat there, his thoughts consumed by a woman who seemed to have no more concern for womanly things than he did.

Leaning back, he pressed his head against the wall. What had he done? he asked himself. He had told Richard Leister he didn't want the land. All because of a breathtaking and bewitching redhead. But the way Richard had spoken to her had made him want to grab the man by the shirt collar and pummel his red-splotched face. And on top of that, one minute she was telling him she only danced with him because she felt sorry for him, and then in the next she proceeded to accuse him of dancing with her merely to get her land.

Honor, mixed with a good dose of pride, surged through him. Wade Alexander doesn't use underhanded methods to get anything, he thought.

But now he faced another trip to try to secure the Patterson acreage. All because of his pride. If only he had stayed calm, he was certain he could have made Miss Montgomery see reason. It should have been a snap to convince the batty woman to sell her land. But no, he had to lose his temper, thinking not of the ranch, but of the obvious fact that the fair Madeline was not some servant girl, not someone trying to help a person who she thought was a less fortunate soul. Instead, she turned out to be a scheming, conniving young spinster desperate for a husband—no better than the rest. Just as he first thought. And to think he fell for it! But most of all, to think how it hurt.

Wade grimaced and stood. Hurt, that was preposterous. He just didn't like being made out to be a fool.

Back in Fielding Wade went straight to the ranch. Hard work under the hot sun was what he needed. Joe Petre, the foreman, along with several ranch hands, looked on with astonishment as Wade attempted to break a wild mustang. After several hours of attempts and being thrown more than once, Wade managed to sit the horse for one complete turn around the corral before he had cooled down enough to venture home.

Wade arrived at the house just before darkness fell. The sun set in the western sky, bringing the day to a vibrant end. Red and orange mixed with a breathtaking blue, slowly turning the firmament to black, leaving him, finally, with a sense of rightness about the world.

The rightness vanished, however, as soon as he walked through the front door, for there, in the tiled entry, sat Miss Esther Merriweather.

At first Wade wondered who she was. Not only had he not given her another thought since he had left that morning, but this woman in no way resembled the one who had arrived to take care of the children.

Gone was the vim and vigor that had so disturbed Wade. Her hair, once so severely pulled back, was now tousled about her thin head. Her spine, no longer so straight, had that slouched curve so indicative of defeat. Her perfectly pressed attire had taken a dramatic change, the skirt no longer so stiff, the blouse no longer so white. Lips that had been pursed in a hard line now curved down on either side attesting to her apparent displeasure. Beady eyes glared at him with malice.

"Finally!" she declared while pushing herself up from the suitcase she perched on.

Wade glanced about the house, suddenly aware that the lights weren't blazing and everything was quiet. "Where are the children? Has anything happened?"

"The children, Mr. Alexander"—she gasped the words, her body so tight she appeared ready to pop—"are upstairs. Not to worry, they are alive. Which is more than I can say for myself." Miss Merriweather pointed toward the stairs. "Up there, Mr. Alexander, is a pack of . . . of . . . heathens who lack manners and discipline. They are terrors, and the only reason I am still here now is that I have never, repeat, *never*, left a position without notifying my employer. Therefore, at this moment you are notified of my departure. I quit, Mr. Alexander. I am leaving this instant for Austin even if I have to walk all the way back in the dark. And let me tell you, every reputable governess west of the Mississippi will hear about this."

Then, without waiting for a response, Miss Esther Merriweather ran a hand over her wiry hair in the futile attempt to smooth it, gathered her belongings with a great deal of ceremony, and stalked out of the house, her chest heaving and her head held high. The heavy oak door slammed behind her.

It happened so fast that Wade had no chance to question her further or demand an explanation. But if the truth be known, it suited him just fine that she was gone. He had no wish to confront another irrational female.

He stared at the closed door and sighed. What next? he wondered, and where was he going to get another governess? He thought of Jack Barnes and wondered if perhaps he had found a relative. First thing in the morning he would go straight to his lawyer's office. Surely someone had turned up.

"You're back!" Phillips exclaimed, entering the foyer with surprising good humor. Quite a contrast to the bedraggled Miss M. "I take it you have already spoken with Miss Merriweather."

The man, who only days before had looked harried and worn-out, now appeared rejuvenated and full of life.

Wade shook his head and eyed Phillips speculatively. "Rather, she spoke to me. What happened here? The kids are all right, aren't they?"

"Yes, they're fine, though I'm not sure I can say the same for the governess." Phillips laughed. "What a lark."

"What is it you find so amusing about this situation?"

"Comeuppance, I believe it's called. The old bag of bones had it coming. After I realized the youths had the situation well in hand, I stood back and watched. Best entertainment I've had in years. Too bad you missed it, sir."

Phillips must have seen the look on his employer's face, for his "life is wonderful" smile disappeared and he burst forth with a rapid explanation. "You should have seen 'er," he said in a rush of words, his carefully practiced accent slipping in his haste. "She was a tyrant, demandin' and hollerin', orderin' everyone around—everyone includin' me." Phillips sniffed his resentment. "You should have heard the things she said to me. Lordin' it over everyone. Acted as though she was better'n me."

"I'm a lot more concerned with what she said to the children, or if I've guessed correctly, what the children said to her."

"Those poor little souls didn't do a thing." The servant's eyes grew fierce. "Not a thing."

"Why do I find that hard to believe? And when did you

become such an advocate for those kids?" Wade asked as he cocked his head in disbelief.

"Well . . . uh . . . I just felt they weren't treated nicely by that old woman."

"Or could it be *you* weren't treated nicely by Miss Merriweather?" he asked, though he didn't expect an answer as he turned toward the stairs. "It's been a long day, and I still have some things to do before morning. I'll deal with the kids tomorrow."

"And how was Austin?" Phillips inquired, his manners and mannerisms back in place.

"Let's just say it's been better." Wade walked to the stairs.

Phillips went to turn down lights, then halted. "Sir, I almost forgot," he called.

Halfway up the stairs Wade stopped and turned. "What is it?"

"I talked to Father Hayes about the children, and he said he would be happy to help."

"I could use a few prayers just about now."

Phillips looked confused. "Not prayers, sir."

"Then what?"

"I don't know. I didn't think to ask. But I expect he'll find a good Christian woman who will come and take care of the youngsters."

Turning back, Wade grunted and continued on toward his room. He hoped the priest would have better luck than he'd had. Wade heaved a tired sigh. Such a well-ordered life, he mused. How could things have changed so quickly?

The hallway was dimly lit, a solitary candle lending eery shadows to the walls. When he turned toward his room, he caught sight of a slice of light shining from underneath a door. His tired sigh turned to a reluctant grunt of laughter. Running his large hand through the dark waves of his hair, Wade could just imagine what had transpired over the last few hours. On impulse, he walked toward the light and opened the door.

The room was large, one of the largest guest rooms in the house. The furniture was dark and massive with dark velvet curtains and huge brass ornamentations; a room better suited to someone more along the lines of Wade himself than the juveniles who just then looked a great deal more like curly headed angels than the redheaded devils he knew them to be. But there they were, huddled about the large four-poster bed, all seven of them, their heads forming a ring of red as they appeared to be carrying on some sort of a serious discussion.

"Uh-hum," Wade announced himself by clearing his throat.

Instantly the room grew silent, all heads snapping in his direction. Once they saw him, eyes grew big and mouths opened in silent "ohs." Wade had to stifle the laugh that threatened to erupt. But the laugh died in his chest when Jimmy, ever the defender, came forward with grim determination to confront the man of the house.

They stood that way for some time, Wade standing so tall and powerful, Jimmy, tall as well, but thin and defiant. Wade felt a wave of regret that he'd had no siblings like these. And then he smiled and reached out and ruffled Jimmy's hair.

"So you ran her off, did you?" he asked the group as a whole.

Every face looked at him suspiciously, not sure if he was ready to shout at them or laugh. Their faces were scrubbed and they were dressed for bed but not yet there. They glanced furtively from one to the other, their dubious gazes resting finally on their oldest brother. Not one of them seemed to know what to say.

It was Grace who broke the taut silence as she raised her tiny hand to her brow and cried, "It was awful, Cousin, simply awful!"

Silence filled the room in one terribly surprised moment before a cacophony of voices clamored for attention.

"Oh, yes! It was," Elizabeth confirmed with serious eyes.

"She's right," Garrett pronounced, looking to Jimmy for reassurance.

"You really shouldn't have left her here, Cousin. She was totally unacceptable." Grace stood with hands on hips, her brow knitted in a scowl, sounding a great deal more grown-up than any almost-six-year-old had a right to be.

Wade wasn't sure if it was the dramatics or merely the thought of how *awful* it must have been, but the laugh that had threatened finally came forth. With the laugh came six squealing youngsters to gather around him.

"She made us eat oatmeal."

"She made us wash our hands all the time."

"And walk! One mile before lunch and another before supper."

"With backs held straight and heads held high."

"I'm exhausted!"

"I'm sore!"

"I'll never walk again."

"And poor Mr. Phillips. She yapped and snapped at him all day long."

"She was awful."

"Simply awful," Grace finished with her hand once again to her brow.

Wade reached down and swept Grace into his arms. "Where, might I ask, did these dramatics come from? I can't imagine Miss Merriweather teaching you those."

"Teach!" Bridget exclaimed, her hair brushed back and braided. "She sat us down before our walks and after our walks, and made us read and write, even after supper!" she cried with a flourish. "No one works after supper. Papa said.

And we told her so, but she wouldn't listen, just sat us in separate places for talking back and made us read some more."

"Did you learn anything?" Wade asked with a smile.

"No," Elizabeth answered shyly. "And Miss Merriweather doesn't know anything. Miss Lorraine told her so."

"Miss Lorraine?" Wade demanded, his smile faltering. "When did you see Lorraine?"

"Just before supper," Grace said. "She came over to see you. And she looked soooo pretty. She wore a beautiful yellow dress with lots and lots of ruffles."

"And the biggest hat I've ever seen," Garrett offered. "Looked like a bird's nest. She slapped at Garvin when he got up on a chair to look for a bird."

"Miss Merriweather told Miss Lorraine she wasn't being proper to come over to our house," Grace announced. "What is proper?"

The two twelve-year-old twins seemed to think this part was particularly funny as they nudged each other and smiled knowingly.

"She shouldn't have come around lookin' for Cousin Wade. A woman isn't supposed to do that kind of thing," Garrett pronounced. "Miss Lorraine doesn't know anything."

"That's not true," Grace denied. "Miss Lorraine told Miss Merriweather that *she* didn't know anything." Holding tightly to his neck, she turned a serious gaze on Wade. "It made Miss Merriweather real mad. That's when she carried on and told Miss Lorraine she wasn't proper. Then Miss Lorraine said things were awful, simply awful." Grace finished by yet again putting her hand to her brow.

"So that's where you learned the dramatics. Well, it doesn't become you," Wade said as he pushed her hand down. "Nor does it become Lorraine," he added under his breath, certain he would hear more about the episode from his fiancée. "Now, all of you to bed. We'll discuss adequate punishment in the morning."

"Punishment!" they cried in unison, all except Jimmy, that is.

"Yes, punishment. You have to learn that you can't go around terrorizing people."

"But you thought it was funny," Garrett accused.

Wade grimaced, not sure how to respond. Coming up with nothing suitable, he said, "I've said all I'm going to say for now. We'll talk in the morning. Now, off with you."

Slowly, dreading what the morrow would bring, the red-headed children began to file out of the room.

"Would you put me to bed, Cousin?" Grace asked, her head drooping on his shoulder and her eyes fluttering closed just as he began to set her down.

With an oddly contented smile, Wade silently walked down the long hall and took young Grace to the room he knew she was using. Pulling back the covers with one arm, he slowly lowered her into bed. After awkwardly tucking the covers under her chin, he reached over to turn down the light, thinking the little girl sound asleep.

"Cousin."

"Yes."

"You shouldn't punish anyone but me. I was the one who was bad."

Wade smiled into the semidarkness. "Now, what would make you be bad?"

"She was mean!" she cried with great feeling.

He wondered if she had been falling asleep at all, or if she had merely pretended, to gain his attention. Somehow the thought didn't bother him as he knew it should.

"You think everyone is mean," Wade responded. "Just the other day I remember you said Elizabeth was mean. You haven't run her off."

"I've tried, but she's still hanging around," she said in a quiet voice.

Wade could barely make out the smile that curved on her lips.

"But you'll keep trying, is that it?" he asked with an answering smile of his own.

The room grew silent.

"No," Grace finally replied most seriously. "I don't want anyone else to leave me like my mama and papa did." The small child hesitated. "My papa's never coming back, is he?" she whispered in a small voice.

Wade's throat constricted and his chest felt tight. The words were like a blow, unexpected and painful. His mind raced to find the right thing to say. What would someone who knew about kids do in the same situation? he wondered. It was one thing to feed them right or punish them when need be, and he was barely managing with that, but talking about people dying was way beyond his nonexistent child-rearing skills.

Failing to come up with some ready-made, polished answer, he reached out and smoothed back her curly red hair, trying his best to muck through the predicament. "No, sweetheart, your father isn't coming back."

Silver moonlight reflected in the tears pooled in her large blue eyes. She looked up at him, eyes intent and searching. "Did he go to heaven to be with my mama?"

Wade felt as though he teetered on a precarious precipice, unsure of what to say or what to do, afraid that either way he went would lead to a fall. "Yes," he finally managed. "Your father has gone to heaven to be with your mother, and right this very minute they are watching over you and will always be with you, right here," he said as he placed her tiny hand over her chest, "in your heart."

She looked down at her chest as if expecting to find her

parents, and then she returned her gaze to Wade. "When my mama died, I was very sad." Her voice grew serious, the tears brushed hastily away. "Papa told me to be strong because he said, 'When God closes a door, somewhere he opens a window.' "

Wade stared down at his wild cousin's young child. Had that tender, heartfelt thought truly come from his reckless, never-far-from-trouble cousin?

Grace's eyes began to close, and he wondered, regardless of where the words came from, what they meant to her. Was it possible for someone so young to understand such things? Did she understand the hope they implied? But regardless of what *she* did or did not know, Wade was realizing more and more just what he didn't know. He who had thought he knew everything, had planned everything, had his days plotted out to the end, at that moment didn't seem to know the first thing about life. He smoothed the covers, then started to leave.

"Cousin?"

"Yes?"

"Does God live in a big house like you with lots of windows?"

His heart burgeoned with emotion for this tiny child who asked so many questions, who tried so desperately to understand how her parents could be taken away from her, tried to understand the incomprehensible. He smiled a sad smile. "I would guess he lives in a much bigger house than this with a lot more windows."

Apparently content with his answer, Grace turned over on her side, pulled up a rag doll that Wade had never seen before into her arms, and closed her eyes. "Good night, Cousin."

"Good night," he whispered, then leaned over and placed a gentle kiss upon his young cousin's brow.

* * *

The sun was up and had cast its long warm rays through the open window when Wade finally woke. Rubbing his hand over his eyes, he wondered why Phillips had not been in to wake him.

Lying there, he strained to hear sounds from other regions—outside, down the hall, possibly below. Nothing. He heard nothing. Then he realized the children were sure to be extra quiet in hopes of delaying their punishment as long as possible.

He remembered Grace's claim that she had been the sole instigator. Such a family that everyone tried to protect the others, even when so young.

But children needed discipline. They couldn't go through life and not learn that they had to take responsibility for their actions. Isn't that what every good parent would do? Feeling certain he was right, he went about determining what penalty they would pay.

After a good ten minutes of deliberation, Wade had no more idea how to reprimand the youths than he had the night before. Wade sighed. It was always something with these kids.

The thought of the children—young Grace and her story, Jimmy and his pride, and every one of their manes of bright red hair—left him with an ache somewhere in the region of his heart. They were Jim's offspring, family, his family.

And then he remembered Madeline Montgomery. Her flowing tresses had been a shade of red that varied just as the children's did. Was it closest to Bridget's? he wondered. Or perhaps he meant Elizabeth. Well, anyway, the younger of the two.

But that was crazy, he chided himself. All of it was crazy. Everything from seven children showing up on his doorstep to the old maid turning out to not be so old at all.

With a grunt, he jerked back the covers and walked with

determined strides to the dressing room. Just as he had planned, he was going to Jack Barnes's office and see what, or rather who, had turned up. After that, he was going to go about pursuing the Patterson acreage. He hoped the price wouldn't have gone up since the man was sure to have found out that the other deal had fallen through. Regardless, it was time to get on with his life, children or not.

Wade didn't make it to Jack Barnes's office that day or the day after that. Something, he always found, came up. He wasn't sure what caused this, and not understanding the reason, he avoided thinking about it at all, pushing the problem from his mind. He had been able to secure another governess, temporarily easing his concern, but she lasted only a short while, and he was forced to find another the day after that.

The driving off of Miss Merriweather had made him laugh, and the second governess actually hadn't been much better. But as the days passed, the keeper situation became less and less amusing as one governess after another was duly run off. No one, it seemed, could control these children.

Eventually, five governesses later, the situation had gotten well out of hand. After the last woman walked out the front door, Wade canceled appointments and went straight over to Jack Barnes's office. "Have you found a relative yet?" he asked as he barged through the door.

"No, nothing's turned up," a startled Jack Barnes said as he looked up from his desk. He looked at Wade closely. "Have a seat. Let me get you some coffee. You don't look so good."

"That's because I'm going crazy. Absolutely insane."

The lawyer laughed. "Well, it happens to the best of us."

Wade looked closely at his lawyer. "Is there a possibility there might be a problem turning the kids over to a relative?"

Jack poured Wade a cup of coffee. "Don't worry yourself, Wade. Any judge around will do what's best for the kids. And anyone with half a brain will agree that married folk are better for kids than a bachelor." He set the cup in front of Wade. "And for now, you need control. That's the ticket. You just need a little control over those kids."

Wade snorted. "Well, if you're such an expert, why don't you give it a try? I happen to be in need of a new governess as of ten minutes ago."

"That must be a record. How many has that been?" Jack looked up at the ceiling while remembering. "Let's see. You managed to keep one all day Monday. But that was only because you weren't around to give notice to. And since then it's been one a day starting on Tuesday and then Miss Wednesday and Miss Thursday and now it looks like Miss Friday didn't last any longer than the rest." Jack looked across his desk. "What are those kids doing over there?"

"I'm not exactly sure. I've avoided them like the plague." Wade leaned back in the chair, closed his eyes, and groaned.

"Maybe that's the problem," Jack said thoughtfully.

"The problem," Wade snapped, "is that those children need a family, not a thirty-one-year-old bachelor and his family retainer."

"Well, I'm looking, Wade, I'm looking all over the country. If there are any relations out there, I'll find them. Not to worry."

Wade stood up and walked toward the door.

Jack stood as well. "If you don't mind my saying so, it might help if you spent a little time with them. The wife was saying that just the other day. It's amazing what a little attention will do."

"Attention?"

"Yeah, you know. Take the boys fishing. Girls love pretty things. Buy them a hat or something. Women love hats."

"Fishing and hats. I come to my lawyer for an update and advice, and he tells me about fishing and hats." Wade scowled. "Leave the kids to me, Jack. You just find me a relative." With that he was gone, through the door and down the steps to the crowded dusty streets of downtown.

Nine

FOUR DAYS HAD passed since Madeline found out Wade Alexander for the scoundrel he was. Every one of those interminable days had left her stomach churning at the thought that she might run into him on the street. Now, thank goodness, having arrived in the small town of Fielding, she was over two hours gone and a good ten miles away from the man, and she finally felt herself rest at ease.

It had taken plenty of talk to convince her grandmother, one, to let her go, and two, to keep her mission a secret from her uncles. But in the end Madeline had prevailed, though only after promising to follow Old Petey Rado and his mail stage—as if the tobacco-chewing, foul-mouthed, tiny little man could ensure her safety. But he meant well, she amended, feeling guilty for such unkind thoughts.

With loose ends tied up in Austin, Madeline had set out on the rut-filled road with an unexpected excitement surging through her veins. And the excitement persisted, despite the two hours of mouth-parching, eye-burning dust she choked on from following Old Petey's rickety stagecoach. She was off on an adventure, perhaps not an African safari, she supposed, but an adventure nonetheless. This, she stated to the scurrying jackrabbits darting across the road, was what life was meant to be!

The opportunity to help the orphans was a godsend. Madeline was more than happy to have a means to escape the suddenly small confines of Austin, however temporary the escape might be.

Out on the road she enjoyed every bump and rut, relishing her freedom. The breeze in her face, the heat on her skin, and a purpose in her soul. Life could be wonderful at times.

Fielding had loomed before her in record time, and after a quick stop for directions to her final destination from a boy on the street, Madeline waved her thanks to Old Petey before pulling up in front of an overwhelmingly large building with just enough time before the lowering sun finally set.

The sun, however, was the farthest thing from her mind when she stopped the wagon and looked up at the gigantic structure. A long gravel drive lined with tall boxed shrubs led to the front doors with pewter handles and a pewter lion's head knocker. The roof was slate gray, and the walls were built from large blocks of hand-chiseled granite. The large mullioned windows looked dark and foreboding.

Madeline left her horse and wagon with a groom who appeared out of nowhere. The well-kept grounds heartened her a bit. Perhaps the place wasn't as ominous as it looked. Regardless, she had come this far, and there was no turning back. So with firm resolve, she took hold of the knocker and announced her arrival.

The door was opened by a middle-aged butler who eyed her despondently. "May I help you, ma'am?" he inquired politely enough.

"I am Madeline Montgomery, here at the request of the Reverend Marshall of Austin and Father Hayes of Fielding."

The butler visibly perked up. "Merciful heavens," he pronounced. "Come in."

Madeline hesitated. Buck up, girl, she reprimanded herself, then resolutely marched through the door.

Though unsure of what she would find inside, she never expected a beautiful residence that would rival any she had seen in England or Europe. Marble floors, curving staircase, carved pillars, crystal chandeliers. Out in the middle of Texas! Not that she cared about such things, just that she suddenly knew with a certainty this was no institution. It was someone's home.

And then it struck her. Someone of this obvious wealth wouldn't need charity work. What could they possibly want with her? She cursed herself for not waiting for more information before jumping in her wagon, unchaperoned, and coming to help. Wouldn't Uncle Richard just love to hear about this little fiasco? She could see him now, his round face red and puffed, ranting and raving, before dragging her home, lecturing her all the way. No, she reasoned, that scenario couldn't happen, this had to work out. And with that thought, the sounds that had only been a faint rumbling in the recesses of her mind burst forth in a plethora of shrill screams as a swarm of children streamed down the stairs.

In something close to shock, Madeline stood transfixed as she counted six bellowing redheaded children, some traveling by way of the banister while others tumbled down the steps, but whatever the mode, they all managed, thank the Lord, to make it to the bottom in one piece. Glancing at the butler, she waited for him to demand order or seek the proper person in charge. It was a moment before Madeline realized he was going to do neither. The man stood quite still with a miserable look of defeat etched across his face.

"Aren't you going to do something?" Madeline asked expectantly.

"What would you have me do, ma'am? These children have minds of their own. I was hoping, however, that they'd go a little easier on you. My employer is kind of desperate at this point. But I guess you'll be leaving now like all the rest of them?"

"What do you mean, 'all the rest'?"

"There has been a string of governesses through here. Each leaving sooner than the last. I guess they just don't make them like they use to. The last one only left this morning." He looked off into some distant place. "I remember the day when a governess would come in and take control, have those youngsters up in the nursery where they belong." Shaking his head, he added, "I guess those days are gone."

During the butler's reminiscing, Madeline noticed a boy she guessed to be about fourteen, who arrived to stand at the bottom of the stairs, making the total number of children seven. He watched her closely. There was a look about him, proud and defiant, yes, but something else, as well. In those green eyes she saw fear and a great deal more responsibility than a boy of his age should have to bear.

Wade Alexander and Uncle Richard were forgotten along with her other concerns and problems. Only the boy and his siblings mattered from that moment on.

Madeline turned to the butler. "When might I meet with the man or the woman of the house?"

"Well, uh, probably tonight?"

"Tonight? Who is seeing to the children during the day?"

"I am," the man replied shortly.

Madeline took in his defensive stance and realized the situation wasn't the butler's fault, but the fault of whoever was truly in charge of these children. No purpose would be served by angering the servant. So she smiled warmly. "And I have no doubt you are doing your best to make things run smoothly."

Phillips relaxed.

"Mr., ah . . . ?"

"Phillips, just Phillips will do Miss, ah, Montgomery, was it?"

"Yes. Well, Phillips, what do you have planned for the remainder of the day?"

He looked at her curiously. "I was going to finish my chores."

"No, no, I meant for the children."

Phillips looked decidedly uncomfortable. "Supper's in an hour," he offered.

The children still raced and roamed, their hollers echoing through the large hall. Madeline felt her dismay grow to anger. What was the benefactor of these youths thinking? No supervision, no planned activities to keep them out of trouble. No attention. No wonder they were having so many problems!

Then she composed herself. It would be counterproductive to fly off the handle. She would deal with the situation calmly and remedy the problems as she had been asked here to do. "Supper in an hour will be fine, Phillips."

Madeline smiled kindly as Phillips instructed her as to where she would be staying, just before two identical young boys leapt from the stairs, shouting something unintelligible, and landed at her feet. "Hello," she said doing her best to stifle her surprise. "Nice of you to drop by."

She turned back to Phillips. "Now, if you could bring my bags in, I'd be most grateful."

The children were no quieter now than before, but Madeline paid them no heed, simply walked past the entire group while Phillips looked on in disbelief.

"Ma'am?" he finally inquired. "What about the children?"

Stopping no more than three steps up, she wiped the grin off her face and turned, speaking firmly and loud enough for all to hear. "They will ready themselves for supper, of course. One hour, have hands washed and don't be late. If you are, you won't get the surprise I have planned for tomorrow." Then she climbed the remaining steps and went in search of her room.

Exactly one hour later Phillips entered the dining room and nearly dropped the platter he held. Amazement stretched across his face, for there before him were seven children with freshly washed hands, sitting around the table. Quietly.

"Who is she?" Garrett asked once Phillips retreated back to the safe haven of the kitchen.

"Our new governess," Bridget volunteered.

"I wonder if she's mean?" Elizabeth speculated.

"I think she's pretty," Grace said wistfully.

"You think everyone's pretty," Garvin grumbled without looking up.

"Mean or not, nothing has changed, we don't need no nanny," Jimmy stated, his eyes determined.

"Then why did you make us wash our hands and come sit down?" Elizabeth questioned.

Jimmy shifted in his seat, not sure himself why he had suddenly told everyone to shut up and get ready to eat. But the way the woman had looked right into his eyes had made him feel something he didn't understand. Not since his mother was alive had he cared about what anyone thought. Now, sitting quietly at the table, he called himself a fool. "Because you want the surprise, don't you?"

"Oh, sure, Jimmy. What kind of a surprise do you think she's gonna give us? It was just a lie to get us washed up," Bridget said with a sneer.

"Well, maybe. But don't worry. Just because we came to eat doesn't mean we still can't show her."

"Show her what?" Madeline asked politely as she walked in.

All seven heads swung around to meet her gaze. No one spoke as she went to stand before the chair that she decided must be for her. Not one pair of eyes left her as she took those last few steps. Once at her seat, she looked around the table, not deigning to sit down.

"I believe," she started, "we have forgotten our manners."

Seven faces looked from one to another in confusion.

When nothing happened, Madeline shrugged her shoulders and pulled out her own chair. "Time enough to deal with that later. First things first. Before we begin our meal, I would like to learn your names. I am Madeline Montgomery and I have come to Fielding for a short time to help out. Now, why don't each of you tell me who you are."

Still no one spoke.

"All right, let's begin with you," she said turning to Jimmy.

Madeline didn't realize she held her breath until it came out in a whoosh when, finally, Jimmy began to speak.

"I'm James Dawson Daniels, Junior. I'm fourteen and old enough to take care of my brothers and sisters."

With a nod of her head, Madeline smiled. "I'm sure you are, Mr. Daniels, and I will rely most heavily on you to inform me of your family's particular needs."

"I'm Bridget and I'm thirteen years old and I refuse to do sums. I'm an artist."

"How wonderful. I look forward to seeing your work."

"My name is Garrett, and he's Garvin," he added, pointing to his brother. "We're twelve and we don't need no help."

Madeline tilted her head. "Twins. How lovely for you. Always having a companion. And I will try to remember that you don't need *any* help."

"I'm Elizabeth. I'm seven. And I hope you're not mean."

"I hope I'm not, too," Madeline replied, her aqua eyes sparkling with humor.

After this pronouncement, all eyes turned to an empty seat next to her.

"Where's Grace?" Garrett grumbled.

Madeline felt a tug on her sleeve. "Ah. I believe we've found her."

The child's cornflower-blue eyes lit up in a smile. "I'm Grace and I think you're pretty."

Pushing back her chair, Madeline leaned over and came face to face with the child. "I think you're pretty, too," she said quietly, touching the girls red curls.

"Are you going to be our new mama?"

Those few simple words took Madeline's breath away—how they touched her heart! She felt tears sting her eyes, and it was all she could do to keep from gathering the child in her arms. In all her life Madeline had never felt such a tug of motherly love—a tug she'd never dared to think she would ever feel. And then the motherly tug turned to protectiveness. This child with no parents, left alone to be taken care of by uncaring hired help, sent her mind careening with the things she would say to whoever was in charge of these children for letting the situation go unsolved and leaving this child to wonder if she was going to get a new mother.

"No, sweetheart, I'm not going to be your new mama, but I would like to be your special friend," Madeline said, her voice tight with emotion. But her glistening tears were banished when the little girl seemed pleased with this answer and threw her tiny arms around Madeline's neck and hugged with all her might.

"Now," Madeline said, her heart still tight in her chest as she sent Grace back to her seat and the youngest, Billy, was duly introduced. "Why don't we start our supper, and then we can decide what to do later."

And with that, Madeline and her seven new charges ventured forth on the trail of a fledgling friendship.

* * *

Wade sat quietly at his desk contemplating his plans. Jack Barnes's words came to mind. Pay some attention to the children. Show them you care.

Working late and dealing with the Patterson acreage had kept Wade at the office late most every night. He hadn't seen the children awake since the night he came back from Austin. The thought made him wince. They were Jim's kids and his responsibility until someone else could be found. The least he could do was spend some time with them.

As a result, whether driven by obligation or choice, Wade put the letter he had been working on in the drawer and his pen in its holder and left, deciding he'd join the unruly bunch for supper.

The streets were alive with activity. People were out walking and riding, most of whom waved their hellos. For a second he thought the priest had waved and he'd run a few steps after him, but when Wade turned in the saddle, the man stood quietly talking to Mrs. Milburn, the town busybody.

On more than one occasion Wade had said that he didn't know which was worse: listening to Mrs. Milburn or not listening to Mrs. Milburn. There had certainly been times when a sticky situation could have been avoided had her words been heeded, or so she said. But for the most part, Wade felt it was better to listen to her with half an ear; otherwise, trouble was constantly stirred up.

He wondered, as he thought of Mrs. Milburn talking to the priest, what she was filling the man's ears with this time. Probably his inheritance. But why let it bother him? he asked himself. Gossip never had before.

The house was surprisingly quiet when he arrived. Could the kids have gone out? he wondered. To the park, to someone else's house? Could Phillips have killed them? The jest made him smile, knowing that while his servant might want the kids out of his way, he wouldn't touch a hair on their various-sized red heads. In fact, he had begun to suspect the man of actually taking to the kids. Hadn't he defended them after running off the assorted governesses? A hardened and determined bachelor of thirty-nine years softened by a bunch of redheaded youngsters. His servant was as daft as he.

His boots echoed in the hall as he walked across the high-polished floor. No sound, no children, not even Phillips was anywhere to be heard. But he didn't have to go far before he heard one quiet voice sounding from the dining room.

Supper must be especially good, he mused, if it was keeping everyone so quiet. Perhaps Cook had laced the meal with laudanum, he chuckled to himself.

But when he stepped through the doorway, unnoticed, time seemed to stop once again when he found not the food working its wonders on his unruly relations, but none other than Miss Madeline Montgomery, weaving a spell of magic as she told her captivated audience some harebrained story.

His heartbeat quickened, the room grew warm. Oddly, it didn't strike him as strange that she was there. Yet again he thought that she could easily be mistaken for one of this feisty clan. The eyes, the hair, even the way Madeline tilted her chin, looked just like his young cousins. And just as hard to deal with, he mused, remembering the words she had flung at him, accusing him of dancing with her to get her land.

His fists clenched at the memory. He had danced with her because she had provoked him, like no other woman had ever done before. He hadn't even known she owned any land. The conniving little baggage!

"And the waves rose in the air some twenty and thirty feet high, rocking the ship to and fro," Madeline told her wide-eyed audience.

"How did you stay floating?" Grace asked somewhat desperately.

"These are grand ships that cross the Atlantic nowadays, built to withstand storms a lot worse than the one we sailed through. Ships a great deal smaller than the *Maiden* have been sailing the Atlantic for centuries."

"Did you sleep in hammocks? And were there pirates aboard?" Garrett queried, bringing hopeful smiles to all those in the room.

"No, we slept in bunks, and unfortunately I didn't see a single pirate, though come to think of it, there was an evil-looking man with a patch over his eye. His name was Sir Wellingham."

"Maybe he was traveling in neato," Elizabeth offered helpfully.

Madeline reached across and patted her hand. "Incognito, and yes, you very well could be right." She turned to Jimmy. "What do you think, James, could he have been a pirate?"

Everyone turned to the oldest for confirmation.

"Hardly. There haven't been pirates around for ages." He was silent for a moment as he glanced around the table at all the disappointed faces. "But he probably was a spy or a foreign agent."

"Foreign agent!" they squealed in delight.

Foreign agent, his ass, Wade thought. Nonetheless, he found himself caught up in the intrigue of the silly story like everyone else—or perhaps he was simply caught up in Madeline's sparkling eyes and tantalizing lips. Just as he had been from the moment he saw her across the room so many nights before.

He wondered what possibly could have brought her to Fielding. It was hard to believe that any woman, no matter how desperate, would follow him to his home for marriage. So it had to be the land, he felt sure. She had acted hastily and now she regretted it, prompting her to travel to Fielding to make amends. Well, the Patterson acreage had already been purchased, he mused with great satisfaction. She had lost her chance. He wondered for a moment why if land were truly the reason, had Ed not sent a wire? But what else could possibly have brought this woman to his home, unless she really was so brazen as to come simply to see him? Although women had boldly contrived to gain his attention for years, this was beyond belief.

"What's a foreign agent?" Garvin asked Jimmy, inter-rupting Wade's thoughts.

"Well, uh, he's an agent that's foreign," Jimmy stated, having only heard the term once and having been fascinated.

"An agent who's foreign!" Bridget cried disdainfully.

"He's right." Wade's deep, rumbling voice filled the room, causing an assortment of red heads to swing around in his direction.

"Cousin!" Grace squealed as she jumped up from her seat and ran to him.

Without thinking, Wade swung her up into his arms and walked into the room. "Phillips, tell Maria I'm ready to eat." He set Grace down in her chair and strode to his own, all the while aware of the quandary that Jimmy was in, not to men-tion the look of what, if he didn't already know better, would pass for sheer incredulity on Miss Madeline Montgomery's face.

Taking his seat, he nodded to Madeline. "Miss Montgom-ery, what an unexpected surprise," he stated with a wry smile as though nothing out of the ordinary had occurred.

She was given no opportunity to reply, not that she could with her mouth hanging open in shocked disbelief, as Wade turned his attention to the children.

"Jimmy's right, and you really have to keep an eye on those agents who are foreign. They're spies," Wade said with grave seriousness.

"Oh!" six children said in unison while Jimmy sat back in his chair, undecided if he was being mocked or saved.

"Miss Montgomery, would you say that Sir Wellingham acted suspiciously?" Wade inquired with an exaggerated sincerity.

"Well, uh, I . . ." she stammered and looked helplessly around the table. "Yes, Mr. Alexander, I believe he did."

"Really?" Garrett asked, leaning forward, looking expectantly at Madeline with a forkful of mashed potatoes halfway to his mouth. "What did he do?"

"Nothing that an unsuspecting soul would notice," Wade volunteered when Madeline appeared to falter. "Just little things like sitting back and observing people, sending coded messages, and dancing with all the pretty ladies."

"Oh, Cousin," Bridget admonished, "you're making all this up."

Wade laughed. "Well, maybe I am, but there are foreign agents out there just as Jimmy said." He turned his attention to his meal. "Roast beef and mashed potatoes. My favorite. Even the broccoli looks good."

They ate in silence for a good five minutes. Only the sound of silverware on china broke the quiet of the room.

"Miss Montgomery," Wade finally said.

Madeline held a glass of water in her hand. At the sound of Wade's voice, she set her glass down rather hard and, unfortunately, on the handle of her fork, the tines of which rested so nicely underneath a piece of broccoli. All eyes watched helplessly, and some disbelievingly, as the errant trunk of green made a short flight through the air. When the projectile vegetable landed just in front of Wade's plate with a muffled splat, the redheaded crew burst into resounding guffaws. Even Wade had to cover his mouth with his napkin to stifle his shocked amusement.

A moment passed before Wade lowered his napkin with great seriousness, reached forward, and, much to Madeline's mortification, picked up the now greatly abused vegetable. "Why, thank you, Miss Montgomery. I would indeed like some broccoli."

Well, if the children were guffawing before, they were falling out of their chairs from laughter at this. Madeline, however, ignored the laughter as she busied herself with the silverware on the table, not certain if she could possibly meet Wade Alexander's dark-eyed gaze without dying on the spot. Of all the people, she raged inwardly, how was it possible that she could end up in this man's home! Yet again she cursed herself for not waiting for more information. What a fool not to have gotten the name of the person with the orphans. She should have guessed that someone as low and vile as he would leave parentless children to fend for themselves.

"Miss Montgomery?" Wade repeated.

"What!" she demanded, giving everyone at the table a start. "I mean, yes, Mr. Alexander?"

"I was just wondering what brings you to my humble abode, aside from your wish to share your vast knowledge of table tricks?" He hesitated for a moment. "Land perhaps?" Wade gazed at her over the rim of his glass of dark red wine, the satisfied smile of a well-fed Labrador pulling at his lips.

"Land?" It was a second before the implications of that one word sunk in. He thought she was there to discuss her land. How could he not know that she was there to help him with the children? How was it that all the man could think of was that stupid piece of land? she raged inwardly.

"Have you changed your mind, perhaps?" he asked.

"Not in your life, Mr. Alexander! You will never get that land. Even if I wanted to sell it . . . even if I was desperate to sell it, I wouldn't sell it to the likes of you!"

His satisfied smile vanished in thin air, an ominous scowl falling easily into place. "You're a real piece of work! Come all this way and then let your pride get to you," Wade bit out as seven pairs of eyes swung back and forth from Wade, at the head of the table, to Madeline at the foot.

"Pride! Pride has nothing to do with it. I am here at the request of Father Hayes, to help you with—" She stopped herself just in time. Having almost finished the sentence with "this mess you've gotten yourself into," she thanked the Lord she had gotten control of her wayward tongue.

"Help me with what, Miss Montgomery?" he asked with disbelief.

"With us, Cousin. Miz Montgomery has come to take care of us." Grace said the words with great authority and knowledge.

"Just for a while," Madeline added. "Just until we can find someone qualified to take care . . ." She glanced at Jimmy and Garrett, who had already informed her of their lack of need of help. "Ah . . . find someone else." She looked at Wade, forgetting her attempts at diplomacy. "Apparently you've run everyone off with your boorish manners."

"I've run them off?" he half shouted. "*They're* the ones who keep running them off."

"Don't blame your shortcomings on these poor innocent children." Madeline's blue-green eyes blazed with anger that he would abuse her darling charges.

"My shortcomings!"

"Yes, your shortcomings! You may have treated me with all the respect deserved of a . . . a . . . toad . . . but I would think even you would be able to deal with young innocent children with a glimmer of respectability."

"Glimmer of respectability," Wade raged. "What would you know about respectability! You ride around in a disreputable old wagon with nary a chaperon in sight. Don't tell me about respectability!"

Madeline burned with embarrassment and rage, but through the haze of emotion she took notice of the children's fascinated stares. She was making a spectacle of herself, and all thanks to Wade Alexander, she blamed unkindly. "Mr. Alexander," she said stiffly. "I believe it would be best if we continued this discussion later."

"Go ahead"—Garrett smiled—"fight all you like. We don't mind. Do we?" he asked the group.

"No," they responded with great enthusiasm.

"We are not fighting," Madeline insisted.

She might as well have told the bunch she was the Queen of England for all they believed her, and when she would have gone on to further dig herself in a hole, Wade cleared his throat and put an end to the discussion. "Finish your meals and then go on and get ready for bed."

"It's still early!"

"Too bad."

"We miss all the fun," Elizabeth grumbled as she shoved the last bite of mashed potatoes in her mouth.

"Mind your manners, Elizabeth," Madeline admonished as if she'd been in the house a million years.

Later that evening, with the children safely abed, Wade and Madeline were somewhat recovered from the initial shock of their situation. They sat across from each other at the dining table. Uncomfortable and annoyed, Wade offered Madeline a brandy.

She hesitated for a moment, but then accepted. "Yes, thank you, Mr. Alexander."

Wade poured her a glass, then returned to his seat. Silence

reigned once again. And through it all, Wade was painfully aware of the woman who sat across from him—aware of the obstinate turn of her lips and the gentle curve of her neck. Aware that she was nothing like what he wanted in a woman. But regardless of his continual mental protests, he gazed across the table as she sipped delicately at her wine, and remembered the feel of her when they had danced. The soft hand that had gripped his firmly. The blue-green eyes that had looked at him so directly. The fiery red hair that escaped and curled about her face, much as it did just now.

Hurricane lamps burned on the sideboard, filling the room with a dim golden light. He pulled out a cigar and cut off the tip while he gazed at Madeline, who sat self-consciously, wringing the napkin in her lap.

"Why don't you start from the beginning and tell me why you're here?" he asked softly. He struck a match to light the cigar, never taking his eyes off her.

"Your Father Hayes sent a telegram to my Reverend Marshall in Austin asking for assistance. Reverend Marshall asked me if I'd come and help out." Madeline held her hands up and added, "And here I am. Simple as that."

Pulling at the heavy smoke, Wade looked at her doubtfully. "But surely you hadn't forgotten my name?"

"Hardly," she said with an unladylike snort. "Your name, however, was not mentioned."

"And Richard let you come?" He looked around. "Alone?"

"Actually, my uncle doesn't know I'm here."

"Oh, so that's it after all," he said impatiently. "You thought you'd sneak out here and put yourself in a compromising situation. When are you going to get it through your pretty little head that I'm not going to marry you. Not by trickery, not by bribery, not by Uncle Richard's shotgun! It would have been bad enough if you had been here because of the land, but to show up in hopes of marriage is beyond belief! You can just pack your bags and take yourself back to Austin."

Madeline clasped the arms of her chair, her eyes narrowing to slits of jade. "Marriage? You think I'm here to *marry* you?" Madeline shook with fury. "You are the most pig-headed, dim-witted, arrogant man I have ever met. I am here for the children—nothing else, you insufferable bore!"

Wade raked his hand through his hair, his eyes filled with malice. "Well, Miss Montgomery, whether you speak the truth or not is irrelevant at this point, since my problem concerns the care of the seven children I have now. I don't need another."

"Another!" she fumed, stung, her porcelain white skin suffusing in red. "I am not the one acting like a child."

"Oh, that's right. I forgot, if you were a child, you wouldn't be an old maid." As soon as the words were out of his mouth, he cursed his stupidity, not to mention his immaturity for saying such a thing. But she made him crazy! Still, that didn't make it any better. She was right. It was he who was acting like the child.

Hurt mixed with anger crossed her face, making his jaw clench. He closed his eyes for a moment. "I'm sorry, Madeline. I'm afraid I haven't been myself lately. Things have been rather . . . unsettled."

Inhaling deeply, Madeline set down her wine, picked the napkin up out of her lap, and slowly set it on the table. With as much dignity as she could manage, she pushed back her chair and stood. "I see now that not only am I not wanted here, but if I remained, I could be of no help to those children under these conditions. Therefore, I will return to Austin first thing in the morning."

And then she was gone, leaving Wade alone in the flickering candlelight, wanting nothing more than to go after her, to tell her not to leave, but knowing to do so would be his gravest error yet.

Redheaded temptresses, he reminded himself once again, were not a part of his plan.

Ten

THE HOUSE WAS quiet. Jimmy pulled his door open a crack and spied the terrain. The long hallway stood dark and unwelcoming—just what he had been waiting for. He crept from room to room, a burlap bag held securely in his hand, and rounded up his brothers and sisters.

"We fell down on the job," Jimmy said once all seven children were assembled in the large room that had become their meeting place. Not practiced in the art of diplomacy, he went right to what he saw as the point. "Everyone of you ooed and gooed all over that new governess."

"She's not a governess, she's only here to help out," Elizabeth explained.

"Whatever," he said with an impatient scowl. "The important thing is we've got to get rid of her."

"I think Cousin is going to get rid of her," Bridget stated pensively. "I don't think he likes her."

Jimmy thought about this for a moment. "You might be right but we can't take any chances. And we're gonna have to work extra hard since you all didn't go after her right away."

"Us," Bridget demanded. "You were the one who stared at her all through supper with silly ol' moon eyes."

"Moon eyes! Moon eyes!" Elizabeth and Grace chanted.

Jimmy blushed crimson.

Garrett snorted. "Made us wash our hands before eating. If it weren't for you, she'd be gone by now."

"You're the one who fell down on the job," Bridget accused with her arms crossed on her chest.

"Well, no sense in throwing blame around now," Jimmy said gruffly. "We just need to make up for lost time. I'll take care of everything, but remember, tomorrow morning, none of this asking anyone to be our new mama," he finished with a glare in Grace's direction.

Grace pulled her rag doll close. "But she's nice and I like her." The tiny tousle-haired child glanced shyly at the circle of siblings. "I want her to stay."

Jimmy noticed Elizabeth looked as if she was on the verge of agreeing, and in an effort to divert the group from a possible split in the ranks, he swiftly spoke up. "She's not staying!"

"Yeah! We don't need a keeper." Garrett was all for no governess.

"Besides," Jimmy said, sitting next to Grace and awkwardly putting his arm around her shoulders, "if we let it happen, she'll be bossing us around, telling us what to do, and we won't have a free second to ourselves for the rest of our lives."

Bridget moved closer. "And scrubbed till we're red. . . ."

"And learned till our brains fall out," Garrett added with sufficient drama.

"You don't want that, do you?" Jimmy asked.

Grace's lip protruded slightly as she was not exactly sure how she felt. "Maybe it wouldn't be so bad to have someone as nice as Miz Montgomery bossing us around."

The rest of the children, including Elizabeth, snorted their disapproval at this, leaving Grace the only deserter.

Standing, Jimmy looked over his siblings like a general would his troops. "Then we're agreed?"

Bridget, Garrett, Garvin, and Elizabeth stated the affirmative, and young Billy mimicked their positive reply. Only Grace held out.

"What's it going to be?" Jimmy demanded.

The young girl wavered, her milky-white face screwing up in indecision, until finally she gave her reluctant nod of consent.

"Good," Jimmy said as he retrieved the bag he had left at the door. Holding it up for all to see, he said, "This should take care of everything."

Unaware of the mutiny taking place under his roof, Wade stood outside his bedroom on the long terrace that wrapped around the second floor of the house. The vision of Madeline after he had called her an old maid loomed in his mind. The pain had been there, yes, but more than that, he had sensed a resigned confirmation of the words. It was as if she knew the truth of his statement and accepted it.

She was past the years when most men would marry her. And though she claimed she had no wish to marry anyway, the look in her eyes had told a different story. Her eyes had been filled with pain—a pain that he didn't know the cause of, but a pain he recognized nevertheless.

The memory of the charred remains of his childhood home reared its ugly head. The familiar grief resurfaced. Still, after all these years, the memory had the power to cut him to the core.

The darkness threatened.

Not this time, his mind raged, not when everything was finally falling into place. With that thought, the darkness receded. He laughed bitterly. Everything *had* been falling into place until the letter had arrived announcing Jim's death, delivering a blow to the foundation of his painstakingly built fortress. Then, to make matters worse, the redheaded

Madeline Montgomery stepped into his life, threatening to topple his already shaky citadel as if it were no more than a house of cards.

He had never heard of the woman in his life, not in all the time he had spent in Austin, not in all the time he had lived in central Texas. And now, out of the clear blue, she pops up at every turn like a bad dream. On top of that, a more simple-minded female he had never met, chattering incessantly about inane topics. And inept—mercy, she had run them into a barn! And this was the woman Father Hayes had suppos-edly sent to take care of the children. What had the man been thinking?

Wade took a deep breath, determined to regain control. He had worked too long and too hard to let his well-laid plans collapse around him. He owed his parents that.

To do so, he had to get the situation in hand. Madeline Montgomery would return to Austin in the morning. Soon another relative would be found to take the children. Field-ing was growing, becoming a better town. Slowly but surely he was cleaning up the houses of ill repute. He was going to bring in doctors and lawyers, ones who held degrees. His ranch was flourishing. The new herd of Anguses was prime, the longhorns were due any day. Railroads were expanding, many times onto land that he owned. And he was getting married. To Lorraine Wilcox. To the woman he had decided to make his bride.

His life was in order.

He knew he should have felt better, but the fact remained that a relative had yet to be found and he couldn't dismiss the truth that Madeline, unlike the stream of women before her, had been able to manage the children like no one else. It hadn't been a dream when he came home to a civilized table.

Realistically he knew he wasn't going to find anyone else, at least not on his own. Word was sure to get around about the impossible children. Eventually no one else would even want the job, no matter how much money was offered. But who was to say Miss Montgomery could find anyone? That thought gave him pause, but then he realized even if she couldn't, she would be here while she tried—taking care of the kids. And surely a relative would be found soon. Jack Barnes had been looking for two weeks now.

Wade massaged his neck. If he was smart, he told himself, he would find an adequate chaperon and keep Madeline there to take care of the kids until a relative was found. He could put up with her for that long even if she was a scheming spinster who would use orphans to get herself a man.

Wade shook his head and gazed out over the shadowed grounds, a cigar clamped between his teeth. It took only a few seconds more until he was decided. Miss Montgomery would remain. He would simply stay out of her way.

Confident that all had been solved, Wade put out his cigar, shut the balcony doors, and sought his bed.

Bright and early the following morning, Madeline went to the breakfast room to tell the children goodbye. Though the table was empty, the sideboard was overflowing with eggs and ham and biscuits, and Madeline was absolutely starved. Hearing no sounds from above, guessing she would have a wait, she decided to eat before leaving.

She loaded a plate. Sausage and pancakes, eggs with melted cheese, and fresh sliced bread dripping with butter. No sooner was her plate filled with food than the table filled with children. She should have known food wouldn't be sitting out on the sideboard if people weren't ready to partake. She shrugged her shoulders and glanced about the table.

Every child sat quietly in their chairs with a suspiciously knowing look stretched across their faces. Madeline eyed each one with a speculative glance. Something was afoot.

"I trust you slept well?" Madeline inquired politely.

"Oh, yes," Garrett supplied magnanimously, his shoulders pulled back, his chest pushed forward. "How did *you* sleep, Miss Montgomery?"

"Just fine, thank you." Madeline wondered how long it would be before she found out what prank they had played, and a prank she was certain of from the looks on their bright smiling faces.

It wasn't long, however, before the slashing smiles gave way to wide-eyed looks of sheer terror when the sound of Wade Alexander, their dear, unyielding cousin, bellowed from above.

"What in tarnation!"

The vibrations from his voice carried through the ceiling, down the walls, across the hardwood floors, and up through their feet, leaving the children trembling in their seats, their eyes sending accusing darts at Jimmy. Madeline sat back and watched it all, wondering what the children could conceivably have done to gain such a heated reaction from their cousin.

Only seconds passed before pounding footsteps moving in their direction rattled the chandelier overhead. Madeline knew she wouldn't have to wait long for her answer.

And sure enough she didn't. Wade stalked into the breakfast room, clothed in nothing more than thigh-encasing pants with the top button undone, and a bright green garden snake dangling from his hand.

His golden brown chest covered with dark curling hair caught not only Madeline's attention but Grace's as well. But where Madeline's voice caught strangely in her throat, Grace's did not.

"Cousin," Grace said in a voice filled with awe or maybe concern. "You're indecent!"

Indecent, true, Madeline thought, but beautiful and

breathtaking, without a doubt. He stood before them, emanating the barely held power of a raging ancient god. And every child there, with perhaps the exception of Grace, was waiting with bated breath to have that rage turned on them. Madeline quickly got hold of her wayward thoughts and took the situation in hand.

"Mr. Alexander, I really must protest," she said in a voice of utmost calm, as if he wasn't standing there taking her breath away. "The least you could do is dress yourself before coming downstairs. Really, what kind of an example could this possibly set?"

Wade threw her a sharp look before ignoring her altogether. He glanced around the table from child to child. Shaking the traumatized snake once again, he spoke with a deceptive calm, and no apparent concern for his state of undress. "Who put this in my room?"

Seven pairs of green eyes grew wide with dismay.

"If this is all you're bothered about," Madeline said, pushing out of her chair and deftly taking the snake from his hand, "then I'll take care of it while you retreat behind closed doors and make yourself presentable."

Wade looked at her with a mixture of outrage and disbelief. "I'm not going anywhere until I find out who did this."

"Good heavens, Mr. Alexander. I think you're getting carried away. Why, just the other day," she said, walking toward the French doors that led out to the garden, "I found one of these poor creatures in my house in Austin. Of course, it was a whole lot bigger than this little ol' thing," she added with a grimace once her back was to the group. If there was one thing she couldn't abide, it was snakes, even if they were harmless. "Nevertheless, they get through the tiniest of openings. I'm surprised you haven't seen any before."

Madeline put the snake on the ground and walked back

and shut the door. "Now, Mr. Alexander, I really must insist you remedy your state of undress."

Wade glanced from face to face with a scowl etched across his own. "Slithered through a tiny crack, my backside!" He ignored the wide-eyed gasps and turned on his barefooted heel and stalked from the room.

Once Wade's slamming door sounded from the upper regions, an audible sound of relief sighed through the room.

"Next time"—Madeline looked at each of them seriously—"you won't be so lucky."

Leaving well enough alone, Madeline set out to finish her meal, encouraging the children to do the same. She would tell them she was leaving once they all were through.

But Madeline never got the chance. Before she had finished her coffee, Wade bellowed once again.

"What have you done now?" she demanded of the still shaky youths.

"Miss Montgomery," he called in a voice that brooked no argument. "I would like to see you. In the study. Immediately!"

The children shrank in their seats, certain their reprieve was being forfeited.

"Hurry up and finish your meal. I'll be back in a moment."

She left the children with a light step and an air of nonchalance. But once Madeline rounded the corner, her step faltered and she had to tell herself there was nothing to worry about. Even if Wade was furious, she would be gone within the hour. This brought a mischievous smile to curl on her lips. Perhaps it had been worthwhile to see the cad so out of sorts.

Pulling back her shoulders, telling herself she had nothing to fear, she entered the study.

Finding a room of supple leathers and a great deal of books, Madeline loved it on sight. What she would give to spend even five minutes perusing the myriad tomes. But she wasn't given so much as five seconds to admire before Wade slammed the door and turned a fierce glare in her direction.

"Why is it, Miss Montgomery, that you have the aggravating habit of infuriating me?"

Well, what could she say to that?! "Why, I don't know, Mr. Alexander. But if you're looking for speculations, I might suggest that possibly it is because, at every turn, you are bellowing and carrying on in such a way that you embarrass yourself."

Her smile was all sweetness and sincerity.

With jaw clenched and hands fisted, Wade stared at this woman who so enraged him. Ideally, despite all his late-night rationalizations and planning, he would send her packing back to Austin with that rickety old wagon and walking tin of dog food she called a horse. But that, he knew, would be like cutting off his nose to spite his face. Though he had suddenly come upon some difficulty in managing his affairs, he wasn't an idiot! He knew he needed her, at least for a while.

Running his hand through thick waves of dark hair, he turned away and strode to the window. "I have decided you should stay."

Madeline wasn't sure she had heard him correctly. "You what?"

"I have decided," he said, each word stressed, "that you will stay."

"Just like that, you decide—"

"Yes, Miss Montgomery, just like that." He turned and took a step toward the door as if the matter were done.

"Mr. Alexander!" she commanded, her hands planted firmly on her slender hips. "It is *not* just like that!"

Wade slowly turned back and would have laughed at her

autocratic manner had it not angered him so. "No?" he asked, one dark brow rising menacingly in question.

"Who do you think you are to tell me what I will or will not do, without so much as one word of consultation with me about the situation? How could you think that after such deplorable behavior as I have witnessed from you, I have any desire to stay?"

He stepped toward her, slowly, ominously. "I did not ask you to come here in the first place. You came into my home and ingratiated yourself with my charges. I am merely complying with your wishes. Don't tell me that you're so fickle that you now are going to up and desert the very orphaned redheads that you so gallantly defended this morning. Which reminds me, Miss Montgomery, in the future, don't think I will ever put up with such flagrant disregard of my authority again."

Her outrage died as suddenly as it had sprung forth. Despite herself, she giggled. "Well, what did you expect me to do? It was intended for me."

The words surprised him, though as soon as she said it, he knew she was right. Their rooms were off the same balcony, and it was not impossible that the children could have gotten the rooms mixed up. He hadn't missed the look of sheer terror that had marred their milky white skin when he had towered in the doorway, the slithering green snake shaking in his hand. He looked at Madeline. "Yes, I guess it was. Did you really find one in your house?"

"Actually the gardener did, but it was outside and he brought it to the house. Wanted to show me the difference between a garden snake and a copperhead he had found the week before. You never know when these things will come in handy."

Together they laughed. The tension eased, and for one heartstopping moment, magic filled the room.

"Will you stay?" he asked softly.

She hesitated. "For now."

"Good, now I'm going over to find a proper chaperon for you. I'll not provide fuel for the gossips."

Just then someone knocked on the door.

"Excuse me, sir," Phillips said after being called into the study. "Father Hayes is here to see you."

Father Hayes and an elderly lady entered.

"Wade," the priest said, not seeing Madeline, "you know my sister, Gertrude."

Gertrude Hayes was a short plump woman with a pleasant smile and gray hair tightly curled about her round head.

"I have taken it upon myself," the priest continued, "to turn to a good friend in Austin for help in the matter of the children. I received word just yesterday that a young woman from Austin should be here at any time. Apparently she's experienced in these matters and will be of great help to you, I'm sure. Since she is not actually a governess, I felt it best to bring a chaperon. You know how the townsfolk can talk. Gertrude has volunteered."

Madeline stepped forward then and extended her hand. "Father Hayes, I'm Madeline Montgomery from Austin."

"You're already here—wonderful."

"Yes, I arrived—"

"She hasn't been here long at all, Father," Wade cut in with a meaningful look at Madeline. "We were just discussing the children."

"I can't wait to see the little darlings," Gertrude said. "We've all heard so much about them."

"Well, good. All's settled," the priest said. "Then I'll get back to the parish and let you three work things out."

Things worked out by Wade leaving for the office, Gertrude ensconcing herself in her newly appointed room and pulling out her crochet, while Madeline rounded up the kids.

"What's our surprise?" Garrett asked, expecting her to have none.

"Oh, yes, the surprise." Madeline casually put her arm around Garrett's shoulder. "We're going to pack a lunch and go to the country for a picnic. Exercise and fresh air. That's what's needed here."

And so it was that by nine o'clock Madeline and the kids had loaded the wagon with a picnic basket and eight bodies and headed for the hills. They barely fit but somehow managed, singing songs and playing games the whole way. Jimmy sat back and kept a watchful eye on the road. He was growing rapidly more concerned with Madeline's ability to control the horse and wagon as each mile passed. "Maybe I should take the reins, Miss Montgomery."

Madeline looked over at him as they were pulled sluggishly up a particularly steep hill. "Have you ever done it before?"

"Well, no. But it can't be all that hard."

"No, it isn't, but right now isn't the best time to begin when we have a load full of children. We'll give it a go later, how about that?"

"That'd be great, Miss Montgomery," Jimmy replied enthusiastically.

"Call me Madeline, everyone does."

However, "Madeline" was a bit more than Billy could manage and by the time they reached their destination, Madeline had become Maddie.

"Here we are," Maddie pronounced as Old Betty ambled to a stop.

Rolling hills, covered with trees and a swimming hole running and clear.

"Perfect, just perfect," Madeline said. "Jimmy, you get

the basket. Garrett, Garvin, you clear a spot. Girls, lay out the food."

They were like cogs in a well-run waterwheel, each one working, everyone laughing, the children forgetting their pact to run off their new keeper.

With enough food to feed an army, they ate until they were sure their stomachs would burst. Cold fried chicken, biscuits with jam, potato salad, and cake, all washed down with gallons of lemonade. After lunch it was off for a swim, though Madeline made them wade for a while until their stomachs had settled. Splashing and diving, the children swam until their skin was wrinkled. Then, eventually, with the sun hot and blazing, they emerged from the water to dry.

"This is the life," Garrett stated as he stretched out, chewing a long piece of grass between his teeth.

"Yeah, just like an adventurer," Garvin commented.

"Maybe so, maybe so," Garrett responded as he drifted off to sleep.

Madeline let them nap before rousing the youths and sending them to search the ground for pecans. Wild pecans. There were hundreds of them. And tomorrow they would make a pie.

After pecans were gathered, the group piled into the wagon and headed for home. By the time the herd drew near Fielding, all but Madeline and Jimmy were sound asleep. Looking over the quiet faces, Madeline smiled.

"Nothing like a full day of activities to tire a person out," she whispered.

Jimmy smiled. "You probably did it on purpose. Hoping to keep everyone out of trouble."

"Such a suspicious soul you are, Mr. Daniels." She smiled. "And maybe just the tiniest bit correct."

"How 'bout letting me take the reins?" Jimmy asked.

"Open roads, no one to disturb my concentration," he added with a meaningful look toward the slumbering passengers.

"I'll teach you, just as I promised, but not until the wagon is empty of all but you and me. I refuse to endanger anyone else's life unnecessarily." The wheel hit a bump, jarring its occupants as Madeline tried to regain control.

"On second thought, maybe I should try to teach myself," Jimmy said with an amused smile.

Madeline scowled before breaking into laughter, knowing he was absolutely correct. "We'll begin as soon as we arrive at your cousin's."

And so they did, just as soon as the passengers and playthings, picnic baskets and pecans, were unloaded. Jimmy held the reins, Madeline next to him, Garrett and Garvin holding Old Betty's head, while Bridget, Elizabeth, Grace, and Billy perched on the steps to observe.

Phillips came out after the first crunch wafted into the house, with the cook and the maid soon to follow. Madeline was no better at giving instructions on how to deal with Old Betty than she was at dealing with the horse herself.

"Oh, well," she said after they plowed through a section of boxed shrubs that lined the drive, "they'll grow back."

"Maybe we should quit now," Jimmy remarked as they waited for Garrett and Garvin to run over and pull Betty out of the shrubs, a branch of holly hanging from the harness. "What is Cousin Wade going to say?"

"Wade! Good Lord!" she cried, clapping her hands to her cheeks as she looked around at the plant life that had sustained heavy casualties during the lesson.

And as if the thought of the man made him appear, Wade trotted up the drive on a beautiful black thoroughbred and stopped directly in front of the wreck site. If Madeline hadn't been so concerned about explanations, she would have laughed at the look on his face. Disbelief, shock, anger, all rolled up into one hideous mask of rage.

Garrett and Garvin knew trouble when they saw it and headed off to the self-preserving distance of the front stoop. Not so far as to miss the action, but far enough away as not to get caught in the cross fire. Jimmy wasn't as smart, or perhaps he was already versed in the ways of defending damsels in distress, for he wasn't about to depart, leaving the fair Maddie to an unknown fate.

"It's my fault," Jimmy began once Wade had managed to dismount. "I insisted Maddie teach me to drive."

Wade hardly bothered to glance in the boy's direction. "Go to the house, Jimmy," he said, his eyes never leaving Madeline.

"But—"

"Don't 'but' me—get to the house. I would like a word with Miss Montgomery."

Madeline noticed Jimmy's wary stance. "Go along, Jimmy. Your cousin and I are going to have a little chat."

Reluctantly the boy jumped down and walked to the house, his hands deep in his pockets, looking back over his shoulder every now and again just in case his knightly skills were needed.

"What are you doing?" Wade demanded once Jimmy was gone. "Someone could have gotten hurt."

"No one got hurt," she responded calmly, ignoring his glance at the ruined hedge. "The boy is fourteen years old, his father has died, he takes his responsibility to his siblings seriously, and he needs to have a little fun. He wanted to learn to drive, so I taught him."

"You, a living testament to the fact that women have no business with reins in their hands, have no business teaching anyone to drive."

"It's Old Betty that's the problem, not me. I've had other

horses that gave me no trouble at all." Madeline glanced over at Wade's sleek black horse. "If you lend me yours, I'm sure I could do a much better job."

"You're crazy if you think for one minute I'd lend you my horse. And I find it hard to believe your ability, or lack thereof, has to do with anything other than your lack of competence."

"Really?" she asked, refusing to get riled. "Then why don't you teach Jimmy yourself?" Madeline stood on the floorboard and held out the reins.

He looked at the wagon wedged in the bushes, Old Betty chomping on the hedge, Jimmy on the front steps, and Madeline staring at him with an impudent smile. "Give me those reins," he demanded, glaring at Madeline.

"I'll just get out of the way." With a swish of her skirts Madeline jumped down and went to the house.

Wade motioned for Jimmy to return, and with that, the new instructor began.

It took as much time to get the horse out of the bushes as it did to finish the lesson, and it didn't take that long to extract the horse.

With a few scraps and scratches from the hedge, Wade and Jimmy climbed warily on the seat.

"I'm not sure what we've gotten ourselves into," Wade muttered as he glanced back at the house and the smiling faces that waited.

Jimmy managed a nervous chuckle himself as he took hold of the reins.

This lesson went no better than the first, and finally, in his arrogance, Wade took the reins himself to show everyone how it was done. Things went from bad to worse, because no sooner did he snap the reins than Old Betty lurched forward—only to stop two steps later. With greater resolve and a flagging ego, Wade snapped the reins again, though with no better results. The old nag, Wade cursed inwardly, was useless. Realizing this, Wade fleetingly wondered how Madeline had managed to get around as well as she did. Obviously there was some trick to it. But he had no opportunity to uncover the magic, because just then the horse decided that something on the other side of the shrubs looked enticing. Throwing Wade and Jimmy back in their seats, Old Betty took off through an, as yet, undamaged section of hedge. "Damn!" Wade bellowed loud enough for anyone within walking distance to hear.

Jimmy, who had sat quietly throughout the hair-raising ride, burst into laughter at this exclamation. "Damn is right! That was one hell of a ride."

"Jimmy!" Madeline exclaimed, having run down from the house to make sure no one was hurt.

"Oh, sorry, I didn't see you there."

"No, I'm sure you didn't," she said with a smile.

But whatever humor had been in the situation before was suddenly vanquished when Wade jumped down from the wagon, his dark countenance explosive. "This horse is dangerous," he raged unexpectedly. "Someone could get hurt. Everyone get inside—now!" Ignoring Madeline's questioning eyes, Wade pulled Old Betty out of the hedge, then went inside without a word.

Madeline watched with growing concern as the children filed into the house with a stormy Wade following. She wondered at Wade's sudden angry outburst, wondered what could cause a man to overreact so. An inner voice told her it was more than a flagging ego that caused the eruption.

Phillips walked down the steps.

"Phillips," she began hesitantly once Wade and the children had disappeared into the house. "Does Mr. Alexander always react like that?"

Phillips thought for a long moment, looking out over the

land. Finally he turned back to her. "No, not always. But the man has some demons nipping at his heels. Until he rids himself of those, I suspect he'll never change."

"What demons?"

"Well, ma'am, that's Mr. Alexander's business to tell, not mine."

Eleven

A CLOCK IN some distant room chimed the hour. Lying in the huge four-poster bed, Madeline counted the bongs—one, two, three—until they reached eleven and the wheels ground to a halt. Closing in on midnight, and she was more awake than asleep. She had studied the dips and peaks in the plastered ceiling and assessed the decor from the blue-gray velvet curtains with silver silk tie-backs, to the various watercolor paintings that hung about the walls, all in an attempt to still her whirling mind.

An unfamiliar bed and foreign sounds kept her awake, she told herself, not the thoughts that spun around in her head like a whirling dervish. The man had come so unexpectedly into her life three times now. And three times now he had threatened to prove her mad. Even in her mind he haunted her—never one to miss a chance, she added with a smile into the dark room.

She tried to push from her mind the way his eyes held hers. She tried to push from her mind the way the man's strong fingers held a glass of dark red wine. But try as she might, visions of Wade Alexander wouldn't leave her alone.

"Ugh," she groaned into the night. "Go away!"

With determination she rolled over and purposely closed her eyes. But it didn't help. Wade Alexander failed to realize she needed sleep and continued to plague her tired mind. So with a frustrated groan, Madeline got out of bed, pulled on a wrapper and went in search of some warm milk. Wasn't that the cure-all for sleeplessness? She had no idea if the drink would do any good, but one heard of it often enough that she thought she'd give it a try.

The hallway loomed dark and foreboding. She didn't dare light a candle for fear of disturbing another's slumber, a specific someone's, she might have added.

With only the moonlight to guide her, she traversed the long corridor and made her way down the carpeted steps. Once in the kitchen Madeline explored the area to find what she needed: milk, glass, pan, and stove. She had only seen the kitchen staff once, and just then she wished to see them again. But that wasn't going to happen. Therefore, after standing for several minutes with a pan of milk in her hand in front of the massive stove and having no idea how to make it perform, she opted for cold milk and hoped for the best.

It was as she sat in the cavernous room, surrounded by huge ovens, stoves, and cold boxes, sipping on the cool milk, that she heard a very familiar stamp and sputter. After a second of careful listening and serious contemplation, she was certain she heard Old Betty. She could hardly imagine what was going on, could only think that perhaps someone was trying to abscond with her dear old horse. So with a start, forgetting her state of undress, she hurried to the door and peeked through the ruffled curtain.

There, in the silver moonlight, was not the thief she expected but the very man who had plagued her mind all night, sitting in her wagon, cursing her fickle horse.

"Men," she muttered for the fourth time since she had been watching. Wade was attempting to coerce Old Betty, with a few choice expletives, to move forward.

"Damn you old nag," she heard him curse.

Without thinking, she opened the door and stepped out onto the porch.

The sound of the closing door caught Wade's attention, causing him to bolt upright with a guilty scowl. He would have cringed with something close to embarrassment had he not been so taken back by the sight that met his eyes. And the sight that met him sent all rational thoughts fleeing from his mind.

Her hair was down, tumbling over slender shoulders like a fiery waterfall, aqua eyes glowing with mischief, neck graceful and white, breasts swelling from underneath the thin material. She looked just like an angel, though he knew firsthand she could be the very devil given the slightest provocation. But angel or devil, she was lovelier than he could imagine, and he wanted nothing more than to taste the sweetness of her lips.

Forgetting the horse, he jumped down from the wagon and approached. Madeline stood next to a huge carved pillar that matched her white gown. She turned slightly and her hair caught the breeze that rustled through the yard, tossing the tresses playfully about her face.

"What brings you out this night?" Wade asked from the bottom step, his voice low and rumbling.

She turned back to him, her hair gently waving in the breeze. "I thought we had a thief on the grounds come to purloin my sweet horse."

Wade smiled. "Sweet, I doubt, and only an idiot would steal that thing." He placed one foot on the next step and leaned forward, his forearms resting on one hard-curved thigh. "You'd have to pay someone to take it off your hands."

"If you weren't stealing her, then what were you doing?" she asked, a smile dancing on her lips.

He glanced casually from Madeline to Old Betty, then back to the beauty on the porch. "Testing her out in case Jimmy ever uses her again."

Madeline's eyes glittered with mischief, her head tilting to the side. "How very thoughtful of you, Mr. Alexander. But I thought you said everyone was to stay away from the horse. She's 'dangerous,' I think you said."

"Well, I'm not convinced the old horse isn't. But Jimmy needs to learn how to drive a horse and wagon."

"Why not use one of yours?"

"I just might, but if the kids are going to be riding around with you, I felt it only my duty to look into this horse problem. You can never be too safe."

"No, I don't suppose you can. If you'd like, tomorrow I'll show you the trick to Old Betty." She looked out into the garden. "Though the trick didn't work too well for Jimmy earlier. Hmmm."

"A trick," he grumbled accusingly. He stepped back from the step and shook his head. "I knew there had to be a trick."

"Surely it couldn't be your ability, or lack thereof," she teased, remembering his similar accusation.

"Never. And I'm not going to wait until tomorrow. Show me now."

"Now? I can't." She looked down at herself. "I'm not properly . . . I . . . I don't have on any shoes," she finished lamely. As if to prove her point, tiny white toes peeked out from underneath her long gown.

Wade chuckled into the sky, and then in one swift movement he was up the steps and whisked her into his arms, before carrying her across the dirt and gravel to hand her up onto the hard seat of the wagon. "Show me this trick," he demanded, the usually hard lines of his countenance melting with a smile.

For the moment her scantily, not to mention, improperly, clad body was forgotten as they settled on the seat.

"Well, you have to sing to her and ask her nicely, just as I showed you the night of the party."

"You're crazy if you think for one minute I'm going to sing to this old horse!"

"Then you're never going to get her to go anywhere. It's sing or nothing."

Wade started to throw down the reins, but after one superior smirk from Madeline, he snatched them tight. He glared at her for one long second, then cleared his throat. Hesitantly, hoarsely, Wade sang a few bars of some old ditty he'd heard in his wilder days. Madeline's eyes opened wide and Old Betty's ears flattened on her mane; not a good sign, Wade mused as he racked his brain for another tune.

After a few gravelly starts, Wade found himself singing a song his grandfather used to sing, and amazingly enough, Old Betty began to jerk her passengers around the graveled drive.

"There," Wade pronounced proudly. "What do you think?"

"I think you've broken my neck."

Wade laughed. "It serves you right after the hair-raising ride you treated me to in Austin."

"Hair-raising? Don't tell me you're so thin-skinned that a few bumps and ruts gave you a scare?"

"I was thinking more of the decimated barn," he said with a meaningful raised eyebrow. "Speaking of the barn, whatever happened?"

Madeline giggled. "I had the man send Uncle Richard the bill. He should be getting it any day now."

Shaking his head, Wade said, "One of these days you're going to meet your match, and he's not going to put up with such silly mischief."

Silence filled the air, neither knowing exactly how to respond to the words, both knowing all too well who that someone was. Wade Alexander.

Finally Madeline broke the uncomfortable silence. "Why don't you try it again?" she said, gesturing to the horse.

With remarkable ease and a great deal more finesse than Madeline had after the months she had been dealing with the horse, Wade guided Old Betty around the house several times. Madeline wasn't sure which Wade was enjoying more—the mastery of the reins or the singing.

Eventually, looking all too pleased with himself, Wade pulled to a stop. Silence surrounded them, the only sound coming from the occasional bark of a distant dog.

"I meant to tell you that you were wonderful with Jimmy last night at supper," Madeline said.

Wade grunted, his pleasure fading as he looked off into the distance. "Was I? If that's true, then it was the first time I've done something right since the kids arrived." Wade looked down at the reins in his hands and his forehead creased with deep furrows. "I've done nothing but rant and rave at those poor kids since I came home the first night they arrived and found them practically swinging from the chandeliers."

Madeline couldn't help the snort of laughter that billowed into the night. "Why don't I find that hard to believe?"

"Because you've seen firsthand what hellions those kids can be."

"And you were an angel at their age?" she asked with her own raised eyebrow. "My guess is you were probably worse. You've certainly caused me enough trouble."

This time it was Wade's turn to snort his laughter. "Maybe not an angel." He leaned back against the seat. "I remember the time Jim, the kids' father, and I rigged a pail of water up over the door. It was meant for our cousin Harold, who drove us crazy."

"Don't tell me. Harold didn't walk through the door."

Wade looked over at Madeline with the sheepish grin of a

troublesome youth. "As a matter of fact he didn't." His grin turned to a grimace as he remembered. "Mrs. Bladewell, the Baptist preacher's wife, walked through that door with a brand-new hat. Jesus, my folks were mad." He hesitated for a moment. "Thank God we're Catholic."

Madeline laughed heartily. "What happened to you and Jim?"

"Jim hotfooted it home, and I was left with a sore back-side and three cords' worth of wood to chop." Wade circled the reins with his thumbs. His mood grew quiet. "My parents never let me get away with anything," he hesitated, "but I always knew I was loved. Why can't I manage that balance?"

Madeline turned on the bench to face Wade, her eyes suddenly fierce. "Your parents had fourteen years of practice before you dumped a pail of water on the unfortunate Mrs. Bladewell's head. Fourteen years, Wade, not two weeks. They started with one child at birth and gradually worked their way from two-year-old tantrums into adolescent pranks. You started with seven children from two to fourteen without knowing the first thing about being a parent. You care, Wade, and you're trying to do the best that you can. That's all anyone can ask for." She looked deep into his eyes. "You're going to make a wonderful father, yet." She pursed her lips, and her voice grew tight with emotion. "After a few rough starts and the inevitable bumps along the way, just as you mastered Old Betty and the wagon, you will master the art of raising children."

"If I could be half as effective as my parents, I'd be happy," he said softly.

She turned away and looked out beyond the house. "Tell me about your parents."

Madeline felt the change immediately, and when she

turned back to him, even in the silvery darkness, she could see his eyes harden. Tension crackled in the air.

"My parents died in a fire while I was away in Austin. There's not much more to say," he replied, his voice suddenly cold and harsh.

"Of course there's more to say!"

"No, there is not."

His words were spoken so ruthlessly, and with such bitterness, Madeline could only manage an "I'm sorry" before she let the subject drop.

Sitting silently alone together in the wagon, surrounded by the dark, she became all too aware of her attire, as well as the man who sat so close on the seat next to her. His profile was so perfect, so handsome, and now so ravaged with pain. She longed to reach out and smooth the creases of anguish away.

He turned then, as if sensing her thoughts, and touched her cheek much as he had done the night they had run down the barn. He looked deep into her eyes, captivating her with his very intensity. Slowly, having no will to resist, she touched his hand. His fingers, under hers, lingered. Madeline swallowed, and the pulse beating wildly in her throat made it hard to breathe. Slowly he reached out with his other hand and touched her rapid pulse. His fingers trailed back to her molten waves of hair. Carefully, almost reverently, Wade pulled her to him, to claim her lips.

"Madeline," he groaned.

He kissed her, slowly, as if not wanting to scare her, until her eyelids fluttered closed. His tongue caressed her lips, gently parting them to taste the sweetness within.

At the foreign touch Madeline tensed.

"Don't," he whispered hoarsely, pulling her close.

Succumbing to the agony she heard in his voice, she forgot all reason and molded her body to his. Hesitantly she flicked his tongue with her own, relishing the feel, reveling in the new and wondrous emotions that flooded her body.

A soft, barely audible moan sounded from her as his strong hands gently caressed her back, moving slowly downward. His tongue became more insistent, pulsating with a rhythm as old as time.

Gradually, breathless, they pulled back as reason set in. They gazed into each other's eyes, each a bit startled, uncomfortably aware that what had just happened should never have taken place.

"Maybe you should go back inside," he said, his voice gruff as he pulled his hands from the waves of her hair.

Madeline died a thousand deaths as Wade moved away from her on the wooden seat. Mortified by her wanton behavior, Madeline pushed back her hair, avoiding his eyes, and started to get down.

She hesitated on the threshold and looked about uncertainly. Glancing from her bare feet to the gravel drive, she shrugged her shoulders with a sigh, then carefully lowered herself from the wagon.

"Ouch," she yelped only a few steps away.

"Damn." In an instant Wade was off the seat, around the wagon, and whisking her into his arms to take her the last few yards back to the house. "You should have reminded me. What kind of a beast do you think I am?" His words hinted at more than the simple question implied.

His steps slowed as he neared the porch, the sweet scent of jasmine filling his mind. He let her down, her body slowly sliding against his hard form, and when her feet touched the wooden planks, he held her tight, reluctant to let her go.

He looked at her, as he had so many times before, as if his dark eyes could penetrate to some truth. He brought his hand slowly up her back and shoulder to trace the line of her jaw. "For some reason that I don't understand, I am drawn to you." His voice was a faint whisper in the night. "And for all that I try to push you from my mind, you plague me at every turn. Why is that, Madeline?" he demanded, his eyes searching, his voice hoarse with emotion. His arm held her close like a band of iron, capturing her to him. "You are not a part of my plan."

He took a long sighing breath before lowering his head to hers as though he had no will to resist and captured her lips with his own. His hands traveled up her arms, trailing a fiery path to her neck, until they came to rest on either side of her face. He tilted her head to accommodate him better and deepened his kiss. Her body leaned into his, and he lowered his hand to draw their bodies together. "Why do you do this to me, sweet Madeline?" he demanded in a harsh whisper, his lips brushing hers.

He watched helplessly as she looked up at him, her eyes glazed with passion and yearning. She reached up to touch his lips. "I'm not a villain, Wade."

He smiled then, though a slow lazy smile laced with anger. "No, not a villain—you're more of a surprise." His dark eyes held her captive much as his arms had earlier. "And my life has no room for surprises." He let her go then and stepped back.

She bit her lower lip as if in indecision, and for a moment Wade thought she would take the small step that separated them and return to his arms. His heart pounded while he waited, wanting her to take the step, even knowing if she did, he couldn't turn back, that he would sweep her up and take her to his bed. But the moment passed, and she took a deep breath and said, "Good night, Mr. Alexander," before she slipped back inside.

"Good night, Miss Montgomery," he responded to the closing door.

Leaning back against the carved pillar, he pulled a cheroot

from his pocket. With a minimum of ceremony, Wade lit the cigar and pulled slowly at the smoke. He couldn't think clearly as disappointment filled him. His body still pulsed with feeling, and the memory of her softness filled his mind.

He tried to remember Lorraine, her lush curves and pale blue eyes. He wanted to forget Madeline Montgomery. But the fiery temptress's image wouldn't cooperate, and it was Lorraine who was hopelessly banished into the night.

Twelve

THE DAYS THAT followed found Wade spending a great deal more time at home. And during that time, much to his surprise, he began to enjoy the children. He ignored the fact that he enjoyed Madeline Montgomery's company as well, and that if it hadn't been for her, they might well have gone crazy by now. Instead, he pushed from his mind any ambivalent thoughts and simply enjoyed the passing time.

One day he found the boys playing with an old set of marbles he'd had as a child. There were only a few left and even fewer that weren't chipped or scratched. The next day Wade rode into town to buy the boys some marbles. The general store didn't have many, but he bought what they had, and while he was there he picked out something for each of the rest of his newfound family as well.

At midday he entered the dining room, his arms laden with gifts, surprised to find it empty. "Where is everyone?" he asked Phillips once he found the man in the kitchen enjoying a cup of coffee with the cook.

Phillips jumped up at the sight of him, spilling coffee as he did.

"You clumsy old fool," Wade said with a smile, belying his harsh words. "Sit back down and quit making a mess. Just point me in the direction of the hellions."

After setting the presents down, Wade found the missing parties in the stable, a small one for horses he used regularly.

Walking through the open door, he was stopped short by the sight of Madeline sitting on a pile of hay, her legs pulled up Indian style under the voluminous folds of her skirt, and seven redheaded youngsters circled around, listening with rapture to, no doubt, one of the woman's mind-boggling tales of adventure.

"Another story?" he asked, bringing welcoming squeals of delight at his arrival, only Jimmy gracing him with the all-too-familiar scowl that Wade was rapidly coming to expect.

Wade mentally flinched when Madeline turned toward him with the wary look that had plagued her eyes every time she had seen him since the night on the porch. He cursed his errant mouth for saying the things he had. What had he been thinking, he wondered, when he had held her intimately one moment, then told her she was an unwelcome surprise in the next? But what was done was done, and Wade refused to think about the reasons behind such a scene for very long. It was just too damn confusing.

Grace and Elizabeth ran to his side, grabbed his hand, and pulled him to the hay. He only half listened to the children as they, all at once, filled him in on the story, wondered if they might ride the horses, and asked where he had been all morning. He looked over their heads and his eyes met Madeline's. Their eyes held for a moment before Madeline looked away and Elizabeth finally demanded his full attention.

"Cousin," she demanded with a long drawn-out, exasperated version of the title. "You weren't listening."

"Sure I was. The story is about a little girl and her garden; yes, one of these days we'll get each one of you a horse," he added, not thinking about the fact that he intended to send the children away, "and I've been into town buying you hellions presents."

"Presents!" The word brought on a deafening cheer and managed to clear the barn out in record time. Only Jimmy got up slowly and followed his excited siblings into the house.

Wade looked back at Madeline, and she cringed each time the screen door slammed in the distance. "So much for my story," Madeline said quietly.

"Maybe you'll finish it later. Perhaps you'll tell it to all of us."

Madeline could feel the warmth in her cheeks. Her heart beat waywardly in her chest, and she wanted nothing more than to reach out and touch the gentle smile that played across his lips, to lose herself in the deep pools of his dark eyes. How wonderful this man was when he wasn't so busy being contrary and enraged.

"Come on," Wade said, reaching out and taking her hand. He pulled her up from the hay and led her toward the house. "We'd best give out those gifts or they might slay each other in the process."

"Where are the presents?" Garrett asked impatiently once Wade and Madeline walked through the door.

"Over there."

The kids found the gifts. Marbles for the boys, dolls for the girls, everyone excited, even Jimmy reluctantly fingering a beautiful multicolored cat's-eye.

"Golly, Cousin," Grace said with great distress. "What did you get Maddie?"

"Maddie?" Wade looked over at the woman in question. He stood there for a bit, clearly bothered by the missing present, until in a flash of inspiration he said, "It's outside. I'll show you."

The whole group crowded out of the house, the wave of bodies carrying Madeline in its midst. They followed as Wade strode with large excited steps toward the barn. And once they arrived, they found Wade pulling out a sleek black mare with black mane and tail.

"A horse for you to use to get around Fielding. Old Betty could use the rest."

"That horse is too beautiful to pull my old wagon," she gasped with pleasure, her hands coming to her cheeks.

Wade laughed. "She's not supposed to pull anything. You'll have her saddled and you can ride."

Her smile disappeared amongst the joyful screeches and cheers from the children. Madeline took a step back. Her hand came to her chest, and her brow furrowed with concern. She looked from the horse to Wade and in a strangely strangled voice said, "Thank you, but no. Old Betty will be fine." She took another step back, darkness threatening her mind, before she turned in a flurry of skirts and ran into the house, the children unaware of her upset.

Wade stared after her and then, without waiting to think better of it, followed her. He took the stairs two at a time and came to her bedroom door just as she slammed it shut. Without knocking, he entered. She stood at the window, only her profile revealed to his searching eyes.

"Would you have preferred a bay stallion?" he asked quietly into the still room.

She didn't turn, appeared not to have heard. But then she closed her eyes, and Wade wanted to take her in his arms and make everything all right. But the impulse that brought him racing up the stairs failed to take him farther.

"I'm sorry," she said. Only that, so simple, as if that were enough.

Wade stepped closer, not understanding the need to persist, knowing that the best thing he could do was turn around and leave her alone. "Sorry for what?" he persevered, unwilling to let the matter go.

Madeline took a deep breath. "For having made a cake of myself over the horse. It was more than kind of you to think of me."

He dismissed her words with a wave, intent not on apologies but, for some reason, on what had caused her reaction. "You didn't make a cake of yourself, Madeline, but I could tell something was wrong. You can't simply clam up and refuse to talk." He stepped closer. "Something happened to you on a horse, didn't it?"

He waited for an answer, but none came. He took another step closer. "You can't let your fears guide you. You have to pick yourself up, dust yourself off, and get back on that horse, get on with your life."

The room grew taut with tension. He could almost feel the muscles in her body tense at his words. But nothing prepared him for the fiery virago that turned on him.

"Who do you think you are to tell me to get on with my life—as if I haven't. Who are you to tell me I must talk about certain events when you clam up and leave at the mere mention of things you don't want to discuss."

His dark eyes grew unfathomable. "Things such as?" he asked, the mercurial change leaving his voice suddenly cold and unrelenting.

Her eyes flashed angrily but with triumph, too. "See, just as I said. You come in here like some paragon of understanding until the tables are turned. Then you turn cold and unreachable, intimidating. And you know damn well what I'm talking about. Your parents and some blasted fire." Madeline cringed, mortified that she could be so callous and insensitive.

His body tensed, his jaw cemented with barely controlled fury.

Madeline stepped back, but the wall blocked her escape. Wade took another step closer. He grabbed her arm, forcing her to look at him. "Yes, my parents and some blasted fire! A ravaging house fire my parents died in while I was in Austin.

And do you want to know what I was doing in Austin? Do you want me to talk about that too, Madeline?"

He held her arm in a grip of steel, his dark eyes wild with wrath. She tried to pull away, but he held her tight.

"I was lying in the bed of some willing female. I don't remember her name, there were so many back then."

Madeline's face grew warm.

"Yes, sweet Madeline, blush all you like, but you wanted to know, so you will hear." Sweat beaded on his forehead, his rage consumed him. "Yes, there were a great many women during those days, and no doubt while my parents were perishing in scorching flames, I laid about, the warm tantalizing flesh of some willing woman filling my hands."

Madeline sucked in her breath and tried to pull away.

"Deplorable, isn't it, my sweet? The truth can be unbearable, as I have learned firsthand."

His rage turned suddenly to a ragged pain. "I was always gone, causing my parents a great deal of heartache that their only child was constantly off satiating wild ways. But my parents always welcomed me home," he said with a sneer, "no doubt hoping I was home to stay. But sure enough I always disappointed them, leaving again, my mother kissing me farewell, that hurt look always in her eyes." He let go of her arm with a jerk and turned to the window, running his hand through his hair. "I'll never forget that look as long as I live. They loved me no matter what. And I wasn't around when they needed me. I could have saved them," he said with clenched fists before turning back to Madeline. "I would have saved them!"

"Wade," Madeline began, her voice a whisper. She reached out to him, but he pulled away and strode from the room, leaving Madeline alone with a glimmer of understanding of the horrible demons that indeed nipped at his heels.

* * *

At one o'clock the following afternoon Madeline and the children commandeered the kitchen. Time had slipped by, and still the promised pecan pie had not been made. But today was the day.

Phillips felt obligated to keep a watchful eye turned toward the group, but Maria and the cook were only too glad to have an excuse to make their escape.

"Let us see now," Madeline said with one finger on her cheek as she studied the kitchen. "If you were ingredients for baking, where would you be?" In her quest for warm milk she hadn't happened upon baking goods, so it took Phillips to point her toward the pantry before Madeline found her way.

Once in the cool, darkened recesses of the large pantry, Madeline found a crate of apples, ripe apples that would soon go bad. "What are the apples for, Phillips?" she called out the door.

"I'm not exactly sure, but Miss Hayes brought them with her, saying perhaps we could make good use of them."

After one mishap- and prank-filled breakfast, Miss Hayes hadn't left the confines of her well-appointed room for so much as a breath of fresh air. She even took her meals on a tray. Given that, Madeline didn't think the apples were in any danger of being used.

"The pecans will save," Madeline told her cooking crew. "And the apples won't. So apple pie it is."

After finding the apples, Madeline found the cabinet filled with every possible baking need.

Surveying the pile of newfound acquisitions along with her seven workers, Madeline decided they needed a plan. "All right. Everyone gets a job. Jimmy, get the knives, and then, you, Bridget, and I will peel the apples. Garrett,

Garvin, you two are in charge of picking out the best pieces of fruit."

"What about me?" Grace demanded, her bottom lip protruding.

"And me?" Elizabeth added.

Madeline thought for a moment. "Yes, what about you two? Hmmm. I know. You can stir the whole mess when we get it thrown together in the big pot." She turned to young Billy. "And you, sir," she said as she bent down to where he sat on the floor, "can supervise us all." Tapping him on the nose, Madeline stood. "All right everyone, let's get to it."

They worked with amazing skill and very little mishap. Apple skins were peeled in long spirals, and Madeline was pleased when not a single drop of blood was shed. After a good thirty minutes, with piles of peeled and sliced apples in front of them, they were ready to make their pies.

"Oh, heavens!" Madeline exclaimed. "We forgot the pie crust." Frantically she looked around, shaking her head in dismay.

"Let's make it now," Bridget said.

"I guess we'll have to but it's best to make it first so your apples don't have a chance to turn brown."

Jimmy gave her a disbelieving look. "Who cares if they turn brown? They're going to get all soft and mushy anyway once you cook them."

"Well, I suppose you're right."

"Uh-ummm."

The group turned to find Phillips standing in the doorway of the pantry.

"I took the liberty of preparing these," Phillips said with two pie crusts held in his hands."

"Oh, Phillips, you wonderful man!" Madeline whisked the crusts over to the counter and duly filled them with the ingredients that had already been so carefully prepared.

After that an apron was tied around Phillips's waist, and he was put to work.

Pies and tarts, jellies and butters filled the kitchen when the proud group finally finished.

"Now to clean up," Madeline announced as she wiped some sugar from her hands.

The bakers looked around them with a groan. The place was covered with dirty pots and pans. A light dusting of flour covered everything and everyone in sight. Madeline eyed the flour-coated youths.

"Jimmy and Bridget. Take your brothers and sisters upstairs and get them cleaned up. I'll tackle this mess," Madeline said as she surveyed the damage.

It was a second before she realized the children were still there. "Come on, get going." But when she turned, she stopped abruptly.

Wade stood in the door.

"Oh, hello," Madeline said quickly as she ran a flour-covered hand over her cheeks and hair, leaving powdered streaks in its wake. She hadn't seen him since their encounter in her room, and just then she had no idea what to say. "Is it time for supper already?" she managed lamely.

"No," he said as he leaned against the doorframe as if the night before had never occurred. "I'm early."

"And I'm a mess," she said.

"You look good enough to eat."

Madeline stared with widened eyes, her mind racing with how she could possibly respond to such a statement. Laughter saved her, however, as the children broke down in huge guffaws, obviously finding his statement the funniest thing they had ever heard.

"Apron and all?" Garret crowed.

"How about the shoes?" Elizabeth offered.

"Tasty," Bridget agreed while Jimmy looked on with a reluctant smile.

Not knowing what else to do, Madeline chased after them, catching Garvin and tickling him. And then they all jumped in, the kitchen erupting with hoots and hollers. Flour flew and Bridget chased Garrett around the butcher's block. Grace, pursued by Billy, sought refuge with Wade, flinging herself into his dark blue-shirted arms in a puff of white flour.

Everything came to a deadly halt when Grace stepped back from Wade, leaving a small child imprint upon him. They waited for him to erupt. But all were surprised when after a moment's hesitation, Wade burst forward and pretended to stalk both Grace and Billy.

"I'm going to get you, and when I do I'm going to tickle you till you cry uncle."

"Uncle!" Grace squealed well out of Wade's reach.

"Unca," Billy yelped in imitation though not nearly as fast.

And then the entire group ran about the kitchen, even Jimmy coaxed into the fun. The children turned on Wade, crushing him amongst them, Madeline sandwiched inside, as well.

Face to face, Madeline and Wade stood entangled in the swarm of children. Their warm breaths mingled. They stood so close that scant inches separated their lips, so easy to lean forward, to feel the intensity that had suffused them before.

"I'm sorry about last night," Wade said softly.

"No, I'm sorry."

"Perhaps we should clean the slate."

"Perhaps," she said, her eyes finding his lips.

Forgetting the children, Madeline's eyes fluttered closed.

"Kiss 'er! Kiss 'er!" Elizabeth and Grace shouted with glee.

"Oooo, yuck!" Garrett and Garvin cringed.

Madeline's eyes snapped opened, embarrassment, or perhaps mortification, turning her cheeks pink, only to find not the seven little children and the strong, formidable Wade, but an unfamiliar woman standing in the doorway.

"My, my, my. What do we have here?" Lorraine stood at the kitchen door, slapping a small fan against the palm of her hand.

"This must be the new governess. How quaint." Lorraine turned her icy gaze on Wade. "Something in her eye? Being the gentleman, I suppose? Or perhaps you were simply trying to help her clean up and wipe that mess off her face?"

The pink turned to red, singeing Madeline's cheeks. "Excuse me, I must look dreadful," Madeline said, mortified at having been caught in such a disgraceful position.

Wade stepped away from Madeline. "Miss Montgomery, may I introduce Miss Wilcox."

"It's a pleasure to meet you, Miss Wilcox," Madeline managed to say, finding it absurd that in the middle of this bedlam Wade could so easily turn to niceties.

"Lorraine will be joining us for supper, Phillips. Have Maria set another place." Wade turned to the children. "Get upstairs and clean up."

The children filed out of the kitchen, glancing back uncertainly from Lorraine to Madeline.

Flour settled, slowly drifting to the ground, taking with it the gaiety and spontaneity that had flown in the air.

Lorraine looked around, her blue eyes snapping with some emotion, her gloved hand waving away the remnants of flour from her yellow and white lace dress. She took a step forward. Her tiny yellow slippered feet sent puffs of flour flying in the air.

"So," she began, her head cocking as if trying to understand the situation before her. "A little afternoon flour fight, is it? A regular activity around the Alexander household these days?"

Wade stepped farther away from Madeline. Madeline unconsciously smoothed her hair.

"Well," Wade began, more confused by what had happened yet again between him and Madeline than concerned about what Lorraine had said. "When's supper?" he asked, choosing to ignore Lorraine's barbed words altogether. He glanced about the kitchen and remembered the huge mess, none of which was caused by a cooking meal.

Madeline followed his gaze, the sight prompting her into action. "Mercy! Look at the mess. I'll have it cleaned up in an instant. Then Maria and Cook can start supper."

Magically Maria and the cook appeared, along with Phillips, who began to roll up his sleeves.

"Yes, in no time. We'll have this mess cleaned up in no time," Phillips offered as he began picking up pots and pans.

Madeline sent him a grateful smile and jumped in alongside him, trying desperately to still her wildly beating heart.

Thirteen

LORRAINE FOLLOWED WADE into a large, rarely used, drawing room. She pretended to admire a painting on the wall, trying to gain a bit of time to sort through her churning thoughts.

She had happened by Wade's office earlier that day and had actually asked Wade if she might join him for supper this evening. She wanted to spend some time with him since he had been so preoccupied lately—preoccupied since he had returned from Austin.

She thought she remembered him mentioning something about a land deal falling through but couldn't recall the details. Thinking business problems must be plaguing his mind, Lorraine thought it wise to join him at his home in hopes of getting some attention. Now, however, after interrupting such a cozy domestic scene between Wade and the new governess, or rather the woman who was supposedly there to help find a new governess, Lorraine wasn't sure what to think. Lorraine didn't like what she had seen, not one bit.

"Can I get you a glass of wine, Lorraine?"

Wade's deep voice rumbled close behind her, but not close enough, Lorraine thought. In the past, she realized, he would have come up to her, wrapped his arms around her shoulders, and pressed a kiss into her neck. She almost leaned back at the memory.

"Lorraine?"

"Oh, sorry. Lost in my thoughts. Yes, I'd love some wine." She turned to him and smiled. "I'd also like you."

His hand hesitated as he poured the wine, but he did not respond. Handing her the glass, he finally said, "I've some matters to attend to before supper. Make yourself at home."

Make yourself at home, she mimicked to herself as Wade turned and departed. Left alone and on her own devices, Lorraine paced the confines of the impeccably appointed room. Intricately designed and woven Oriental rugs covered most of the high-polished hardwood floor. Crown molding and picture windows added to the beauty, but most of all, it was the Louis XIV escritoire overlooking the sprawling green lawn that always filled Lorraine with longing. From this desk she planned to spend a good deal of time writing letters, answering invitations, and commanding the great house that was soon to be hers. Or at least that had been the plan until she had walked in and witnessed the unnerving scene in the kitchen. Could the temporary governess be threatening her future? Lorraine asked herself, her smooth brow creasing with worry.

Lorraine paced a few more steps. The woman's red hair and pale skin came to mind. Somewhat *freckled* skin, she thought unkindly. And her height. Good God, she was an Amazon. Relief slowly began to trickle in. The woman had none of the qualities that Lorraine knew Wade was partial to, the classical features that she, Lorraine, possessed in abundance. She smoothed her hair in the mirror, took a deep breath, and smiled. No need to worry, she told herself, Wade Alexander was hers.

But as the minutes ticked by, and an hour passed with no sign or sound from other regions, Lorraine's assurance turned into concern. By the time Wade returned, Lorraine was beside herself with worry that showed itself in anger.

"A little bit of work to attend to? The governess perhaps?" she asked when Wade walked through the door, her voice seething.

Wade looked at her for one long hard moment. "Jealousy doesn't become you, Lorraine."

Only that, nothing more, no explanations or apology, just a caustic remark to make her the miscreant, and Lorraine became all the more enraged. When he held out his arm to escort her to supper, it was all she could do to retain some semblance of calm, knowing to do anything else would be a mistake.

The dining table was almost entirely surrounded by well-scrubbed faces when Lorraine entered on Wade's arm. No one spoke as Wade helped her into the chair at the foot of the table. Wade had just pulled out his own chair when Madeline skidded to a halt at the doorway. She had been heading straight for the same spot Lorraine now occupied.

Red slowly colored Madeline's cheeks. "Oh, excuse me," she stammered when everyone turned to look at her. With a quick smile, Madeline tried making a hasty escape.

But Wade stopped and quickly assessed the situation, then pulled out the only available chair.

"How nice," Lorraine remarked with a tight grimace, her pale blue eyes snapping with displeasure.

Phillips entered with a tureen of thick stew.

"Stew!" Grace said, her face all scrunched up like a prune.

"Grace Daniels, mind your manners," Madeline responded immediately.

"Well, it's yucky," Grace persisted, all the while Lorraine looking on with irritation.

"If it's not to your liking, then you can go upstairs and wait for tomorrow's meal and see if you like that one better." Madeline took a good-size helping for herself. "Phillips, this looks wonderful. Send my compliments to Cook."

"Yes, ma'am."

Grace sulked but remained seated.

Madeline concentrated on her food.

The only sounds were the clinking of silver on china and an occasional heavy sigh from Grace.

"All that flour was sure hard to wash off," Elizabeth said sometime later. "Stuck all over. Covered my arms and clothes, and I found big globs in my hair. It was like glue."

"Is that what all that bellyachin' was about?" Garrett stated between bites. "Could've sworn you were being kilt."

"Don't swear, Garrett," Madeline reprimanded. "And it is killed."

"That's what I said."

"You said 'kilt,' " Wade corrected.

"Oh," Garrett said with his head tilted in thought. "Killed, kilt. What's the difference?"

"Correct and incorrect grammar." Madeline turned to Wade. "I think it's time to start looking into a school for the children. What type of school do you have here in Fielding?"

"Aren't you from Fielding, Miss Montgomery?" Lorraine asked from down the table.

"No, Miss Wilcox. I'm from Austin."

"Austin?" Lorraine glanced from Madeline to Wade. "Were you a governess in Austin? Is that how you found out about this position? Or was it from Wade himself when he was in Austin so recently—twice."

"I certainly didn't find out about anything from Mr. Alexander," Madeline remarked caustically.

Wade narrowed his eyes and would have snapped a retort about her own duplicity when Madeline turned back to Lorraine and said, "Actually, I heard about the children from Reverend Marshall. I work with him in Austin five days a week helping the less fortunate."

"Less fortunate," Lorraine minced dryly. "How nice."

"Nice, no, Miss Wilcox, but necessary all the same." Madeline stared into the flickering candlelight as if the flame held some answer. "It breaks my heart that there are so many needy children with no roof over their heads or food in their bellies. And it seems the more one does, the more one finds needs doing."

"A veritable font of goodwill, I see," Lorraine said through clenched teeth and a forced smile.

But Wade didn't hear Lorraine's words or her tone, for it came to him in an almost blinding flash of unequivocal and inexplicable relief that Madeline had not lied to him. Obviously the work she had spoken of that was hard to deal with on a day-to-day basis was doling out to the needy. A strange elation brought a wide grin to his lips. "That's the work that's hard to deal with?" he asked Madeline, interrupting Lorraine in the middle of something she was saying.

Lorraine fumed, and Madeline looked at him curiously.

"What did you think I meant?"

Lorraine sat back and watched. Her concern grew with every spoonful of stew that disappeared from the various plates around the table. She realized then that she had made a grave mistake in telling Wade she wanted nothing whatsoever to do with the young hooligans, because this governess, in doing so, had become more a part of Wade's life than she. The way he looked around the room, eyeing each child fondly, not to mention the way he looked at Miss Montgomery, made Lorraine's blood chill with foreboding.

And so it was, in between the irritatingly perfect apple pie and the children being dispatched upstairs, that Lorraine came up with a plan. She was going to play mother herself.

Surely it couldn't be for too long. Surely they were on the verge of finding a relative to take the children. She'd have to go over and talk to Jack Barnes and see where things stood. Anyway, she was certain she could manage for a few days, maybe a week, all in the effort to prove to Wade that Miss Montgomery wasn't the only person good with children. Goodness gracious, she mused, how hard could it be? And no better time to begin than the present.

"Wade, why don't you join me upstairs? I thought I'd read the children a bedtime story."

He turned to Lorraine, surprise etched on his face. "A bedtime story? You?"

Throwing her napkin on the table, she pushed back her chair with a scrape and stood. "Yes, me," she said, somewhat disheartened when Wade made no attempt to follow. "Then just stay down here, but I think those sweet children could use a story before they fall asleep."

"It's still light outside, Lorraine," he remarked, his brows furrowed in a doubtful frown.

"Oh," she said, bemused, looking toward the window. "Well, then, a pre-bedtime story," she added, not to be deterred from her present course of action, and glided from the room.

"Who is that woman?" Madeline asked once Lorraine was out the door.

"My fiancée," Wade responded absently as he poured two glasses of port.

Madeline flinched as if he had threatened her with a blow. She sucked in her breath and sat back in her chair, trying to make sense of his simple words. "Your fiancée? The woman you are to marry?"

Wade set the crystal decanter aside and glanced at Madeline. "Yes."

"Since when?"

"What do you mean, since when?" He set a glass of the sweet, dark red wine in front of her.

"I mean, how long have you been engaged? Were you engaged when you were in Austin . . . riding around with me and . . . and . . ." Her words trailed off and her eyes blazed like jade fires.

"I wasn't engaged *that* night," he said with conviction.

"Not that night?! When, the next night or the night after that? Or do you expect me to believe that out of the clear blue you just decided to get married?"

Wade looked at her in confusion.

"No, of course you didn't just decide to marry her. You intended to marry Miss Wilcox the night you met me!"

"I suppose so," he said in a lazy drawl, his eyes unfathomable as he continued to watch her, before taking a drink of port.

"You suppose! You were as good as engaged to another woman, but you danced with me, rode in my wagon, sat under the moonlight, and . . . and . . . harnessed my horse," she finished lamely.

He hesitated for a moment. "*You* asked me to dance, and *you* insisted on taking me home. I didn't ask for a ride."

"Well, you could have said no."

Wade leaned forward and looked directly into her eyes. "I tried!"

"Tried, my foot! You lecherous . . . cad!"

Madeline threw her napkin down and pushed out of her chair, much as Lorraine had, but instead of a clean, dramatic exit, the chair fell to the floor with a crash, catching her skirt and rending the hem.

"Let me help," Wade offered, coming forward.

"I don't need your help!" She flung the words at him, anger and hurt warring on her gentle features, leaving Wade to stand nonplussed in the dining room once she had yanked herself free and fled.

Lorraine walked down the hallway, determined to make her plan a success. After the long drawn-out meal she had just experienced, spending so much as one second more with those kids was the last thing she wanted to do. But it couldn't be helped. She hoped they'd keep their grimy hands off her new dress. Just the thought of candied fingers touching her caused a shiver to run up her spine. But she knew what she had to do, so she held her chin high and went gracefully in search of the children, hoping that some miracle might occur and they would all be sound asleep.

The golden glow of an early evening sky caught her attention, proclaiming with its hints of sun just how much of a miracle it would have to be. "Well, it is possible, isn't it?" she asked out loud. "Don't little children need their rest?"

Walking down the hall, her heels were soundless on the thick rug. She ran a finger lovingly along the wainscoting, straightening already straight pictures possessively. Soon this would be her new home. And she knew she had to do whatever it took to keep it that way.

Lorraine stopped at a door. Knocking quietly, she hoped no one would answer.

"Come in," a voice called from beyond.

Lorraine grimaced. "Oh, well."

"Miss Lorraine," several children said in surprise.

Searching the room, ignoring the kids, Lorraine found a bookshelf filled with old leather volumes. "Let's see. What do we have here?" She flipped through book after book, closing each with a snap when she determined they were too difficult for her to read.

"What are you doing, Miss Lorraine?" Elizabeth asked.

"What does it look like I'm doing?" she retorted unkindly. "I'm trying to find a book."

"What for?"

"To read to you."

"Here's one," Grace offered while the others looked on with distress.

Lorraine strode toward the children and took the proffered book. *"Grime's Fairy Tales."*

"Grimm's!" the group exclaimed.

"Grimm, Grime, what's the difference? Now, quiet so I can read."

"Are you sure you can?" Garrett asked suspiciously.

Lorraine glared at the twin. "Of course I can. Now, everyone gather round. No, no, not there, you're on my skirt. Careful for my shoes. Ouch! Careful. In fact, why don't you all sit down on the floor. I'll sit here on this stool."

"But then we can't see the pictures."

"I'll hold them up. Now shush. Once upon a time." Lorraine smiled at the sound of her voice. "Oh, this is going to be fun. Where was I?"

"At the beginning," Bridget supplied helpfully.

"This!" Billy toddled forward, thrusting a small book into Lorraine's hands.

"But I've already begun."

"This!"

"Oh, well, let's see." Lorraine opened the book to the first page. She stared at the page filled with relatively small print and looked a bit disconcerted.

Grace leaned forward and sweetly said, "If you'd like, I'll read it."

"Yeah!" Elizabeth exclaimed. "Grace is good at reading."

Lorraine looked at the small girl in astonishment and not a little disbelief. "You're too young to read."

Grace blushed with pleasure, but when she would have taken the book to prove her prowess, Lorraine pulled back and began to read. "Once upon a time there were—"

"Read this," Garrett interrupted, thrusting another book forward.

"No," the girls moaned. "This new one that Maddie brought."

Lorraine bristled. "And what 'new one' did Maddie bring?"

"This!" Elizabeth said excitedly holding out a leatherbound volume.

"That's a girl's book," Garrett stated with disgust.

"It is not."

"It is so."

"Children!"

"I'm going to my room," Bridget stated with a huff.

"So am I," Elizabeth said, close on her sister's heels.

And before Lorraine knew what had happened, she was sitting alone, her yellow satin dress with perfectly puffed sleeves spread becomingly around her, with no one left to read to. "This mothering thing is going to be easier than I thought," she said out loud with a laugh before setting the books aside and going in search of Wade.

She found him standing before the window, swirling a glass of brandy, looking out at the darkening sky, unaware of her approach. All that was needed, Lorraine thought, was a fire burning in the grate and a hunting dog curled up on the floor to make the picture complete. Well, maybe not the dog, she amended, what with their smell and all, but the fire and a handsome man swirling brandy added just the right touch to the vision she had of what her life should be.

A well-connected, highly sought-after male. Elegant home, lots of money. And since she planned to continue her travels with her mother, she hoped he would not be too possessive. Well, maybe just a little, she thought with a smile. And she wasn't about to lose it on account of a few measly kids who were only going to be there temporarily and a governess and her sickeningly sweet smiles and good works.

Walking up behind him, she slipped her arms around his waist. "Anything interesting out there?"

He turned in her arms. "Not particularly. How are the children?"

"Fine, simply fine."

"How did the story go?"

Lorraine thought for a moment before she answered. "Fine."

After setting his brandy aside, he set her at arm's length. "You don't sound convinced."

"No, really, it went just fine. And then, before too long, they were off to bed easily enough."

"It seems you have a way with children after all."

"Of course I do, sweetheart. I was just so shocked when they first arrived. You understand, don't you?" Lorraine took hold of his lapels in her tiny fists and demurely lowered her head.

"Yes, I understand. We all were shocked."

"I'd like to make it up to you and the children. I'd like to help you take care of them. At least take them to the park and such things. Show them we all care."

A sense of relief washed over Wade, though a relief born more from the idea that his well-ordered life indeed was well ordered, that years of planning were not unraveling before his very eyes, than that Lorraine wanted to take care of the children. "I think that's a wonderful idea. And I'm sure the kids will love it."

"Then it's all settled. Tomorrow I'll come over at ten-thirty and show them around town, then take them out for tea. Now," Lorraine said, "the children are in bed and the servants are doing whatever it is they do, and we have the rest of the evening to ourselves." She ran her hands up his arms. "Let's pretend we're married."

Several weeks ago he would have laughed before dipping his head to taste her painted lips. But several weeks ago seemed a lifetime away. "It's getting late. Your parents said to get you home early."

"They always say that." A hint of defeat flickered in her eyes.

"I have a lot of work to do tonight, so it's best. Come on, I'll take you home."

Lorraine hesitated. "Everything's all right, isn't it, Wade?"

He looked at her for a moment before pulling away and walking over to retrieve his hat. "Everything's fine, Lorraine."

Taking her by the elbow he led her to the buggy waiting outside.

Madeline decided getting seven children bathed and dressed was no easy task. Not that any one of them was difficult to handle, it was more that there were so many of them, and limited bathtubs and time. But she was determined that the children look their best when Miss Wilcox arrived to take them out.

She pressed clothes, polished shoes, brushed hair, laced up boots, and tied bows.

"Aren't we a good-looking group?" Madeline said as she stood back to observe her handiwork. "Now, what's this? Come on, shoulders back, and wipe those frowns off your faces."

"Ah, Maddie"—Jimmy sighed—"we don't want to go with Miss Wilcox."

"He's right," Bridget agreed. "Why don't you take us?"

"Because Miss Wilcox is. And none of this whining. You wouldn't want to embarrass Cousin Wade, would you? I want you to go out today and be the ladies and gentlemen you know how to be. Am I understood?"

No definite words could be made out of the mumbling that issued forth.

"I can't understand you," Madeline admonished with a loving smile.

"Okay," Jimmy stated reluctantly, his hands shoved deep in his pockets. "But only because you're making us."

Madeline filled with love that instantly turned to longing. "Go make me proud," she said, then quit the room before anyone saw the tears that gathered in her eyes.

Eleven o'clock passed, then eleven-thirty, and by twelve the seven youths had pretty much destroyed Madeline's handiwork. But just when the group was about to forget Miss Lorraine altogether and get on with something worthwhile, the door knocker sounded. All seven redheaded children gathered together, then sulked down the stairs.

"Children," Madeline called from above, a warning in her eyes.

"All right," Jimmy said with a half smile.

Phillips opened the door to let Lorraine in.

"Good morning, Phillips," she chimed.

Phillips glanced at the clock, noting the late hour, and gave a slight shake of his head.

"Where are the children?" Lorraine looked toward the stairs. "Oh, here they are." She hesitated, her forced smile slowly melting. "You're all a mess!" she said with great irritation.

The children looked down at themselves.

"Quickly. Go straighten up. We don't have all day."

Having overheard the conversation, Madeline descended the stairs like a mother bear after her cubs. "Go wait out front," she said as she shooed the children out the front door, while Lorraine stood speechless, her mouth opened with outrage.

Closing the door, Madeline turned to confront the other

woman. "Miss Wilcox. If you had arrived when you said you would, they would not have had a chance to get messed up. And I will not have you make them feel inadequate because you were late."

Lorraine stood straighter. "You will not have it, will you? Well, let me tell you something, Miss Montgomery. You will not 'have' or 'not have' anything related to these children. You are not a part of this family. Do I make myself clear?"

"Is there a problem here?"

Both women turned to find Wade standing in the doorway leading to the kitchen.

"Why, Wade, darling," Lorraine cooed as she smoothed her hair, managing a pointed glance at Madeline, daring her to say anything. She stepped forward to greet her fiancé. "I didn't realize you were here. What a wonderful surprise."

She reached for his hand with both of hers. He looked over her head to Madeline. Their eyes met and held as Lorraine chattered away. A protectiveness that Wade didn't begin to understand surged through him. He had heard the heated tones but had not been in time to make out the words. And why, he asked himself, was he certain the blame lay at Lorraine's feet?

"Aren't you taking the children out, Lorraine?" he asked while still he gazed at Madeline.

"Well, yes," she said with a hint of indignation. "They're waiting for me outside."

"Then you'd better not keep them waiting any longer."

Not knowing what else to do, Lorraine dropped his hand and turned on her heel. Madeline moved out of the way, going to the stairs, taking them as fast as she could.

After Lorraine left, Wade went to the stairs and started to call after Madeline but stopped himself. What was he doing? he wondered. What would he have said? What could he possibly say? That he was filled with a strange inexplicable relief that she hadn't tried to lie to him the night of the party, that perhaps she was as good as she appeared on the surface? Or that he couldn't get her out of his mind? That he thought of her constantly, playing over in his mind the feel of her body as she trembled in his arms, of the softness of her lips when he had kissed her, of the desire he felt harden his body whenever she was near? No, he couldn't, or wouldn't, say any of those things. Because none of it made any sense.

He could not identify the capricious, obscure, utterly illogical reason why he could not shake Madeline Montgomery from his mind no matter how hard he tried.

He paced back and forth across the marble floor trying to make sense of the situation. And then it came to mind that perhaps if he took her into his arms once again, the mystique would wane. Satiate the hunger and the hunger would cease. And it was with that thought that he took the stairs two at a time in pursuit of the fair Madeline.

The rooms were empty and the house was strangely quiet. How long had the children been there? He smiled. Long enough that he had gotten used to the racket they made. The house seemed lonely suddenly. The realization surprised him.

He continued down the hall. Every room empty. Madeline's door stood open, but she was nowhere within. He heard steps from above, from the attic. His only thoughts being of his need to find her, Wade followed. Narrow steps led to the upper regions, and he wondered when he had last come this way. The rooms held boxes and an assortment of furniture, but nowhere did he find Madeline. He walked to the very last room and found her standing at a dormer window, looking down on the front drive, waving soundlessly to the children's disappearing carriage.

Her shoulders shifted, affording him a glance at her face.

Tears reflected in long rays of sun. Her grief banished his callous pursuit. He felt he should leave. But despite his better intentions, somehow he couldn't bring himself to turn around and walk back down to safer regions.

"Are they gone?" he asked quietly, his voice echoing in the hollow space.

The sound startled her, and furtively Madeline wiped at her eyes.

"They'll be back, you know. Back to spill their milk and chatter until they drive me insane." His voice teased and caressed.

She hiccuped a laugh. "Possibly sooner than later."

"What? Drive me insane?"

Madeline leaned against the windowframe, snorting a short burst of laughter. "That as well, perhaps, but I was referring to their return from the outing."

"You're probably right," he said, stepping into the room. "I give them an hour."

Tilting her head, she considered. "Forty-five minutes."

He came closer. "It's a bet."

"I'm not the betting kind, Mr. Alexander." She turned to face him, to look his dark eyes. The sun glimmered in her hair. "But I suppose there's always time for a first."

Wade stopped before her. If he raised his hand, he could touch her creamy white skin. "Or a second," he whispered, his eyes on her lips.

The words hung between them, their meaning sending jolts of feeling through them as they remembered the night she found him trying to master Old Betty in the dark.

He reached out then, able to hold himself back no longer, and lightly touched the fullness of her lips. With that touch they were lost to a flood of emotions strong enough to threaten their balance. His fingers gently trailed a path across her cheek, her eyes closing at the feel. She leaned toward him, losing herself to the passionate storm that raged within as his hands cupped her face and he lowered his head, pressing his lips to hers. She leaned into him, her hands coming up to tentatively touch his chin. He smelled of spring, like fresh grasses waving in the breeze. She sighed.

"Oh, Maddie," he groaned, pulling her tightly to him. "Why can't I get you out of my head?"

But Madeline's only answer was to cling to him, fiercely, as if she would never let him go.

Time stopped, the world blurred, nothing existed but the moment, the feel, each other.

He trailed a fiery path from her lips down her neck, her head falling back. He wanted her with a passion that burned beyond control. "Damn you, Madeline. I want you so badly," he said as his lips passed from her neck to her shoulder, his strong hand coming up to cup the fullness of her breast.

Her surprised gasp echoed in the empty room, causing Wade to pause. Moments passed as the echo stilled, leaving his ragged breath the only sound. Slowly, with every ounce of strength his powerful body possessed, he put her at arm's length, to force some distance between them. He knew his theory that holding her again would banish her once and for all was false, but he was unable to let go just yet.

He looked into her eyes, stormy and turbulent as a raging sea, and saw her confusion. It took every ounce of willpower he had not to pull her back to him, to hold her, to let her know how much he wanted her. But that was the problem. That wouldn't do. It was Lorraine he wanted, Lorraine he had set out to win! It was Lorraine who was a part of his plan, not the redheaded warrior who had turned his life upside down.

The vision of cards tumbling through the air filtered

through his mind. Indeed, his house of cards leaned precariously, the foundation gravely weakened. Though not beyond repair, he told himself, his hand tightening on her arms.

"My apologies," he said stiffly, before he let go of her and strode from the room, blocking from his mind the pain he saw in her blue-green eyes.

Fourteen

WHEN THE TEA partiers returned forty-five minutes later, they brought not only children's guilty smiles and Lorraine's shrieks of outrage, but a downpour of rain. Wade ignored it all and told the children to go upstairs before pulling his fiancée into the study.

The feel of Madeline raged in his mind, but only because he had been without a woman for so long, he told himself emphatically, trying desperately to find another means to explain away his infatuation. He had simply forgotten how pleasurable it was to kiss Lorraine.

"What are you doing?" Lorraine demanded as she was pulled through the study door. "Haven't you heard a word I said? Those children are beasts. Simply awful. Something must be done. I have never been so mortified in my life. First, they—"

Wade silenced her protests by taking her into his arms and kissing her, a fierce, demanding kiss. It was a moment before she responded, and when she did, she pressed her body up against his, moaning, her hands circling down his back.

He kissed her harder, frantic, as if searching.

"Wade . . ." Lorraine giggled as his lips went to her neck. "I've never seen you so . . . worked up. You've missed me?"

"Hush," he said, putting from his mind the growing thought that it was no good, that it hadn't worked. But still he tried.

"Oh! Excuse me."

The voice was like ice-cold water splashed over a body that was lukewarm at best.

"The door was open, and I . . ." Madeline held her hands to her cheeks as if doing so could cover the red that surged there.

Madeline's blue-green eyes met Wade's, neither aware of Lorraine looking on in anger.

"I'll come back . . . when it's more convenient." Madeline turned on her heel, her sensible skirt swirling around her ankles, and fled through the door that had been carelessly left open.

Wade watched her retreating form, his heart pounding hard, wanting to call after her, to wipe away the hurt that had darkened her eyes. But he wouldn't do that—he couldn't.

The first step of the massive stairway caught Madeline's foot, and she nearly fell to the ground. After catching herself with one arm, she gathered her skirt and took the stairs, trying desperately to gain control. The complaints of the children went unnoticed as she passed them by and went to her room and quietly closed the door.

The image of Wade holding Lorraine Wilcox in his arms played havoc in her head. She felt betrayed. Only minutes before he had held her in his arms. Only minutes before she had known his heated touch, his demanding kiss. She had been lost to the strong arms that held her tight, lost in a world that had the ability to make her forget her resolve. She had forgotten herself, wanting nothing more than to see where the moment would take them.

But he had pushed her away, probably for her wanton ways, disgusted that a supposed caregiver of children would so easily fall for an engaged-to-be-married man. She was a fool. A stupid, wanton fool. Embarrassment intertwined with her hurt.

A knock sounded at her door.

Madeline whirled at the sound. "Who is it?"

"Us!"

Madeline closed her eyes for a moment and took a deep breath. As she expelled the air slowly from her lungs, a smile quivered on her lips, battling with the pain. So egocentric were they that they assumed she would know who "us" was, and of course, she did. Resolutely she pushed Wade from her mind.

"Come in, Us."

The door flew wide on its hinges, banging against the wall and bouncing back, doing much to push her concerns away.

"Careful, careful," Madeline said as she opened her arms to the herd of children, welcoming the unequivocal love they offered.

They spoke all at once, sending a cacophony of sound echoing through the room. Laughing, Madeline held up her hands. "Quiet, one at a time. I can't understand a word you're saying."

"It was awful."

"She's mean."

"We had to sit in hard chairs . . ."

"Foreeeeverrrr."

"And the cakes . . ."

"Were disgusting."

"Filled with slimy cheese."

"Now, now, children. You weren't gone all that long. Miss Wilcox was nice to take you to tea. You should be appreciative. I hope you remembered your manners." Madeline glanced from child to child, their eyes suddenly unable to meet hers.

"What did you do?" Madeline asked suspiciously.

"Nothing."

"Jimmy?"

"Aww," the boy said, his head wagging back and forth. "Just spilled some tea on Miss Lorraine's dress is all."

"What happened then?"

"Well, she kinda jumped up and hit the table, and everything kinda went flying around the room."

"Yeah!" Garrett added enthusiastically. "You should have seen it! There were these cookies, little flat things. Boy, they must have stayed in the air at least five minutes," he exaggerated. "Good thing they didn't hit no one. Mighta chopped off their head."

Both Garrett and Garvin gave great whoops of appreciation for the image this remark brought to mind. The girls squealed their disgust, Jimmy merely shook his head, while young Billy became angry that he didn't seem to know what everyone was talking about. But Billy was given no chance to make a scene, for Madeline rounded the group up and marched them downstairs to apologize.

"You all know better," she said as they took the stairs. "You tell Miss Wilcox how sorry you are, understand?"

"Ah, Maddie, do we have to?" they wailed.

"You most certainly do! You'll not embarrass your cousin with bad manners. I will not have anyone calling you bad-mannered heathens. Do you understand me?"

"Yeah," they mumbled, sulking.

"Pardon me?"

"Yes, ma'am."

"That's better."

Once that was settled, Madeline remembered the scene she had walked in on earlier. What if they were still . . . in the throes of passion? The words made her cringe, then they made her mad. The man must go around chasing anything in a skirt. One minute carrying on with the governess, the next with his fiancée. Or maybe he was one of those—a man who dallied with the help. Madeline held tight to the banister. How dare he!

Wade and Lorraine stood in the foyer, relieving at least one of Madeline's concerns. The couple turned at the sound of their approach. Wade looked at Madeline. Madeline looked away. Lorraine looked at the children before she realized Wade was looking at Madeline. Nothing was said.

"Children," Madeline began with tight lips, "don't you have something to say to Miss Wilcox?"

They shifted from foot to foot.

"Sorry," Jimmy practically grunted.

"Sorry for what?" Madeline prompted.

"Sorry for havin' no manners." Jimmy said this more to Madeline than Lorraine.

Lorraine stepped forward, clearly trying to control her anger. "Miss Montgomery. The children have no need to apologize to me," she said stiffly. "In fact, I was just coming up to ask them to play a game. Outside."

"But it's raining," Garrett protested.

"There seems to be a break in the storm. The fresh air will do you good." She turned to Wade. "Don't you think so, dear?"

He looked at Lorraine. "I thought you just said—"

"Said I was going to find the children. Come along, what shall we play?"

No one responded.

"Croquet!" she announced. "Out on the lawn. You do have a croquet set, don't you, Wade?"

Croquet was duly set up on the lawn, the children unenthusiastically taking mallets and balls. However, it only took a little while before the children forgot their earlier outing and the boys got into the swing of things. Jimmy, Garrett,

.

and Garvin smacked the balls around, aiming more for toes than tiny gates.

"Children!" Lorraine screeched after the third ball had knocked her dainty slipper. And then she smiled, a forced smile that failed to reach her eyes. "I think we've had enough croquet."

Seven sets of green eyes glowed with excitement.

"Tomorrow we'll go to the town square for a stroll in the park."

The excitement was extinguished by a chorus of moans.

Lorraine, however, paid them no mind as she picked up her skirts and headed for the house, leaving the children on the back lawn to grumble their discontent.

"I think I'm getting sick," Garrett announced.

"Me, too," Garvin seconded.

"What do you mean?" Elizabeth asked, concerned.

"He means that they don't want to go to the park tomorrow with Miss Lorraine," Jimmy explained.

"Oh. I feel kinda bad, too," Elizabeth said with a smile. "And Bridget, you look awful, just awful."

And in seconds their grumbles changed to bursts of laughter.

"I want to play!" Grace sat in the middle of the floor, multicolored marbles all around her.

"No, Grace. Go play with someone else," Jimmy said with barely held patience.

"*No!* I want to play marbles, with you!"

"Well, you can't, ya little brat. Now get out of here before I throw ya out by the seat of your pants."

Pools of tears gathered in her eyes, and her lips puffed out and quivered. Jimmy ignored her and began gathering up the marbles.

"I'm going to count to three, Grace, and by the time I do, you better be out of here."

Grace didn't move.

"One . . ."

Grace crossed her arms.

"Two . . ." he continued, his face becoming red with anger.

Grace glared.

"Th—"

Grace jumped up from the floor, scattering the remaining marbles. "I hate you, I hate you! And I never want to see you again." With that, Grace raced out of the room, her wail of displeasure filling the house.

Jimmy grumbled as he rummaged around, finding the rest of the marbles, then leaving the room to go upstairs. He'd had enough of the stupid game.

Someone knocked at the door just as he reached the top of the stairs. He turned back to go to the door, but Wade was there before he made it down a step.

"Jack," Jimmy heard Wade say. "What brings you out here?"

"I found a relative of the kids."

Wade was silent for a moment, and Jimmy didn't see the scowl that crossed his cousin's face. "Let's go to my study."

Jimmy followed the men silently and stood outside the door once they were inside.

"Tell me the details," Wade said once the door was closed, unaware of the third party listening outside.

"Well, there are some relatives all right, but they say they can't possibly deal with all seven. If there just weren't so many of them, Wade."

Jimmy's throat became suddenly tight. He closed his eyes, then turned to the stairs. He didn't wait around to hear the rest. Wade was going to try to pawn them off on some other relatives. With his mind churning with thoughts, Jimmy went to his room to determine what he should do.

The words he had flung at Wade the night of their arrival came to mind. "I can take care of us," he had said so defiantly. But now, the reality of feeding and clothing himself and six other children proved a daunting thought. How could he possibly do it? he asked himself. He didn't even have a job. And at fourteen, how could he do anything that would make enough money to support so many kids?

Jimmy laid down on the bed he had come to think of as his own. *If there weren't so many*, he remembered Jack Barnes saying. Yes, Jimmy thought, if there weren't so many of us. Jimmy felt certain he could take care of himself, and if he did, if he left, then maybe Wade would keep the rest of them. It was only him that Wade didn't like.

So young James Dawson Daniels, Jr., packed his few things, wrote a simple note, and quietly left the house in search of a new life.

Wade paced the confines of his study. Back and forth, with Jack Barnes standing off to the side.

"I won't split the children up," Wade finally said. "And that's final. Now find me someone who can take all of them."

But as Jack Barnes left the room, Wade wondered if he could bear to part with the kids at all. He had grown so used to their outrageous pranks and contagious laughter. But these children needed parents to love them and guide them, not a single thirty-one-year-old bachelor and his obviously unmotherly betrothed.

The thought of Lorraine and the attempts she had been making to be with the children came to mind. It was that very effort, more than anything, that had proved to Wade that Lorraine was not meant to be the mother of these children—perhaps not of any children.

He thought of Madeline. The words *smart, bright, intelligent, knows her own mind* filtered through his head. The word *headstrong* made him roll his eyes at the understatement. The woman was as bad as the kids. But he smiled nonetheless. It wasn't that he wanted a stupid woman, he just wanted someone who . . . what could he say, what did he mean? he suddenly wondered. All the things he had sought in Lorraine no longer seemed so appealing. It was Madeline Montgomery who plagued his mind. But he was given no more chance to contemplate the meaning of this when the shrieks and wails of one of the children sent him flying up the stairs.

Grace sat on the floor, crying inconsolably—not another soul in sight. Where were the others when you needed them? he wondered. Not knowing what else to do, Wade sank to the floor next to her and asked what was wrong.

"Jimmy," she wailed. "He's gone and I'll never see him again. Just like Mama and Papa."

Wade tried to assimilate her words, panic filling him, thinking she meant that somehow Jimmy had been killed.

"He left and it's all my fault. I told him I hated him and never wanted to see him again."

Wade noticed the note on the floor. The words were written haltingly, but Wade realized that Jimmy had run away.

Through her muffled sobs and a downpour of tears, Wade extracted the whole tale from the weeping Grace. He knew that Jimmy wouldn't have run away simply because of a fight with his young sister. No, there was more to this than Grace realized, but what?

"Nothing you said or did made Jimmy leave. There's no reason to blame yourself." But his words had little or no effect on his young cousin, and he realized that until he found

Jimmy and brought him home, she wasn't going to believe him.

Wade hadn't noticed Madeline's arrival in the doorway. And it wasn't until after Grace had extracted the promise that Wade would go and bring Jimmy home, and she had run from the room, that he noticed Madeline.

"You should heed your own words," she said quietly, all thoughts of her hurt and his betrayal forgotten in the face of someone in need. "You are no more responsible for your parents' death than Grace is responsible for Jimmy's disappearance."

Wade's eyes opened wide for a fraction of a second before his jaw tightened and his fist clenched at his side. But Madeline was not to be deterred. "You are a wonderful person, Wade. Every young man has had his wild days."

In a flash Wade smashed his fist into the wall, rattling the pictures, startling Madeline. "I have no idea what has brought on this absurd comparison." His voice was like sharpened steel, unrelenting and deadly. "Regardless, how can you possibly compare a child's spat with the death of my parents?"

His anger filled the room, and Madeline would have stepped back from the force had she not been determined to stand her ground and help this man see the truth that he failed to see.

"Because both of you feel guilty over something you had no control over. The difference is that Grace will go on and forget all about it. You'd rather walk around with your grief than admit you can't control everything around you. Terrible things happen in life whether you like it or not."

"Ha!" he said with a toss of his head. "Call it what you like, but a man has got to take care of what is his, watch out for the welfare of his family." Wade's voice grew harsh and intense as he paced the bedroom like a caged animal. "And if my father had been more concerned with his family and built a house out of stone like I told him instead of staying in that wooden tinderbox, my parents would still be alive today."

Madeline brought her hand to her chest when his surprising words sank in. Wade stopped in his tracks and closed his eyes, the anger evaporating into the new house built so sturdily of stone. "Something so simple. But he was too concerned with the ranch to think about what was best for his family." Wade leaned up against the wall.

Madeline wanted to reach out, to smooth away his pain, but she was stuck where she stood, unable to move as this strong man stood before her, ravaged with pain and memories.

"My father was a great man. So much better than me. He was always here, working hard, providing for his family. How could he have let it happen?"

A chill crept into Madeline, filling her, leaving her desperately cold. She finally reached out and touched Wade's arm, wanting so badly to take him in her arms and comfort him, finally understanding the full extent of the demons that had tormented the man for so long. Not only did he feel guilty for gallivanting around the country while his parents worked hard at home, he felt guilty for being angry at a man whom he loved and whom he felt was a great deal better than himself. His father had stayed at home and worked hard, unlike Wade years ago. But the man he most admired had made a grave mistake, and Wade didn't know how to reconcile these two facts—and he didn't know how to forgive.

"It's all right to be angry with your father," she finally said. "That doesn't mean you loved him any less. Great men make mistakes just like everyone else. Accept that, Wade."

A wave of emotion contorted his dark features as if he desperately wanted her words to be true. Wade looked at Madeline with his hard searching eyes, and for a moment she thought he would reach out to her. But the moment passed and he turned on his heel and stalked from the room to search for the missing Jimmy.

The rain had started up again, rapidly turning the dirt-filled roads to pools of mud. The streets were deserted, the townspeople having sought drier parts. Wade rode straight to the stage depot, assuming the boy knew of nowhere else to go to make his departure. But Jimmy was nowhere to be found.

Wade continued through the rain, along every street, to the church and General Store and everywhere else he could think of the boy might be. But it wasn't until he reached the outskirts of town, on the road to Austin, that he caught sight of his quarry hunched over against the rain.

When Jimmy saw him, he renewed his futile efforts to escape. Only seconds passed before Wade had jumped from his horse and was at Jimmy's side. Wade caught his arm and turned the boy around with an angry grip as he remembered Grace's tear-filled pleas. Wade and Jimmy stood facing each other, the pouring rain surrounding them, each filled with a formidable anger. Their eyes shot daggers, and their strong jaws clenched.

"What are you doing, boy?" Wade demanded harshly.

"What's it to you?"

"I happen to be responsible for you and your brothers and sisters, so it means a great deal to me."

"Like hell it does." Jimmy tried to jerk away.

"Like hell, nothing. Tell me why you left!" Water soaked Wade's hair, leaving black licks of hair flattened across his head.

"Leave me alone," Jimmy ground out, then managed to pull away.

Wade grabbed the boy's shoulders and turned him back

around. "Just leave you alone while Grace sits at home crying because she feels she's to blame?"

"That's crazy," Jimmy spat, his eyes suddenly wary. "She has nothing to do with it."

"Then go home and tell her." Wade's anger did not diminish. "As far as she's concerned, you left her just like your mother and father did, and this time it's all her fault."

"Damn," the boy cursed, looking miserable. "Just leave me alone."

Wade looked down at the boy, who suddenly looked as though he carried the weight of the world on his slim shoulders. Wade sighed. "I can't do that, Jimmy," Wade said, his anger lost to the turbulence he saw in his young cousin's eyes. "You can't leave. How would I keep those kids in line?" A kind smile suddenly played lightly on his lips.

Jimmy scowled. "They don't need me. They'll be better off without me. Then maybe you won't try to get rid of the rest of them. Then they'll have you."

Wade grimaced when he realized that Jimmy must have overheard some of his conversation with Jack Barnes. And what could he say to that? Deny that he was looking for someone to take them? Lie? Never. But how could he explain all the reasons for looking for someone in the first place? He hardly understood his reasons himself. It all seemed so selfish now, keeping his life in order, maintaining his smooth path.

Telling himself he was trying to please his dead parents.

The thoughts washed over him like a scalding bath.

Or had he been trying to maintain the perfectly ordered life to keep at bay the anger he felt for his father?

Wade shook his head, unable to face those thoughts just then. Jimmy was his primary concern.

He focused on the boy. "Regardless of what happens, your brothers and sisters need you. I could never take your place. And I will never split you all up." Wade looked directly into Jimmy's eyes. "I promise you that."

Jimmy's eyes filled with a cautious hope. His shoulders relaxed. "Really?" the boy asked.

"Really," Wade promised, pulling Jimmy close in a tight embrace.

A wary truce settled between them as Wade took Jimmy home on the back of his horse. They arrived to shrieks of joy from Grace and the other children, who had finally learned of the trauma.

Wade glanced at Madeline as he walked past the gaggle of children to the stairs. Suddenly he felt so tired. More exhausted than he had in years. Lorraine, Jimmy, the kids . . . Madeline. And now his father. His mind filled with conflicting images, and just then he didn't have the energy or the know-how to straighten them out. All he wanted was sleep.

Wade slept through the night, and when he woke the next day, he rode to the ranch in hopes of finding some peace and quiet from his raging thoughts. He stayed late, and when finally he turned for home, Wade arrived to a darkened house. With tired steps he climbed the stairs in search of some much needed sleep. At the top of the steps he noticed a slice of golden light coming from one of the children's rooms.

Deciding to say good night, Wade went to the door but was stopped by the clear sound of Madeline's voice. The sound sent a shiver of pleasure up his spine that pushed at his exhaustion. His mind filled with visions of her hair and her eyes, but most of all, her lips as they had touched his so fervently, so full of passion.

"You see, Garrett," she was saying, "as my grandmother told me, life is curly, and no matter how hard you try to straighten it out, it curls right back up again."

Wade wasn't sure what they were talking about or how

Garrett responded. His mind whirled back to the day before. He remembered Madeline's words to him about his father, about the guilt he carried around. The pain that he had felt at her words resurfaced in all its ragged glory. But more amazing to him was the fact that the little slip of a woman in there talking to his children knew more about life than he did. A man well traveled and worldly. A man who had known every kind of pleasure. How was it possible for her to know so clearly what he for years had failed to see?

He walked to his room without saying good night. The memories that had plagued him so for years no longer seemed so dark. He went to a chest and opened a drawer. He carefully pulled out the irreplaceable china doll the children had been playing with the night they first arrived. A smile flickered on his lips when still the darkness didn't threaten. Then, with determination in his eyes, he reached farther in the drawer and found a piece of folded flannel. Reverently he unfolded the cloth to reveal something that glimmered in the dim light. Strips of gold and silver intertwined to form a ring—his mother's wedding band. He closed his eyes and remembered.

He saw his mother pull the ring from her finger and show him the place where the gold and silver had broken free. She had hated to part with it, even for the short while it would take the goldsmith in Austin who originally made it years before to repair the treasured piece. Wade had teased his mother, telling her she was entirely too sentimental. "Don't worry," he had said, pulling her close and kissing her forehead. "You will have it back in no time." But she had never worn the cherished twists of gold and silver again. She had perished in the flames before the ring had been returned.

Wade squeezed his eyes shut and felt a heart-wrenching sadness at the loss. But for the first time it was a sadness void of guilt. And he knew then he could go on with his life.

He realized as he stood in the dimly lit room, his body exhausted and his mind crying for sleep, that he could stop trying to live for his dead parents as if he were trying to make everything up to them. And, yes, his father should have built the house out of stone, just as he had told him, but every man makes mistakes, just as Madeline had said. He must accept the fact that no man can completely control his surroundings. Wade had to learn to forgive his father and, in doing so, forgive himself.

The long-held anger and guilt fell away from him leaving him weak. He must stop forcing his life into a cookie-cutter mold, he suddenly realized. He must simply live.

Relief filled him. It all seemed so clear now. Lorraine hadn't been the woman for him, but the woman he thought his parents might approve of. Had he changed so much in the last few weeks? he wondered. But he shook his head in answer. No, he hadn't changed. He had simply become aware of the things that were truly important in life.

And then it hit him. The best way to deal with this new life was with Madeline Montgomery at his side. And with Madeline as his wife, he could keep the children. The thought sent a surge of pleasure through him that almost made him laugh when he realized how much a part of his life the little hellions had become. He pushed from his mind the kind of pleasure that surged through him at the thought of Madeline as his wife, telling himself she was merely the perfect solution to a problem—nothing more. If he broke his engagement to Lorraine, married Madeline, and kept the children, all his problems would be solved.

Yes, he thought with a smile curved on his face, all his problems would be solved.

He felt better than he had in years. He had come up with a plan to bring his life back in control. Just a shift here, and an adjustment there, and once again he had brought order back into his world.

Fifteen

LORRAINE CLICKED HER shiny nails on the table, again and again.

"Lorraine, dear," her mother finally said, "please stop that. It's most irritating."

Lorraine glared at her mother, clicked her nails one last time, then pushed out of her chair and left the room.

Catching sight of herself in the mirrors she passed, she went up the stairs and down the hall, thoughts of Wade running through her head every step of the way. Wade Alexander and his awful children, that is.

Her attempts at mothering had been disastrous. Even Lorraine could see that. Why, just yesterday that fat little baby had ruined yet another of her favorite gowns. Lorraine grimaced. It didn't matter that it was Lorraine who had insisted Billy could have that last sausage at the fair in hopes of quieting the boy. Bridget had said it wasn't a good idea, and Lorraine had ignored her. Apparently Billy's stomach had sided with Bridget and decided it needed to rid itself of the contents. Ugh!

It was midmorning, and she still wasn't dressed. Her flowing robe and matching nightdress swirled about her ankles as she lowered herself prettily onto a chair. She could hardly remember the feel of Wade's arms around her or the taste of his lips molded against hers. She could hardly count the harsh kiss Wade had pressed on her a few days before.

For all it had excited her, Wade hadn't been truly involved. If there was one thing she knew about, it was a man's attentions, and Lorraine knew Wade hadn't been very attentive. And not just during that kiss, she added with a frown of concern. Lorraine knew she hadn't truly held her betrothed's attention since the children had arrived. Or was it since Wade had returned from Austin?

Lorraine thought back as best she could. Her stomach churned. Was it possible, she wondered frantically, that it wasn't simply the bratty children Wade was growing attached to but Madeline Montgomery as well?

This time when Lorraine tried to ease her fears with thoughts of the other woman's Amazon height and awful red hair, it didn't quite work. In fact, it didn't work at all. No accounting for a man's tastes sometimes.

Lorraine's heart pounded. Wade Alexander was the best catch around, and she couldn't afford to lose him. With that most disconcerting thought, Lorraine's mind began to race, determined to figure out a way to hold on to her betrothed.

Hurriedly she jumped up and began to dress, deciding the best thing to do was get over to Wade's house and use her winning ways to ensure her position with him. Lorraine smiled. How could the man resist when she was really trying?

She dressed in Wade's favorite gown and arrived at his house an hour later. Unfortunately, he was long gone into town. Oh, well, she thought, perhaps just as well. Maybe the person she really needed to talk to was Miss Madeline Montgomery herself.

Lorraine went in search of the woman, walking past a disconcerted Phillips.

"Miss Montgomery, just the person I wanted to see," Lorraine said once she found the woman from Austin upstairs in her room.

Lorraine's smile did nothing to put Madeline at ease. "What can I do for you, Miss Wilcox?" Madeline asked politely.

Lorraine laughed. "You could start searching for someone permanent to take care of the kids instead of trying to become permanent yourself."

Madeline's eyes grew wide with alarm.

"Yes, I can see it in your eyes. You want my fiancé and his passel of children. Everyone knows," she lied. "Have you not realized the stir of gossip you have caused? Everyone in town is talking about the young, single female staying with the bachelor—engaged bachelor, I might add—who is trying desperately to snag the man herself. Everyone in town also knows you arrived the night before Father Hayes brought his sister over the next morning. You're damaging not only your own reputation, which is none of my concern, but Wade's and the children's as well, which is."

Lorraine noticed the dismay in Madeline's face. So she took a chance that the woman really was as sweet and as much of a do-gooder as she appeared and went for the kill with something she hoped would work. "If you're not careful, then you're going to force Wade into marrying you simply to save reputations, despite the fact that he loves me. Why, just the other night Wade told me how he couldn't wait to set a date for our wedding, but couldn't until things were settled with the children," she lied again with a put-upon smile. "You don't want to come between Wade and his only true love, do you? Besides, those kids are on their way out. It's only a matter of time before a relative is found to take them. Then Wade and I will be married. And that little scenario, Miss Montgomery, has no room in it for you. Do I make myself clear?"

Madeline's surprise and dismay turned to anger. When she had been told she would help out with the children until someone permanent could be found, no one told her that someone was another relative to pawn the children off on like old clothes! Why had she been wasting her time interviewing other governesses if this had been Wade's despicable plan all along?

"You make yourself quite clear, Miss Wilcox," she said through clenched teeth. "If there is nothing else, I have things to do."

When Lorraine didn't respond, Madeline turned on her heel and left without another word, leaving Lorraine alone in the hallway to wonder if she had won.

Madeline walked into her room, or the room she was simply using, she reminded herself. Anger warred with dismay. Anger over Wade's apparent attempts to get rid of the children and dismay that everything Lorraine said about Madeline's intentions was true.

Mercy, how she wanted to stay. How she wanted to remain in Fielding, remain with the children, but most of all, remain with Wade. If she was truthful with herself, Madeline knew her dreams had been full of Wade, the children, and herself becoming one big happy family. And the pain was almost too much to bear when she realized what she had been doing and how fruitless it was.

It was true that she had interviewed several governesses and had found, for one reason or another, that none had been good enough. Lorraine was right, Madeline realized. She had wanted to become permanent herself. And what if because of the gossip Wade did succumb and think to marry her instead of his only true love? How could she face a lifetime of knowing he had been deprived of his love because of her? Especially faced with the knowledge that in the end she knew she could not marry him anyway.

Shame engulfed her. To have been so thoughtless. But then reason entered in as she told herself, surely no man would marry because of rumors and children, especially children he planned to send away.

And with that the anger returned tenfold. The man was a beast. He was planning to send those dear children away. How could the man live with himself?

Wade was waiting at Lorraine's house when she returned home. For the merest of seconds her heart leapt with excitement. It had been so long since he had just dropped by to see her. But one look at her handsome fiancé's face told the telling tale. He was not there to prize her with gifts or lavish her with kisses. No, the man was there with bad news.

Lorraine's mind raced. Perhaps another relative had died, and as usual he was merely upset. A small burst of hope surged forth but was quelled when Wade asked her mother if he could see Lorraine alone. A death could be discussed in front of her mother, she thought heartlessly.

Maybe he had come to tell her that a relative could not be found and he was going to keep the children. Lorraine's heart stilled at the thought. No chance was she going to be a mother to that bunch of bratty kids! The last few days had been sheer hell. She would not stand for one more day of *faux* motherhood, let alone a lifetime of it. No, the kids would have to go—somewhere.

Wade waited until her mother had left the room. He cleared his throat uncomfortably. The man was clearly ill at ease.

"Lorraine, please sit down," Wade began quietly.

Lorraine tried to hide her apprehension as she walked over to the sofa and gracefully lowered herself to the cushion. "Now, Wade"—she forced a laugh—"you're making me nervous with all this seriousness and stern looks. Everything's all right, isn't it? Just like you said it would be."

The midday sun glared, its long rays filled with floating

dust slicing through the room. Wade looked out the window, then forced his eyes back to her. "No, Lorraine, everything isn't all right. I think you'll agree that things have changed."

Lorraine's straight spine stiffened. Her eyes narrowed. "What is it you're trying to tell me?" she asked, her voice as stiff as her spine.

With a sigh he moved toward her, lowering himself to the cushion to sit next to her. "Lorraine, you are a beautiful and desirable woman. There's not a man around who wouldn't agree. But you and I know that you'd be miserable with the children."

"But the children aren't staying." Her voice rose an octave.

"Well, as I said, things have changed. The children *are* staying."

"And when did this turn of events take place?" she demanded as she rose from the sofa in a swirl of skirts and strode to the window.

Reluctantly Wade followed. "I realized just the other night that I couldn't give the children to some other relative. They've been through too much as it is." Wade shifted on his feet. "And I wouldn't be totally honest unless I admitted that I've grown fond of them."

Lorraine turned like a she-cat, her look of apprehension gone. "Fond of them or the little nanny you suddenly find in your home—or is it in your bed?"

Wade stiffened. Only the years of practiced control held him in check. "I will ignore that remark. You're upset. You don't know what you're saying."

"I know damn well what I'm saying. It's all because of that little upstart from Austin that things have changed."

"Lorraine, there are many men out there who will sweep you up in a moment. Tell them all you tired of me and broke my heart. Tell them whatever you like. But we both know that if we were to marry, you'd be miserable with the children. You will be happier with someone who can give you the life you deserve." He looked closely at her. "I'm sorry, Lorraine."

"You're sorry!" she hissed.

Lorraine paced the room. Her mind raced. What was she going to do? she asked herself. And then it came to her. She'd bide her time. The fact remained that no matter how infatuated he was now, the other woman was nothing like the type of woman Wade wanted. It was obviously some kind of novelty thing going on. He would lose interest in the little governess, and then she, his true love, would be there to welcome him back with open arms.

Yes, Lorraine smiled inwardly. She'd be patient. She wouldn't tell anyone about the broken engagement, and then no one would ever know about the little tiff they'd had. She'd become Mrs. Wade Alexander just as she planned, maybe just a little later than expected.

"Would you like me to tell your parents?" Wade asked, breaking into her thoughts.

"Oh, no! I mean, no, that won't be necessary," she said, her voice having suddenly grown sweet once again. "I'd like to tell them myself."

The weary conversation dwindled to a close, and within minutes Wade was out on the road. He was anxious to get home. Despite the distaste he held for having to break his engagement with Lorraine, he looked forward to getting home to start his new life with Madeline.

Some little voice inside his head told him that Madeline meant a great deal more to him than a perfect solution to his problems. But he ignored the voice and whistled all the way home.

* * *

"Madeline," Wade said that night as they finished supper.

The children looked up, all aware of a certain unfamiliar tone in their cousin's voice.

"Yes?" Madeline responded.

"Would you please join me in the study?"

"Can we come?" Elizabeth asked with wide, hopeful eyes.

Wade laughed and pushed back his chair. "No, Elizabeth, you can't."

Wade walked over and pulled out Madeline's chair, then led her from the room.

The windows were open in the study, letting in a slight breeze from the cool spring evening. Trees were growing greener and the days were getting warmer, but at night the breezes still whispered of the past winter.

Madeline stepped into the room, apprehension making her tense.

Wade walked over and poured two brandies. He handed one to Madeline. "Come, sit with me, Madeline."

She followed him to a supple leather sofa and carefully sank to the cushion. Glancing out the window, she took a tiny sip of the strong drink.

"I broke off my engagement to Lorraine," Wade said with no preamble.

Madeline didn't realize she sucked in her breath or that her hand clutched the short crystal stem.

"Aren't you going to ask me why?" Wade smiled a bit.

"I don't think that's any of my business."

"When it has to do with the children . . . or with you . . . it is your business."

Madeline looked at him in confusion, though through her confusion she felt a heavy dread begin to fill her. "I don't understand."

"For some time now I've been looking for another relative to take care of the children."

Madeline tensed at the words.

"As a bachelor, I felt I wasn't qualified to take on the responsibility of raising children, much less seven of them." Wade smiled. "You might agree I wasn't doing the best of jobs when you arrived."

Madeline didn't respond.

"Anyway, I've decided to keep the children myself. I've grown rather fond of the little hellions." Wade looked down at her. "And I want you to be their mother . . . and my wife."

The anger, confusion, dread, and disbelief came together in a crash, leaving Madeline nonplussed. She sat on the supple sofa, the brandy snifter held forgotten in her hand, and could do nothing more than stare at Wade as though he had simply gone mad. When her mind finally made sense of his words, it was all she could do to set her snifter down without snapping the stem in half or smashing the glass on the ground.

"Just like that, you've decided to replace Lorraine with me? Why? Because I get along with the children and she doesn't?" Her voice rose dangerously.

And then a thought occurred to her that almost sent her staggering back. Lorraine had been right. He would marry her to save reputations and in doing so lose his only true love.

"Well, I can't be their mother, or your wife," she said, ever so close to tears. "I won't let you make that mistake."

Then before she could make a complete fool of herself, she rose from the sofa and walked from the room, leaving Wade to stare after her, having no idea what he had done.

Madeline took the stairs as fast as she could, not caring if anyone was watching. Once her door was closed securely behind her, she flung herself onto the bed and wept. She

wept for an eternity, crying not only for the man's extremely
unromantic proposal of marriage, but for all her lost hopes
and dreams as well. For all that she would never have. To
have been teased with the kind of life most women take for
granted made her reality all the more painful to accept. And
now to have to face the fact that Lorraine was right. Obviously Wade felt pressured into marrying her because of rumors and gossip. But more than that, Madeline raged, she
felt certain that the only reason Wade would succumb to
such pressure was to secure her land. Yes, with one fell
swoop he would ease unseemly gossip, have a permanent
nanny to tend the children, and would get the land he so desperately wanted.

She remembered their stolen kisses, the love and longing
she had felt, and had thought that in some small measure he
had felt it, too. But no. He had only been using her, hadn't
loved her at all.

And then her traitorous thoughts emerged. How she
wanted him, how she wanted to stay regardless of the fact
that he loved another. She would hand over her land, serve
up her life, just to be near him. Oh, how she wanted to stay,
to be his wife and the mother of the children. But that, she
knew, would be the ultimate betrayal.

She cried until no more tears would come and finally she
drifted into a restless sleep.

The crescent moon rose in the sky, providing a glimmer of
light to display the land. In her sleep Madeline turned away,
flinging her arm back behind her head. She moaned and
whimpered as dark images filled her dreams.

Galloping along, laughter in the wind, her laughter, her
smiles, until in one fateful moment the horse was no longer
under her but rearing above her body. Pain. Darkness. Until
sometime later a doctor leaning over her. Mother crying. Father worried. Doctor saying something, Madeline trying des-

perately to understand. "But at least she's alive," her father said. Madeline wrenched from her dream with a cry.

It was some minutes before Madeline realized she wasn't dreaming any longer and that Wade, not her father, held her in his arms, in those strong arms that had made her feel cherished and safe. And with a blinding flash, she realized she loved this man. But why, she wondered, was she surprised? Hadn't the feeling been brewing within her for weeks now? But her feelings had been mixed together—attraction, then pity; anger, then desire; and now dismay mixed with a love that she never dreamed she would have the opportunity to feel. Yes, love, God forbid. Though she knew she shouldn't.

Tears threatened and she pressed herself closer to his massive chest, trying to feel safe. She could feel the pounding of his heart as he held her secure.

"Hush, now," he whispered into her hair, holding her tight. "I'm here."

Gently, with his arms around her, he rocked her as he would a child, rocking her fears away. He tilted her head, and he looked down into her eyes. He looked down at her not as a child, but as a woman, and Madeline could see the desire in his eyes as clearly as if he had spoken of it aloud. Slowly he bent his head and kissed her on the lips. Softly, gently, barely felt, but sending a shiver of longing through her so strong and forceful that it made her gasp.

Wade pulled back at the sound, desire clearly warring with concern. Pushing all else from her mind, Madeline reached up and pulled him to her, and with a passion that surprised them both, she pressed her lips to his. With a groan he pulled her close, his hands holding and caressing frantically, as if wanting to touch every inch of her, to know her completely.

They were awash in a wave of passion, swirling and rolling as the tide tossed them up only to pull them down into the depths, drowning them in the strength of their raging desire. He kissed her lips, then left them to tease her ear, his warm breath teasing and tantalizing.

How she loved this man, she thought through the haze of wanting. But her haze was cleared when Wade pulled back, his brow furrowed. He took a deep breath before kissing her softly on the forehead. "Not yet, my sweet Maddie. And if we don't stop now, I'll have to finish what I've begun." He kissed her again and then gently set her back on the pillows. He stood over the bed and stared at her for an eternity before he turned and walked from the room, without ever saying good night.

He left her alone in the darkened room, leaving fragrant traces of his cheroot and brandy. Her mind filled with images of him as the man she loved, the man she wanted, and then, too, as the man who was fast becoming a wonderful father. He had gone from not knowing what to do with the children to dealing with them with an ease that surprised even her.

How had it all happened that the lonely outcast from the party had come to be so important to her? How had she let herself fall in love with a man, want to marry this man, when she knew better than anyone that marriage wasn't an option for her? Despite all her wishes, she could never be so selfish.

The old pain resurfaced, and it was as if her dreams still held her tight in their grip. But no matter the wanting, she had to leave. As soon as she could. Tomorrow she would find a governess for the children, and she would return to Austin and let Wade go back to Lorraine.

And sure enough she did, hiring a woman no better or worse than the slew of others who had been through the door. With the children out at the ranch with Wade, Madeline jotted a quick line of farewell and departed, never looking back. The sheer pain that ravaged her body made it impossible.

Sixteen

THE OUTING PROVED to be a huge success. The children turned out to be surprisingly capable when it came to ranching, never balking, even when asked to do the most menial and unpleasant of tasks. And once they returned to the house, all seven of them leapt from their horses, eager to share their exploits with their beloved Maddie. Oh, the stories they had to tell.

They skidded on the high-polished floor as they flew into the house; only Jimmy retained a bit of decorum and walked quickly up the stairs.

Wade was left in the saddle shaking his head. The horses grazed on the shrubbery with reins caught around their ears. It would seem there was a lesson yet to learn—that of grooming and stabling one's horse after the ride was through. But the lesson could wait. The day had been good, and he wasn't about to be the one to spoil it for them. With a chuckle and another shake of his head, Wade called the stableboy and every other available man to help round up and put away the grazing horses.

Once the horses were stabled, Wade eagerly followed the children. His steps faltered when he remembered his talk with Madeline and his subsequent proposal of marriage. Some look he couldn't quite put his finger on had crossed her delicate features. For a second he had thought it disbelief and distress. But that couldn't be, he told himself. Her very kisses told him her true feelings. She wanted him as much as he wanted her. She was only shocked by his sudden offer.

He cursed himself for having proposed so soon after breaking his engagement to Lorraine. But he had been so eager to make Madeline his, to right his life, and make his house a home. Now, he promised himself, he would go slowly with her, show her that she would make the perfect addition to his family.

Wade opened the front door expectantly. The laughter he expected to hear, however, was missing, replaced instead by cries of anguish.

"What's happened?" he demanded as he rushed up the stairs toward the sound.

"She's gone!"

"She left!"

Wade approached Madeline's door, where the children huddled together. His heart pounded, his pulse raced. What had happened to her? he wondered, fear tightening his chest.

It wasn't Madeline he burst in on, however, but a little old lady with soft white hair and an expression that clearly bespoke her distress, sitting next to Father Hayes's sister, Gertrude.

"She's gone, Cousin!" Grace cried.

"Forever!" Elizabeth added with cries of her own.

But Wade ignored the children, for he saw a note in Jimmy's hand. Without a thought for the boy, Wade grabbed it away and read the missive—once, twice, and finally a third time before the import sunk in.

"She's left us," was all he said.

He stood motionless until finally the chaos caused by the children pierced his hazy bubble. "Quiet!" he roared, then turned back to the new woman. "Who are you and what are you doing here?"

The woman's hand quivered and shook, but Wade was beyond comprehension of the anxiety he was causing. "Speak up, woman."

"I . . . I . . . I'm Mildred Hawthorne. Hired by Miss Montgomery to care for the children."

Gertrude Hayes confirmed the words.

"No!" the children cried in unison. "We want Maddie! Cousin, bring her back!"

Whatever pain laced his eyes before was gone when he turned from Mildred Hawthorne to the children, the pain replaced with a dark hardness that had not been seen for some time. Now it had returned, though darker and harder.

"I will not go and bring her back. She has left us, plain and simple. That's her choice. Now leave it be. Miss Hawthorne is here now instead." With that, he turned away and quit the room.

Dumbstruck, the children turned as well. They walked from the room, their small feet dragging, their young shoulders slumped.

"Why would she leave?" Elizabeth asked in a small whisper. "How could she do this to us?"

"What did we do to make her go?" Grace asked no one in particular.

"We didn't do anything," Bridget insisted.

"She just didn't like us is all," Garrett determined as they headed down the long hall.

Jimmy didn't contribute to the sorrowful conversation, but the light that had only recently started to glow in his green eyes glowed no longer. Everyone always leaves, he thought, always.

Wade leaned against the windowframe, the glass panes pushed open into the garden. Night had fallen, though it seemed a lifetime since he had walked into Madeline's room and found her gone.

The pain. But, no, he raged inwardly. There was no pain at her loss. He was simply outraged by such inconsiderate and selfish behavior, or so he tried to tell himself over the hours that had passed.

He pulled on the pungent smoke of his cheroot and looked out over the land. Gently rolling hills cast shadows on the deep valleys. The sounds of night that normally filled him with the rightness of the world left him feeling empty and alone.

The moonlight faded, the sliver of light obscured by the passing clouds. Darkness fell around him. And the darkness seemed to overcome him, seeping into his soul, filling him with despair.

He had offered to give her his life, to marry her, to make her the mother of the children, and what did she do? She fled, with no more than the simple words *I have to go. I have to go*, his mind screamed. Why, damn it, why? He threw the cheroot savagely into the dirt of the garden. There were going to be no answers, because the one person who could provide them was gone.

The following morning Wade came down to breakfast, his face stern and set. The noise from the breakfast room was enough to deafen a elephant. He looked in and found the table full of wild children, Phillips bringing towels to clean up spilled milk, and Mildred Hawthorne trying fruitlessly to bring her charges to heel. On seeing Wade, Phillips ran over, soaking-wet towels dripping in his hands.

"Thank God, you're here. The kids have gone mad. What are we going to do?" Phillips asked.

Wade stepped away from the pool that began to form at his feet. "Lock them in their rooms, send them out to play, buy them a house of their own. I don't care, Phillips, do what you want." Wade turned and left the house, leaving an open-mouthed Phillips staring after him.

Wade galloped his horse the whole way into town, tossing the reins to an unsuspecting stableboy when he arrived. He strode to his office without so much as a tipped hat or good day and snapped orders the minute he walked through the door. He worked relentlessly on projects and proposals, never lifting his head even when someone brought some new file he had sent for. Only when a quiet knock on his door and Lorraine's voice filtered into his brain did he bother to look up, and then with no more than barely held patience at having been disturbed.

"What can I do for you, Lorraine?" he asked bluntly.

"Well . . . I . . ." she stammered, not used to being spoken to in such a manner. "I just wanted to come by and see if perhaps you'd like to come to supper this evening. I'm going to cook. All your favorites."

Her hopeful smile did nothing to lighten Wade's foul mood. "I didn't realize you knew how to cook, or for that matter, that I had any favorite foods."

"Of course I can cook," she said with great feeling, her hand to her ample bosom. "What woman can't?"

He started to say *you*, but managed to hold his tongue and said instead, "Thanks, anyway, Lorraine. But I've got work to do."

She moved closer, her pale pink taffeta skirt swishing seductively. "You have to eat sometime, and I would so desperately like to see you. I've missed you, darling."

The clock announced the quarter hour, then all was silent as Wade looked across his massive desk at the woman he once planned to marry. How, he wondered, could he have thought this woman could possibly have been for him? For that matter, how could he have thought his parents ever would have approved? Good God, they were decent honest people. People like Madeline. The thought seared him anew.

He tossed down his pen, ink splattering when it hit, and looked at Lorraine standing before him, clearly uncomfortable in the awkward silence.

"It's over Lorraine. I told you that the other day."

"It can't be!" she cried, her chest heaving with the first true emotion Wade had ever seen her experience. "Mother and Daddy are expecting us to join them for the award banquet in Austin. You know how much this means to Daddy. We can't disappoint him and not attend."

"You won't disappoint him because you can go whether I do or not."

"But it will crush Daddy if on this special occasion he has to find out you have terminated our betrothal."

"You haven't told your parents yet?" Wade asked, his brow coming together in an irritated frown.

"How could I? Not now, not yet. I can't spoil his special moment. After all, in the last year, since you have been over at the house so much, you have become like a son to him."

Wade missed the triumphant look that crossed Lorraine's face when he cringed at her words. He had indeed spent a good deal of time with her father. And despite the way the judge made the law fit his own means, Wade actually liked the older man. The least he could do for him was to attend the award ceremony with his family as he had promised to do months before.

"All right, I'll go. But once we get back to Fielding, you have to tell your father that the betrothal is off, or I'll do it myself like I wanted to in the first place."

"Oh, Wade." Lorraine laughed as she ran around the desk and threw her arms around his hard waist. "Daddy will be so pleased."

And so it was that Wade traveled to Austin with the Wil-

cox family, the children left at home with yet another governess and Phillips, who was ready to pack his bags and search
out new employment.

After procuring rooms at the hotel, the Fielding contin-
gent arrived at the banquet to much ado. Judge and Mrs. Wilcox were in their element amongst all the praise and
recognition. Lorraine didn't do badly herself. But Wade
wanted nothing more than to leave the blasted city that now
held memories of another time, of another woman.

He sat at a table with Lorraine and several others he hadn't
seen in a while. The conversation carried on around him, re-
quiring only an occasional nod or murmur. And it was just as
the meal was served that he saw her. There, across the room,
at another table with another man, sat Madeline, her smile
and laughter like an arrow straight into Wade's heart.

As the evening progressed, Wade watched the conundrum
of a woman who plagued his every thought. His anger
mounted with each passing word, each gesture of her hand,
and each faint laugh emitted from her full red lips. He failed
to notice that each word was strained, each gesture was
forced, each laugh was hollow; and it was all he could do to
hold himself back from pummeling the other man and dragging Madeline back to Fielding and demanding they marry.
But he managed to restrain himself until three dances into
the night, and he could stand it no longer.

He pushed back his chair, startling Lorraine, then strode
onto the dance floor, roughly tapping the other man on the
shoulder, then taking Madeline into a dance of their own.

"Wade," she whispered when his arms pulled her close.

His name was like a caress, immediately filling him with
joy, smoothing away his anger, and for a moment he couldn't
speak. He looked down at her, and it seemed to Wade as
though, despite it all, they were bound by a common thread,
that she was the other half needed to make his whole com-

plete. And he was suddenly deeply aware that there was a great deal more between them than he had been willing to admit.

He twirled her around the dance floor, his eyes never leaving hers, the air heavy with thoughts unsaid.

"What are you doing here?" she finally asked.

Her words shattered the fragile spell, reminding him of her betrayal. Instantly his jaw cemented.

"A better question is, what are you doing here?" he snapped.

"I'm dancing, as you can see," she answered with matching asperity.

"Yes, I see. You're dancing, merrymaking. Having a grand time. I should have stayed with my original assessment of you."

"And what was that?"

His arm tightened around her waist, his eyes boring down into the depths of hers, as a cold smile curled on his lips. His low laugh was contemptuous. "A scheming, conniving strumpet concerned for no one but herself."

With surprising speed she pulled her hand away to slap the derisive smile off his hard, chiseled face. But her effort was for naught when Wade caught her wrist in a deadly grip and pulled it to his side.

"Careful, my dear. You're making a scene."

"I don't give a damn who's watching. Now, let me go." She jerked herself from his arms and left him alone on the dance floor to stare after her with deadly rage.

"My, my, my," Lorraine's voice sounded behind him. "And to think at one time you said she meant nothing to you." Lorraine's eyes narrowed with malice. "I think, Mr. Alexander, you mean nothing to her."

He turned to her then, anger distorting his face. But he said nothing before walking from the room.

Lorraine went back to her table, her mind racing with plans. But she didn't get very far when Wilbur White stepped in her path and asked her to dance.

She looked him up and down and tried to remember what she knew about the man. A good five years older than her father and twice widowed was all that came to mind. Hmmm. But then she remembered he was widowed without children and he had made a wagonload of money selling hardware around the state. And he lived in Austin.

Right that second the thought of moving to a larger city did wonders for Lorraine. Move away from the knowing glances that were sure to result when everyone finally found out that she and Wade were no longer to be married. Her mind burned at the thought. Though she would tell everyone she had rid herself of the man, people would know that she had lost him to Madeline Montgomery. And that was not tolerable. How she would love to make Wade Alexander pay.

She focused on Wilbur White. Perhaps, she thought with a sly smile, he was just the man she needed. "I'd love to dance, Mr. White," she said, bringing an elegant lace fan to her face. "I think we might dance well together." And with that, Lorraine Wilcox was lead to the dance floor with the man she decided would take Wade Alexander's place.

Wade stood on the terrace of the governor's mansion fighting off his confusion. He told himself it was simply anger. But when he had seen Madeline's blue-green eyes, he could only think of this strange and inexplicable bond they shared. He asked himself again, what was it about this slip of a girl, so unlike anything he ever dreamed he wanted, that could so draw him to her? What was it about her that made him feel whole when she was in his arms?

A reluctant smile found his lips. She made him laugh

when she was near, and he had never felt so miserable as he had since she had left.

Wade turned to look out over the garden, breathing in the night air, hoping the coolness would banish Madeline from his mind. He waited for his heart to still, for his breath to slow. He waited for the sweet memory of Madeline to fade from his mind. But unlike the night he first saw her, this time it didn't happen. This time he knew too much of her, the feel of her skin, the touch of her lips, to ever be able to banish her again. But damn her, he cursed to himself, she had left the children and she had left him, and that he couldn't forget.

Wade returned to the ballroom, where he found Lorraine happily ensconced in the arms of a man Wade gauged to be as old as her father, but a man he knew had plenty of money and was in need of a wife. With a shrug of his shoulders, Wade felt a sense of relief. Lorraine was taken care of, and now all he need do was go back to the hotel and leave at first light.

The long night lying in bed proved no better than the award ceremony. Wade tossed and turned for hours only to find himself getting up in the wee hours to sit on the windowsill. He smoked a cheroot and could think of nothing but the infuriating Madeline Montgomery. And the more he thought about her, the more frustrated he became.

Gradually his frustration turned back to anger, and by the time the long orange rays of morning began to stretch across the countryside, Wade knew what he was going to do.

After a quick shave and bath, Wade found directions to Madeline's house, then walked the few blocks to give the irresponsible woman a piece of his mind. He didn't notice the neatly kept lawn or the unusual architecture as he marched up the flagstone path. He pounded the brass knocker on the door with enough force to wake the sleeping guests at the hotel several blocks away. And while the guests probably jumped from their beds, it was a good few minutes before he heard any sounds from within.

Eventually, a woman with a hurriedly donned robe pulled around her cracked open the door.

"I'm here to see Miss Montgomery," Wade stated with an arrogant authority.

"Well, you can come back at a decent hour, and we'll see if she's receiving," she retorted, obviously unimpressed.

Wade stared at the woman through the few inches of space between the doorjamb and the barely opened door, the surprise of her words the only thing saving her from a severe rebuke at her insolence. And he might have gotten around to it eventually, if she hadn't started to slam the door shut. Only Wade's quick wits sent a hand out to hold it open.

"I'm afraid you don't understand, ma'am. I am Wade Alexander and have come to see Miss Montgomery."

The woman eyed him more closely but seemed no more inclined to open the door now than before. Yet another woman who didn't know a woman's place, he thought irritably. And to think that at one point he actually respected Richard Leister. It was a good thing he had found these things out before he had made the irrevocable mistake of binding himself for life to such a woman.

He shook his head over the idea that he had ever been led to believe Madeline was good for the children. He pushed from his mind the fact that the only time the children had had a modicum of civility was when she was around.

"So," the woman said with a whistle and a shake of her head. "You're Wade Alexander." She looked him up and down through the gap in the door, and Wade was almost certain she smiled. But no sooner had she almost smiled than it was gone and she said, "Miss Montgomery is not available. Now, get your hand off the door." She pushed with her ample weight against the hard plank, obviously intending to shut the door, fingers in the way or not. And she almost succeeded until Wade realized what she was doing and held the door firm.

"Selma, who's there?"

Wade heard Madeline's call in the distance. The sound of her voice momentarily banished his anger. Suddenly he wanted to throw open the door and close the space between them. He wanted to take her into his arms and ask her never to leave him again.

But the lapse was only temporary.

Madeline was selfish and unfeeling, he told himself firmly, reining in his wild heart. She thought of no one but herself when she up and left the children, damaging them more than they already were. He was only there to tell her so.

"Selma," she called again. "Who's there?"

"Nobody important, dearie. Just the milk boy wanting his money early is all. Now, go on back upstairs."

And with that Wade heaved open the door, having to grab the woman by the arm to prevent her from falling. He heard a small gasp, and when he looked up he found, as always when he came upon Madeline, the most beautiful sight he had ever seen.

She stood halfway down the stairs in a vivid blue dress. The hair that he so often longed to run his hands through tumbled over her shoulders and down her back like a blaze of fire against an early morning sky. She looked down at him, clearly startled, and for a second Wade thought he saw a flicker of hope. But then the look was gone, making him believe he had only wished for it, and that made his anger return tenfold.

"Sir!" Selma demanded furiously. "If you do not leave this instant, I will send for the sheriff!"

Wade ignored the woman and took a step toward Madeline. "I have something to say to you," he said with an unnatural calm. "And if you don't come down here, I'll come up there."

Selma gasped.

"It's all right, Selma," Madeline said with a sigh. "I'll be fine. Perhaps you could put on a pot of coffee."

Selma seemed to waver before she sniffed, then stiffened her shoulders in turn, and finally huffed off toward the kitchen.

"Why don't we go into the garden room. It was just finished," Madeline said, taking the remaining steps down the staircase and slipping past Wade.

He followed her and came upon a room filled with plants and a wall full of windows that looked out over the garden. A white latticed archway covered in jasmine led to the green beyond. For a moment he was taken back as he remembered the many times he had filled his senses with the scent of sweet jasmine when he pulled Madeline into his arms.

"Isn't it beautiful?" she asked with a sigh. "There is something so splendid about such a wild, unwieldy vine."

Wade shook his head, thinking it figured that out of all the flowers in the world, Madeline Montgomery would love such an unruly plant.

Abruptly she turned away from the windows, giving him no opportunity to respond, and sat down in a white wicker chair.

"You wanted to say?" she asked.

Not "How are the children?" or "How are you?"—simply "You wanted to say?" as though she was anxious to have their encounter through. And with those few words his anger boiled over. "I wanted to say that you are selfish and irresponsible. How could you simply up and leave the children like that? For all the good you did while you were there, your desertion has undone all the progress and made the situation worse. The children are devastated by your departure. You're worse than their parents. They, at least, left unwillingly. You simply packed your bags and didn't even bother to say goodbye." Wade paced the room, his jaw tight, his eyes dark as coal.

"I had to leave," Madeline said in a small voice.

"Why?" he demanded.

"Because . . ." she began, then looked away. "Just because."

"Just because?!" His voice echoed through the room. "Just because you care for no one but yourself! And to think I ever thought you were different! Time and time again you prove to me how wrong I was."

Madeline visibly cringed at his harsh words, but still she didn't defend herself. She swallowed hard and took a deep breath and looked out through the window. Her eyes locked on the jasmine vine, its tenacious strength and beauty enhanced by the white lattice that it clung to for support.

The morning dawned brightly. An early morning breeze rustled through the velvety blooms, promising a warm day.

Wade paced again, his anger slowly dying. The rage that had consumed him couldn't fight the overwhelming need he felt to protect her as he watched her sitting in front of him, more beautiful even than in his dreams. His anger dissolved completely, leaving him confused yet again.

"Why, Madeline?" he asked, his voice hoarse and rough. "Why did you leave?"

She looked at him then, unshed tears glistening in her eyes. Minutes ticked by while she didn't answer, merely sat in her seat, a maelstrom of emotion crossing her face. When finally she spoke, her voice was a whisper. "I had to" was all she said.

Only a few feet separated them, but Wade didn't know

how to close the distance. His feet wouldn't move, and his hand wouldn't reach out.

Looking away, Madeline bit her lower lip, her brow creased with emotion. She seemed so uncertain and so miserable that Wade wondered how he ever thought she would leave because she was selfish. There had to be an explanation.

"Why, Madeline?" he asked again and finally took the steps that separated them. "Why?" He lowered himself to his knee before her and reached out to gently turn her face to his. "Tell me why," he demanded softly, gazing into her eyes.

He expected an answer, a whispered response that would answer his plaguing question. Instead she reached out and touched his hair, barely, her hands trembling. With one finger she traced a path that seared his soul, from his hair down his cheek to his jaw. "You have such strong features." She hesitated, staring at her finger. "I've missed you so."

And then the answer no longer mattered. His only thought was to hold her as he longed to, to pull her into his arms and never let her go. With a groan he took the hand that caressed his face and pressed it to his lips. He trailed a path of demanding kisses up her arm.

"Madeline," he murmured, his breath a warm caress on her skin.

Slowly he pulled her from the chair to kneel with him as the morning sun brightened the room. His mouth hovered over hers. "I hated that you left," he whispered. He gave her no chance to reply when he hungrily covered her mouth with his. An intensity overcame him, and he felt he could never hold her close enough.

Through his dazed senses he felt her tense at his fervent response. And with a restraint he didn't know he possessed, he gentled his kiss to a slow seductive journey. He pressed his lips to her forehead and then to the curve of her delicate ear. His warm breath sent tremors through her body, and after teasing her with raindrop kisses about her face, he reclaimed her lips once again. This time his kiss was gentle, coercing her to respond. Her hands trailed back and wrapped around his neck. Hesitantly she responded, shyly kissing him back.

He kissed her until kissing was no longer enough. He buried his face in her hair, wild jasmine filling his senses. "I was afraid I'd never see you again," he finally said, his voice barely a whisper.

For a moment neither moved, then Madeline hugged him tight. "I didn't think I'd ever see you again, either. Not you or the children." She gently pulled away to sit in the chair. "I found life to be awfully boring without the little hellions to liven up my day." Her voice was taut with emotion. "I've missed them terribly." Again, she traced his cheek with her finger. "I missed you terribly, as well."

He looked into her eyes, his brow furrowed, his jaw set. When his searching gaze found no answers, he asked, "Then why, Madeline? Why did you leave?"

"Well," a demanding voice interrupted. "What do we have here?"

Madeline hastily turned toward the door, where Selma stood with a tray filled with coffee and cups. Wade remained where he was, the tension slowly returning.

"Did you lose something, Mr. Alexander?" Selma asked as she approached to set the tray down on the table. "Here, now, get up off your knees. I'll have the maid look for whatever it is in a bit. Here," she continued as she poured two cups of steaming coffee, "have a cup, sir. Can't start the day without a spot of hot coffee to spur one into action."

Wade pulled himself up, restraining himself from coming down on the old woman with all the anger and frustration that he felt.

"There we go," Selma said as she pulled another chair up to the table. "Have a seat. How about a little sugar?"

Wade glanced from the cup Selma held to Madeline and noticed the tears that once again had started to brim.

"Madam, if you will please leave us," Wade said in a voice that brooked no argument.

Selma stammered beneath his heated gaze. "But . . ."

And then Madeline jumped from her seat, knocking the low table as she did. "I'm sorry, Wade," she said in a whispered cry, then she fled the room before he could reach out and pull her back. And when he would have followed, Selma stepped in front of him. "Don't, Mr. Alexander. It's best this way."

"Best!" he said with great incredulity, anger shimmering in his eyes. "Best for whom I'd like to know."

But the spell that had allowed him to reach out to Madeline was broken. And with that he stormed out of the house, closing the door between the two halves needed to make the whole.

Seventeen

MADELINE RAN UP the stairs and down the hall to her room, shutting the door against all her churning emotions. How was it possible, she wondered, that the mere sight of the man could send her resolve tumbling in confusion? She had had no choice but to leave Fielding, she reminded herself. It was best for everyone.

But none of this eased her aching heart. She longed to run after Wade, tell him to take her back, to love her and cherish her for the rest of her days. But that would be foolish.

It was too hot, not to mention too late, to lose her heartache to sleep, and she had no energy or enthusiasm to go to Guy Town to help Reverend Marshall. She shifted aimlessly about the room until a soft knock sounded at the door.

"Come in," Madeline called as she lethargically straightened her dressing table.

"Good morning, dear."

Madeline turned to her grandmother. "Good morning, Gran. You look lovely," she said, glancing over the lavender dress her grandmother wore, trying for some enthusiasm. "Off to something special?"

Gran seemed to hesitate before approaching her granddaughter. Then, with resolute eyes, ignoring her granddaughter's question, she went straight to the point. "I haven't asked why you came home in such a flurry of unhappiness. I thought it none of my business. But now I have heard, along with everyone else in walking distance, that you left seven children without so much as a goodbye, and I find I must speak.

"Madeline, we both know you are not one to shirk your duties. So I find myself wondering if . . ." Gran seemed to flounder but then pulled her shoulders back and continued. "Did that man . . . was that man improper with you in anyway?"

Seconds ticked by while the import of her words sank in. When they did, Madeline's eyes grew wide with dismay. "No! Absolutely not, Grandmother." She may not have been the perfect lady what with wanting to kiss the man at every turn, but that wasn't his fault, was it? "Not to worry, Gran. He is in no way to blame for my leaving." And then she looked away. "At least, not in the sense you're concerned about."

Relief stretched across Gran's face, the lines of tension vanishing from her forehead. "I am relieved," she began but was stopped when Madeline closed the distance between them and put her arm around her grandmother's shoulders.

"I feel terrible that you ever had to worry with such a thought. Wade was always perfectly proper. It was just that . . ." Madeline looked away. "He was engaged to another woman."

"*Was* engaged?"

Madeline grinned humorlessly. "Yes, *was* engaged."

"What happened?"

"I got in the way. Rumors, damaged reputations, obligations to preserve his good name, all forced him to break his engagement."

Gran looked concerned and not a little skeptical. "I may not know this man well, but I've been around him enough over the past years and overheard him say enough today to know that he is not the type of man to succumb to public criticism."

"How would you know that?"

"Wade Alexander and your uncle Edward have been friends for ages. And I know for a fact that Wade Alexander, for good or for bad, is ruled by no one but himself. There must be another reason he broke his engagement to his fiancée." Gran looked at Madeline meaningfully.

However, the meaning that Madeline saw was different from her grandmother's. "Maybe he wouldn't succumb to the pressure if that was all, but Gran, Lorraine was terrible with the children. She hated them as much as they hated her. And family is important to Wade. He's decided to keep the children himself." Madeline shrugged her shoulders to hide her pain. "I got along with the children, so I was useful."

"Hogwash!" Gran snorted. "No man is going to leave a woman he loves because in a matter of a few weeks she can't get along with some kids. Why can't you face the truth and accept the fact that the man wants you?"

"For my land," she blurted, then turned away for fear that sudden comprehension would show in her grandmother's eyes. "He wants my land."

"Obviously you're going to see what you want no matter what is true." Her grandmother sighed and patted Madeline's tightly clasped hands. "Regardless of what you think Wade Alexander wants or doesn't want, the fact remains that you left seven children for no good reason other than feeling sorry for yourself. I find that unfair and not a bit like the granddaughter I have grown to love, but more important, to respect. You owe those kids an explanation, dear. And a proper goodbye."

"I can't go back, Gran," Madeline said, her voice a thin, reedy whisper, her eyes filling with tears. "I just can't."

Gran took Madeline's shoulders and turned her so they

stood face to face. "Look at me, girl," she demanded. "It's not that you can't, it's that you won't. You *chose* to leave, and now you are *choosing* not to go back. There's a difference. You have to accept responsibility for your actions."

Madeline squeezed her eyes shut, trying to block out the words. She knew her grandmother was right. She didn't want to go back, to bury herself in the fruitless joy of being near Wade and the children. But she knew, as she must have known all along, she had to go back and right her grievous wrong. She couldn't hide from it any longer. She had been desperately unfair to the children, and it was her duty to go back and make things right.

Yes, she thought as she opened her eyes, she would return to Fielding.

"You're right, Gran. And thank you for making me face what I didn't want to see." Madeline smiled a bit. "It's hard to see a painful truth when it is something you'd like to think yourself incapable of." Suddenly she felt a great deal older than her mere twenty-six years. "I'll pack and be on my way."

Gran grinned uncertainly. "I took the liberty of sending for Old Petey the mail carrier. He should arrive any time."

Madeline shook her head and had to laugh. "You think you know me, do you?"

The smile and laughter disappeared from Gran's face, replaced with a fierceness that surprised Madeline. Gran took Madeline's hand firmly in hers. "What I know is you are a caring woman who puts the rest of us to shame for all your good." She shrugged her shoulders. "Now, go get packed before I start to cry."

Gran left Madeline filled with a mixture of pride and love. What a feeling, she reflected, to be so loved by another. With the pride still surging through, Madeline pulled out a small valise and began to fill it with a few clothes. But with every item packed inside, the pride was gradually replaced by trepidation. She was going back to Fielding—to Wade and the children. Good God, she moaned aloud, how would she gain the strength and determination ever to leave there again.

It was well into the day by the time Madeline had everything squared around and was able to leave. Old Petey, the mail stagecoach driver, grumbled impatiently in the foyer, stepping outside now and again to spit a wad of tobacco into the bushes. He had almost spit on the floor the first time, but Selma's look of outrage sent him stomping out the door, muttering about know-it-all women, to spew a stream of brown tobacco. He wiped his dirty sleeve across his bearded face as he walked back inside. Selma grimaced at the sight but said nothing, merely stood guard with a fierce scowl for fear the man would purloin something valuable.

Gran's promises that the man was harmless went unheeded by the dour-faced Selma. And she stood in the foyer watching the ill-kempt man until he and his dilapidated old wagon rambled down the drive with Madeline in her wagon following close behind.

Selma shook her head and harrumphed past Madeline's grandmother. "As if gallivanting around town with nary a chaperon is not enough. Now she's rambling across the state in a beat-up old wagon with a man of visible disrepute—all with your blessin'!"

Gran only smiled, hoping against hope she had done the right thing, then walked out into her rose garden to tend her precious flowers.

Madeline and Old Petey rode the whole way to Fielding much as they had the first time: Old Petey and his stage sending up a constant cloud of dust, Madeline and Old Betty choking on it the whole way. Madeline hardly noticed, how-

ever, as her thoughts were well occupied. Where the last trip
had her mind filled with orphans who needed her, this trip had
her mind filled with Wade Alexander. How would she face
him? she wondered. After all the hateful things he had said to
her, would he even let her in the front door?

Lying, scheming, selfish. She couldn't remember the rest.
And she didn't much want to. He had been one angry *hom-
bre*, as they were fond of saying in Texas, when he had
barged into her house that morning.

But then there was that look in his eyes just before Selma
had entered with coffee. The look that she had seen there a
hundred times since she met him. Looking into her soul,
searching, wanting something Madeline didn't understand.
But what was it that he wanted? A keeper for his children—or her land?

Well, it didn't matter now, she told herself, shaking such
thoughts from her mind. She was returning to Fielding to set
straight a terrible wrong, and then she would leave, return to
Austin, and put her energies into a school.

Madeline waved her thanks to Petey once they reached
Fielding. From there she could make it on her own. She traveled through the quiet town until she came to the intimidating heights of Wade Alexander's home.

After pulling through the high wrought-iron gates and
up the drive, a groom appeared to take her conveyance.
From the corner of her eye she noticed the damaged hedge.
The memory brought a reluctant chuckle bubbling in her
chest. Someone had made an attempt to lessen the battered
look. Madeline wrinkled her nose when she realized the
hedge would never be the same.

Deciding that she was procrastinating, doing anything to
prolong the inevitable confrontation, Madeline grasped her
skirt firmly and walked up the steps. Before she could falter,
she took hold of the brass knocker and banged at the door. At

first there was no sound, and it was a few minutes before the door swung open.

"Miss Madeline!" Phillips practically cried in surprise. The faithful servant's eyes brimmed with joy. "It's so good to see you, miss." He pulled her inside with great familiarity and relief, forgetting himself and his position, and shut the door. "Oh, how we've missed you. The place just hasn't been the same."

As if to prove his point, bickering and crying could be heard in the distance along with tiny feet being stomped at most probably someone not getting his or her way.

"Thank you, Phillips." The sounds from upstairs grew louder. "I suspect I'd best go see what trauma has occurred."

"Grand idea, Miss Madeline. And tonight we'll have a fine supper to celebrate," Phillips said as he galloped off to the kitchen.

With a fortifying sigh, Madeline climbed the stairs. One flight proved inadequate to find the squabbling children, though the querulous sounds had grown louder, leading Madeline to determine they were in the attic. Up she went until, reaching the higher regions, she found the gaggle of siblings bickering and crying, as they halfheartedly attempted to play a game.

"It would seem you've forgotten your manners," Madeline said with a loving smile.

The room grew perfectly quiet for a split second while the children jerked around to see who it was, to see if perhaps their ears had deceived them.

"Maddie! Maddie!" they cried once their eyes confirmed their ears, before running to her at full force.

"You're back!"

"I knew you'd be back!" Garrett said faithfully.

"Me, too," Garvin agreed quietly.

Madeline caught herself on the door and hugged each child as best she could. "How I missed you little devils," she said through tears as the group huddled together, pulling her into the room.

"I missed you desperately!" Grace cried dramatically.

"I know, pet," Madeline said, reaching down to cup the little girl's chin. "I missed you, too."

They talked and laughed, and Madeline listened to the tumultuous stories coming at her all at once. And through the muddle of almost deafening sound, no one noticed when Wade arrived to darken the threshold.

Earlier, in an attempt to escape the noisy children, Wade had gone out to the stables. With the dark mood he was in he was afraid of what he might do to one of the unruly youths. But then the noise had gotten louder, and he'd had enough. The children had to learn. So he stalked into the house, up two flights of stairs, and found not just his unruly charges but his maddening Madeline Montgomery, too. When would he fail to be surprised at this woman's unexpected appearances? he wondered.

He would have smiled if he hadn't suddenly remembered that very morning when he had stormed from her house, promising himself he'd never see her again. In addition, he had promised himself he would stay away from Austin even if it meant riding all the way to Houston for supplies. He had sworn unfairly that he'd never speak to Edward Leister again for having invited him to the damn party in the first place. And he had cursed the ship captain who had brought Madeline Montgomery across the Atlantic Ocean from the safe distance of England. The British deserved the headache.

But now, standing in the doorway, he found his anger warring with a smile, the anger quickly losing out to the overwhelming joy at her return. It didn't matter why she was back; he only cared that she was.

"Look who's back!" Grace cried when she caught sight of Wade.

Madeline turned to the door and found Wade, more handsome than any man had a right to be. Grace ran over to him and yanked at his hand, trying to pull him toward Madeline. "Look, Cousin. Maddie came back."

"So it would seem," he said, his voice deep and unreadable.

He still wore the same riding clothes he'd had on that morning: black pants encasing his massive thighs and a white shirt open at the neck. Madeline had the urge to reach out much as she had done that morning. Instead her hand came to her hair as if to brush the dirt from the unruly tresses.

The children glanced from Wade to Madeline, then back to Wade, uncertain at what was happening. "What'sa matter, Maddie?" Garrett inquired. "You look kinda sick."

Madeline turned from Wade to Garrett. "Mind your manners, young man," she reprimanded with an embarrassed smile.

"What did I do?"

"It's not polite to discuss such things," Madeline said, not knowing what else to say.

" 'Specially to a lady," Elizabeth added, condescension dripping from her voice.

"That's right," Grace added with her own fierce glare at her older brother. "It's not polite to talk about vomit in public."

Everyone, including Wade, cringed. "Uuggh," several groaned.

"Ugh, is right," Madeline said. "Now, everyone downstairs."

* * *

That night Phillips lived up to his promise, and supper indeed was fine. They feasted on veal cordon bleu, stuffed potatoes, fresh asparagus with a creamy sauce, and fresh-baked rolls. The children dressed themselves in their very best clothes with almost every button buttoned into the corresponding buttonhole. Shoes were mostly unscuffed and ribbons mostly matched. And every sock, with the exception of Billy's, made a perfect pair. Even Madeline dressed in a festive violet gown.

The evening flew by, leaving Madeline and Wade no opportunity to be alone. But through each bite of food and tidbit of conversation, each was aware of the other. Madeline put the children to bed with the exception of Jimmy, who lingered downstairs in the study with Wade.

Wade and Jimmy didn't say much, but when Madeline glanced in the door later, the scene made her heart tighten with love. Rather than break up the unexpected camaraderie that had sprung up between the two cousins, Madeline tiptoed up the stairs and readied herself for bed.

She lay awake for some time. She relished her return, and as she had feared, plain and simple, she wanted to stay.

She loved the children as if they were her own. And most of all, she loved Wade Alexander despite his domineering, infuriating manner, despite the fact that she knew she shouldn't.

No, she shouldn't.

Dark images threatened. She closed her eyes, willing them away. But the voices still came. *"At least she's alive."* But just then, just being alive wasn't enough. She wanted to spend the rest of her days with Wade Alexander. For just once in her life she didn't want to think about what was right for everyone else.

And in that moon-streaked room she made a decision. "Call me selfish," she whispered into the silver light. "For once I'm going to forget what I *should* do and do what I want."

The darkness retreated, and she squeezed her eyes closed tight for just a second before opening them with a smile. She wanted to be with the children, and she wanted to be with Wade, to enjoy what little time they might have together, wherever the moment might take them.

Yes, for once in her life, she was simply going to enjoy herself, not spend her time trying to do what was right for everyone else.

With visions of being held in Wade's arms, Madeline fell fast asleep with a gentle smile curved upon her face.

Eighteen

MADELINE ROSE EARLY the following morning to wake the children. Throwing back the covers, she leapt out of bed, certain of a glorious day. Once she was dressed and ready for anything, she pulled open her bedroom door and stepped into the hallway. For the first time in years she didn't think about what could not be in her life; she thought only of the moment. And the moment held the children and Wade.

Going from room to room, Madeline roused the children, pulling them up from their dream-filled sleep. She dressed them in old clothes, then led the group to the kitchen.

"Good morning," Madeline said cheerfully to a startled Phillips and kitchen staff, who weren't used to seeing anyone else up this early.

"What's this?" Phillips asked from his seat while looking over the rag-clad group.

"Yeah," Garrett groaned groggily, rubbing his sleepy eyes. "What're we doing?"

"It's too early," Garvin added.

Madeline laughed and grabbed Garrett and Garvin's hands. "We're starting a project today! A wonderful project that will be lots of fun!"

"A project?" Garrett asked hopefully, a little life beginning to emerge. "Like building a tree house?"

"Or a sailboat?" Garvin inquired.

Jimmy skeptically eyed his raggedy siblings. "Don't hold

your breath. From the looks of us it doesn't look like it's
gonna be too fun or too wonderful to me."

"But there you are wrong, my skeptical friend," Madeline
said with a mischievous smile. "Any project can be fun if
you choose to make it that way."

Phillips groaned and Garrett and Garvin moved away with
identical grimaces.

Jimmy smiled reluctantly and looked at Phillips. "It's
gonna be worse than I thought."

Phillips quickly covered his mouth after a short burst of
laughter escaped at Jimmy's words.

Madeline glowered at the two but only for a moment.
"Pessimists, the both of you. I promise that if each of you
tries, we'll have a grand time. And if not, at least we'll have
a grand time with the results, for we are going to turn that old
dusty attic into a school!" Madeline finished with a great
look of triumph and a tilt of her chin that could only mean
she absolutely, without a doubt, thought this was grand
news.

"A school!" all seven children cried in true horror.

"Yes, a school. And don't worry. Everyone will be in-
cluded in the project." Madeline surveyed all those in the
kitchen, including the kitchen staff and Phillips.

"But we don't want a school," Elizabeth wailed.

"Things are fine just the way they are," Garrett added.

"Nonsense. Of course you want a school." Madeline
looked at them closely. "This is going to be a fun school."

"Fun?" Bridget asked, clearly disbelieving.

"Yes, fun."

Madeline turned to Phillips, who quickly stood from his
chair and grabbed his cup of coffee. "No, thanks, little lady.
Cook and Marie have to deal with the house and meals,
and I—"

"And you, what, Mr. Phillips?" she asked suddenly formal.

"I've got to reorder Mr. Alexander's study," he said with a look of inspiration on his face. "And that's where I'm off to right now." And with that he was gone, leaving Cook and Marie to fend for themselves. They instantly turned back to the kneading of dough and scraping of carrots, announcing as clearly as Phillips they had no intention of getting involved.

Madeline shrugged her shoulders. "Oh, well, we'll do it ourselves."

She sat the children down to quickly eat their meal before herding them up the stairs until they reached the very top.

Madeline surveyed her surroundings. Upon truly inspecting the place, as she hadn't done before, she found it in worse shape than she remembered. Well, nothing to do but get started, she told herself.

"All right, everyone. Let's begin. Jimmy, you and I will move the furniture out. Bridget will get cleaning supplies. Garrett, Garvin, you're in charge of getting buckets of hot water. Elizabeth and Grace, open all the windows." Madeline turned to young Billy. "And, Billy, once again, you are in charge of supervising."

Downstairs, Wade walked into his study to find Phillips ensconced in the high-backed leather chair, the daily paper spread out over the desk. "Busy at work?" Wade asked with one eyebrow cocked curiously.

Phillips looked up, concern etched on his face. But then he saw Wade. "Oh, it's only you."

"Expecting someone else? And is this what you do when I'm not around?"

"Well, of course not!" Phillips said, clearly insulted. "I was just getting this old body out of the way. I tell you that woman is trying to work us all to the bone. Up there starting a school, right here in this very house."

Wade's eyes narrowed in disbelief. "A school? Who's starting a school?"

"Miss Maddie, I tell you. She's up in the attic now giving out orders like a drill sergeant. Got the kids working away, not that she isn't, too, of course. But mercy's sake, a man's got only so much strength."

Wade, however, wasn't listening any longer. He marched out of the room, his large hand flexing at his side. The woman was trying to turn his house into a school, he raged inwardly, remembering all too well her desire to start a school for less fortunate children. Well, not in his home, he mumbled under his breath.

He took the stairs two at a time, with hardly a change in his breathing by the time he arrived. He saw her immediately, and for a heartbeat he was taken back by the sight, his purpose forgotten. Then he shook his head to clear it. Not this time, he ⬤proved himself. He would not have her turning his house upside down.

"Madeline!" Her name pierced the room, its resonance quivering in the air.

Madeline looked up in surprise, but when she caught sight of him, the surprise quickly melted to pleasure. "Good morning," she said with a sweet smile.

The smell of soap mixed with dust hung in the early morning rays of sun. The small group worked like a whirlwind, the children hardly stopping to acknowledge his arrival.

"You can't start a school, Madeline," he began, barely managing a stern look. "I can't have every kid in town traipsing through my house."

Madeline leaned back on her heels, a soapy scrub brush in hand, and said, "Oh, no. Not for the town's children. This school is just for ours."

Ours. Madeline blushed. The word hung unretracted in the air, neither Wade nor Madeline able to turn away. Ours. Not his or mine, but ours. And with that one word the dam that had kept Wade's emotions mostly in check burst open, allowing everything he felt, in all its uncertain terms, to flow forth, threatening to consume him with all its intensity. Nothing in the past mattered just then. Only Madeline. And he knew he must have her.

"Yes, ours, Madeline," Wade said, his dark-eyed gaze locking with hers, trying to force her to accept the truth of his words.

Madeline hastily brushed a strand of hair back from her face, leaving a streak of soapy bubbles across her chin. She wiped at it with her apron, then with a furtive glance back at Wade, she leaned forward to vigorously scrub the floor as if unable to face his words.

Wade watched her for a moment and almost reached down to pull her up and make her face the truth. But not now, not here with all the children around. So he smiled and walked the length of the floor with measured steps before he turned and left without another word.

The small group worked tirelessly. Madeline worked as hard at banishing thoughts of Wade from her mind as she did at cleaning. To do so, she had them all singing songs and telling jokes, and little by little the old attic room looked more and more like a schoolroom rather than a storage room. Every crack, crevice, and flat surface was dusted and readied. The floor was scrubbed, along with the windows, while Jimmy, Garrett, and Garvin took the rugs and curtains outside and beat them within an inch of their lives.

The boys enjoyed this activity immensely and probably would have been at it the rest of the day had Phillips not finally decided he could no longer, in good conscience, stay in the study while the rest of the family worked so hard.

His first job was to bring a halt to the rug fight and return the rugs and drapery along with the boys to the top floor.

Madeline smiled gratefully at Phillips's appearance before going after another section of floor. Once the cleaning had been accomplished, Madeline, Phillips, and the children stood back to admire their work. But their happy smiles slowly faded.

"The walls look awful," Grace stated. "They've got marks and stuff all over them."

"Yeah," Bridget agreed. "They need to be painted."

Madeline groaned. "Painted?" She shrugged her shoulders and sighed. "I believe you're correct. A fresh coat of paint would be the perfect finishing touch." Turning to Phillips, she asked, "Is there any paint around here?"

"Well, there is," he said, a grimace stretching across his face as he looked over the filthy dirty children. "But . . . maybe it's not such a good idea for the . . . everyone to do the painting." Phillips suddenly perked up. "In fact, I know a fellow who could do the painting himself."

"Heavens, no, Phillips. I could not spend Mr. Alexander's money."

"But he has plenty—"

"No, Phillips. We are going to do it ourselves." She turned to the children. "Isn't that right?"

"Yeah!" they cheered in unison.

And so, with a handful of hours left of sunlight, the small crew began the task of repainting the walls. Now, a great deal more was painted than was intended and by the time all was said and done, the children could have stood against the wall and been camouflaged if it weren't for the glowing smiles that slashed across their precious faces, interrupting the smooth flow of color. Even Phillips had been supplied with a few strokes of paint.

They finished painting just as the sun went down, leaving the team of nine exhausted. All Madeline wanted to do was soak in a hot tub before crawling into her soft bed and sleeping until morning. She hadn't realized how much work needed to be done. But before she could come close to her bed, there were seven children who had to be cleaned up.

"All right, everyone, outside. And don't touch anything on the way out. Phillips, could you bring some old shirts down to cover them up after we divest them of their painted clothes?"

"Good idea," Phillips responded before he headed out the door.

"Now, line up," Madeline called. "We're going to file out of here in hopes of lessening any possible damage. No paint smears on the walls."

The children scrambled to line up with the exception of Jimmy. "You're crazy if you think I'm gonna march down the stairs like a baby."

The word *baby* caught everyone's attention, and Madeline's line disintegrated before her very eyes. No one else was going to be a baby, either! Madeline hung her head for a moment, then looked back at them with raised eyebrows. "But, Jimmy, babies can't line up, they're too young, they don't know how. It's grown-ups, military types, who are able to form a straight line and march in unison. Isn't that what you meant?"

All the younger children looked from Jimmy to Madeline, then back to Jimmy, wondering what his answer would be. Jimmy half smiled at Madeline and gave a short nod. "Line up, officers," he called as he stood at the door with shoulders back and chin held high.

Somehow they all made it down two flights of stairs and

out into the yard without too many casualties. But if
Madeline was proud of herself for managing the line, her
ego was punctured when she tried every tactic in the book to
divest the children of their painted clothes.

"But you can put these shirts on immediately," Madeline
said with not a little exasperation in her voice, holding up
old shirts that would easily cover each child from head to
toe, and some a bit more.

"I'm not taking anything off," Bridget said with arms
crossed and a mutinous glare to her eyes.

Only Billy stood in the yard naked as the day he was born
and heading toward the pond at an all-too-rapid pace. Phillips caught him and swung him in the air to much squealing
and giggling before the boy was wrapped in one of the shirts.

"One down, six to go," Madeline muttered under her
breath.

"Bridget, you and the girls go into the stable, then, when
you're finished, the boys will do the same. How about that?"

Bridget thought this over, then reluctantly agreed. "But
keep everyone away from the door," she demanded.

"Of course, of course. Now, get on with you."

The chore was accomplished shortly thereafter, then the
group was sent off inside and upstairs to get cleaned up.
Night was upon them, and Madeline wondered where Wade
could be. They hadn't seen him since he left them to their
project.

After supper and still no Wade, Madeline kissed the children good night and added the admonition to stay in their
beds instead of creeping about the house as she had heard
they had begun to do in her absence. Then she made her way
to the tub that lay waiting with hot scented water. Slowly she
peeled off her old clothes, dust and cobwebs falling off as
she did. Gingerly she stepped into the water, the heat sting-
ing the skin that had been cut and chaffed during the day of

work. But the slight sting was negligible compared to the feeling of luxurious warmth that enfolded her body. Sinking down until the water lapped at her chin, Madeline closed her eyes and relaxed. Visions of Wade danced in her head. One minute frustratingly overbearing, the next smiling and laughing. He was an enigma, but for some reason, that did not displease her.

She must have fallen asleep, for when she became aware of the water again, it was lukewarm, almost cold, sending a chill up her spine. Quickly she grabbed the soap and scrubbed vigorously.

With her bath finished, she pulled on a wrapper over her gown, and went to the window. The night air beckoned. Madeline went to the French doors leading to the terrace that ran along the second floor. She stepped out into the night, leaned up against the railing, and pulled the night air into her lungs. She closed her eyes and held her wrapper tightly closed. The dark enfolded her, and eventually she heard the sounds of the night. Sounds in the distance, sounds that, while she stood there, seemed harmless and unthreatening.

A gentle breeze rustled through her wrapper, and the faint aromatic smell of cheroot wafted over her. Wade's cheroot. Her eyes opened with a snap, and she turned toward the scent. And there he stood, one hip leaning against the railing, his dark eyes boring into her. Her heart skipped a beat.

"How long have you been there?" Madeline asked with a strangled voice.

He didn't answer at first while he pulled on the cigar and watched her closely. "Long enough to wonder again how any one woman can be so lovely."

The words made her dizzy with longing. She felt warm inside. Wade stood away from the railing and crushed his cheroot into a planter. She took a deep breath when he turned to her and slowly closed the space between them.

"I was hoping you'd still be up when I returned."

His voice was a caress, and Madeline almost closed her eyes at the feel.

"I went to Austin," he said. "To get you a surprise."

"A surprise! What did you bring?" And then Madeline blushed. "I'm as bad as the children."

"Or as good," he said, taking another step forward.

"I don't think that's a compliment," she replied breathlessly.

"Perhaps not a compliment in the sense you mean," he said, reaching out and lightly touching her cheek, "but I'd have it no other way."

His eyes caressed her body. "I'd have *you* no other way."

Her breath caught at the words; her head felt light. Her fingers trembled as she reached up and touched his strong hands. She closed her eyes. He pulled her close to him then, pressing her head against his massive chest. Gently he stroked her mass of cascading curls. She listened to his heart. It seemed to gallop in his chest, pounding against his ribs, matching hers in cadence. The pounding told her more than words ever could.

She stayed in his arms, unwilling to move away. They stood entwined, the silver moon and flickering stars shining on the union. A sense of peace filled Madeline. She felt as though she was finally home, where she belonged, in the arms of the man she loved with an intensity that was almost painful.

She pulled back a bit and looked up into his eyes and started to speak, deciding to bear her soul, to tell this man all she felt. But her words were lost when seven children tumbled in a heap at the corner of the house-long terrace. Madeline twirled to face them as they tried to untangle themselves from each other. Garrett was the first to extricate himself to stand, with a guilty smile and a shrug, next to the tangle.

Wade leaned once again against the railing, watching the spectacle with a mixture of outrage and amusement flickering across his face. "How is it that I ever forget that just around every corner lurk my young cousins?"

The humor was lost on Madeline as she walked toward her charges, the thought that she had been about to bear her soul pushing her on. "What is the meaning of this?" Her voice was harsh, and the children instantly looked chagrined. "Have you ever heard of privacy?" she demanded angrily.

"Madeline," Wade said softly, though with a force that commanded.

She jerked around to him, and it was a second before she realized she was making a fool of herself. The children didn't deserve her wrath, and in fact it truly wasn't them she was angry at. She saw in his eyes that Wade knew this, and she cringed at her unfair behavior. She was upset with herself and had taken it out on the children. "I'm sorry," she said to the children before walking back through the French doors and closing them with a bang.

The children vanished magically, leaving Wade on the terrace, the night sky his only companion. He sighed and pulled another cheroot from his pocket before he realized he wasn't alone. Hesitant steps shuffled, and Wade turned to the sound. Jimmy stood where the children had so recently disappeared. Wade smiled his encouragement to make the boy feel welcome.

"Sorry 'bout that, Wade," Jimmy said hesitantly.

It was the first time Jimmy had called Wade anything, or at least anything to his face, Wade amended with an inward smile. The fact filled him with hope. "I appreciate that. But if I were you, I'd be apologizing to Madeline."

They were silent for a while, Wade looking back to the countryside, Jimmy hovering at the corner.

"Look out there," Wade said to Jimmy, hoping to draw him near.

Jimmy came up next to him and looked out at the land.

"Out there is the ranch, all thirty-four thousand acres of it."

"That sounds huge," the boy responded with awe in his voice.

"Yeah, it is."

They stood next to each other, leaning against the railing, a comfortable silence falling between them.

"You love her, don't you?" Jimmy asked suddenly.

The cigar stilled in Wade's hand before he took it in his mouth once again and pulled hard at the aromatic smoke. He blew the smoke into the air in one heavy gust, and in that second, prodded by a young boy half his age, Wade realized it was true. For all that he told himself he needed Madeline and he knew he certainly wanted Madeline, he had pushed from his mind that perhaps there was something more. And now the realization washed over him like a tidal wave, leaving him helpless to resist.

"Yes, I suppose I do," he finally answered before crushing out the cigar and ruffling Jimmy's hair. "Yes, I suppose I do."

The sun was not yet ready to make an appearance when Madeline woke the following morning. She stayed in her bed wondering again how she could have behaved so badly. Oh, how she wanted to roll over and go back to sleep. But she wouldn't succumb to the coward's way out. No, she would get up, dress herself, then go down to breakfast and face them all.

And she did, though for as long as it took her to get there,

Wade and the children were well into their meal. The children were regaling Wade with tales of their cleaning and painting exploits. Even Jimmy provided a story or two. Wade listened with his full attention.

"Good morning," Wade said when he caught sight of Madeline.

She blushed at the innocuous words and hurried to her seat, not bothering to wait for one of the males to pull out her chair.

"Good morning," she said with a small smile.

"Wade and Madeline sittin' in a tree . . ." Elizabeth began to sing.

Wade cleared his throat meaningfully, and Bridget swatted her sister on the head. Madeline's red face turned a dangerous shade of vermilion.

"Maddie!" Grace exclaimed, worry etched across her face. "You look like you're gonna explode!"

Madeline laughed then, and the rest of the group joined in. Not another word was said about the encounter last night. And with her worries gone, Madeline realized she was starved.

She dished up a plate of eggs and ham, pancakes laved with butter, then covered them in syrup until it was pooling at the sides. Phillips poured her a steaming cup of coffee and she even asked for a large glass of milk.

"Milk?" Garrett asked with his face wrinkled in disgust.

"Yes, milk, and every one of you needs a glass, as well."

"Oh, great, Garrett," Bridget reproved. "Now, look what you've done."

"Yeah . . ."

But the argument was avoided when Wade deftly stepped in and said, "Enough," and miraculously it was done.

Wade turned to Jimmy, as he had so many weeks ago, expecting some recognition of his prowess. This time he wasn't to be disappointed when, although Jimmy didn't comment, he emitted a reluctant smile, which was good enough for Wade. On the heels of that success, Wade turned to Madeline with a nod of superiority. This time the rolling of eyeballs came from Madeline, breaking the quiet table up into gales of laughter.

"Jimmy," Wade said as the laughter began to die away, "why don't you come out to the ranch with me today? I could use your help."

Excitement animated the boy's face. "Really? Work with you on the ranch?"

"Really," Wade responded, then turned to Madeline. "That is, if you don't have any other plans for him."

Jimmy turned to Madeline with hopeful eyes. Madeline smiled. "I think that's a wonderful idea. The schoolroom is finished, and we won't start school until Monday. I think it's a perfect time to go out to the ranch."

"I want ta go, too," Garrett stated.

"Me, too," Garvin added.

"Yeah, us, too," Elizabeth said, indicating the rest of the children.

Wade glanced at Jimmy and noticed the boy's hopeful excitement dim just a bit. "Later, kids. Today it's going to be just me and Jimmy."

Jimmy almost smiled, then sat back importantly. "I'll tell you all about it when I get back."

A keen joy filled Madeline. Wade was so good with the children, and they were gradually growing to trust one another. Madeline shifted uncomfortably in her seat and had to remind herself not to think of the future.

"And now for the surprise," Wade announced.

The children squealed their delight and jumped up from their chairs, *where, what,* and *hurry,* coming from their mouths. Wade laughed and looked over their heads at Madeline. "A schoolhouse surprise up in the schoolroom."

The room cleared in a flash, leaving Wade and Madeline alone. "I told you last night that I brought you a surprise, but you never got to see it."

Wade held out his arm, and Madeline jumped up, much as the children had, excited to find the surprise.

"Look, Maddie, tables!" they cried once Madeline and Wade arrived.

"Tables," she stated, confused. And then she glanced around the room to find indeed several tables lined up in the room.

Wade looked on with a smile. "When I was up here yesterday, I realized that you didn't have any desks. So I rode over to Austin yesterday and bought every table Joe's Mercantile had to sell."

"When did you get them up here?" Madeline asked, clearly astonished.

"Amazing things can happen in the middle of the night." Wade smiled and Madeline would have blushed again had Wade's grin not been so boyishly pleased.

"And each one has a name on it, all shiny like," Garrett noticed.

"Look," Elizabeth squealed. "Here's mine."

Every child found his or her table with a shiny brass nameplate tacked to the wood. They went from the youngest child at the front to the oldest at the back.

"Wade, they're perfect." Madeline looked at him with a mixture of disbelief and gratitude. "I'd forgotten all about desks."

"I guessed as much, so I took it upon myself to find some." He hesitated for a moment. "You don't mind?"

"Mind? Good heavens, I'm ecstatic." Madeline reached

out and squeezed Wade's hand and offered him a smile that would have melted the coldest of hearts.

Wade didn't let go of her hand and pulled her to the back of the room, where a row of windows looked out over the back lawn. "And now for my next surprise."

He pointed down into the yard, and when Madeline's eyes followed his direction, she found a white lattice archway, much like the one she had so recently finished in her own backyard, with vines of yellow jasmine starting their way up the sides.

"Oh, Wade, it's beautiful!" she cried, before turning to this unpredictable man, throwing caution to the wind, and reaching up to wrap her arms around his neck.

He picked her up and twirled her around, his laughter filling the room and bringing the children to circle around. "Had I known," he whispered for only her ears, "I would have planted some jasmine before."

Not understanding what was going on, and for that matter, not really caring, the children pulled Madeline away, intent on showing her the new acquisitions.

Wade leaned back against the wall and watched his new-found family. Nothing in his life had ever felt so right. The kids needed him, that couldn't be denied, but what he was coming to find was that he needed the kids as much or more. They brought with them from the wilds of Nebraska a sense of rightness and purpose to his life. The thought amazed him as he had always thought of himself as a man with a purpose. But now, standing back and watching life and happiness pulse through his house, he realized his purpose had always been a hollow one. He still wanted to raise the finest cattle in Texas, but no longer did he feel that every waking hour had to be spent proving to his dead parents he was worthwhile.

And sweet Madeline. She stood in a shaft of sunlight, caressed by the golden light. He remembered how he thought she looked just like the children, could easily have been their mother. Now, with her standing so lovingly surrounded by those very same youths, he knew he had been right, and though they were not issue of her loins, they were as much hers as any child could ever be.

As if she sensed his gaze, she looked over at him and smiled. His heart seemed to still; her breathtaking beauty was almost painful. Jimmy had asked him if he loved her. The simple word *yes* seemed inadequate in conveying all he felt. He loved her as he had never loved anything before. And he was reminded again of his inability to ever let her go. He shook his head in wonder. Everything he had told himself he didn't want in a woman and would succumb to only because he needed her for the children's sake, all those qualities—headstrong, opinionated, tall, redheaded—he found he loved. What a treasure she was. And with that thought came the piercing realization that he had gone about his proposal of marriage all wrong. He had set before her a business transaction that would benefit all those involved. No romantic, get-down-on-one-knee proposal from him. The memory made him wince.

If he wanted Madeline to be his wife, which he did with all his soul, he knew he must woo her, cherish her, show her that he loved her. He had to court her, and court her he would, he decided with growing anticipation.

Wade remembered his trip to the ranch with Jimmy. There was no way he was going to break his promise to the boy. As a result, he would have to put off his courting until they returned. And then, as if Jimmy had some second sense, he turned to Wade and said, "Why don't we all go to the ranch? You and I can go alone another time." Jimmy spoke with a bit of a swagger and a great deal of importance, and Wade had the urge to hug the boy tight.

"If you're sure?" When Jimmy nodded his approval, the

children, who must have been holding their breaths, sent out whoops of joy and danced in circles like a bunch of wild Indians.

"What do you say, Maddie?" Wade inquired with a lopsided grin. "How would you like to see the ranch?"

Madeline rewarded Wade with a smile full of happiness and joy. "I would love to."

The children's cries grew tenfold, threatening the very structure of the house.

"I'll make a picnic lunch while the rest of you go get ready," Madeline stated as she rounded up the children and pressed them toward the door.

The children filed out with Madeline behind them, and just as she walked past Wade, he reached out and gently took her arm. He didn't say anything, merely looked into her eyes for an eternity. They stood that way for long minutes until Grace shouted from halfway down the stairs for them to hurry. In one swift movement Wade leaned down and placed a gentle kiss on Madeline's lips. "Better hurry up, Maddie," he teased. "You're holding everybody up."

And then she was gone, leaving Wade to stand back and marvel at the unexpected turn his life had taken.

Nineteen

WADE, MADELINE, AND the seven children descended on the ranch by midday. Wade, Jimmy, Garrett, Garvin, and Bridget were on horseback; Madeline, Elizabeth, Grace, and Billy were in the wagon. Wade had better sense than to ask Madeline to ride, but again he wondered what caused her fear.

None of that mattered, however, as the boisterous crew toured the huge expanse of land. With the pride of a new father, Wade led them around, showing off the workings of his well-run ranch. Madeline had never seen so many head of cattle and had never laid eyes on the ones with the long horns.

"What kind of a cow is that?" she asked, pointing out the unfamiliar beast.

Wade grinned like a schoolboy. "Longhorn cattle, the pride of Texas. They just arrived. In fact, that's why I needed your land."

The land. It seemed for a second that the sun dimmed, though when Madeline glanced up, the sky was almost painfully blue. The land. Her spirits plummeted so rapidly and so thoroughly that she almost missed his next words.

"Thankfully, Herb Patterson didn't prove to be as difficult a seller as you," he said with a meaningful grin. "He sold me his tract, and for less money than I was willing to pay for yours."

She stared at him, slack-jawed, as the import of his words sunk in. Her breath caught and a feeling so joyous and so wonderful burgeoned within her that she nearly fell off the seat of the wagon. He already had his land!

Wade pointed to the north. "See the second rise in the distance?"

Madeline managed to turn herself in that direction. "Yes."

"That's where the new land starts. It's a good piece of property and I'm pleased. Next week we're going to start building fences so we can move the cattle." He seemed unaware of Madeline's emotional state as he turned to Jimmy. "What do you say to coming out to help with the fences?"

The boy beamed with barely contained pleasure, his green eyes shining, his carrot-red hair brilliant in the midday sun. "That'd be great, Wade."

Wade turned back to Madeline and found her staring off into the distance and then at him.

"I thought all this time you wanted *my* land," she said breathlessly.

"Did you?" Wade asked with a teasing smile.

A bright shade of red crept into Madeline's cheeks, but she didn't look away. Wade guided his horse closer to the wagon and reached out and took her hand. "You made it perfectly clear from the start—well, let's say from the first time I met you and knew who you were," he amended with one raised eyebrow, "that you had no interest in selling, at least not to me. I've never been one to butt my head against a rock wall. In fact, I finalized the deal with Patterson shortly after I saw you in your uncle's office in Austin."

"You mean you already had the land when I arrived to take care of the children?"

Wade chuckled, remembering the night. "Yes, I did. And when I saw you sitting there, I relished the idea of telling you I no longer needed your land."

"Why didn't you?"

"You never gave me a chance. Before I could get the childish barb in, you had stomped off with the intent of high-tailing it out of there first thing in the morning."

All Madeline wanted to do was tell Wade how happy she was, how much it meant to her that he wasn't after her land. But the words wouldn't come. She could only bask in the bright rays of warmth that the knowledge brought. And with that knowledge one more pillar holding her defense against the man crumbled.

The day was filled with fun and good cheer. No one could have asked for a more perfect afternoon. The kids and Wade raced horses and swam in a stream, and even managed to coax Madeline into joining in a game of stickball. Darkness was upon them when they finally pulled through the wrought-iron gates of the house, ready for a banquet, a bath, and a bed.

They dragged themselves up the front steps and through the door, Wade carrying a sound-asleep Grace while Jimmy carried the snoring Billy, Elizabeth leaning contentedly against Madeline. But all good cheer came to a careening halt when Wade stopped dead in his tracks.

He didn't speak at first, and when he did, though Madeline was unable to see around his massive shoulders, she knew something was terribly wrong.

"What brings you out at this time of night, Harold?" Wade asked, his voice unnaturally calm as he took in not only Harold Mackenzie but a middle-aged couple as well.

Madeline moved forward and found two men and a woman springing up from their seats in the foyer.

"Wonderful news, Wade!" Harold exclaimed with great excitement.

"Madeline," Wade said, harshly cutting Harold off before

he could say anything else. "Please take the children upstairs. I'll be up in a moment."

Madeline looked uncertainly at Wade before taking Grace from his arms. "Come along, children. Let's go up and get ready for bed."

"But I'm hungry," Garrett moaned.

"We all are, and just as soon as we're cleaned up, Phillips will have a wonderful meal for us. Fried chicken and potato salad. And a triple-layer chocolate cake."

This information brought grumbling approval and got the kids started up the stairs, but not without worried glances at the man and woman in ill-fitting clothes who stood looking extremely uncomfortable under the glaring gaze of Cousin Wade.

"Who are they, Madeline?" Bridget asked quietly.

"I don't know, Bridget. Probably someone who has a problem in town and wants your cousin to straighten it out."

Bridget looked dubious.

"Nothing to worry about. Whatever it is, your cousin will take care of it," Madeline said with a smile that didn't quite reach her eyes.

Once the children were well out of hearing distance, Wade motioned for Harold and the couple to follow him into his study.

Wade eyed the couple as they lowered themselves into the leather chairs. The man was short and didn't look to Wade as though he'd missed many meals. His clothes were made for a slimmer man and strained to keep the man's girth within the confines of the straining coat and pants. The woman was no better, and her dress strained a good deal more.

"What can I do for you?" he asked politely.

Harold clasped his hands together, his eyes wide with triumph. "I wanted to show you I could do something right. So I took it upon myself to find a relative to take the children off your hands." He spread his hands to encompass the un-known man and woman. "And here they are!"

Wade stared at Harold. "You what!?"

Harold stepped back, then froze, his triumphant eyes turning rapidly to orbs of distress.

"I'm Nestor Siringo," the fat man interjected when it appeared Harold wasn't going to say anything. "And this is my wife, Hamrah." The woman yanked at her tight sleeves. The man reached over with lightning speed and smacked his wife on the arm. "Act like the lady yer suppos—are." He looked back at Wade with a crooked smile and shrugged. "Women."

Wade took a step forward.

Mr. Siringo hurried on. "Ya see, Mr. Mackenzie here got ta holt of us 'n we're here to take our dear departed relatives' babies home to Missouri." Mr. Siringo smiled, showing sparsely toothed gums.

"Missouri?" Wade asked, brows knitted.

"Yes'um, and we came right fast," Hamrah said, receiving yet another smack for her effort.

"If you strike your wife again, Mr. Siringo, I will call the sheriff and have you locked up." Wade had to hold himself back from reaching out and smacking Nestor Siringo or perhaps simply wringing his neck.

Wade strode to the window and looked out onto the darkened lawn, his hands clasped behind his back. In the distance he could see the stables, lanterns lighting the area as the groom put away the horses and Madeline's wagon.

Once he had regained his composure, Wade turned back to the visitors. "I apologize for any inconveniences you have incurred by traveling to Fielding. But the children already have a home. Here with me."

"But, Wade, I thought . . ." Harold faltered.

Nestor Siringo jumped from his seat, his shirt collar

straining, his face suffused in a dangerous red. "Already
have a home! Like hell they do. They're coming with me.
Just like Mackenzie said. I care for the kids, you pay for the
upkeep. By golly, I'm not leavin' without 'em and some
money for my troubles."

Wade's worst suspicions were confirmed. The man was
after the money. And to think he had set this turn of events in
motion in the first place. He thanked God once again he had
seen the light before irreparable damage could have been
done.

"You will be reimbursed for your travel expenses, but as I
said, the children are well taken care of and you are no
longer needed. Now, as I think our business has concluded,
Harold will show you to the door."

Wade turned to Harold. "I'll talk to you in the morning."

In the face of Wade's implacable countenance, Nestor
Siringo and his wife followed Harold to the door. But just
when Wade thought all was going well, Siringo turned and
said, "It's not that simple, Mr. Alexander. And you haven't
seen the last ta me yet."

Wade barely contained his impatience as they quit the
room. He told himself they could do nothing, that they had
no rights involving the children. Jim had left the children to
Wade. But he couldn't help but hope that he would never
have to see the Siringos again.

A sleepless night did nothing to ease Wade's mind about
the Siringos. He had tossed and turned as Jack Barnes's
words came to mind, again and again. *"Don't worry yourself, Wade. Any judge around will do what's best for the kids.
And anyone with half a brain will agree that married folk are
better for kids than a bachelor."* The thought sickened him.

What if he hadn't changed his mind and decided to keep
the children himself? Would he have selfishly sent them off
with a couple of ill reputes like the Siringos to fend for them-

selves? he wondered. Would he have been so wrapped up in his well-ordered life that he would have sacrificed the well-being of the children to maintain his peaceful existence? What would have happened had Madeline Montgomery not come into his life to show him the selfishness of his ways?

But that was water under the bridge at this point. None of it mattered now, he told himself firmly. He was keeping the children and providing them with all the love and happiness he could, and that was all that mattered.

When Wade arrived at his office, Jack Barnes was already there.

"Wade," Jack called, pulling his ample girth up from the chair. Jack smiled as he reached out to shake Wade's hand. "I suspect you're mighty pleased just about now. Harold did a fine job."

At the mention of his name Harold timidly knocked on the open door.

"Here's the man now." Jack walked over and slapped Harold on the back, nearly dislodging his spectacles. He pulled Harold toward a chair before he picked up a cup of coffee. "He had to run an advertisement to find them, cost a pretty penny. But it was worth it in the end 'cause now you got yourself a relative to pawn those hellions off on."

Wade slammed his fist down on his desk just as Jack was taking a sip. Jack sputtered and spewed hot coffee out of his mouth.

"The relatives, as you call them," Wade said through clenched teeth, "who hardly know each other, have no interest in the kids other than the money they will bring. I've decided I'm not giving up the children after all, and when I told Mr. Siringo and his . . . wife this, they were none too pleased."

"But, Wade," Jack began hesitantly. "You said—"

"I don't give a damn what I said. I'm not giving up the children." Wade looked at Barnes with an unwavering gaze. "Is it possible they could get the children anyway?"

Jack Barnes sighed and turned the cup in his hand. "Well, they've got proof of kinship, and what with them being married and all, there is a possibility. As I told you before—"

"I know what you told me." The fear that had been niggling at the back of Wade's mind was confirmed. "Damn Harold!" He finally turned to the other man. "What were you thinking? Any idiot would know those two are frauds. And now I have to contend with their threats and vows to take the kids. An advertisement, for Pete's sake!"

Dragging his hand through the waves of his dark hair, he turned back to Barnes. "What did they use as proof of relation?"

"Birth certificates and a signed document stating they indeed are relations to Gwen Daniels, James Dawson Daniels's wife."

"Those could have easily been forged."

Jack shifted his weight uncomfortably. "Now, that's true, Wade, but you'd be the one to have to prove they're fake. They look pretty darn authentic right now."

"Then prove it, and fast. As I said, I'm not giving up those kids."

Jack and Harold left the office, and Wade went outside to walk off his anger and think. It was as he stepped out the door that Lorraine hurried past on the boardwalk.

"Good morning, Lorraine," Wade said distractedly.

Lorraine looked up, startled as if she hadn't seen him until just then. "Wade," she said, her startled eyes turning rapidly to slivers of ice. "How's everything over at your little house?" Sarcasm dripped from her voice.

"Fine, and congratulations on your upcoming nuptials."

Lorraine surveyed him closely as if to measure his sincerity. "Well, thank you," she finally bit out. "Wilbur is a wonderful man." She looked out over the town. "I hear you've finally found some relatives. I guess that changes everything?" She turned back to Wade with clearly hopeful eyes.

"People who claim they're relatives," Wade said with a deepening scowl. "But it doesn't matter one way or the other. I'm not giving up the children."

Lorraine's hopeful eyes turned cold again. "Well," she said with a huff, "if you'll excuse me, I have business with my father." Lorraine smiled suddenly. "Yes, business with my father." Then she turned in a swirl of skirts and set off toward the judge's chambers.

Her mind raced as she traveled down the boardwalk, not bothering to look when she stepped out on to the dusty road to cross. Fortunately the hour was still fairly early, and only a few riders and wagons had to swerve to miss her.

She banged into the town courtroom without so much as one word to anyone who stood about, before she barged into her father's chamber. "Daddy!" Lorraine demanded before the door shut completely. "I was talking to Father Hayes this morning, and it seems some relatives of those kids have been found."

Cornelius Wilcox sat back in his chair and looked at his daughter over wire-rimmed glasses, a scowl furrowing his brow. "What are you talking about, Lorraine?" he asked after some moments. "What kids?"

Lorraine stomped her tiny foot and gave one great heavy sigh. "Daddy! Wade's cousin's children. You know, all those seven little brats that came between me and my marriage."

This was still a sore subject around the Wilcox household.

"A relative has been found, you say?"

"Yes, and it's about time." Lorraine turned slightly toward a window, not wanting her father to see her face. "But I just saw Wade, and he still refuses to give up the children." She hesitated for a moment. "And to think this situation will continue, then. It's a shame the way Wade has been carrying on with that governess. Living in sin, I've heard more than one person remark. Why, just yesterday, Mrs. Milburn was saying Wade is setting an awful example, not only for those poor innocent children he's got living there, but for the rest of the town as well. Good heavens! Fielding is a respectable town, and we can't have such flagrant disregard of morality taking place right under our very noses without doing anything. As I said, if something isn't done, this situation will continue." Lorraine sighed.

Judge Wilcox tapped his fingers against the desk. When Lorraine moved a step, he looked up as if he had forgotten she was there. "Don't you have some tea or sewing things you need to be doing?" he asked impatiently.

"Of course, Daddy." Lorraine came around the desk and leaned down to kiss her father on the cheek before she turned with a smile and left.

Twenty

A KNOCK SOUNDED at the door. Wade halted in midstride as he paced back and forth across the length of his office.

"Mr. Alexander," the courthouse messenger said importantly. "Judge Wilcox would like to see you in his chambers, sir."

Wade tossed the boy a coin and turned to the window. The talons of unease clutched at him. The judge's summons bode no good, especially coming from a man who, as Wade had commented on before, made the law fit his own means. The man had had plenty of opportunity to discuss the broken engagement with Lorraine and hadn't. Why now did he want to see him? The children and the so-called relatives, he felt certain.

Wade walked over to the courthouse and was ushered in to see the judge as soon as he arrived.

"Wade," Cornelius Wilcox began, not bothering with pleasantries, "it has been brought to my attention that relatives of the children have been found—married relatives," he added with a meaningful look at Wade.

"I suspect they're frauds, Judge."

Cornelius hesitated for a moment. "Frauds, you say? I've been looking into the matter this morning, and I see no problems with their credentials."

"With all due respect, sir, I'm certain I can prove otherwise. It's not unheard of to buy forged papers."

The judge looked closely at Wade. "Is that one of the things you learned while you were out gallivanting around the country?"

Wade held his temper with a tight rein. To antagonize the man would do nothing to help the children. "One of the things."

"And was another breaking betrothals to young impressionable girls? Did you learn that in some den of inequity?" Judge Wilcox's brow furrowed, his fists clenched on his desk.

"Did you call me here to discuss the children or your daughter?"

Judge Wilcox slowly sat back in his chair and exhaled a long, heavy breath. "The children, as a matter of fact. And the relatives who've been found."

Wade took a step forward, his jaw tight as a whip. "I'll prove they aren't who they say they are."

"You do that, Wade. In the meantime, the Siringos have petitioned this court to have you live up to the promise made on your behalf by Harold Mackenzie. And since it is my opinion that the children are in better hands with married relatives than a bachelor and his unmarried governess, I've decided the children are going with the Siringos."

The room suddenly seemed too small, and Wade had to close his eyes to steady himself. He couldn't let this happen, not to the children, his children. His and Madeline's.

"I will be married within the week," Wade said, fury threatening to overflow. "And since Jim left the children to me and I will be married, you can have no objections."

Wade and the judge stared at each other across the massive oak desk. Nothing was said.

"If there isn't anything else," Wade finally bit out, "I have a wedding to plan."

Wade left the courthouse, his head swimming in anger. Of

all the spiteful, small-minded things he had endured in his life, this was the worst. Fury riddled his body. Yes, he would be married by the end of the week, but he had wanted Madeline to marry him for himself, not because of any sense of obligation.

Well, then, the courting was just going to have to speed up. And that infuriated him all the more. He wanted the time to show her his love, prove to her that they were meant to be together. Let her come to him when she felt ready. But now, because of a vindictive old man, he would have to forgo such luxuries.

Later that evening Wade stood on the terrace overlooking the land. No matter how long he stood there, no matter how hard he tried to calm his mind, the unease persisted. And it was more than just the children.

Leaning against the column, Wade pulled out a cheroot, trying to turn his mind to things that were simple and easy to understand. As easy to understand as his life had been before the night of Ed and Rosalind's party when he met Madeline Montgomery. Truthfully though, he knew the turmoil hadn't started with Madeline, but with the letter that had arrived telling of Jim's death.

He had been overcome by a feeling of emptiness that none of his well-laid plans could fill. And then he had met Madeline, and like the waters behind a broken dam, she burst into his life and filled it with turbulent waves. She had sent him reeling from the force, and he had cursed her more than once for disrupting his once calm world. But Wade saw now that she had saved him from himself—brought new life and meaning into his parched existence.

He felt certain he could work out the situation with the children. Even if he had to buy off the dubiously authentic relatives. Judge Wilcox couldn't award the children to the

Siringos if they quietly disappeared from town, better off than they came, on their way back to wherever they really came from. The idea made him want to pummel the heavily jowled face of Nestor Siringo, though to do so would get him no closer to keeping the children. It would simply provide one more mark against him in the judge's eyes. And if money was the only way out, then so be it.

Madeline, however, was proving to be an entirely different story indeed. He had told the judge he would be married by the end of the week. Right that second he stood a better chance of marrying the town busybody, Mrs. Milburn, than Madeline Montgomery. And he hardly understood why. One minute he felt certain all was going well and it would be only a matter of time before she would agree to be his wife, then in the next she proved as elusive as a butterfly.

She wanted him as surely as he wanted her. He had seen the truth in the depths of her blue-green eyes. Why, then, he asked the heavens not for the first time, did she pull back from him as if she could go no further despite her wish to do so? Such restraint she had, such control over herself. But again, he didn't understand why.

He pulled on the heavy aromatic smoke, the puffs of white floating through the night air in swirls and eddies until they finally disappeared. He turned sideways from the column to lean his hip against the balustrade, and as he did so he saw her. His pulse raced, and it was all he could do to keep from throwing his cigar in the bushes and taking the few steps that separated them.

She wore the same white cotton nightgown covered almost entirely by a matching white wrapper that she had worn that night she found him trying to master Old Betty. And like that night, bare feet peeked out from underneath the white ruffled bottom. His pensive countenance lightened with a smile.

"Do you ever wear slippers?" he asked softly, his voice deep and smooth.

She glanced down at her feet as if surprised by their appearance. And then she smiled, too. "Actually I do. But like that last time, while packing in haste, I forgot them."

A cicada beckoned to its mate somewhere in the dark.

"Were you in a hurry to return?" He gazed at her across the dimly lit expanse, his eyes sparking with hope for an instant before he shifted uneasily and his fathomless eyes returned.

Madeline stood very still, unanswering. Wade cursed himself for being so much like a hopeful youth. But when he started to turn away, turn back to the familiar black sky, she took one tentative step away from the door that led from her room, one step closer to Wade.

"Yes," she whispered into the night, "I was in a hurry to return."

The spark of hope rekindled, and though it was more difficult to hold himself back, he did. He knew that she must come to him at her own pace, of her own volition. He willed her closer, and hesitantly she came forward until she stood directly in front of him. As if not knowing if she should continue but afraid to stop, she reached out, and he could see the tremor in her hand as she touched his cheek. "Yes," she repeated, her breath shallow, "I hurried back."

Wade covered her hand with his. He turned his head until his lips brushed her palm. He felt as much as heard her intake of breath. His hand left hers, going to her forehead, to smooth the worry away. Her fingers fell to her side, and he leaned down and gently kissed the same path his fingers had taken.

She smelled like a cool spring breeze laced with jasmine, her hair just dry from a washing. So sweet, so innocent. He took a deep breath and turned her around until her back was pressed against him. His strong arms circled her shoulders, and he leaned down to bury his face in the thick waves of her hair.

Ever so softly she took his work-roughened hands and placed light kisses on each calloused finger. He held her tighter, afraid to speak, afraid to let go for fear the magic spell would break, causing her to take the few steps back into the sanctuary of her room.

So they stood quietly together, each holding on tight, the darkness and sounds of night wrapping them in a cocoon of serenity, providing Wade with the sense of peace he had long been missing.

"I love you, Madeline," he said after some time.

He felt her quiet body still even further. The world seemed to stop while minutes ticked by and Madeline didn't respond. Finally, after what seemed like an eternity, Madeline turned in his arms and looked up until her eyes met his. His breath caught at her fragile beauty—yes, fragile, he thought, despite her usually outrageous and certainly less than ladylike ways.

He reached down to wipe away a tear that streaked a glimmering path down her cheek. But his finger stilled when she spoke.

"I know," she whispered, confusing him, for at that second he didn't know what she knew at all. As if discerning his confusion, she said, "I'm amazed to find that I do know you love me . . . for nothing more than myself." Her voice broke on the last word, and an unbearable pain filled her eyes.

"Madeline, what is it, love?" he demanded, his voice strained. And when she would have looked away or perhaps pulled away, he thought uneasily, he tightened his grip, unwilling to let her escape from him yet again.

"Madeline," he demanded, "I love you." He turned her

chin until she was forced to look into his eyes. "I want to share the rest of my life with you. I want you to be my wife."

The pain in her eyes only intensified. In desperation, grabbing at any possibility that might be the problem, he added, "And not because of the children or the damn land." His voice took on the ominous undertones of steel. "I love you and want you for you, just you, for no other reason—despite your aggravating ways."

Her pain mingled with the threat of laughter, causing her face to contort as she half laughed, half sobbed her sorrow. He clasped her head to his chest. He murmured soothing sounds into her hair, stroking her back, comforting her until she calmed.

When Madeline pulled back, her eyes were a deep, dark green and red-rimmed from crying, though filled with love, Wade felt sure, but something more as well. Determination, he thought in some recess of his mind but was given no chance to contemplate this when she reached up and touched his lips.

"Love me," she whispered.

His heart seemed to stop as his mind assimilated her words. "Madeline," he said, his voice tight and oddly strangled.

"Love me, Wade," she demanded softly, "tonight."

"Sweet Madeline," he groaned before he swept her up into his arms and carried her into his room, her gossamer thin gown and wrapper trailing in their wake.

Long beams of moonlight cast the room with a silver gloss. He kicked the door closed with his booted heel, leaving only one shaft of silver slicing through the open curtains.

Reverently he set her upon the bed and stretched out beside her, looking deep into her eyes. Searching, questioning. He saw her fear, but with it he saw her undeniable love. He leaned over and kissed her eyelids, filled his senses with her sweet scent. Gathering her in his arms, he felt complete, felt as though he had finally come home after a long lonely journey.

"Sweet, sweet Madeline," he whispered into her hair.

He held her body close. His body began to burn, slowly, intensely. He wanted her then as he had wanted her months ago on the sandy bank of the gently rippling river in Austin. But unlike then, he knew he must control himself, to honor her body and respect their love by waiting until they married.

Wade rolled over and pulled Madeline with him. He lay very still without letting her go, willing his desire away. "Soon, love. We'll be married soon."

A shadow passed through her eyes, and when Wade would have questioned her, she leaned down and kissed him, not on the cheek or forehead, but on his lips, demanding, pleading, bringing a groan from deep within his chest.

"Madeline."

She kissed him again, persistent, until he fiercely pulled her to him, rolling her underneath his massive form and molding her body to his.

"God, how I love you," he murmured hoarsely, his hands and lips frantic in their quest.

He tasted her sweetness, he felt her body, the hard planes and angles of his pressed against the curves and valleys of hers. It was all he could do not to tear the thin material from her body and move within her. Instead, he trembled as he brushed his mouth against the pulse in her throat.

"I shouldn't," he said in a tormented whisper, pulling back to look into her eyes, running his hand up the length of her thigh, the white gown gathering against his golden skin. "Not yet." But he couldn't let her go, the sweet feel of her body searing his palm. Not yet.

His hand continued its heated journey, brushing the curve of her hip, teasing her narrow waist, finally resting on her side, just under her arm, the heel of his hand pressing against the soft swell of flesh. He watched as her back arched like a bough of a graceful willow, seeking more. Her hands came up to caress him. Gently, with one strong hand, he pushed her arms back above her head, and leaned down to inhale her sweet fragrance before he pushed her gown aside and opened his mouth on the soft underswell of her breast.

The small gasp of pleasure that emitted from his love, and the feel of her gracefully curved leg between his, tested his restraint. She moved slightly beneath him. And if there had ever been a moment he could have turned back, it was spent, his noble intentions utterly and thoroughly lost to his desire.

His clothes melted away as he finished divesting her of the remnants of her gown. He looked down on her, caressed by silver light. "You are exquisite." And with a groan he came down on her once again, his hands fisting in the waves of her hair as they came together, joined as one, making complete each of their empty lives. Their love was an odyssey of revelations, opening up a world of feelings neither knew existed.

The moon waxed in the black sky, slowly, until it reached its zenith, caressing everything beneath with its silver glow, proclaiming the rightness of the world. And then, as always, though in no way diminished, the moon gradually descended, leaving Madeline and Wade lying together, bodies entwined, replete from their lovemaking.

Silently, clasped together, they began to drift off to sleep. Just as the moon disappeared into the blackness, Wade contentedly asleep, Madeline shook the drowsiness from her mind and pulled herself up to look on the sleeping man. She ran her hand delicately over his high cheekbones and around his strong jaw, which was no less formidable despite his slumber. A tear glistened in her eye.

"Always remember that I love you," she whispered to this man she loved like no other before extracting herself from his arms, pulling on her wrapper, and quietly slipping from the room.

Twenty-one

WADE AWOKE WITH a start, his peaceful sleep disturbed by darkness and uncertainty, by visions of trying to reach out to Madeline, who stood elusively just out of reach. Desperation filled him as she moved away from his grasp.

He turned on his side, the covers falling away, the cool morning air whispering against his skin. He reached out to pull Madeline into his arms.

But Madeline was gone.

The dream came back to him in full force. His eyes narrowed, and he told himself it was only a dream.

Glancing about the room, Wade expected to find her curled up in a chair or leaning against the sill watching the early morning sky. But the chair sat empty and the sky stood unwatched, causing Wade's heart to lurch in his chest as he remembered all the times she had disappeared. He took a deep breath and forced himself to relax. After what had transpired in this very bed, he knew she was his; to make their union official was all that remained.

He pulled himself from the covers and went to the cedar chest to find his mother's ring. It felt solid and heavy in his hand—the perfect gift to show his love.

He dressed quickly before searching for Madeline. She was in the schoolroom, at the same window where he had found her waving silently goodbye to the children as they rode off with Lorraine so many weeks before. It seemed like a lifetime ago that he had taken the stairs two at a time to prove to himself he was only intrigued by what he felt he couldn't have. He smiled at the thought. How wrong he had been.

The shiny brass nameplates gleamed in the rising sun. Soon the children would sit at the tables, Madeline there to teach them. He looked silently upon the woman who would share his life. She stood there before him, partially turned to the window, her face almost obscured. He took the few steps that separated them without faltering, eager to have her set a date.

But when he touched her, she started. She turned to look at him and instead of the glow of happiness he expected, he found a palpable pain, though a pain he refused to accept. To prove to himself their happiness, to erase the pained look on her face, to erase the remnants of darkness left over from his dream, he pulled her to him and buried his face in the fiery cloud of her hair.

"Why did you leave me?" he asked.

Madeline didn't answer at first, merely wrapped her arms around his strong frame and held tight. "I didn't want the children to find me there," she finally said.

Wade emitted a short burst of laughter that reverberated through the schoolroom, relieved at the obvious truth of her words. "Yes," he whispered into her hair before pulling back and smiling. "Good thing one of us could still think coherently. How could I forget how often those little redheaded devils turn up underfoot."

The windows stood open, and the warm morning air filled the room, lifting the curtains slightly, then dropping them back down again, only to lift them once more. Mockingbirds sang their morning songs, fluttering and chasing, confident in the new day. Squirrels chattered and raced up and down trees, excited by the springtime air.

Wade ran his strong hands down Madeline's arms before reaching into his pocket. "I have something for you." He pulled out the ring, the gold and silver reflecting the sun. "It was my mother's."

He felt her body tense and saw her eyes fill with desperation.

"Oh, Wade." Her voice trembled.

When he tried to explain her actions away, she pulled back, not accepting his gift, and looked at him, her eyes telling the tale that he dreaded to hear. His dream resurfaced as she pulled away from him, completely.

"I can't marry you, Wade." Madeline took a deep breath and her voice steadied. Then she stepped even farther away, beyond his reach. "It would never work." She went to her new desk and straightened an already straight pile of papers. "As soon as I can find a suitable replacement, I will return to Austin. I plan to tell the children this morning."

Wade reeled from the shock. The darkness of his dream threatened to overwhelm him. Her words barely registered. His only thought was that she was leaving him—again. "I love you," he said in a disbelieving voice. "I want to spend the rest of my life with you."

The papers she held slipped from her hands and drifted to the floor in a slow fluttering seesaw, back and forth until they settled on the newly polished floor. Madeline watched the papers, her fingers slightly outstretched as if trying to reach out but unable to move.

"Madeline," he began, but couldn't think of what else to say. After everything, after all they had shared, words failed him. He didn't think about the children or the complications that her departure would bring about; he only thought of the pain of losing her—yet again. And with that, his shock and pain quickly turned to anger, insinuating itself in the fine cracks in his heart. White-hot fury racked his body, replacing the uncertainty and pain.

"You're leaving!" he demanded, his fist clenching and unclenching at his side. "Just like that you tell me you're leaving."

It was a long time before she answered. "It's for the best, Wade," she finally said without looking at him, still looking at the papers that lay scattered on the floor.

Memories of their night together filled his mind, their bodies entwined, the ultimate avowal of their love. "What about last night?" His voice was like steel, its cold iciness slicing through the room.

Still she could not bring her eyes to meet his, and she started to lean down to gather the scattered papers. With a few fleet steps he was next to her. He grabbed her arm to keep her from kneeling and pulled her to him, gripping her arms, tightly. "Look at me," he commanded. "What about last night?"

She moaned, a strange strangled sound, and she looked into his eyes. He saw her pain, and with it his rage died as quickly as it was born. "I thought you loved me."

Madeline turned from the pain in his voice. How she wanted to throw her arms around this man she loved like no other, to press her cheek against his solid chest, to feel his strong arms wrapped around her body, making her safe. She wanted to cry out for the unfairness of it all. How she wanted to spend the rest of her life with him. A life filled with love and happiness, fulfillment and the children. This man who alternately humbled her with his love and infuriated her with his stubbornness. To have a house with children always underfoot, the smell of baking bread and snatched cookies from the cooling rack. The smell of Wade's fine cheroots filling the room. How would she live without them? she wondered again as she had wondered every moment since she extracted herself from Wade's strong arms that morning and hurried from the room.

But all of that was a dream, wonderful fantasies of a life she couldn't have. She knew how badly he was hurting just then—she felt it herself. But she knew as well that this pain could never compare to the lifetime of disappointment and regret he would feel if she married him. No, not at first, perhaps, but eventually, she felt sure, as the newness of their love diminished and betrayal set in. And would not betrayal be what Wade felt when he learned the truth?

Visions of the dark night and a horse rearing above her threatened at the edge of consciousness. She pushed them back. Not now. And with that her faltering resolve stiffened.

"Madeline," he demanded, his grip still firm. "I know you love me."

And with those few words the moment had arrived, the moment that she had desperately hoped to avoid. But she knew from the look in his eyes she had no alternative, unless she chose to tell the truth, and just then, despite her innate dislike of lying, she knew she couldn't. Instead, she said in a voice of steel to match his, "You're wrong. I don't love you. I only hoped that you would buy my land."

His eyes opened wide, then narrowed into unnatural slits. His jaw tightened. He freed her arms and stepped away. "Why are you lying?"

This time Madeline's eyes opened with surprise. "I'm not," she finally said, her chin tilting with defiance.

"You're lying, Madeline."

"I'm not!" Her voice of steel wavered, her eyes showed their uncertainty.

"You are! You love me, Madeline, just as much as I love you. You have loved me since the night you pulled back your shoulders and walked across the room and asked me to dance."

"I did not," she insisted, though her brow furrowed and her chin quivered dangerously.

"You have loved me as no other woman has loved me, for no other reason than for myself."

"No," she denied breathlessly, tears glistening in her eyes.

"Madeline," he whispered, standing only inches before her, "you love me as I love you. We are meant to be together."

"No!" she cried, her tears turning to sobs. "That can't be."

She started to turn away, to escape, but he reached out and caught her arm and whirled her back to face him. "I won't let you run away from me again, Madeline. I love you!"

"Perhaps now." Her voice was bitter, her eyes snapping wildly, and she tried to wrench away.

His grip was like bands of steel on her arms, keeping her prisoner. "What do you mean, *perhaps now*?"

"Let me go." She pulled at his grip, tears brimming in her eyes.

"No, Madeline," he said fiercely. "I love you, do you hear me? I love you."

"Not for long!" she cried, throwing the words at him. "Not once you found out I can't give you children of your own." Her eyes blazed with shimmering anger; her cheeks streamed with tears.

"What are you talking about?" he questioned, his brow furrowed as he tried to understand.

"About children!" she cried in a voice unnaturally high. "Your own children. I've seen how you've come to love your cousins. You enjoy their company just as you laugh at their jokes. You love those kids, you've become a wonderful father, as if you were made for the role."

"Of course I love the children," he said in confusion, "and I can only hope I will be a good father to them. Isn't that what you want?"

She covered her face with her hands as if to block out the pain. "Yes," she moaned. "Yes, that's what I want. But don't you see?" She took her hands away from her face and looked at him as if he were an errant child. "You are a wonderful father, and you will want children of your own! Children that I can't give you!" she wailed.

Wade leaned down against the edge of the desk, his hands still locked on her arms, as understanding slowly dawned. He remembered her irrational fear of horses and her nightmares that left her weeping. An accident that had left her barren. And suddenly it all made sense. Her declarations that she would never marry, despite the love he saw in her eyes. Her need to be near children, and the looks that hinted at yearning whenever she was with his cousins.

His heart ached for her. He longed to take her in his arms and smooth the hurt away. To make her safe. To let her know that it didn't matter.

And it didn't.

Slowly, gently he loosened his grip and ran his hands up her arms until they rested on either side of her neck. He tilted her chin with his thumbs, forcing her to look into his eyes. "I already have children of my own, our own, seven of them, who—like me—love you very much."

A heartfelt wistfulness stretched her perfect features in a painful mask. "Every man wants sons of his own, Wade," she stated softly, resignation having set in. "Children from his loins to carry something of himself into the future—especially someone like you with all your love of family." A sad hollow smile flickered on her lips. She placed her hands on his and looked into his eyes. "I love you too much to take that away from you."

He closed his eyes for a moment, then opened them again with a glowing fierceness. "I love you! I will not lose you! And as for carrying something of myself into the future, I have Jimmy and Garrett and Garvin and Billy!" The fierceness softened a bit, though he still held her tight. "Or perhaps with you for a mother, it will be Bridget or Elizabeth or Grace who will take over the most unladylike task of breeding cattle and taming wild horses. Don't you see, Madeline? We already have our family."

His words or perhaps his softness conquered the final remnants of her flagging determination. Her eyes closed tightly as she tried to regain control, but the harness that Madeline had for years kept so tightly on her feelings about her inability to have children finally snapped, and her streaming tears turned to heaving sobs. "But I always wanted a baby!" she cried, covering her face with her hands, her shoulders shaking with her misery.

The words tore at his heart. He moved her hands away. He felt helpless knowing he could do nothing more than hold her. But hold her he did, trying to give her some of his strength, murmuring sweet nothings into her hair.

The sun stretched its long rays into the room until the golden orb was well into the morning sky. He rocked her until her racking sobs calmed, and when she stirred he hugged her tighter.

Eventually she quieted, her body worn to utter limpness. He spoke then, in a clear soft voice. "Someone very wise once told me a story that I will always remember, about how when God closes a door, somewhere he opens a window."

It was some time before she responded, and when she did it wasn't with words but a red-rimmed, puffy-eyed look of blinding hope. Wade smiled and smoothed her hair. "Yes, love. God has given you seven redheaded children who need you very much. Just as I do."

She closed her eyes one last time, and when she opened them again, it was as if she expected Wade to be gone. At the sight of him, sitting there, his solid strength holding her, she flung her arms around his massive shoulders with one last great sob. And when she quieted once again, he looked into her eyes with all the love he felt. "Marry me, Madeline Montgomery."

Her tear-filled snort of laughter carried through the room, and for a moment Wade was taken back.

"Always making demands, Mr. Alexander. Have you not learned to ask?"

He pulled her close with a growl and whispered in her hair all his love and desire, and then when he had finished, he added one word—*please*.

Epilogue

HAROLD MACKENZIE BURST into Wade's study, his pale green eyes glowing with excitement. "Wade, I've received a telegram with proof that the Siringos aren't who they say they are! I've just seen the frauds off on the morning stage. Now you don't have to get married!"

A startled gasp caused Harold to whirl around, away from Wade, to find the bride-to-be in a quiet corner reading a book.

"Oh, ma'am, I'm so sorry. I didn't see you sitting there. If I had—"

"Enough!" Wade's command shimmered through the room. He looked at Madeline, her vivid beauty so fragile as she sat curled up in the chair, her brow creasing with worry. Damn, he cursed to himself. Just when things were going so well.

"Wade," she said, her voice unsure. "What's he talking about?"

With tired hands he raked his fingers through his hair, throwing a derisive glance at Harold before he took a long sighing breath. He held out his hand to her. "Come here, love."

Harold stood where he had stopped, the telegram clutched mercilessly in his hands. "Perhaps I'll just go now." He started to leave.

"You're not going anywhere, Harold," Wade snapped.

Harold flinched.

Madeline set her book aside and went to Wade.

"Madeline, it's not what you think," Wade began.

"I don't know what to think," she said, distressed.

"Harold, give me that damned telegram."

Wade quickly read the missive and snorted his approval. And then he turned back to Madeline and explained all that had transpired with the Siringos and the judge.

"Why, those blackguards!" Madeline exclaimed, her worry forgotten, replaced by outrage for the children. "How could people be so heartless!"

She turned to Harold. "Thank you, Mr. Mackenzie," she said fervently, "for pursuing this issue and bringing Wade the proof he needs so . . ." Her voice slowed. "He . . . doesn't have . . . to get married."

Wade took her hands and turned her to face him, wanting nothing more at that moment than to erase the uncertainty in her eyes. "I didn't need proof, Madeline. If it came down to it, I would have paid them off. Whether the Siringos were still here or not, I want nothing more than to marry you, to make you my wife." He pulled Madeline between his granite hard thighs.

Harold shifted uneasily. "Perhaps I should go now," he repeated.

Madeline jumped as if she had forgotten the other man's presence.

"Yes, why don't you?" Wade said with an exasperated scowl.

"Thank you again, Mr. Mackenzie," Madeline called after him as she nudged Wade meaningfully in the ribs.

"What?" Wade inquired, feigning ignorance.

Madeline sent Wade an imploring look as if he were a recalcitrant child.

With a sigh and a noise that sounded suspiciously like a snarl, Wade added, "I appreciate your efforts, Harold."

Harold Mackenzie stopped at the door, his pale green eyes beaming with pleasure. "Thank you, Wade," he said enthusiastically, starting to pull the door shut behind him. "And don't you worry, I'm already on the next project."

Wade groaned as the door clicked shut. He shook his head, and when Madeline laughed, he growled and pulled her back between his thighs. "Now look what you've done!"

"At least he means well. Besides, somehow things always manage to work out in the end."

"So far, though I still haven't gotten you to the altar yet."

Madeline ran her fingers through his hair. "Tomorrow, my love. And speaking of the wedding, my family should arrive anytime."

Madeline's heart fluttered with anticipation as Rosalind and Bridget circled around her, putting the finishing touches to her gown.

"You're beautiful, Maddie." Bridget stood back and looked on with wistful eyes.

"Yes, you are, dear," Rosalind added with a loving smile.

"Thank you both. Now, Bridget, why don't you go and make sure all our bouquets are in order?"

In the kitchen Bridget found Elizabeth and Grace fighting over one of their meticulously made bouquets.

"It's mine!" Grace wailed.

"Not either, it's mine!"

Elizabeth made to grab for the flowers, but Phillips stepped in just in time and deftly snatched the whole thing from destruction.

"The bouquet is Elizabeth's, and this," he said, picking up a basket of blossoms, "is for you."

Grace ran her tiny hand through the silky petals and seemed content.

"Now to find those boys," Phillips said, turning on his heel, leaving the girls to admire their handiwork.

He found Garrett and Garvin stretched out on the study floor in their best coats and pants, playing marbles with young Tommy Teeple. "Boys! Get up, get up! Or you'll be a mess by the time the wedding begins."

Ed and Richard entered the study just as the boys grudgingly pulled themselves up from the floor.

"Run along, kids," Edward said as he went to the desk.

Richard plopped down in one of the leather chairs. "I still can't see how Wade could possibly let Madeline build a school on that piece of land. And to think he's going to surprise her with the building contracts! Maybe you should try to talk some sense into the old boy now that you're his lawyer and all."

"I happen to think it's a fine idea, and Madeline will love it."

"What's this world coming to? Well, at least Madeline was smart enough to ask me to give her away."

Edward immediately looked away to hide the grin that appeared. He wasn't about to tell his brother he had convinced Madeline to do just that when she had approached him late last night.

The door swung open, bringing Wade and Jimmy in its wake. Wade walked over to his desk, where Ed was sitting, reached in the top drawer, and pulled out the worn piece of flannel. He pulled out the gold and silver ring.

"Jimmy, I'd like you to hold on to this until Father Hayes and Reverend Marshall ask for it."

Jimmy beamed with pleasure. "Sure, Wade. Don't you worry about a thing."

Wade reached over and grasped the boy's shoulder. "I won't, son."

The house was brimming with guests. The townspeople came bearing gifts of cured hams and wild chickens, anything they could gather up on such short notice. Father Hayes and Reverend Marshall stood together in an arched window that overlooked the lawn. Wade paced nervously before them, hardly able to believe his dream was finally coming true. Jimmy stood by importantly, his hand continually checking for the ring in his pocket. Grandmother Leister sat proudly in the front row with a blubbering Selma beside her.

"I'm just so happy," Selma sniffed into her handkerchief.

Gran admonished her about such a display and added, "The ceremony hasn't even started yet."

But then the music began, and Gran was forced to pull out her own handkerchief.

Richard stood at the bottom of the curving staircase as first Elizabeth, then Bridget came down the stairs, fragrant bouquets of sweet jasmine in their hands. Grace followed, looking about shyly, tossing jasmine blossoms as she went.

The music heightened, bringing Madeline to stand at the top of the steps. She drifted down the stairs in a cloud of white, tiny ribbons of yellow intertwined at the waist, a full bouquet of jasmine clutched in her hand. Richard's cantankerous countenance softened, and when she reached his side, he leaned down and whispered in her ear. "You're beautiful, dear," he said, clearly proud.

Madeline smiled her thanks, and then she turned and found Wade and she had eyes for no other. Their eyes met and held, much as they had that first night, never wavering, aglow with love. The promise of the future was felt by each.

The vows were said with a beauty and clarity that brought a tear to more than one person's eyes. And then, as the gold and silver wedding band was slipped on Madeline's finger, Wade realized his life was truly in order.

*If you enjoyed this book, take advantage
of this special offer. Subscribe now and...*

Get a Historical

No Obligation

411